Lilith Unbound

Edited by Elaine Cunningham

POPCORN PRESS
PO BOX 12
Elkhorn, WI 53121

Lilith Unbound copyright © 2008 Elaine Cunningham. All individual stories and poems contained herein copyright © 2008 by their respective authors.

Cover design by Katheryn Smith

Typesetting by Lester Smith

All rights reserved. No part of this publication may be reproduced or transmitted in any form or by any means, electronic or mechanical, including photocopy, recording, or any information storage and retrieval system, without permission in writing from the publisher.

"The Shiksa," was originally published in *Ancient Enchantresses,* copyright 1995 by DAW books, reprinted by permission of the authors. "Looking for Lilith" was originally published in *Lenox Avenue* magazine, July 2004, reprinted by permission of the author.

Request for permission to make copies of any part of the work should be mailed to the following address: Popcorn Press, PO Box 12, Elkhorn, WI 53121.

Printed in the United States at www.qualitypod.com

ISBN: 978-1-4276-2755-1

TABLE OF CONTENTS

Introduction	5
1181 Lilith, *Marsheila Rockwell*	7
Trophy Wife, *Elaine Cunningham*	9
A Lovers' Quarrel, *Jonathan Moeller*	21
The Shiksa, *Mike Resnick and Lawrence Schimel*	35
Looking for Lilith, *Nisi Shawl*	41
Alone, *J. Robert King*	49
The L.I.L.I.T.H. System, *Lara Gose*	61
The Cashier's Tale, *Robin Bridges*	71
Delta: A Story in Verse, *Lily Hoang*	77
Death of the Madonna, *Christina McCoy*	93
Screech Owl Serenade, *Lorne Dixon*	111
What Dreams May Go, *Ed Greenwood*	123
What I Did This Summer, *Marcus Ewert*	137
So Weeps the Thunderbird, *T. L. Morganfield*	141
Exiles, *Nancy Schmidt*	157
The Girl in the Mirror, *Stephen D. Sullivan*	165
When Hell Comes Calling, *Jackie Kessler*	179
When the Wind Blows, *Eirene Donohue*	191
Mother of Vampires, *Jennifer Greylyn*	209
The Right Thing, *Hannah Goodman*	215
Confirmation, *Tracy Woelfel*	227
A Day at the Fair, *Clint Collins*	239
Man-Underground, *Kate Riedel*	243
Reconciliation, *Lynn Hawker*	259
Nocturne, *Lester Smith*	267
About the Authors	268
About Popcorn Press	272

Introduction

About twelve years ago, I was asked to write a Lilith story for an anthology of alternate creation tales. We were living in Los Angeles at the time—a strange and foreign land as far as I was concerned. I was particularly fascinated by the pervasive shadows "The Industry" cast over the inhabitants. In *Trophy Wife*, Lilith buys into this mindset in very thorough fashion. She works in reality TV, reads Oprah-recommended books, and communes with angels who commandeer her screen in the guise of sitcom characters. It's a quirky story, to say the least, but while researching and writing it, I was struck by the storytelling possibilities in the Lilith mythology.

Lilith, the First Woman, the wife Adam discarded when she refused to submit to his will. Lilith, the goddess of storms, the night bird. Lilith, the succubus who haunts men's dreams and steals their souls. Lilith the child-slaying monster, the mother of demons. Lilith the feminist poster girl. Lilith the muse.

The stories in this collection cover all these aspects, sometimes in unexpected fashion. In *So Weeps the Thunderbird*, T.L. Morganfield melds Lilith lore with Native American mythology. Nisi Shawl goes *Looking for Lilith* in the savannas of Africa; Jonathan Moeller visits early 18th-century Boston in *The Lovers' Quarrel*. Lilith inspires dancer Isadora Duncan in Christina McCoy's *Death of the Madonna*, inventor Bryce Bryce Wildenstone in Ed Greenwood's *What Dreams May Go*, and untold thousands as a motivational speaker and self-help author in *The L.I.L.I.T.H System*, by Lara Gose. In these stories Lilith is a divorce attorney, an aspiring author, a giant snake, a vengeful asteroid. And of course, she's the ultimate shiksa.

As one might expect, most of the stories are fantasy tales. But in *The Right Thing* by YA author Hannah Goodman, a modern-day, teenaged Lilith struggles with issues as old as Eden. It's not quite clear whether or not there's magic in Eirene Donohue's *When the Wind Blows*, other than the enchantment of a beautifully told tale. Some of the stories venture into the realms of horror—*Screech Owl Serenade* by Lorne Dixon will make Chuck Palahniuk fans very happy—and *Confirmation* by Tracy Woelfel is urban fantasy with a touch of noir. There are also three poems—Marcy Rockwell offers a sly little villanelle, Lily Hoang a mosaic, and Lester Smith a wistful finale.

More information about Lilith lore and legends can be found at www.elainecunningham.com/lilith.htm.

1181 LILITH

by Marsheila Rockwell

...the asteroid belt is so huge that the chance of running into one is less than one in a billion...if you want to come close to an asteroid, you have to aim for one...

> –S. Alan Stern
> Associate Administrator, NASA
> 2 June 2006

...or it has to aim for you...

> –Marcus A. Stern
> Captain, Hibernation Vessel *New Eden*
> 14 July 2413

The last of Adam's children
Of weak Eve's blood, near devoid
(His first wife? Long forgotten)

Their home turned cold and rotten
They blast, bold, into the void
The last of Adam's children

In search of a new garden
Silver sleep ships all deployed
Their first life long forgotten

By gravity begotten
Fiery fate they can't avoid
Those last of Adam's children

The impact, always certain,
With a main belt asteroid–
That first wife, long forgotten

Pity a passing thought, then
She broke orbit and destroyed
The last of Adam's children
First wives won't be forgotten

Trophy Wife
by Elaine Cunningham

Sunset tints of rose and gold were fading to silver when Lilith pulled into the driveway of her trim Spanish villa, a "gift" from her latest ex-husband. She gathered up her purse and a sack of goodies from the upscale grocery in town, then nudged open the car door with the toe of her Manolo Blahniks.

The evening breeze swept over her as she rose, carrying with it the scent of the ocean, the neighbors' roses, and the eucalyptus trees in the nearby park. Lilith drew in a long breath and held it, savoring the complex perfume. This, in her opinion, was heaven—or as close to it as she was ever likely to get.

A burst of shrill, frantic barking shattered the evening calm, and a pocket dog of some sort scuttled out from behind one of the jade trees framing her neighbor's driveway. It scooted to a stop a few feet from Lilith, its tiny body bouncing with each accusing yap.

Lilith grimaced. Small dogs reminded her of short men: they made a lot of noise and took themselves far too seriously. Come to think of it, if Stan, her latest ex, swapped his comb-over for a Pebbles Flintstone topknot and a baby blue ribbon, he and the yard rat could pass as litter mates.

She shifted her grocery bag onto her right hip and extended a perfectly manicured hand to the little dog. Still barking, it hopped closer to take a sniff.

A pulse of energy burst from Lilith's fingers, slicing the dog's final yip into a slim, staccato burst—the audio version of an exclamation point. Lilith straightened, gazing with satisfaction at the whiff of acrid smoke—all that remained of the Stan's canine alter ego.

"Makes you wonder why anyone bothers with divorce attorneys," she murmured.

A rift of recorded jazz drifted out into the soft evening. Lilith glanced toward the neighbors' house. An attractive blond woman hurried into the yard, shadowed by her much older husband. Lilith knew the type: white hair in a ponytail, two kids in preschool.

The trophy wife caught sight of Lilith. She smiled and waved, as oblivious to danger as her dog had been.

"Hi! I'm looking for Muffin. Have you seen him?"

Lilith slid a dismissive glance over the blonde, then locked eyes with the husband and turned up the heat. The trophy wife's soft, startled gasp amused Lilith. Most men who were willing to cheat on their first wives happily stepped out on numbers two and three and so forth. Somehow, most promoted mistresses failed to pick up on this.

"I heard something yapping," Lilith responded vaguely. "I'll keep an eye out. No doubt 'Muffin' will come sniffing around sooner or later."

That prediction, made potent by a pointed, sidelong glance at the husband—and a dose of innuendo heavy enough to make a soap opera vixen stand up and applaud—brought a mixture of outrage and panic to the young woman's eyes. Lilith had seen that expression many times before, but it never ceased to gratify. It was, after all, an important step in the process. Few things made a man's life more uncomfortable than an insecure and suspicious wife.

Smiling now, Lilith let herself into her house and dropped her purse onto the hall table. She shrugged off her jacket and kicked off her pumps. With a grateful sigh, she flexed the owl-like talons on her feet.

The tiled floor felt deliciously cool to the scaled skin of her feet, and her talons clicked delicately as she walked across the living room to the kitchen. She opened a nice bottle of pinot noir and poured herself a glass. Sipping as she backtracked, she sank down onto the sofa and glanced at the latest Oprah-recommended book, which lay open and face down on the coffee table. A quiet evening with a well written, thoroughly depressing book sounded, for lack of a better expression, heavenly.

Lilith reached for the book, then hesitated and picked up the television remote instead. After ten mind-numbing hours in court, followed by the frustration of a Los Angeles commute, a sitcom rerun seemed the more appropriate intellectual challenge.

She clicked. Images of a half dozen beaming Gen-Xers danced across the screen to music she considered only slightly less annoying than the ex-dog's yapping. She leveled the remote at the offending perkiness with deadly intent.

But at that moment, the music died, and Joey, Chandler, and Ross turned to gaze somberly and directly at the camera. Something in their collective stare froze Lilith's finger on the OFF button.

"Woe unto you, demon and harlot!" proclaimed Joey.

Lilith doubted this was the line called for in the script. Not even the last two seasons were *that* badly written. And there was something disturbingly familiar about that voice, even cloaked as it was by the actor's pronounced Brooklyn accent.

"Semangelof?" she said tentatively. "Is that you?"

"No, *Chandler is* Semangelof. I'm *Senoy*," Joey informed her.

"Oh. Well, that figures," Lilith murmured in a dazed tone. Of the three avenging angels—Senoy, Sansenoy, and Semangelof—who'd been sent to retrieve her after she'd ditched her first husband, Senoy was undoubtedly the best looking. He'd probably grabbed Joey's body before the other two guys could shrug off their wings. Semangelof was the funny one. Small wonder—even an angel needed to deploy humor as a defense against a name like that. Lilith had never been able to see any reason for Sansenoy, which, considering the celluloid avatar he'd chosen, also followed.

She let out a resigned sigh. "So. How'd you guys find me?"

"Always have you found a place of repose in the desert," intoned Senoy. "Thus has it been from the days of Gilgamesh the Sumerian." His Joey avatar had a bit of trouble getting out the big words, but Lilith got the basic idea.

"In other words, we staked out Vegas, figuring you'd stop by sooner or later," Semangelof paraphrased, punctuating his remark with Chandler's trademark smirk. "If nothing else, Lilith, you're predicable."

Lilith cut loose with a few evocative phrases in Aramaic and chugged the rest of her wine. Thus fortified, she placed her glass next to the Oprah-recommended book and faced down the angelic trio in her television.

"All right, what am I being blamed for *this* time?"

"Your crimes against God and man are too numerous to list," Joey/Senoy said sternly. "There is no foul deed you have left undone."

"I try to touch all the bases," she agreed. "What foul deed are we talking about?"

"None," the angel admitted. "You have turned to aiding the abandoned and the friendless. Frankly, we are puzzled."

Lilith's smile held an edge that could have cut diamonds. "And you said I was predictable."

"That was Semangelof," Senoy pointed out.

"Behold the wonder of divine grace!" Ross/Sansenoy spoke up at last, an expression of transport on his lugubrious, borrowed face. "Miracle of miracles, that even such as Lilith can turn her foot from the path of evil!"

"Hey, I wouldn't count on it," she advised him.

But Sansenoy would not be deterred. "What joy your redemption will bring to the angelic host! We must retrace your steps, and learn what brought you to this place of light."

"Bitch, *please*. Not another flashback episode!"

Lilith brandished the remote with a fervor usually associated with silver crosses and vampires. The trio of familiar faces blinked off the screen, to be replaced by a garden scene of such beauty that even Lilith's brass-plated heart quickened.

For a moment she beheld Paradise, lush and green and filled with the murmur of running water and the joyous lilt of birdsong.

"Lilith! Liiiiiilith! Where are you?"

Even now, thousands of years after their divorce, Adam's voice still had the power to set her teeth on edge. She watched—albeit with the same fascination that prompts motorists to slow down and gawk at accident scenes—as a curtain of vines parted and her first husband strode into view.

He looked good. That, she couldn't deny. Tall and golden brown, with the body type every studmuffin on Venice Beach dreamed about in the shower. But when it came right down to it, Adam was about as interesting as a bagel without a schmeer.

As Lilith remembered it, there really hadn't been all that much to do in Paradise, and Adam wasn't exactly innovative when it came to the main form of entertainment. With him, it was plain old missionary sex with golden boy on top. Lilith had tried to introduce a little variety.

Adam wasn't having any. All things must be as he decreed, or he'd sulk until the cosmos in general and Lilith in particular came around to his way of thinking. The sulking and the posturing had been bad enough. One night he stopped pouting and tried to enforce his boring conjugal rights.

As Lilith watched that long-ago confrontation play out on the plasma screen, her ancient, unforgotten anger swept through her like a red tide. She snatched up the remote and clicked rapidly, switching from channel to channel. Every station carried the same nightmare. She tried turning off the set. Another futile effort.

Furious now, Lilith prepared to heave herself off the sofa. She couldn't budge.

"Watch, learn," implored a disembodied angelic voice. "Only by confronting and renouncing your sins can you avoid damnation!"

"Too late, Sansenoy," Lilith muttered. "Play some Neil Diamond in the background, and you've got hell nailed."

Obligingly, the strains of "You Don't Send Me Flowers

Anymore" began to waft through the room.

"Um, excuse me, Sansenoy," drawled an equally invisible Semangelof, who was still using Chandler's voice, "but do you remember all those times I tried to explain *sarcasm*?"

There was a long pause as the more serious angel tried to absorb this. "The demon was jesting?"

"Something like that, yeah. Just let her watch the movie, okay?"

The muzak switched off abruptly.

"Now we're talking," she approved. "Since I'm quite literally stuck here, any chance you could top off my wine glass?"

Her goblet was instantly filled with a deep red liquid. She sipped tentatively, grimacing as supermarket-quality Passover wine assaulted her palate.

"Sarcasm is fun," Semangelof observed in a smug tone, "but irony is so much more satisfying."

Lilith sighed and put down the goblet. "Let's get this over with."

The action on the screen picked up a bit then, and Lilith watched as her younger self "defied Adam," which was a tidy, Talmudic way of saying she kicked him in the nuts. But the Talmudic scholars got the next part right: filled with the elemental power of her fury, Lilith transformed. Her feet changed to a raptor's talons and wings sprouted from her naked shoulders. Free and wild, Adam's first wife—now a "demon"—flew away toward the Red Sea, a place full of lascivious spirits and wild revels. Sort of like Marina del Rey during the Seventies.

"There you engaged in unbridled promiscuity," Joey/Senoy said in an accusing voice.

"One man's party girl is another man's goddess." A dreamy smile curved her lips as she reminisced. "Babylon was fun, but *damn*, but I miss those Sumerians."

"A harlot is a harlot, whoever tells the tale." Sansenoy's disembodied voice still retained the hangdog drawl of his Ross avatar. It suited him so well that Lilith doubted he'd ever be able to shake it. "Even the Sumerians attest that you bore a demonic brood, producing more than one hundred Lilim a day!"

"Play all night, labor all day," she said flippantly. "Are we finished here?"

"Sorry, not yet," Chandler/Semangelof said.

The scene on the television screen changed into a vastly different but equally familiar landscape: an aerial view of rocky hillsides peppered with sparse vegetation, surrounding a long, narrow body of water. There was no getting around it—the Red Sea district had some pretty dismal real estate.

Still, Lilith had to admit it had been a good time. Back then she'd looked pretty good, too. Her bright red hair was a slash of color against the endless gray sky, and the giant, hawk-like wings nicely complimented her curves. By Bhaal, she missed having wings! There were so few places a demon could wear them these days. She really had to get down to Mardi Gras this year.

Nostalgia tightened Lilith's throat as she watched herself fly. A rare spring rain fell over the Red Sea as the young Lilith soared and wheeled and danced in giddy celebration. For centuries Lilith had been known as a storm demon, and she still got off on extreme weather. Too bad that some forgotten scribe had botched a translation, transforming her image into a creature of the night.

Three wet, bedraggled angels winged toward her younger self.

"Adam is lonely," announced a young and very earnest Senoy.

"Small wonder. Adam is boring."

"That may be so, but God demands your return."

The young Lilith considered this, her bright head tipped to one side. "And if I don't?"

"Then we are to drown you in the Red Sea," Sansenoy said.

"Hmm. Let me think that over," she said dryly.

All three angels nodded. Back then, not even Semangelof recognized sarcasm. The winged Lilith continued her circular flight, doing her best to look deep in thought. But each circle took her subtly higher, moving her into position for an attacking dive. The angels awaited her response with heavenly patience, and, it might be added, surreptitiously enjoyed the view. It was hard to get clothes on and off over wings, and Lilith usually didn't bother to try.

When Lilith had gained enough height to make a dive count, she spread her talons into rending hooks and attacked, feet first.

After the first startled moment, the angels rose to meet her in a rush of soggy wings and righteous indignation. Lilith managed to get in some good hits, and more than a few angelic feathers flew as she kicked and clawed and bit.

In the end, though, simple mathematics decided the matter: there were three of them and one of her. Despite garish wounds and tattered wings, the angels managed to get Lilith pinioned in mid-air, Senoy holding her wrists above her head, and Sansenoy and Semangelof each clinging to a slim ankle and struggling to keep beyond reach of her talons.

Lilith watched the television screen in helpless rage as the world's first and quite possibly worse divorce settlement played out on the screen. It took a while to get the concept of "irreconcilable differences" through to the angels, but they finally conceded possibilities other than death by drowning or the more lingering torture of life with Adam.

She was granted her life and her freedom, but a hundred of her "demonic children" would be destroyed each day. The Lilim, those beautiful creatures Lilith had nurtured in her image, would soon be no more. Furthermore, it was arranged that an amulet inscribed with the names of the three angels would act as a sure ward against retaliation. Any child of Adam's line who wore such an amulet could not come to harm at Lilith's hands.

After all these centuries, this "compromise" still infuriated Lilith. She glared in the general direction of the invisible trio. "And this never seemed slightly unfair to you? Maybe even a tad—oh, I don't know—*hypocritical?*"

"Just watch," Sansenoy said shortly. He didn't make any admissions, but at least he had the grace to sound uncomfortable.

Somewhat heartened by this small victory, Lilith settled back on the sofa and turned her reluctant gaze back to the television.

Again the scene changed. Centuries zipped by, centuries in which thousands of women shrieked and prayed their way through childbirth. It was sort of like an extended episode of *ER,* with one difference—each laboring woman clung to the amulet meant to protect her life and that of her babe from the demon Lilith.

It didn't end there. Her name was vilified every time these Daughters of Eve sang their babes to sleep: the very word "lullaby" was an insult, fashioned as it was from ancient words for "Lilith, be gone!" Babies who smiled in their sleep were awakened for fear that Lilith had lured them into her sphere of influence and was playing with them or tickling them in their dreams. And so it went, from the earliest years of humankind well up into the seventeenth century. By then her own babes were long gone—thousands upon thousands of Lilim killed or hounded into hiding.

At last the disturbing litany came to a close. A familiar coffeehouse scene filled the screen. The three celebrity avatars were sitting shoulder to shoulder on a sofa, sipping from over-sized mugs and casting surreptitious glances at the door.

Lilith smirked. Coffee wasn't *exactly* a sin, but it was closer to the good stuff than these guys usually came. She cleared her throat, enjoying the guilty haste with which her tormentors set aside their mugs.

"Thus did you torment the descendants of Adam," proclaimed Joey/Senoy. He paused to wipe a bit of latte foam from the corner of his mouth. "Your fearful shadow fell upon the cradle of every child of Adam. Yet this evil, grievous though it was, was not your only sin. There was an earlier one."

"Here it comes," Lilith murmured resignedly. She'd been expecting this; after all, her sexuality was her main claim to fame, and the issue that had started this mess in the first place.

Once again the scene changed. Impenetrable gates barred the entrance to Paradise. Outside stood two beautiful, golden brown people, weeping and shrieking as they lobbed bitter recriminations back and forth.

"Behold the agony of Adam's penitence," the Ross sound-alike said in hushed tones. "Many years after their banishment, the pain of their separation from Paradise was still an open wound."

Lilith snorted. "Penitence, my ass. If you could hear what Adam and Eve were actually saying, you'd have another take on the matter. When they were tossed out, Eve cut him off. For more than a century, nothing. Nada. Zip. Not even the routine missionary stuff."

"Even so, only a truly wicked creature would exploit a sorrowing man," Sansenoy persisted. "Your evil hoard of succubae and incubi sought out Adam and Eve in their sleep. Thus were born into the world foul spirits that plague mankind even unto this day: giants, demons, succubae, even vampires."

"Let's not forget street mimes," she added caustically. "I get blamed for a lot, but not one of your Talmudic scholars listed me among Adam's supposed seducers. Or Eve's either, for that matter. Not that I swing that way."

"Yet there is reason to number you among these foul creatures of the night," Sansenoy said sternly. "Why else would the belief persist that it was dangerous for a man to sleep alone in a house, lest Lilith get hold of him?"

She shrugged. "A need to transfer guilt over naughty dreams? A last-ditch line to use at the local bar? 'Come over to my place, baby, because if you don't, Lilith will get me.' It's been centuries since someone hung an amulet over a cradle or recited 'bound is the bewitching Lilith' to stave off night visitations. After all these years, why should you care?"

The angels fell silent. For a long moment, there was no sound at all, but for the regular whir of passing cars and the plaintive howl of a coyote up in the Santa Monica foothills. Even the picture on the television screen was frozen, depicting two figures trapped in an ancient moment of knowledge gained and illusions lost, of sorrow and anger and sudden, bitter truths.

That's how Lilith saw it, anyway.

The screen split, so that half held the image of Paradise lost, half revealed the coffee-swilling avatars.

"Eve was very beautiful," Senoy/Joey said wistfully. "The perfect woman, fashioned for Adam by the very hand of God. Is that why you hated her, Lilith? Because she succeeded where you failed?"

Even as Lilith sniffed and sneered, she had to admit—privately—that maybe Senoy was on to something. She'd never quite sorted through her feelings about Eve, which was odd when you considered now many centuries had passed since the little bimbo had returned to dust.

Although, strictly speaking, "returned to dust" was not entirely accurate. Adam had been molded from the earth, as had Lilith. Eve, on the other hand, had been custom built around one of Adam's ribs.

"No wonder the biblical accounts make such a big deal about the rib thing," Lilith mused. "The writers wanted to stress that Adam's new wife was not made from the same stuff as he was. Eve was constructed from spare parts, and we're not just talking ribs here. She was made from Adam's fantasies, designed to suit his whims and wishes. You might say she was the ultimate trophy wife."

"And so you hated her, as you hate all women who supplant the first wife in their husband's affections," Senoy concluded.

A small, knowing smile lifted the corners of Lilith's lips. "Actually, I'm quite fond of some of them."

"Teach me how I am wrong," the angel implored.

Lilith took another sip of kosher wine. "Well, for starters, I have nothing against women who seduce married men. I've been the second wife more times than you can count."

"I know of some of these adulterous unions. You ruled as Queen of Zemargad and of Sheba. You were the bride of Samael the Demon King."

"And don't forget my crowning achievement," Lilith taunted him.

A long moment of silence followed. "We do not endorse as literal truth all the writings of the pre-Zoharic gnostic Kabbalists," Sansenoy said defensively.

"Who could blame you?" Lilith retorted. "Those guys claimed that the Matronit—the female aspect of God—went into exile with the Hebrews after Jerusalem fell. They'd also have you believe that God was forced to accept yours truly as a consort in place of the Matronit. Forced, mind you! Do I look like someone who has to resort to *force* to get a guy?"

"A metaphor," the Ross-shaped angel insisted. "Nothing but a metaphor. If any of it were true, you would be dead. The same scholars say that when the messianic era came, God and the Matronit would be reunited, and Lilith cast out and utterly destroyed."

"Cast out, I can't argue with," she said dryly. "But as you can see, I'm not dead yet. You might say that the case is still under appeal. The Jews and Christians have a hung-jury thing going about whether or not the messianic era has actually occurred."

"So you owe your existence to a legal loophole," mused Semangelof. "I'm beginning to understand why you went to law school."

Lilith aimed a slow smile at the Chandler-clad angel. "There is more to life than self-preservation, sweetie. I'm in the revenge business."

"How so? By advocating reasonable divorce settlements, you aid the men you profess to hate!" Senoy protested.

"Put aside my profession for a moment, and look at my personal life. I was a first wife once and a second wife more than a thousand times. Believe me, I found ways to make the life of every one of those men a living hell. And they deserved every moment of it."

"We've had a pile of complaints about your latest ex," Semangelof/Chandler admitted. "But is vengeance against the Sons of Adam so important that you would lower yourself to marry a schmuck like that?"

"Well, I'll admit that Stan was a step down from God, but who wouldn't be?"

The angel let the dig pass. "Our question remains: What's with the new career?"

Lilith gestured to the left half of the television screen, which still depicted in heartbreaking clarity the frozen tableau of Eden lost. "Adam got his perfect trophy wife, and look what it cost him."

"Some might say a woman like that is herself a Paradise," Senoy said tentatively.

"Yeah, a lot of men think along those lines. Eve might have been a size-four brunette with perky tits, but I'm not exactly hard on the eyes, myself. I've found thousands men who were willing to be seduced away from wife number one and boy, did that get old! So I learned a better way."

"Which is?" asked Senoy.

Lilith smiled coyly and picked up the remote. "Mind if I turn on the DVD? I have something that might clear things up for you."

In response, the images of cheerful coffee house and the locked gates of Eden faded from the screen, to be replaced by the *Seinfeld* rerun in progress. Lilith quickly pressed the buttons that switched from TV to DVD, driven to speedy efficiency by the possibility that Senoy, Sansenoy, and Semangelof might shanghai the show's male characters as avatars. That would be bad. Jerry could probably pull off the angel shtick, and George as a chubby, venal cupid was almost obscenely appropriate, but c'mon—an angelic *Kramer*?

The camera panned over a courtroom scene, and a baritone voice-over announced, "We now return to *L.A. Divorce*, Judge Evelyn Walker presiding."

As the judge recapped the settlement terms, Lilith's thoughts drifted to the events of last few hours. The three angels' visit, if it had accomplished anything, had confirmed in her mind the validity of the path she'd taken. During her long history Lilith had been woman, wife, mother, goddess, demon. Times changed, and like most of the Old Gods, she adapted.

She turned her attention back to the screen. The camera passed quickly over the too tan, too taut visage of someone's First Wife to linger on her attorney, Lilith Morgenstern.

"I still don't get it," Semangelof/Chandler said, a hint of a whine in his voice.

"What better career for a sex-and-blood demon than a divorce lawyer?" Lilith said smugly. "If you don't mind a little redundancy, that is."

"There's that," he admitted. "I understand why you represent the first wife, but why don't you torment the guy?"

"Been there, done that. A thousand times and change, if you recall my career as a second wife. You've heard the expression, 'So many men, so little time?' I can't be everywhere. That's what the Lilim were about, remember? To ruin the lives of men I couldn't get to? Well, times change, and so do female demons."

The television camera, as if on cue, pulled in for a close-up on the newly divorced man and the very young, very blond woman who was congratulating him with great enthusiasm.

"She looks familiar," Semangelof said in a troubled voice.

"Imagine her with bright red hair," Lilith prompted, fingering one of her own flame-colored locks as she waited for the angels to see the family resemblance.

There was a collective gasp as they made the connection, followed by a long silence.

"We got all the Lilim," Semangelof said tentatively. "That's the official story."

"Uh-huh. I keep that file in the same drawer as my copy of the Roswell report," Lilith sneered.

The demon's smile broadened as she watched the future trophy wife going about the family business. "Why ruin him in divorce court, when there's a longer, slower, more poignant vengeance in store for him? He wanted his Eve, and he got her. Given time, he'll be just as miserable with the deal as Adam was. I'm an immortal being: I can afford to be patient."

Lilith clicked off the set. Another silence followed while the invisible angels fumed and the demon savored the moment.

"We'll have to write up a report," Semangelof said at last, his disembodied voice sullen. "Do you have any idea what a hassle this will create? The Big Guy will have us checking out every second and third wife in Los Angeles! And for what? Surely not all of these trophy wives are Lilim..." His voice trailed off uncertainly. "Or are they?"

The mother of demons merely smiled.

Semangelof sighed. "Maybe just this once we should fudge the report. How about this: *Lilith believes every man deserves a second chance, and she wants all mankind to be as happy as Adam was with Eve.*"

Lilith chuckled darkly. "I couldn't have put it better myself."

A Lovers' Quarrel

by Jonathan Moeller

The house was locked, the windows shuttered. Even so, Lucas heard the screaming.

A Welsh serving girl answered his frantic knock. He pushed past her into the hall. "Dear God, Gwen, what's happened?"

The girl looked at Lucas with solemn eyes. "Dr. Williams, oh, it's good you've come. It's Mrs. Williams, sir. The baby. He seemed so healthy, and then…"

Lucas raced up the stairs. He heard Marianna scream again, the sound filled with despair. Lucas rounded the landing and found Henry pacing before the hallway mirror.

"Lucas?" said Henry. He seemed dazed. Henry had sailed from Boston town to Spain and Istanbul and India, had never lost a ship to storm or pirate. Never had Lucas seen his brother looked so crushed. "What…what are you doing here?"

"I had heard Marianna delivered a son," said Lucas. "I rode at once for Boston, to offer my congratulations. What happened?"

Henry resumed pacing, his big hands opening and closing. "The delivery went well, or so the midwife told me. The boy seemed healthy. And then…and then…he died in his sleep." He shook his head, face working. "It was hard. Three years we've been married with no children, and she's had two miscarriages before this. She was so happy. I fear the grief has driven her mad."

"Henry," said Lucas, staring at the bedroom door. "How long ago was the boy delivered?"

Henry frowned, brow furrowing. "It was…eight days? Yes, eight days. She was going to name him after me."

"Eight days," whispered Lucas. He knew what that meant, even if Henry and Marianna did not. "Did you have the baby baptized?"

"No," said Henry. "We go to Reverend Thompson's church."

Reverend Thompson was Congregationalist. The Congregationalists did not believe in baptizing children until the age of reason. Damned fools.

"I don't think you can do anything, Lucas," said Henry. "The doctor already came and went. I wish you had been here for the delivery. Maybe you could have seen something, done something…"

"I wish I had been here, too," said Lucas. "Let me see her."

Henry nodded. "Yes. You were always better with words. Maybe you can say something to comfort her."

Lucas doubted it, but he followed Henry to the bedroom anyway.

Marianna sat huddled by the window, sobbing. The sight made Lucas's heart twist. She was a year younger than Lucas, but now seemed older than Henry. Her face looked hollow and gaunt, her eyes puffy and shadowed. She held a small bundle cradled in her arms, a bundle with closed eyes and tiny blue lips.

It felt terribly cold in here. Lucas wondered if Henry felt it. He crossed the room and knelt besides the sobbing woman.

"Hello, Marianna," he said, laying a gentle hand on her shoulder.

She blinked up at him. "Lucas?"

He nodded.

"Thank God you're here," she said, desperate. "You can help my baby, can't you? He's sick. Can't you help him?"

Henry made a sound that might have been a groan, or a sob.

"Marianna," said Lucas. "Your baby died."

Then he saw it—a faint haze of shadow that covered the dead infant like a veil. He was quite certain neither Henry nor Marianna could see it. But that was nothing new. At the age of five, Lucas had seen the dead crew of a lost merchantman rise from the harbor and march through Boston's streets, and ever since, he had seen things no one else could.

"Can't you help him?" said Marianna, weeping. "Can't you do anything?"

Perhaps....

No, he dared not risk it. Infants died every day, did they not? It couldn't be helped.

But those children died of illness. The shadow veil proved that no illness had slain the baby. And he had never seen his brother like this. Or Marianna.

"I promise you," said Lucas. "I will do what I can."

"Thank you," whispered Marianna. She began weeping again, bending with the sobs

Lucas stood and crossed to Henry's side. "Stay with her. In her state of mind, there's no telling what she might do."

Henry blinked. "What will you do?"

"She can't sit here with a dead child forever. I will make the necessary arrangements, and return in two hours." Or he might not return at all.

"Thank you," said Henry. "You are a loyal brother. I scarce find the strength within myself to stand, let alone to make the…the funeral arrangements."

Lucas nodded and walked into the hallway, shutting the door behind him. He paced to the landing, running shaking fingers through his hair. This was madness. The Salem hangings had not been so long ago. If Henry had even the slightest inkling, if the truth came out, then Lucas would hang as a witch.

He turned, and saw Gwen staring at him.

"You know, don't you, Dr. Williams?" the serving girl said. "How the baby really died?"

Lucas nodded.

"I tried to warn Captain and Mrs. Williams," she said. "I made up the charm against the dark ladies, as my mother taught me, and hung it over the cradle, but Captain Williams would have nothing of it. Said it was papist superstition, and made me take it down. I'm sorry, sir."

"You did what you could," said Lucas, fighting the urge to curse. A baptism would have been enough. Gwen's charm would have been enough.

The girl's eyes widened. "You're going to do something, aren't you, sir?" She knew what he was, even if Henry and Marianna were too blind to see it.

"Yes," said Lucas. "My horse is tied outside. Take both the saddlebags to the attic, and hurry. Do not look inside them. Once I am in the attic, do not let anyone inside for any reason. Anyone! Do you understand?"

Gwen nodded and hurried off.

* * *

A short time later Lucas stood alone in Henry's gloomy attic, the saddlebags at his feet. Old crates stood against the walls, and in one corner an ornate looking glass sat beneath a dusty sheet. It had stood in the bedroom, Lucas recalled, until Marianna's first miscarriage.

Lucas pulled a piece of chalk from his saddlebags and drew a double circle on the floor. Between the circles he scribed various sigils of protection and warding. Inside the smaller circle he drew a pentagram, using the edge of an empty crate as a ruler. At each of the pentagram's five points, he placed a fat red candle.

He sweated in the attic's stifling air. When the preachers warned against the dangers of diabolical forces, they probably had no idea just how right they were. If anything went wrong…

Now or never.

Lucas began the ritual.

It went on for some time. Candles lit, powders tossed, chants spoken. Lucas produced a fat book from his saddlebag and read aloud, first in Latin, then in Greek. He sang a very specific chant in Hebrew, sang it again backwards. The hot, heavy air began to stir.

The candle flames dimmed, and the chalk lines seemed to glow.

Lucas took a deep breath and spoke the name. "Samael!"

An icy breeze flickered through the attic. The air smelled very bad. Yet the pentagram remained empty.

And then, all at once, the demon was there.

For some reason, he—or perhaps it—chose to take the form of a dandified French nobleman clad in rich velvets, a powdered wig crowning his head. All illusion, of course, but Lucas was relieved. Samael's true appearance would have been unsettling.

"You have extended a most gracious and formal invitation," said Samael, voice smooth. "How could I possibly decline such courtesy?" He glanced at the attic window. "Ah. New England?"

Lucas nodded.

"Tight-lipped, I see. Excellent. I am usually summoned by grandiloquent fools. To what purpose have you summoned me, might I ask?"

"Knowledge," said Lucas.

The demon smiled. "That is easily obtained. Though not cheaply. They say you New Englanders are positively devils for business." He chuckled. "As it happens, so am I. I'm sure we can come to a reasonable arrangement."

"I seek information about the Lilim," said Lucas, "and their mother, Lilith."

The demon's expression did not change, but the candles flickered and almost went out.

"Do you, now," said Samael at last.

"I already know much about her," said Lucas. "The legends are…disparate, let us say, but a common thread weaves throughout. The Lord created Lilith to be the first wife of Adam. But she was proud, and haughty, and refused to submit to Adam as a wife should. So she was seduced by a demon named Samael, who taught her the secrets of dark magic, and fathered monsters upon her. When Adam learned of his cuckolding, he told the Lord, who in his wrath cast Lilith from Eden, and castrated Samael."

The demon's lip twitched, once, and frost began to form on the rafters.

"Afterwards, Samael returned to her, but she scorned him, and withdrew to a cavern located Outside the circles of heaven and earth," Lucas continued. "Here she reigns over her Lilim, her monsters, and the souls of those she takes from earth. Because Lilith can never bear a human child of her own, she sends the Lilim into the earth to harvest the souls of newborn children. For eight days, an unbaptized infant is subject to her power."

For a long time Samael said nothing. Lucas wondered if he had pushed the fiend too far. Demons, like men, had their pride.

"A fanciful tale," said the demon at last. He smirked. "But a tragedy for your race, no? For in lieu of Lilith, Adam wed Eve, who lured him into sin and death, and made your race subject to my Master. But, come. You craved knowledge." His voice thickened with scorn. "If I can presume I teach one already so learned."

"You will tell me," said Lucas, "how I might travel Outside."

Samael laughed. "Step within this circle, mortal man, and you will see more of the Outside than you ever wished."

"A courteous invitation, but I think not," said Lucas. "Specifically, you will tell me how to reach the realm of Lilith."

"A foolhardy endeavor," said Samael. "Why would you wish to visit that harlot?"

Lucas told him.

"The way is known to me. I could share it with you." Samael grinned. No dandified Frenchman ever had teeth so sharp. "For a price. Can you meet it?"

"Yes." Lucas swallowed hard. "I can."

* * *

After Samael departed the pentagram, Lucas crossed to the looking glass. He snatched away the cloth and gazed into his reflection. Henry had brought back the mirror from one of his voyages. From Venice, perhaps, or Calais. An expensive luxury, to be sure, but it was nothing more than silvered glass in a wooden frame.

But according to Samael, it could become a doorway to Lilith's realm.

Lucas drew a pair of pistols from his saddlebags and tucked them into his belt. Each had been loaded with specially prepared shot. Around his neck he hung an amulet of Egyptian design. According to the old books, it had the power to turn aside beguiling enchantments.

He would put it to the test soon enough.

Lucas drew a knife, pricked his finger, and began to chant. A drop of blood splattered against the floorboards. He kept chanting, repeating the words Samael had taught him, and gazed into the mirror. His reflection gazed back.

Then his reflection was gone. In its place stood a naked woman.

Lucas stepped back, his chant faltering. The woman's skin was white as chalk, her hair and eyes like wet tar. The black eyes fixed on his face, and Lucas wondered what that white skin would feel like beneath his hands, the pale lips against his.

He clutched the amulet, breathing hard.

The mirror rippled like mercury, and the Lili stepped into the attic. Her bare feet made no sound against the floor. Lucas saw his reflection in her featureless black eyes.

"You called me," whispered the Lili. Her voice made Lucas sweat.

"I did," said Lucas, stepping back again.

The Lili glided toward him. "What do you desire, mortal man?"

Lucas stepped backwards yet again. "Daughter of Lilith, I wish only to talk."

"We can do more than talk," said the Lili, reaching for him. Lucas stumbled backwards. "So much more."

"Look down," whispered Lucas.

The Lili stopped, looked down. A vicious spasm went through her limbs. Lucas had led her into the center of the pentagram.

She shrieked, jaw yawning like a python's. A tongue like black leather lashed the air. "You will suffer for this, mortal dog! I will find those you love and tear out their hearts! I will..."

"Shut up," said Lucas, retrieving a bridle with an iron bit from one saddlebag. The Lili snarled, but did not speak. Taking care not to step within the circle, he leaned forward, rammed the bit into the Lili's mouth, and looped the bridle over her head.

The creature's black eyes promised his death, but she made no move to stop him.

"Now," said Lucas, "by this sign and this symbol I compel you. You will lead me Outside the circle of the world, and take me to your mother's realm." Or so Samael had claimed. Demons were liars, but Lucas hoped Samael hadn't lied about this.

The Lili's fangs grated against the bit as she turned toward the mirror. Lucas gripped the reins in his left hand and followed. She stepped into the looking glass once more, the mirror rippling. For an instant Lucas expected his hand to shatter the cold glass. The Lili pulled him in after her.

Lucas felt an instant of shocking cold, followed by a stab of agonizing pain. For a dreadful moment he felt himself falling, plummeting through an endless void. Then his vision snapped back into focus. He stood in a narrow cavern of dark rock, illuminated by faint, shimmering will o' wisps of blue light. The Lili stood a few paces away, smoke rising from her mouth.

An unsettling thought came to Lucas. He had bound the Lili with the power of the circle and pentagram. But Outside the circles of the world, those symbols might not carry the same power…

The Lili confirmed his suspicion by spinning around, flinging a clawed hand out in a vicious backhand blow. He leaned away, but even a glancing blow was enough to fling him back against the cavern wall.

He slumped to the floor, gasping. The Lili surged towards him with an enraged shriek.

Lucas wrenched a pistol from his belt and fired.

The silver ball tore through the Lili's chest. The demon-thing staggered, black hair billowing behind her. Lucas drew his second pistol and squeezed the trigger. The ball tore away the top half of the Lili's head. No blood came forth, but something like liquid darkness splashed against the cavern floor, followed shortly thereafter by a slender, crumbling body.

Silver, even Outside, retained its efficacy.

Lucas climbed to his feet and took stock of his surroundings. Against the cavern wall he saw the hazy, shimmering image of Henry's attic, close enough to touch, yet very far away. So long as the mirror remained intact, he could return to the circles of the world. If he lived that long, of course.

The narrow stone passage led down into a vast cavern, one that appeared many times larger than the grandest church in Boston. A will o' wisp drifted past his head, and Lucas jerked away. Within the sphere of pale of light he saw the face of a dead infant.

Lucas reloaded the pistols, gripped one in each hand, and followed the will o' wisps downward.

Soon a maze of crystalline light filled his vision. Thick, sticky webs choked most of the great cavern. One of the will o' wisps drifted up against the strands, and transformed at once into a fist-sized blue gem, alive with light. Lucas saw thousands, tens of thousands of gems imprisoned in the webs. Were these the souls of all the babies Lilith had claimed since the Fall?

It would have been beautiful, had it not been so ghastly.

A stone stair wound its irregular way upwards. Lucas took the stairs, climbing higher and higher, past the webs and the thousands of imprisoned spirits. A low murmuring filled his ears, like a sighing sob, or constant mocking laughter. Then the stairs ended in another great cavern, and Lucas found himself before the throne of Lilith.

Thousands of Lilim filled the cavern, sleek and pale. The other spawn of Lilith wandered the cavern, shapes gaunt and terrible, creatures that did not look even remotely human. The walls and ceiling blazed with the blue light of imprisoned souls. Three of the Lilim glided towards him, eyes blacker than hell, mouths opening into dagger-edged pits. The charm against his breast grew warm. It must have been working, because Lucas felt no desire.

Just terror.

Lucas leveled the pistols. The three Lilim stopped, but more circled around him.

"You slew our sister," one said.

"You shall pay for that," said another.

"Perhaps," said Lucas, trying to keep the pistols trained on all of them, "but before that, two of you will die. Your demon blood will not save you from silver."

"You will die here," they purred.

"But not alone," said Lucas. "Who will join me? Let's not be bashful." Sweat dripped into his eyes, but he dared not wipe it away. "Come, now. You can either kill me and two of you will die…or you can give me free passage to your mother."

The Lilim laughed again. "You should have let us slay you, mortal," one of them said. "We would only have killed you. Our mother will show you no such mercy."

They demon horde parted to form an aisle. It ended in a dais of red marble, atop which rested a throne of translucent alabaster. And on that throne sat Lilith.

The sight of her hit Lucas like a blow. He could not look away. She was not beautiful. She transcended beauty. Her hair shone like molten copper, her eyes cold and bright as emeralds.

The amulet against Lucas's chest grew hot, painfully hot.

"So," murmured Lilith. Her lips moved, but Lucas heard the voice inside his head. "It finally has come to pass. Some intrepid fool dared to follow my daughters here. And now you've come to challenge me for the soul of your precious whelp, no doubt." She appeared amused.

Lucas leveled both pistols at her chest. "You are older than sin itself, but you are still a woman of flesh and blood, and you are still subject to death."

That amused the thing on the throne even more. "I'm sure it comforts you to think so. Tell me, which screaming whelp do you hope to pry from my wicked grasp?"

A murmur of amusement rose from the assembled Lilim.

"The son of Henry and Marianna Williams," said Lucas, "taken this morning."

Lilith seemed surprised. "Indeed?" She reached up and plucked a shining blue gem from the web. "This one? He is not your son."

"Regardless," said Lucas, keeping his hands steady, "you will release him."

"Why?" said Lilith.

Lucas gestured with the pistols. "Madam, I should think that obvious."

"Perhaps," said Lilith, smiling, "but not to you. What is the child's soul to you? He is not your son."

"He is my nephew," said Lucas. "That is enough."

"Is it, now?" she said mockingly. "You must be a learned man to have come here. Let me add something to your learning. I was Adam's first wife, when the world was young. Do you know why he set me aside?"

"Because you were barren," said Lucas. "Because you were seduced by the demon lord Samael."

Lilith laughed aloud and waved a hand at the Lilim. "Do I seem barren to you? Samael was pathetic. As are all his kind. Samael was a…convenience to me. I would have abandoned that wretch Adam in any case. The lord over all creation," she said, her mouth twisting in scorn, "and he was a prevaricating weakling. I was to submit to him? I was to let that spineless fool breed sons upon me? It was an insult. So when I was cast from Eden, when Eve came to bear his sons, I promised revenge. He would have his precious brats…until I took them from him. Is there any pain greater than a father looking upon his slain son?"

"I know this story," said Lucas. "It has nothing to do with my nephew, whose soul I cannot help but notice you have failed to hand over."

"Where is the child's father? Why has he not come in wrath to rescue his offspring?"

"He lacked the means to travel here," said Lucas. "I did not."

"And so you came," said Lilith. Her green eyes flickered, and the amulet grew almost unbearably hot against Lucas's chest. "You traveled beyond the circles of the world. Few can boast of such a feat. And what drives men to great deeds? Passion? Madness?" She smiled. "Love?"

"Enough," said Lucas. He raised the pistols. "The soul, now."

Lilith flicked a finger.

The pistols shivered in Lucas's hands. The triggers dissolved into powder even as he squeezed. The grips shattered into splinters, and the barrels fractured into broken shards. The silver balls clattered against the floor and rolled away, followed by the shards of his protective amulet.

He felt Lilith's gaze drilling into his, her eyes digging into his thoughts.

"Pity," said Lilith with a lazy smile. "Silver is proof against dark magic, but it seems that steel and wood are not."

Lucas took a step back, heart hammering. He heard the Lilim closing in a circle around him. Lilith rose, the glowing gem in her right hand, and laughed.

"You have come to your death," said Lilith, "and you do not even know why." She lifted the gem. "You wish this were your son, do you not?"

Lucas said nothing.

"You loved her," said Lilith. "You loved her from the moment you first saw her. But you were just a hungry student, and your brother was captain of his own ship. So she married him, and you could only watch." She almost sounded sympathetic. "You watched, and you yearned for what you could not have."

"No," whispered Lucas.

"Yes," said Lilith. "And now you have thrown your life away for a child that is not yours, for a brother who thinks little of you, and a woman who loves you not."

The assembled Lilim laughed, their derision echoing through the glowing cavern.

"Then kill me and be done with it, damn you," said Lucas.

"I could," said Lilith. "Or you could give your soul to me."

"And spend eternity imprisoned in your webs? Hardly appealing."

Lilith laughed. "A mere demon might take your soul. Give your entire self to me." The green eyes blazed. "Your brother has no sons, but you shall father a new race of Lilim upon me. And I can give you your heart's desire."

She blurred, her form wavering, and became Marianna.

Lucas's breath fled.

She did not look as Marianna did now, gaunt and drained from grief. She looked as Marianna had the day before her wedding, fair and young and strong. The broken amulet might have warded Lucas from the allure of the Lilim, but nothing could have stopped the desire that raged through him now.

"The world has scorned you," said Lilith, "now come to me."

Lucas staggered towards her. He did not want to, but he could not stop himself. No, he did want this, more than he had ever wanted anything. Lilith came into his arms, cold eyes alight with triumph.

"Bold fool," she whispered, "you are mine now." She lowered his face to hers and kissed him.

When their lips touched, a surge of dark power roared up from within Lucas and plunged into her. Lilith shoved him away, blurring back into her original form, green eyes wide with sudden alarm.

"What is this?" she snarled.

Lucas waited. Lilith was mortal. For all her power, for all her great age, she was still human, still subject to death.

And subject to demonic possession.

"Greetings, my darling." Lilith's mouth moved, but it was Samael's voice that came forth. "It has been far too long."

"You!" shrieked Lilith. "You dare! Leave at once!"

"Oh, I think not," answered Samael. "Surely the mighty Lilith can drive a mere pathetic dupe from her flesh."

Lilith lunged at Lucas. "You fool! You brought him here!"

Then she jerked backward, reeling and trembling. Lucas could almost see Lilith and Samael wrestling for control of her body.

"My dearest love," said Samael. Lilith's hands came up, trembling, the nails long and sharp. "I've missed you so." The blue gem tumbled from her grasp. "Your eyes are like emeralds. I think I'll take them first."

Samael plunged Lilith's thumbs into her eyes. Her scream of agony made the cavern shudder, the glowing webs tremble.

The Lilim rushed towards Lucas and Lilith, shrieking. Samael bellowed a snarling, grating incantation, and the cavern shuddered again. A rip appeared in the air, a hole into nothingness. A sulfur stench flooded into the icy air, and the hosts of Hell, the demons subject to Samael, poured forth from the tear. The Lilim screamed and grappled with their nightmarish enemies, even as Lilith writhed and jerked, her bloodstained face contorted as she struggled with Samael.

Lucas ducked, seized the fallen gem, and ran.

He half-leaped, half-tumbled down the great stairs. The cavern trembled like a dying man, strands of web snapping free. Lilith screamed again, and Lucas rolled down the last thirty feet of stairs. He stumbled to his feet, every muscle aching, and sprinted.

He passed the withered husk of the Lili he had shot. In the stone wall he saw the image of Henry's attic, cloudy and indistinct. Lucas risked a glance over his shoulder, and saw a horde of enraged Lilim and a throng of maddened demons racing after him.

Lucas threw himself at the attic.

He endured a moment of agonizing pain, followed by a wave of burning heat and again by terrible cold. Then he was rolling across the attic floorboards, shards of broken mirror raining around him. Lucas flopped onto his back, gasping for breath, broken glass grating against his coat and boots.

In his right hand, the glowing blue gem shivered and vanished like morning mist.

And, below, he heard a baby begin to cry.

* * *

"A peculiar illness, no doubt," said Lucas. "Though a cruel one, to make you worry for naught. Sailors come to Boston from halfway around the world. No doubt one picked up some strange Oriental disease and carried it home."

"You really think so?" said Henry.

Marianna kept crying, but not for grief. The baby gurgled in her arms, and Lucas doubted she saw anything else. Henry himself looked thunderstruck. Lucas was grateful for that. Neither husband nor wife noticed his disheveled condition.

"Yes," said Lucas, "I do." He hesitated. "I should go. Both of you have suffered quite a shock…"

"No," said Marianna. "No. Please, I beg you, stay a few days. In case the disease returns. I should feel much better if you did."

Henry gripped Lucas's shoulder. "I shan't trust these Boston quacks again. Telling me my son was dead. Ha!" He grinned. "Put all of them together, and they'd still only have half your wit."

Lucas found himself blinking back tears. "Yes. I'll stay for a few days." He grinned back. "I'd wanted to make the rounds of the bookshops anyway."

He closed the door and walked back into the hall. Gwen was waiting for him with anxious, awed eyes.

"That was no illness, I'd swear to it. The poor boy was dead. What did you do?"

"What I had to," said Lucas. "It would be best if we never spoke of this again."

"Yes," said Gwen. "Yes, of course, you're right, sir." She blinked a few times, then smiled. "Such a bold fool. We will finish our kiss one day, you and I."

Lucas seized her arm. "What did you say?"

"Sir?" Gwen frowned. "I'm...I'm sorry, sir. I just felt so dizzy for a moment. Did I say something impolite? I'm terribly sorry if I did."

"No. Nothing of the sort." Lucas let go of her arm. "Perhaps you should see if Captain Williams has any brandy in the house."

Gwen hurried off, passing the mirror at the end of the hall as she did so. Lucas stared at the mirror for a moment, and then hung his coat over it

The Shiksa

by Mike Resnick and Lawrence Schimel

"And I said to God, 'Go ahead, make my day.' Just like that I said it. 'Make my day.' I sounded better than Clint Eastwood. 'Make my day,' I said, and God, He split the light from the darkness. So I said to him, 'That's pretty good.'"

Morton Goldberg, who I've known since we went to college together and who also does our taxes for us, laughed and laughed.

"*Daaaaaaddy!*"

"Cain!" I bellowed towards the hallway. "How many times have I told you not to hit your brother?"

I turned to face the other direction and yelled toward the kitchen, where Eve was trying to cook stuffed cabbage and, judging from the smell, the cabbage had lost in straight falls. "Can't you do something about your sons? We're trying to take care of some business in here."

Eve came through, wringing her hands in her apron. She did so only in part from frustration, I knew; she also wanted them to be properly dry. I listened for the resounding smack against Cain's behind and at last turned back to Morton and spread my hands in a gesture of helplessness. "What can you do? You know how children are these days."

"All too well," Morton said, and we nodded our heads and sighed until Eve had crossed back and disappeared into the kitchen, with Abel clutching her skirts, even though he'd already grown taller than his mother.

I shook my head at the boy as he disappeared into the kitchen, then turned toward Morton. "So back to business. Golf tomorrow at eleven?"

* * *

"He doesn't like my cooking, can you believe this? My own son tells me he doesn't like my cooking!"

I had no idea who Eve meant when she said this—I was just tuning her out, as usual—but that didn't stop her from nattering on. She was in a mood, and she was going to complain. As part of her retribution she plopped a second stuffed cabbage onto my plate as she continued, "And after I braved God's own wrath to sneak back into Eden and pick him some fresh apples because I know that apple pie is my son's favorite, and could I do any less for my son?" She smiled at Abel, and patted his head, before glaring at her other son and continuing, "I brave God's own dire wrath to sneak back into Eden, not to mention nearly getting killed by a flaming sword and a *messuginah* archangel, and does my son care? No, he tells me he doesn't like my cooking and doesn't want any!"

She spooned a baked apple onto Cain's plate and then disappeared into the kitchen with the tray of them before I had a chance to grab dessert. I stared down at the lumpy green cabbage on my plate and wondered briefly if my imagination was strong enough to pretend it was a baked apple (and if my stomach could survive if my imagination was that strong).

"Daaaaaddy!"

The moment Eve's back was turned, they had to fight.

"Knock it off, Cain. How many times have I told you not to hit your brother? Now sit on your hands until you learn how to behave properly." I glared at the kitchen, where Eve had disappeared, leaving me to deal with the kids while they were fighting. I sighed and turned towards Cain, hoping to distract him with conversation. "So tell me, what did you do today while I was slaving away to keep food on your plate and a roof above your head?"

"It's Saturday, Father. And anyway, you're retired."

"Just answer the question, and spare me the back talk."

"I met a pretty girl today."

I put my fork down and orchestrated a heavy silence upon the room as I stared at my son. I could hear, in the kitchen, that Eve had stopped cooking at this news.

"What did you say, Cain?" I asked. I kept my voice measured and slow.

"I said, 'I met a pretty girl today,' Father."

"That's what I thought you said." I contemplated the salt upon the table. "This girl—is she Jewish?"

My son looked me in the eye and said, "No."

Before I had a chance to say anything, Eve had come roaring in. "What did you say?" She grabbed Cain by his ear and turned him to face her.

He shrugged out of her grasp and looked up at his mother. "I said she's not Jewish," he said defiantly.

Eve threw up her hands, as if to berate God. "For this I lay in pain and agony? Three whole days of labor I was with you, but do you care? I feed you and clothe you and teach you proper manners so you don't embarrass yourself in the world, and do you pay any attention? This is too much! All I want to do is dance at your wedding and see at least one Jewish grandson. This is so unreasonable for a mother to want? After I changed your diapers all those years, gave you milk from my own breasts. These very breasts." Eve shook her ample bosom for emphasis. "I can't stand this!"

Eve swooned, falling across the couch. Abel leapt immediately to his mother's side, and began fanning her face and loosening her apron strings to give her air.

"Look what you've done to your mother!" I said to Cain. "Is that what you wanted—to send her to an early grave?"

"But you always say '*Shiksas* are for practice,' Father. I hear you tell Uncle Marvin's children that all the time."

I could hear that Eve, who had begun to breathe again over on the couch, had gasped and suddenly stopped breathing once again, and I knew that I would be hearing about this again later in the evening. I sighed and fed my second helping of stuffed cabbage to the dog. I looked at the beast as it wolfed down the table scraps, and I hoped we had an understanding that it would sleep on Eve's side of the bed tonight.

"What is okay for Uncle Marvin's children is not okay for my children," I told Cain.

"But why, Father?"

"Because I said so."

Cain was dissatisfied with this answer, and since I couldn't think of a better excuse, I changed the subject.

"This female person, she's pretty?"

"Very pretty, Father."

"This female person, she smokes only in moderation?"

"Yes, Father."

"This female person, she drinks only in moderation?"

"Yes, Father."

"*Aha!*" I said, raising a forefinger in triumph. "What kind of nice girl drinks and smokes?"

"A *shiksa*, Father."

He didn't miss a beat, my son, and much as I wanted to slap him, I was proud of him for that. But I knew talking with him was hopeless. This girl had her claws too thoroughly into him. I knew the feeling quite well.

"Son, let me tell you about *shiksas*. Once, when I was much younger," I began, "*much*, much younger, many years before I met your mother," I added, for Eve's benefit, "I went with a *shiksa* for a short while.

"It was back when Eden was newly planted, before I had named even a tenth of all the plants, and I hadn't even started on any of the birds or the fishes. An angel came to me—or at least I *thought* he was an angel; back then demons were so newly fallen from grace that they still looked like angels, and it was only much later that I realized he was a foul demon, but by then it was too late. Anyway, this demon smuggled me out of Eden into the World. I'd never been into the World before, so of course I was excited and anxious to explore this new territory. It had been quite lonely in the Garden of Eden, with only animals to talk to, and working all hours of the day, naming everything in sight. So I was ready for a break when this demon came up. I was also quite naive back then, since I'd never been to the World before. Anyway, this demon took me to a club, where this woman was. This *shiksa*."

I paused in my story, remembering Lilith.

"She was much worse than just any *shiksa*. Much, much worse.

"Anyway, the club where I met her was one of the real hotspots of Gomorrah; it was called Paddles. It was one of those kinky-sex clubs, you know, one of those S&M dungeon type of places." Eve squeaked again on the couch, and sat bolt upright, but I continued with my story before she had a chance to interfere. "I'm sure you know exactly what I mean. I still remember what young men talk about in the locker room.

"But I didn't know any of that when this demon-who-I-thought-was-an-angel brought me to this place. I caught on pretty soon once I was inside, but I couldn't very well leave, because I didn't know how to get back to Eden without my guide to bring me back. So I followed him through the various dungeons until we came to a room where a pretty girl sat all by herself in the corner, and while my guide was busy watching the whipping occurring on the bed, I went and talked to her.

"She had long jet black hair down to her waist, eyes like dark pools, and beautiful dark skin. I sit down next to her and say, 'What's a nice Jewish girl like you doing in a place like this?' She laughs at me, and it's only later I learn that she was neither nice nor Jewish.

"Lilith had kinky tastes from the start. She liked uncircumcised men. How unhealthy, how unclean! But that wasn't the worst of it. Talk about unclean, Lilith liked to sleep with demons. We're talking tails and cloven hooves, which didn't make them kosher, I'll have you know.

"And she always, *always* insisted on being on top. She wore these thigh-high boots with five-inch heels—and we won't even *invent* boots for another four thousand years. And the ointments! My God, one smell of them could do more to your libido than six years of your mother's cooking."

Eve gave a little moan, which sounded remarkably like "ungratefulsonuvabitch!" and began crying again.

"And at one point she asks me if I'm having a good time, and I catch my breath long enough to answer that I am having about as good a time as anyone has ever had, and probably better, and she smiles and says Good, that helping happily married men have a good time is one of her prime functions in life, the other one being to show us that we weren't so happily married after all."

Well, I described some of the things she taught me, like the Jivaro Passion Grip (which will become all the rage just as soon as God gets around to inventing Jivaros), and the Penetrable Forest, and the Moebius Trip (which she assures me will drive someone called Einstein wild in 1906 A.D., whatever an A.D. is), and when I finished my story, I recognized the gleam in my son's eye, and I instantly knew that no good would ever come of Cain.

I sighed and asked him, "This girl, what's her name?"

At least I will have something to hate, this *shiksa* who had led my son away from the path of righteousness. Not that he needed much coaxing. So prone to violence, to domineering control. Just the type to be turned on by some *shiksa* dominatrix.

"Lilith, Father. Her name is Lilith, and she said to say Hello to you if you still remembered her." Cain gave me a wicked smile. "I'll tell her you remember everything."

Looking for Lilith
by Nisi Shawl

    Not a word. Looks, gestures, grimaces or blank stares; that was all she got. Everyone was making baskets or printing "James Brown—Superbad" tee-shirts, or coming up with new recipes for hot sauce or wrinkle cream. Some of them didn't look busy, wearing out raffia chair-bottoms or tumbling pebbles in a heap of gravel. Still, one could never be sure. Not all work is visible.
    But either they were preoccupied, or rude, or they didn't want to admit that they couldn't help. It was clear that if they had ever known the answers to her inquiries, they didn't remember them. She was pretty sure that once, they had known.
    She stayed in the hotel several weeks, and finally everyone got used to the crazy light-skinned girl and her persistent questions. And she was persistent. Down at the station at dawn, out at the clubs till two in the morning. She was tired, but she dared not sleep her fill. She might miss a whim, an evanescent urge to help.
    It was George at the Sous Venir Boutique who gave her her first real clue. She was standing inside, watching the dust collect on new and old curios in his front window; useless things for useless people. A weathered, walnut-bark-skinned man walked past, balancing an ancient rattan suitcase on his head. It appeared to be held together by clothesline. His eyes stared fixedly forward, his jaw was locked tightly, stubbornly holding onto his many secrets.
    George nodded. "He knows."
    At once she flew out of the shop. But the burdened old man was nearly out of sight. The battered case bobbed over the heads of the crowd, bouncing down the hill, deeper into the decaying core of the tourist sector. Sidewalk gave way to crumbling concrete, then to brick. The suitcase disappeared into the courtyard of a deserted hospital. Racing through the colorful throngs of foreigners and natives, she ran under the grey arch.
    The old man was resting on the edge of a dried-up fountain. She came to his side and sat, waiting. When they had both caught their breath she asked.
    "Where is Lilith?"
    He met her piercing eyes with his dull ones. "I know. I show you the way. Come in here." He rose and led her under palms that

had found the moisture lost by the fountain. They entered the bathhouse. "Here. Look. I made it."

She stared, beneath her feet, over her head, all around her, absorbed in the mosaic and the story that it told. Every part of every part mattered, and if you looked at a piece it made sense, and if you looked at the whole it made more sense.

She saw a tree before a mountain lake, high above a plain, flowering whitely. From below its stem a river tumbled and twisted, feeding the tree's far-reaching roots. Hollows darkened the cliff behind the falls. Water and wood intertwined harmoniously, following their common path. The tree's flowers burned brilliantly, casting shadows of the lower branches upon the flatlands. There were shadows, too, behind the tree, in the waters of the lake. The shapes of these shades were larger, bulkier, yet streamlined. All was lapped about by green darkness.

She walked forward and looked more closely, her steps hollow and gritty in the ruined bathhouse. Light fell through gaps in the roof and showed her tiny specks of black in the green border, specks swarming for a mass of mottled red. Ghostly, skeleton-like shapes were woven with snakes. There were spaces between the snakes. She slipped off a shoe and placed her foot in one of these spaces. A perfect fit.

She changed positions. Some of the tiles representing the savannah were glazed differently, though the glazes covered identical colors. Some tiles were shinier, or duller, or rougher than others. Depending upon her point of view, she saw the differences as spirals, ripples like heat waves rising from the grasses, or tall mounds pierced with fatal-looking blackness. Crouching, she seemed to see the blades of brown and green fashion themselves into other shapes: slings, sandals, baskets, nets and lassoes.

The empty pools were tiled in black, veined with silver and gold.

Over all was a likeness of the sky, broken by the sky itself. Between expanses of blue, changeless clouds were interrupted by changing ones, leaving her to wonder at what might be missing from the picture.

On the walls and floor, too, pieces were missing. But these seemed almost to have been removed on purpose; this was not vandalism, nor was it the destruction of the elements. It was an act of deliberate mystification. Still, she thought she recognized the patterns, some as concrete as antique sidewalks, some more abstract: accompaniment, betrayal. Some were simple and straightforward, others knotted about themselves, too complicated to be seen, only felt.

When she understood it all, she looked outside. She had expected the old man to be gone, but he was there, watching her. "Can you take me?" He nodded.

Eight fevered days later, they left. The way lay upriver, first through jeweled jungle, then savage savannah. The old man, Joe, led her, but this was not entirely necessary, for once on the proper path, she found that all was as she had been shown. Fearful adolescents accompanied them, young relatives of Joe's, in his command. They were as unfamiliar with the wilderness as she was, and not as driven. She did not rely upon them completely, nor upon the stores they carried. She studied the signs and watched for signals.

Joe still bore his rattan suitcase, keeping it always at hand. Pitying him somewhat, she asked if one of the youths might not carry it for him, but he would not allow it. And in truth, his burden seemed to buoy his steps.

They passed dead villages. Human bones filled huts, spilled out of ceremonial circles, dragged onto the trail by scavengers.

It was the untamed and the unknown that scared her crew; they were not at all put off by these sad, familiar remains. They helped themselves to any ornaments and tools that they came upon, sharing them amongst themselves. Perforce, she accepted an ivory toothpick pressed upon her by one well-muscled youth. It was prettily carved, and stained with dark dyes. She decided that this was a signal to her that she must stop abstaining from flesh. Under the shiny leaves of gigantic trees, she joined in a feast of warm, salty stew.

Joe nodded his approval to her across the small, bright fire. There were rules that had to be broken. She had to make them to disregard them. Sometimes it didn't seem worth the trouble she took, prohibiting the pronunciation of different diphthongs, the contact of certain bodily parts. Especially when she had to disobey her own ultimata soon after they were born.

It took so long. There were so many little pieces, so many formalities, so many observations to make. But if she had gone the same way in a hurry, she wouldn't have gotten were she was going.

She did not hasten, but neither did she hesitate. There was danger all around, and she had to deal with it, and learn from it. She memorized the patterns woven by snakes, and found how to place her feet to avoid their inevitable strikes.

Incredibly minute insects plagued their path. As she had been instructed to do, she carried a lure before her, sweet-smelling meat that attracted and held the biting flies. Their concentration upon the lure enabled her to pass untaxed.

The savannah was inimical to human life. The river misbehaved itself, winding in fractious turns; to follow it strictly would have meant spending months on the hot, hostile plain. Often nothing appeared on the surface of things but a dry, gravelly bed. The true river ran belowground in these places.

At night, gases emanated by the grass destroyed all extraneous matter with which they came into contact. Fortunately, the fumes clung low to the ground, never rising above knee level. It was possible for the band to clothe themselves in tightly woven sandals fashioned from blades of the grass. In this manner, they were able to shield themselves from the effects of the gases, though the rough edges chafed their skin. During the day they rested, licking their wounds. They had little water.

A woman became ill during the night. She doubled over under her load, grunting, then collapsed to the ground. At first they thought that the gases had dissolved her skin, causing the flow of blood that issued from her thighs. But when they lifted her up it was seen that there had not been time for them to act. The bearer was in the throes of a spontaneous abortion. It was necessary to bathe her with their last bit of water, and to carry her on in a grass sling. The sick woman made an awkward burden, tossing and moaning in the darkness. At last the sun rose and a breeze blew, breaking up the deadly vapor.

Joe was gone. The plain extended in all directions, emptily. In the light of the new day the plateau was visible, distant though it was. But of her guide there was no sign. The width of waving grass could not easily hide him yet did not show him. Unperturbed, she settled herself down in the flickering shade. Soon, she slept.

She woke alone. The adolescents had deserted her, taking with them all the equipment except a couple of empty water containers. Undoubtedly, their desire to complete the journey had left with Joe. She remained calm. All would proceed as it was meant to.

Heading for the nearest open stretch of river, she made her way among the mounded entrances to deep burrows. Bald, conical, they hunched up warningly in her path. From time to time starlight struck brightness from beady eyes perched on these mounds, waist high and higher. They did not frighten her. Had her followers still accompanied her, they might all have fought together to fend off the creatures, as she had been shown in the bathhouse mosaic. But it was not so, and so to fight would not be necessary. As it was, she kept her distance from the mounds, knowing that the rodents could not attack her through the flesh-melting fog. And when the dawn came and the misty barrier retreated, it seemed they must have other things to attend to, as she had anticipated. She filled her empty water containers from the peaceful river, secure in her belief that the burrowers would not be hungry for some time to come.

Looking for a place to rest for the day, she came upon proof of her conviction: the fugitive crew. The crossing of their path with hers was easily explained by the presence of water. The fact that they remained there when they had been so eager to return to the city was due to their inability to leave. Parts of them protruded from the openings of the burrows. Their limbs and torsos jerked as the carnivorous rodents below struggled to drag in as much meat as they could before the poisonous mists of evening dissolved the bodies. The burrowers were industrious animals, and she was sure that many of the adolescents were already safely buried in chambers far below. Their packs had been rifled, all the sweets pilfered, or spoiled and scattered. She salvaged what she could and continued.

At last she stood at the foot of the waterfall. It towered above her, its heights remotely grand, its base thunderous, overwhelming. All was just as she had thought to find it. Moments passed. Nothing changed. There was something wrong; the dam's spillway remained open and the white torrent continued to pour down from the head of the falls. She could not enter.

She camped, waiting. Sooner or later, the spillway would have to be closed. The rains were not due yet, not for some time. The flow would have to be cut, or at the very least, slowed. She waited, picturing the Lake of the Clouds receding from its shores, the lotus blossoms sinking lower and lower with each passing day. Surely the giant turtles would be called to their harnesses and instructed to pull shut the great underwater gate? Surely the lake would not be emptied simply to keep her out?

It was not. As she was sitting, watching, nearly tranced by the changeless flood, it thinned to a mere rivulet. Revealed now in the face of the cliff, the entrance to the tunnel yawned wetly before her. Smiling, she rose and took the path within.

There was no light. Dodging dangerous projections, stepping with the precision needed to avoid the numerous chasms, she made her way in and up.

The tunnel debouched upon a natural amphitheater. White sand covered the ground where she stood. She was in the arena. She tensed, looking around with dilated pupils. That shadowy shape, she decided, must be Joe, seated on one of the many curving stone benches that surrounded her.

And there, that was Lilith, dressed in flowers. At first she could not tell, with her dazzled eyes, what was the color of Lilith's hair, what hue her skin. Then her eyes adjusted, and she saw.

Lilith's skin was black, so black it reflected the world, like deep, still water. Her hair was like a nest of petals, white and glowing, shedding its immortal glory on the blossoms she wore. In her shining face, her eyes were wide, drawing secrets into their softness. Her high brow was smooth, clear as volcanic glass. But beneath her proud, arching nostrils, the corners of Lilith's blackberry mouth drooped in a pouting frown.

Panic struck through the supplicant. Why had she come here? Why had she sought this potent female force, a demon, as some said, or a goddess, even? What was her business here, her intention, her own name? It seemed as though she hadn't asked herself these questions for a long, long time; and now there were no answers.

A terrible silence hung around them. Suddenly, she sank to her knees. It was all she could do. She had come, she knew not why. Perhaps the motive for her journey was another's. She could only trust that her persistence would be enough, even without comprehension.

At her action, Lilith relaxed her frown and made a motion with her right hand, the side where Joe was sitting. The movement was vague, yet imperious, and Joe quickly left his seat, lifting the familiar suitcase. With ceremonial precision, he came down the steps. His bare feet slapped on the grey stone, then silenced themselves in the sand. The rattan case rustled. He placed it before her in the ring and resumed his place, all without meeting her eyes.

Helplessly, she stared at the knotted clothesline that held the case shut. She cast her eyes about her. There was no sword, no blade of any sort. She closed her eyes and reached blindly for the knotted mass. The silence was patient, no longer terrible, as she worked the bindings loose. The lines fell free, and she opened her eyes again, blinking in amazement. Hesitantly, she placed her hands on the case's foremost corners, then looked up to Lilith for approval. Lilith nodded.

Taking a deep breath, she lifted the lid of the suitcase. She looked within it. It seemed to be packed with grey and white feathers, gently stirring in the wind. But, no, the feathers stirred of their own accord, lifted, formed themselves into gently beating wings. Geese uncrooked their necks, arched their pinions and flew out of the suitcase. One, two, three, and then more, faster and faster, clumsily at first, but with gathering grace. An entire flock of geese flew up into the air and circled above the amphitheater. Bright feathers and quiet ones floated down into the arena. Then the entire flock, having organized itself into the proper formation, flew away to the Lake of the Clouds.

She searched the faces of her audience. They appeared to find the suitcase's contents as marvelous as she herself had.

The feathers lay motionless on the sand. Stooping, she picked them up, placing some of them in her hair and retaining other between her fingers. Then she performed for her guide and goal. She danced the dance she had been taught by the snakes of the jungle, the meandering of the river, the abysses within the tunnel, the knotted cord. As she finished her dance, she realized she had not come for this. She had come to come. She had made the dangerous journey not to reach the end, but to travel to it. She bowed, sweeping her feathers in the sand.

Lilith was alight with approbation. She clapped her hands. "Well done, well done," Lilith said. "I had not been led to expect so much from you." Lilith glanced toward Joe, who only bowed his head. "You will shine as an example to others."

Again Lilith made the vague, imperious gesture. The old man came back down to the arena. This time he faced her squarely. "Did not meant to doubt," he told her, dull eyes apologetic. "You come through. Thank you." He paused a second, putting both hands on her shoulders. "Maybe you come through again."

Then he pushed her down gently, collapsing her and folding her neatly together. Reverently, respectfully, he placed her inside the suitcase and began, once more, to tie the knots.

Alone
by J. Robert King

His name is mud. That's what the Lord God calls him: Adam. Mudman. That's because Adam is made of mud, which is a sticky kind of ground that comes from dead plants and dead animals and poo.

I love my mudman.

I'm made of something else. There's another kind of sticky ground called clay. It doesn't come from dead things or poo but from wind. Wind grinds rocks to sand and then to dust and then drops the dust in hollows and mixes it with water and presses it into clay. I'm made of clay, so I am called South Wind.

I am Lilith.

Me and the mudman are made for each other.

Well, really, we are *separated* from each other. That's how the Lord God makes things—by separating them: light from darkness, water from land, mud from clay, male from female, mudman from me.

We're separated, but we're supposed to be together. It's not good for someone to be alone. So we've got parts that put us together.

Adam's got a penis. I have a vagina. They're opposites. One goes out and the other goes in. They fit together.

Adam shows me how they fit together, pushing me on my back on the grass and flinging up my feet like hands spread toward the sun. He shows how we fit together by fitting us together over and over with a frustrated look like he's proving something.

It doesn't take long to prove.

Adam nods to himself and sits back and lies down on the ground.

This is good. Adam has shown me how we fit together. I'll show him another way.

I swing my leg over him and sit down.

"Lord God!" says Adam. He sounds like he means it, but I'm not sure what he means—happiness or madness or excitement. It seems like all at once. "Lord God, what kind of mate is this you gave me?"

That's the way we speak to the Lady Goddess. (I call her Lady Goddess because I'm female. Adam calls him Lord God because

Adam's male. We are saying the same name, but my voice is smooth and Adam's is rough, so the same name comes out different.) We talk to the Lady Goddess because she's everywhere and always listening and she's trying to figure us out while we are trying to figure ourselves out.

The Lady Goddess says to Adam, "She is a fine mate."

"Look at her," says Adam, and he looks at my breasts while I show him how we fit together. He blinks like he can't remember what he is saying. Then he says, "She's sitting on me!"

"Not sitting," I say. "Bouncing!"

The Lady Goddess says, "Don't you fit this way?"

"No. She's beneath me," Adam says.

"I'm above you," I correct.

"You're supposed to be beneath me."

"But we fit," I point out. I show him again and again, and he can't remember what he is saying. Then his eyes open wide and he is nodding like he understands, but then he frowns and pushes me off and says, "I need a new mate."

This is surprising. I have shown him three ways we fit together, and he has shown me one. That is four ways. How many ways do we have to fit together to be mates?

"I need a new mate."

The Lady Goddess says for me to walk with her, and we leave the mudman, and we walk in the cool of the garden.

"He can't need a new mate," I say to her. "We are made for each other."

The Lady Goddess says, "Lilith, you are made of old stuff. Clay is old. It came before any living thing. Adam is made of new stuff—mud that lies on top of clay. That is why he wants to lie on top of you."

"We fit other ways."

"But mud wants to lie on clay."

So I go back to Adam and let him show me the one way he thinks we fit together, and each time his face is tight like he is making an argument and then his face relaxes like he has made his point.

"I get your point," I tell him, "but there are other ways." I show him and show him and show him. It's not just me on top, but each of us on a side, or one up and one down, or all kinds of ways. Adam nods and smiles as I show him these ways, but afterward he frowns like all my ways have disproved his one way, and he scowls and says, "I need a new mate."

So, the Lady Goddess says for me to walk with her, and we leave the mudman and walk in the cool of the garden.

"He doesn't need a new mate," I say. "I have shown him thirty-three ways we fit together."

The Lady Goddess says, "Yes. He doesn't need a new mate, but he must be shown that fact." And so she makes all the animals—all the beasts of the field and the birds of the air and everything that creeps upon the earth or swims in the sea. I get to see it happen. I get to see creation. And she brings these new creatures to Adam to offer them as mates.

Adam looks at the first one, which is a scaly lizard with spines jutting out and eyes that pivot in different ways. "I can't mate with this prickly, ugly, cold…gecko." And so the gecko has a name, but Adam does not have a mate. He flings the gecko away and picks up another creature, a slimy amphibian with a blown-up throat. "I can't mate with this boogery, swamp-stinking, croaking…bullfrog." And he throws away the bullfrog and picks up a little bird. "I can't mate with this yellow-bellied sap sucker." And lifting another: "I can't mate with this buck-toothed, flat-tailed beaver."

The Lady Goddess's plan is working.

Adam thinks the fish are too cold.

He thinks the birds squawk too much.

He thinks the marsupials smell too strong.

He thinks the mammals are too furry.

When Adam has named and tossed away all the other mates, the Lady Goddess whispers to me, "Now, go back to him."

So I go back to Adam and show him the thirty-three ways we fit together and show him three other ways that are enjoyable even if we don't quite fit.

One second after he is nodding and saying, "Yes! Yes! Yes!" Adam rolls away and says, "I need a new mate."

"Sophia!" I say, which is the true name of the Lady Goddess. I say it like I mean it: happy, mad, and excited all at once.

So the Lady Goddess says for me to walk with her, and we leave the mudman and walk in the cool of the garden.

"Adam and I are made for each other," I tell her. "Why does he want a new mate?"

The Lady Goddess says, "You are made by erosion: rocks broken down by wind. He is made by corruption: bodies broken down by death. He does not love you because you have no corruption in you."

"But he does not want the codfish or the newt or the buzzard or the wallaby or the meerkat."

The Lady Goddess seems weary and says, "Then I will have to make for him a woman of mud, who will have corruption in her. It is not good for the man to be alone."

The Lady Goddess makes Adam fall asleep, and she scoops out part of his side and makes it into a mudwoman. And the Lady Goddess breathes life into the mudwoman and lays her beside Adam.

Adam rolls over in his sleep and lies down on the mudwoman, and they fit together. They're *asleep*, and they fit together. They are not just made *for* each other. They are made *of* each other.

Adam wakes up, and he sees the woman and wakes her up, and they fit together again.

The Lady Goddess says, "It is very good."

But I do not think so. I go to Adam and say, "Who is this mudwoman?"

"She is bone of my bone and flesh of my flesh. She is my mate."

"She is not your mate. She is *you*. I am your mate. We fit together in thirty-three ways."

"I don't want to fit with you. I want to cleave to her."

And so I turn to the mudwoman and see that she *is* bone of his bone and flesh of his flesh. "I will show you that she is you!" And I push her on her back on the grass and show her two ways that we fit together. Before I can show the other thirty-one, Adam kicks me off and bellows like a lion.

That's the name he gave to one of the animals he didn't want to mate with.

I run away and hide behind the Tree of the Knowledge of Good and Evil. It is the one tree that is forbidden in the garden, so that's the place I will be safe from Adam.

"It is not good for him to be alone," I say to myself, remembering what the Lady Goddess said about Adam. "But what about me? I am alone."

I am not alone. There is a creature here, a serpent that puts its moist fingers on me and slithers around my thigh. I catch it in my hand and look it in the eye and say, "You are not made for me."

The serpent does not answer. It is an animal. Animals do not have language. I do not expect a voice from it, but I hear one anyway, a voice saying, "We *are* made for each other."

"Who is speaking?" I ask, and the serpent is gone.

"It is I," says a white-robed being who stands before me. He looks like me and the mudman, but he glows as if he is made of sun rather than of mud or clay, and he has wings. "I am just as you are. I have done no wrong, but I am alone in paradise."

"You are bright," I say.

"That is my name," he says. "I am Lucifer, which means 'Light Bringer.'"

"How are you like me, Light Bringer?"

He smiles and approaches me. "I would not bow to Adam, just as you would not bow to him. You would not let him be your master, and I would not let him be my master."

"Yes," I say. "The Lady Goddess has made a new mate for him."

"And the Lord God has banished me from heaven, but not from paradise. We are not alone," says Lucifer, taking my hand and lifting me up to stand beside him. "Taste of this tree. Let it balm you."

"I will not!" I say, looking at the sickly yellow fruits that hang above my head. "The Lady Goddess has forbidden it. She says that if I eat of this tree, on that day I will surely die."

"Aren't you hungry?"

"I am."

"What then may you eat?"

"I may eat from the fruit of any tree in the garden except the Tree of the Knowledge of Good and Evil."

And Lucifer turns and goes to the Tree of Life and says to me, "You can eat of this tree?" He takes down a pomegranate and splits it open in his hands and holds out the bleeding fruit.

I take the fruit from the Tree of Life and eat it and wipe my mouth on my arm and say, "I am full."

"Yes—full of eternal life," says Lucifer. "You have chosen well. Two trees—one that gives death and one that gives life—and you have eaten of the tree that gives life. I wonder: which one would the mudwoman choose?"

"She has corruption in her," I say. I am not lying. It is not kind, but I am not lying. Just then, I see the mudwoman coming up the path. "Here she comes," I say, but Lucifer is gone. I am alone except for the serpent that wraps its moist fingers about my feet.

"Lilith," calls the mudwoman. "Lilith?"

"I am here," I tell her, and she comes to me beneath the Tree of the Knowledge of Good and Evil, and the serpent crawls toward her toes.

The mudwoman does not look at the serpent but at me, and she looks at my breasts the way Adam does. They are the same person. "We fit together," she says.

"Yes," I say. And I show her thirty-one more ways, and also the three ways that are enjoyable even though we don't quite fit. "See?"

"I see," she says.

"Maybe Adam will see, now," I say.

The mudwoman shakes her head. "Adam won't see."

"But you are the same person. If I am your mate, I am Adam's mate."

"You are not my mate."

"But we fit together!"

"Adam is my mate! I am his mate!"

I try to show her the thirty-three ways and the three other ways, but she yanks out my hair and scratches my face and kicks my belly and roars like a lion, and I run from her because she and Adam are the same person and I am afraid of both.

But I do not run far. I hide behind the Tree of Life and pluck a pomegranate and eat the bleeding fruit and rub it on my face and my head and my belly to heal me.

But the mudwoman is talking to the serpent. It has put its moist fingers on her, and it is climbing around her body, and it is whispering to her. I cannot hear what it is saying. The mudwoman walks to the Tree of the Knowledge of Good and Evil, and she plucks off the big yellow fruit and bursts it open on her knee and eats the bleeding meat.

And Death shadows her face.

She takes the halves of the yellow fruit and holds them over her breasts. "Cover me! Cover me!" she screams to the serpent, and it wraps its moist fingers around her thighs and covers her vagina. She bellows like the howler monkey and runs, and the serpent falls from her as she scampers into the woods.

The serpent smiles and scuttles toward me and says, "She has corruption in her, and she has chosen death. She will die, and you will be Adam's mate...."

"But they are the same person," I say. My heart splashes in me. "If the mudwoman dies, the mudman dies."

"Then I will be your mate," says Lucifer.

I grab a pomegranate from the Tree of Life and run for Adam. He could die this day, and I love him, and if he dies, I will be alone forever.

It is not good to be alone.

But when I see him, the mudwoman is already there with him, and she takes the two halves of the yellow fruit from her breasts and holds them out to Adam. He stares at her breasts and can't think what to say.

I rush up beside her and break open the pomegranate and hold it out to Adam and say, "Don't eat the fruit she offers! It is Death. She is going to die, and you will die if you eat it. Eat the fruit I offer. It is Life. I will live, and you will live with me."

He looks at my breasts and can't think what to say.

The mudwoman holds out the yellow fruit to him. She says simply, "I am your mate."

Adam takes the yellow fruit from her and eats.

Death shadows his face.

He shouts, "Cover me! Cover me!" and he runs away into the woods.

The mudwoman presses the yellow fruit to her breasts and shouts, "Cover me! Cover me!" and runs after him.

I am left alone.

Then the Lady Goddess comes walking in the cool of the garden and sees me standing there with the halves of pomegranate and says, "You have chosen wisely, Lilith, to eat of the Tree of Life."

"But my mate has eaten of the tree that gives death."

"What did he do?"

"The mudwoman gave to him, and he ate."

Death shadows the Lady Goddess's face. "Then, they will die, this very day."

"Don't let him die. Let him live."

"If they remain here, near the Tree of Death, its poisons will kill them this very day. If I banish them from the garden, they will live longer—a hundred years, perhaps a thousand, but at the end of their days, they will die."

"Banish Adam and leave the mudwoman."

The Lady Goddess looks sadly at me. "Adam would not go without his mate."

"*I am his mate!*"

"The mudwoman is his mate."

And the Lady Goddess leaves me and strides through the garden and calls to Adam, and he cowers in a bush.

"Because you ate the fruit I forbade to you, you must leave the garden today or die."

"Where will I go?" he cries.

"Out into the world, where you will work for every morsel you eat and at the end of your days will die and return to dust. Why did you eat of death?"

"I ate because my mate ate."

"Where is your mate?"

The mudwoman calls out from another bush. "I am here."

"You are banished with Adam," the Lady Goddess says, "and he will fill you with his seed, and you must bear his children, for you and Adam will die, but your children must remain upon the earth."

"Will they live, then—my children?"

"They will die as you will die. You were made of corruption and have chosen death, and so death will be handed down to your generations," the Lady Goddess says. She is in despair. "Why didn't you choose life?"

"The serpent offered me, and I ate."

The Lady Goddess reaches into the wood and pulls forth the serpent and strikes off its legs and flays the skin from them and makes clothes for Adam and the mudwoman.

And no sooner are its legs struck off than the serpent changes, becoming once again the man made of light, except that his arms and legs are gone and his body is long like a snake, and his tail is as a shining sword.

"Guard the gates of the garden, Lucifer, lest Adam and his brood seek to return. And ever while they live—these mortals and their offspring—you must do all in your power to drive them away from paradise."

The feathered serpent flies into the air and drives Adam and the mudwoman from paradise and perches on the gate and swings his scythe tail to slay them should they return.

And as they leave, Adam turns to his weeping mate and says, "I will name you Eve, for you will be the mother of all living."

But the Lady Goddess turns to me and says, "She will not be the mother of all living, for you have in your womb the quickening seed of Adam—from before he had eaten of death. You will bear children, too, and they will be the immortals, and they will be the rulers of men."

I smile at the Lady Goddess and say, "I will no longer be alone."

* * *

In nine months, they begin spurting out of me, from my vagina, where Adam planted them. His seed is strong and bears many children from me.

I'm frightened when the first one comes. I think I'm dying. My belly snaps tight like it will split, and the babe rips out and makes blood shoot from me. The babe emerges, and I grip him in slick fingers, and he shines so yellow in my hands that he seems the sun. He comes at morning like the sun, and he shines like the sun, and I name him Ra. And Ra sets his blue eyes to the blue skies while he suckles at my breast.

But even as I hold him to me, another child grows within. Adam's seed is strong. And the child jets from me and hits the earth squalling and struggles in her bag of waters and is mud-mantled by the time I sweep her up. The mud must have gotten into her being, because she is a child who will always slosh in mud and water, who will forever pour water and shit and blood out across the desert to make it bloom. And I name her Tawaret.

And while I am still nursing Tawaret and Ra, other children come from me. Adam's seed is strong. They come from me—Osiris and Zeus and Odin, who are immortal sons of Adam, and Isis and Hera and Ve, who are his immortal daughters.

I love them all and tend them in the garden.

And while I bear these children of Adam, Eve bears others: Cain who murders Abel, and Seth, and a host of mudmen. They grow quickly, like a brood of dogs—who are puppies beneath their first moon and mongrels beneath their twelfth. They intermarry and spread out across the land and make cities and make war. At first, they turn their murderous ways on each other, but in time, they come to the garden to make war on us.

Many a morning I sit with my children by the gates of the garden and look out over a field glowing with campfires and bristling with war tents. Many a noon I watch as Lucifer flies down from the gate and reaps the heads of the soldiers with his scything tail.

But this morning is different. This morning, the mudmen fill the world from horizon to horizon, and they wheel siege engines to the banks of the Tigris and Euphrates and look as if they will take the garden at last.

And the Lady Goddess comes to me in the cool of the garden and says, "Lucifer cannot defend the garden alone. You live here, too, you and your brood. You must send your children out to fight alongside Lucifer."

"I do not want my children to be killers," I say.

"Either they kill some children of mud, or all children of mud will enter the garden today and die."

So I send them out—my sons and daughters to kill their half-brothers and -sisters.

It is sport for my immortal brood. As the children of mud charge across the grasslands toward the garden, Ra blazes above them so they crack and wither, and Tawaret floods their blood out over the cracked earth to feed the grass. As the children of mud sail their warcraft down the Tigris, Osiris rises in the river and topples them into the water, and Isis wells the tide so that they are carried away into the sea. So fight my sons and daughters, side by side—Zeus and Hera, Odin and Ve—and the children of mud in their multitude cannot stand against their immortal kin.

And my children delight in the spoils of war—the metal weapons so cleverly forged and worked, the silk robes so patiently woven and dyed, the chariots and boats so masterfully hewn and strewn.... My boys delight in lying with the mudfolk women and filling them with immortal and uncorrupted seed. My girls delight in lying with the mudfolk men and being filled with their corrupted seed. And so are born the Nephilim—the giants and champions of men: Aeneas and Odysseus, Gilgamesh and Goliath and Samson, Rameses and Romulus and Remus, Hercules and Alexander....

But the sons of Adam hate my sons, just as Adam hates me. The mudfolk cry out to the Lord God to kill us, but the Lady Goddess loves us and will save us.

"If you remain here, there will be war forever between you and the children of Eve," she says. "And so, I am splitting up paradise and setting the pieces at the corners of the world."

So the Lady Goddess separates Eden like a pomegranate and creates other hidden realms—the Heavens and the Underworld and Olympus and Asgard—and my children, two by two, leave Eden to dwell in these places. They are grown and raised and gone.

* * *

And once again, I am left alone in the garden. It is not good to be alone. Without my children—creatures made *of* me—I long for the man made *for* me.

Adam is nine hundred and thirty years old, now, and Eve is dead, killed by the poisons she ate in the garden. The children of Eve have filled the world like a gnat swarm, but Adam is alone now, just like me.

Unlike me, he is dying.

I go to him.

His ancient back is bent above the hoe, his skin striped with the scars of time, his bones craggy and caved. Still, I love him—I, who am still beautiful and young and naked and unashamed.

"Adam," I say to my mudman, "Adam."

He looks up with cloudy eyes. His arthritic fingers tighten on the hoe handle. He listens with withered ears that sprout hairs and lifts a bald head and blinks into the clear air. "What?"

"Adam. I'm the one who was made for you."

"Eve?"

"No," I say, letting my glowing, naked form appear before him. "I'm Lilith."

"Who?"

"Don't you remember? When the world was newborn, we were, too. We were made for each other."

"God made me," Adam says proudly, thumping his chest. "I was the first man."

Adam doesn't remember me. I cannot be angry. His brain is full of poison. "I was the first woman."

Adam blinks, surprised. "You were there?"

"I was there."

Bliss smooths his face, drawing back the corners of his mouth and the corners of his eyes. "There was this place, a garden—beautiful and perfect. And I was young and naked, and there was this young and naked woman, this perfect woman—not my wife, but another woman."

"I was that woman," I tell him. "I *am* that woman."

His eyes become teary crescents in his craggy face. "A fine woman, she was. A damn fine woman. She knew thirty-three ways we fit together. Not like Eve, who knew just one. That woman knew thirty-three ways, and three ways that we didn't even fit but that were enjoyable anyway."

"I *am* that woman," I tell him, and there are tears in my eyes as well. "We were made for each other."

He looks beyond me. "That's just what she said. She was so desperate to be with me, but I thought I could find better." He takes a deep breath. "I couldn't.... What I wouldn't give to be with that woman one last time."

"Be with me," I tell him, and I draw the rags back from his old body—his withered skin and shrunken muscles and broken bones—and I enfold him in my arms and legs.

And the mudman, the one I was made for and the one who was made for me, has one last moment of joy as I lie with him. His face is clenched, but he doesn't seem to be trying to make a point. He is trying to understand one. His eyes open wide, and he rocks on me as if he is saying *yes*, and he understands at last.

"We were made for each other," he says to me.

"We are mates," I say to him.

But I do not know if Adam hears me. I cannot ask if he does, for suddenly his fingers go slack on my arms, and his nine-hundred-thirty-year-old body slumps against me. I hold him, and I weep. I have waited almost a thousand years for this moment—the time when Adam knew he was made for me, just as I knew I was made for him. But the moment comes too late.

Adam is gone.

And now, I am alone forever.

* * *

In nine months, I give birth to the first of Adam's spent seed. The boy is human like Adam, but in all other ways is like me—beautiful and honest and tragic and alone. I speak to him, and he does not hear. I hold him, and he does not feel. I weep for him, and his eyes are dry.

So I lay my son in a human crib. Surely the mudwoman can reach him. She suckles the babe and sings to him and holds him, but even in her arms, he is alone.

He bears my curse.

And more children come from me, more changelings fill human cribs. Mothers sing "Lilith be gone"—lullabies to keep me from their cribs, but I cannot bear these children alone. At first, the changelings are one in a million, and then one in ten thousand, and then one in a thousand, and now one in a hundred.

The mudfolk mothers can't save them anymore than I can. They can only hold these unfeeling ones to their breasts and sing lullabies to unhearing ears.

The L.I.L.I.T.H. System
by Lara Gose

The applause was deafening, as usual. Throughout most of the show I had felt that my performance was a little off, however, and I was ready to be done with it. I bowed, waved and then left the stage. Griffen, my personal assistant, met me with a warm, wet hand towel and said, "Great presentation, Lil. You were really great."

I sighed. "We've had this conversation hundreds of times, Grif, and I can't believe you're making me have it again...It wasn't great. I wasn't great. Quit telling me what you think I want to hear instead of telling me what I need to hear."

He lowered his head and proffered me the towel. I grabbed it and began wiping my hands. It's the only perk I require when I'm speaking. You can discover the details of any number of contracts on websites like The Smoking Gun, and you'll read about really picky things that aren't at all required in a dressing room—such as the number of flower arrangements and the flowers that can or can't be in them or the kind of M&Ms that should be provided including colors that aren't allowed in the mix. But all I demand is a hot towel waiting for me after the show, like you get when you fly first class or dine in a Japanese steakhouse. Public speaking makes me need to wash my hands when I'm finished more than any other activity I've tried in my life. Maybe it's the feeling that I just shook thousands of very dirty, very mortal hands.

I continued walking back to the dressing room, Griffen keeping pace, even though the applause had turned into the rhythmic clapping that signals the crowd wants an encore. They wanted more of me than I could give. It had been a long week, and the tour for the new book had only just begun. Twenty-five cities in twelve days.... Fortunately some of those visits would happen via satellite. But even an immortal gets weary.

"Tell them I'm not going back out," I told Griffen. "And if there's a meet-and-greet after this, cancel it. I'm not in the mood."

"I can get you out of the former, but I won't do the latter. You have an interview tonight. There's no way out of it, Lilith." He pushed his horn-rimmed glasses back up his aquiline nose.

Again, I sighed. "Fine time to develop a backbone, Grif."

He smiled. "This one's going to be important to you. The president of your national fan club, Missy Harper."

I couldn't help but wince. Not just a fan, but an uber-fan. *The* uber-fan. Griffen was so right about this.

"Where am I meeting her?"

"She was at tonight's presentation. Security will be bringing her around to your dressing room. I can give you…say, fifteen minutes to yourself before she gets back here."

I nodded and pushed open the door to the dressing room. "Make it so. And thanks, Grif."

I watched his leonine head bob in return, and then he rushed off. Ours was a strange relationship, one that had evolved through the years, much like our physical forms. In truth, I had no better friend in the world, and I have hoped on occasion that he might say the same about me, despite everything.

Inside the dressing room, I was blessedly alone. An embarrassment of riches waited for me in the form of gift baskets and flower arrangements. Once in an interview I had said that I enjoyed the *tecolote ranunculus*, and ever since then I had received enough bouquets in tribute to make Caesar Augustus envious. At least I had learned that lesson before I had the chance to say anything negative about something I cared little for.

Griffen had arranged things in the room, which was really an antechamber to the smaller, more private one where I had dressed and had two assistants fix my hair and apply my make-up, as was expected. You can't disappoint the masses. There are just some things they expect, and that was one reason I wouldn't be changing into sweats and a tee-shirt or something else a little more comfortable than my black silk power suit and heels for this interview. I suspected that Griffen had removed a few flower arrangements to make it seem less like a jungle. The furniture was grouped to create a cozy space for conversation, and on the coffee table he had laid out a tea service and an assortment of sweets. He always paid attention and took care of details like that.

I paused to admire a few flowers before taking a seat in the fashionably overstuffed loveseat in the room. I kicked off my shoes and closed my eyes. For just a few minutes I wanted to be anything but "on" for an audience.

My mind wandered. What would she want to know about, this Missy Harper, president of the L.I.L.I.T.H. fan club? I could make an educated guess or two. They usually wanted to tell me how much my system had changed their lives, and they asked me what had made me decide to reclaim my name, turning Lilith into something other than a word signifying a demon out of religious history. It didn't matter to them that I talked about that decision in my presentations and in my books. What mattered was that I gave them the opportunity to tell me their stories and that I told them mine personally. Had I realized how tiring this cult of personality could be, I might have done things differently when I made the career change that had placed me on this path. But The L.I.L.I.T.H. System had treated me well. Given where I had come from and where I had ended up…

A knock on the door roused me from my reverie. I stood and quickly put my heels back on just before Griffen entered, followed by a couple of the security team that traveled with us. I found their headsets, tasers, infrared goggles and other gadgets a bit ridiculous, but I hoped their presence would deter any too-curious mortal, if not others of my kind. They were followed by a young blonde dressed in linen—black slacks and a crisp white blouse, both fitted to her trim figure. So much effort goes into the creation of fine cotton linen. My opinion of the uber-fan rose a tiny bit.

"Ms. Harper, allow me to introduce the author of the New York Times bestseller, The L.I.L.I.T.H. System…" Griffen began.

I stepped forward, cutting him off so that he could avoid using the surname that custom made necessary in this day and age. I held out my right hand to take hers.

"Yes, of course, Ms. Harper. It's so very nice to meet you. Call me Lilith, please. I hope you enjoyed the presentation."

We shook hands.

"I did, of course, although I thought it seemed a little forced tonight. I mean, it went well, the crowd loved it, but I believed it more when I saw you in Chicago last winter when you were lecturing at the university."

I laughed and made eye contact with my assistant. "See, Griffen? What I need to hear."

Turning back to my guest, I explained, "My assistant Griffen will stay with us, but if you don't mind, the security detail will wait outside."

"That's fine with me, Lilith."

"Please, take a seat," I gestured at the pieces of overstuffed furniture. The men in black left the room, Ms. Harper moved to the chair beside my loveseat, and Griffen took a post not far behind her. She had not balked at calling me by name, as others sometimes did. That interested me.

"You were in Chicago earlier this week. I live there. I should apologize in person for having to cancel our interview. Something came up. It couldn't be helped. I am grateful to you for rescheduling."

I chose to ignore the fact that Griffen had not reminded me of the canceled meeting. Her candor further intrigued me. Even Griffen rarely spoke to me so directly. It was refreshing to encounter in a fan.

"Well, Missy, I'm pleased that we were able to reschedule so easily. Yours is an important position in the fan club, and we all certainly value your contribution to the success of The L.I.L.I.T.H. System," I said, reaching for the teapot. "May I offer you some tea? And please help yourself to some goodies. I find the caffeine and the sugar help replenish my energies after a presentation. I drink it strong and sweet."

"A cup of tea would be lovely, thank you," she responded. I poured two cups as she gathered a few cookies onto a plate.

Leaning back into the comfort of the loveseat, I held the saucer in one hand and raised the teacup with the other. Why not return candor with candor, I supposed.

"Look, Missy, I don't mean to be inhospitable, but we will probably both have a more interesting time together if you direct the interview where you want it to go. I'm a bit tired from this week's touring, so I'm happy to let you lead. If you stumble across anything I don't want to discuss, I promise you that I won't take offense unless you try to push the matter after I tell you I'd rather not talk about it. Agreed?"

I saw Griffen raise his eyebrows, a look of surprise darting across his face. I wanted to laugh but thought better of it.

"I think I can abide by those ground rules, Lilith," Missy paused to sip her tea. "I suppose I have a dual purpose being here, speaking with you. I mean, I'm here on my own and also for the club, after all."

I nodded and sipped my tea.

"I've wanted to tell you how much your work has changed my life…"

I swallowed some more tea, using this effort to stifle the groan that so desperately wanted to climb out of my throat. Such promise, wasted.

"I'm sure you hear that all the time. I get it myself, from time to time. I run a program for at-risk high school students, as they're called. Truly, they're kids who need an outlet, a helping hand, something that they don't get at home or in school, for whatever reason…"

"That's admirable work," I replied as she paused to take a bite of a peanut butter cookie.

"Thank you. It was you who inspired me to do it."

I noted that my cup of tea was going dry and refilled it, certain I would need the camouflage to hide behind as she continued to speak. Best to get it over, I thought.

"You're right," I said. "I do hear that sort of thing frequently. But each story is unique. Please do tell me yours."

Griffen's eyebrows flashed again. I worried that I didn't sound sincere enough. Then she started again.

"When I consider where I am now, it's almost difficult to understand where I was just a few years ago. Nothing had ever been easy. My parents were killed in a car accident when I was twelve years old. My dad's sister refused to take me in, so I became a ward of the state. I married young, right out of high school, and we had two children—twins—right away, not because we planned it but because we were pretty careless. My husband and I were users. We lost our apartment and ended up on the street. He OD'ed, and the children were taken away from me. I was pretty sure I had hit rock bottom, and then my in-laws got custody of my babies. Even now that I've turned around my life, I will probably never see them again except through a private detective's dossier."

I recognized the faraway look in her eyes and the quiet tone of her voice. So many of the people I encountered were survivors of similar stories. While I understood their pain, I always had to fight to suppress the part of me that became enraged at the audacity these mortals had to compare their travails to mine. Our stories were similar in theme but vastly different in magnitude. I fingered the pendant I wore on a fine silver chain. A nettle seed nestled in a clear glass bead to hold a memory: the stinging plants I harvested for soup and tea, for fibers to make a linen as best as I knew how, to be strong for my babies, to give them rough blankets made with a mother's love so that they might have something of me before they were taken from me…

Griffen gestured behind her, and I refocused my attention on Ms. Harper. She sat still, paused. We had to continue. This had to end soon. I had a plane to catch at 0-600 so that we could get to San Francisco for an interview on a morning news show.

"More tea, dear?" I offered to re-fill her cup. "Loss has left a deep mark on your life."

She nodded, and lifted her teacup.

"I couldn't have gotten through it all without The L.I.L.I.T.H. System. Do you ever marvel at the lives you've touched? I mean, in only a handful of years, you've created a phenomenon as big as anything Oprah's ever done."

Ah, Oprah. There's a comparison that gets made at least once with every book tour. I nodded.

"It's humbling."

"It's so simple, really. But I couldn't figure it out on my own. I mean, I might have, but you helped me find it sooner. Life Is Living In Thine Happiness…It was February, freezing outside, I had a bad cold and a stomachache, but I was walking around outside because the shelter I usually stayed at was closed." She laughed, sharply. "They had to fumigate."

I sipped my tea and nodded encouragingly.

"I had managed to scrape together some change, and I wanted coffee or a bowl of hot soup. So I was walking downtown looking for someplace where I could get something like that and have time to warm up. And then I saw a big window display with a cutout figure of you standing in the window next to a stack of your first book. I stopped to look. I think it was something about you that caught my eye. This is embarrassing…"

She paused, her cheeks and neck beginning to blush. I couldn't imagine what she could have to say.

"Just spit it out," I said. "Being direct is so often the best way to get past being embarrassed."

"Well, it's just that it can't possibly be true. I mean, for a long time after my mother died, I looked for her face in every woman I met. But I never found it. Then I saw this cutout of you, and there was something…the color of your hair, the shape of your face, that reminded me of her. My reaction was so visceral that I just stood on the street crying as the tears froze on my face."

She paused, caught up in her reflections, and sipped her tea. I waited.

"I was a bit delusional at the time, in retrospect. I remember thinking that I had to go in the store and see my mother. So I found myself spending far too much money on a large paper cup of organically grown hot coffee for the opportunity to sit inside the bookstore's café and page through your book, *The EVE Principle: How Not to Be Absolutely Dejected and Miserable*. It would be too much to say that I walked out of that bookstore a changed woman, but I did leave with something to think about. And not long after that, I found that I was able to just flip a switch in my head and change the way I had been feeling and thinking. I made plans and set goals and did everything I could to become the better person I could be instead of continuing to be the lesser person I had been…"

I noticed that Griffen was following our conversation intently.

"It's a marvelous feeling, isn't it? That moment of initial realization that you can choose to be more than you are is so…empowering!" I raised my teacup as if making a toast, and Missy responded in kind.

"It is. It truly is. And I cannot thank you enough. Which is one reason why I decided to form the fan club and after that the foundation that supports my work with at-risk youth. Would you believe that most of the funding for the foundation has come from L.I.L.I.T.H. System fans? I don't know how much of the community you are able to experience…but the support, the network…well, it's all amazing."

I leaned forward, resting the teacup and saucer on my knees.

"You have really inspired a multitude, Lilith, and the ripple effect adds astronomically to that number. Honestly, I can't think of anyone I've met through the club or at your lectures who isn't using his or her inner strengths to help others, even just in small ways."

She laughed, and I raised my eyebrows to question the source of the joke. She caught the gesture and responded.

"Maybe your ideas have spread so efficiently because so many of your converted are ex-junkies!"

"I've certainly been accused of worse things than selling crack," I said with a straight face. I could only hold it so long. Her laughter was golden and contagious. I realized that I wanted to continue to share her company. It was too soon for our interview to end.

"So tell me about your work," I suggested.

"It's simple, really," she said as she grabbed another cookie to munch. "I trained as a social worker, finishing my degree in two and a half years instead of four. And I set up the foundation while I was in school. It was my senior honors project. As difficult as things had been before, they became that much easier after I started following the system. People seemed to want to help me. I wasn't mean or angry, and I didn't rebuff them or scare them any more."

"Yes, change your attitude and change the world around you," I said. "It surprises me how something so simple can be so difficult to achieve for many people."

"My thoughts exactly, Lilith," Missy replied, emphasizing her point by waving her index finger.

"I've always appreciated how you talk about rehabilitating your name as a way of rehabilitating your persona. I mean, I had disappointed and crossed people in my past. I needed to be rehabilitated. Pretty much from the ground up—my personality, my reputation. And that's why I decided to do something to help teenagers.

I moved my teacup and saucer to the coffee table and shifted forward in my seat.

"Maybe some of them can figure out how to flip that switch and have an easier time of it. They can spend more of their lives living in their happiness. My work helps others, and by helping others I help myself because maybe some of those people will understand how I have changed, how I have done my part to help, and they will see that they, too, can facilitate change in their own lives."

I could do it. I believed her. I could change. I believed her. And realizing that saved me.

As did Griffen, who cleared his throat and said, "Lilith, I hate to break this up, but you do have an early flight to catch…"

Missy Harper set down her teacup and saucer, looked at her watch, and said, "Oh, goodness! I didn't mean to keep you so late. I know your schedule is full. I've really enjoyed just talking with you, but I should be going. Look, it's a terrible imposition, but what if we reschedule the interview? Or I could e-mail you questions, and Mr. Griffen could get back to me on your behalf. It's for the magazine, the interview, or I wouldn't ask."

I felt muddled. I nodded slowly, standing as she stood, holding out my hand to shake hers. "I think Griffen will find some time for us to meet again. We're traveling a fair bit over the next several weeks, but maybe there will be a layover in Chicago.…"

"That would be wonderful!" she said, grasping my hand with both of hers. "I look forward to it!"

And then in a whirl she was out the door and being escorted to her car by security.

After a long moment, Griffen broke the silence. "Well, Lil?"

"She's one of mine, isn't she? A child of one of my children's children…"

He nodded. "I think so. She has a way of drawing people to her. It reminds me of you."

I realized that I was staring at the door, as if I could see through it after her. "This is…unexpected. It's been so long."

Griffen nodded.

"You knew?"

"I suspected. And I thought you should meet her."

I kicked off my heels and sat down in the loveseat again, still for a long moment. "She got to me," I said as I poured more tea.

I took a sip and then another, thinking. "Find time in the calendar, Grif. Whatever it takes."

I had believed her. Even I could change.

The Cashier's Tale
by Robin Bridges

In my last incarnation, I was a cashier at Green Garden Grocery, working graveyards. It was on a full moon night, and I was at the first register in my ceremonial red smock, ringing up a customer when I first heard Her voice.

Maggie...

It wasn't the assistant manager on the PA system. The voice called again. *Maggie, my daughter. Tell the people I require a new sacrifice on my altars.*

I looked at my customer, a purple-haired, elderly lady in a matching purple muumuu. Oblivious to any celestial voices, she was lifting her third bag of chicken legs (sixty-nine cents a pound for a ten-pound bag) out of her buggy and plopping it onto the belt.

"Double bag those, will you, sweetie? They're dripping blood all over my asparagus."

"They're dripping blood all over the store," Todd, the stock boy, grumbled. "I've been following her all over the store with this damn mop."

Luckily, the purple-haired lady hadn't heard him. Todd mopped his way back down aisle eleven. I gave the lady her receipt and heard the voice again as I chucked her double-bagged chicken back into her buggy.

Maggie...tell the people...

I started cleaning the chicken blood off my register belt for the fortieth time that night, and couldn't help but feel a little thrill. The Goddess was talking to me! I'd been Wiccan since middle school, and I'd never heard Her voice before. I never dreamed She would give me such an odd message, but hey, a message is a message.

What could She want for a sacrifice? I thought of all the customers I'd checked out and all the groceries I'd scanned: rice cakes, industrial-sized cans of pork and beans, cottage cheese, cat litter. None seemed to be an appropriate sacrifice for a goddess.

Still musing, I closed off my register, leaving the two 5-11p.m. cashiers in charge of the front. I had to go clean the bathrooms before the girls went home.

Todd had already started cleaning the men's room, which reeked of pine cleanser. He was throwing out empty packages that evil shoplifters had left for us: a Listerine wrapper, three film boxes, an empty cigarette carton, and a plastic pantyhose egg. It took more than some hosiery in the men's bathroom to shock us. The stock boys once found a naked old man taking a sponge bath at the sink. "Full moon," Mike, the assistant manager had said, sighing. "Brings all lunatics within a forty mile radius into this store."

Well, here it was, another full moon night, and I was one of those lunatics, hearing voices and searching for the perfect sacrifice for the Grocery Store Goddess. Actually, at the moment I was standing on a beer display, holding a bottle of Windex and scanning the aisles for Mike. Why was I standing on a mountain of beer? Armed? Because a rat the size of a watermelon was looking for a six-pack. Or maybe his Wheaties.

"Miiike!" I yodeled over the aisle tops. I could see him on aisle four stalking something. A rat? A shoplifter? His next ex-wife?

"MIKE!" I screamed again, louder, and he came running. "What?"

"He's gone now," I said, jumping down. "But you've got to put out some D-Con or something for these rats."

"Want to see the one I just got over on aisle four with a toilet plunger?"

"No, thanks." I started to head back to my register, and then remembered my goddess' mission. "Hey Mike, what are you going to do with that rat?"

Todd stuck his head around the corner. "Throw it in the meat grinder, wrap it up and sell it as hamburger. You know—the usual."

Mike rolled his eyes. "Todd, go finish mopping. Mags, go back to the front and tell the other girls to pull their tills and go home."

The rest of the night was quiet, but my morning relief called in sick. The store manager, Mr. Davidson, pleaded with me to work just until the eight o'clock cashier came in. I told him I'd do it if I got a free breakfast in the deli. He agreed and even tried to ring up a few customers for me while I went on my break.

Actually, I was too tired to eat anything, but I needed to sit down. In the deli I fixed a large Diet Coke from the fountain and slid into a vacant booth. The regular breakfast crowd, elderly men from the retirement village across the street, had settled in. They were griping about Medicaid and Medicare, and which one paid for false teeth.

I closed my eyes and tried to meditate. *Ommmmmm...Grocery Store Goddess, grant meeee sereniteee...*

My serenity was shattered by the cook's shriek. "Aeii! Get out of here!"

Instinct made me jump up onto my chair. Mike and Todd materialized instantly with toilet plungers and a garbage bag. The Denture-Club-For-Men never noticed what was going on.

The morning got hazier after that. I remember checking out lots of customers, and I remember asking Mr. Davidson if Todd had taken the rat home with him. And I remember Heather coming in at eight o'clock, but for some reason, I didn't get to go home. Since it had gotten so busy, Mr. Davidson must have forgotten about me, and I'd been too tired to remind him.

A dull fog settled over my brain. I saw the store and the customers in a sort of 3D tunnel vision. A caffeine buzz hummed in my ears and muffled out the crying babies, cussing old ladies, and the opening and shutting of cash register drawers and automatic sliding doors. Even the buggy boys slamming grocery carts against the wall seemed far away. And in the back of my mind, the Goddess still whispered in my ear.

Maggie...

I remember Todd coming back in to work. It must have been around two. And I remember Mr. Davidson yelling at him about something. Nothing unusual about that, but this time, Todd was yelling back. And his voice sounded...wrong. Very wrong. I left my register to run after them.

When I got back to the meat department, the fight had escalated. Todd and Mr. Davidson were throwing punches behind the two-way mirrors. Todd was babbling about predators and prey. Mr. Davidson was yelling that Todd was fired.

"She wants a sacrifice!" Todd said, circling around the meat-cutting table, trying to corner our manager.

"You can hear Her too?" I shouted happily. "That's great, because I was starting to think I was just tripping on Diet Coke." Probably laced with rat poison.

Maggie, tell the people...

"Yes? What does my Lady require?" There were a few bouquets of shriveled up mums left in the floral department. Or maybe some chocolate?

Blood, Maggie. Her voice was a soft, seductive purr. *I must have blood. And I want a body of my own.*

Oh. Shit.

"Mags!" Mr. Davidson howled as he dodged a roundhouse punch. "Call for help!"

The stock boy's eyes were glazed over. He looked possessed, or controlled, or maybe just under the influence. I was starting to have a very bad feeling about my Grocery Store Goddess.

As I reached for the intercom phone, Todd grabbed my hair and yanked me away. He gazed lovingly at the meat grinder, then, with a terrible smile, began to stalk Mr. Davidson again.

"A sacrifice," he whispered, "for the Lady Lilith!"

It figures. Six years of scrying and meditating and studying Goddess books, and *this* is what I channel?

"Mags!" There was an edge of panic in Mr. Davidson's voice.

Good thing I'd studied a few extracurricular subjects, too. In the corner was a grocery cart full of shopbacks, items that needed to be put back on the shelves. I rummaged through the cart, finding a few items I could use.

"Here we go!" I waved the spell components at Mr. Davidson, who'd climbed the meat freezer to get away from Todd.

Mr. Davidson looked like he was about to cry when he saw what I held. "Sudoku?"

I grabbed a pencil off the inventory clipboard and found the puzzle I wanted. "This is not just a puzzle. It's a magic square."

If anything, this made him look even more nervous. "Just call the cops."

I ignored him and emptied a canister of Morton's Salt around me in a large circle. No Dark Goddess was gonna mess with my grocery store.

"Lilith, I evoke you!"

An eight-foot-long, emerald-green snake appeared, coiled up within my circle of salt. I gasped, not sure what I had expected.

"Pick me! Pick me!" Todd shouted. "My life for the Goddess!"

There was a large rumble on the other side of the two-way mirror. The door shook and swung open. A pregnant woman entered, wearing a white eyelet top and faded maternity jeans. She took in the snake without fear or surprise.

"What have you done now, Lilith?"

I felt a tingling up the back of my neck. The lady looked familiar. She'd been in here before, buying the industrial size can of apple-pie filling and a tub of Cool Whip. I had figured it was a pregnant craving.

She stopped at the salt circle and looked at me, her deep blue eyes mischievous. "Release her to me."

I hesitated. I knew it would sound rude, but I had to ask. "Who are you? Are you a goddess, too?"

The snake laughed. I think. "*Thissss* is your Grocery Store Goddesssss, Maggie. I will reward you greatly."

The pregnant lady snorted. "She'll give you nothing but misery, my girl. I may not be your Grocery Store Goddess, but I'm known by many names. You can call me Eve."

"Go back to your garden, bitch," the snake said. "Thissss is my domain now."

"This planet *is* my garden. You are the one who's not welcome."

Eve dug into her macramé hobo bag and pulled out a tattered newspaper clipping. She handed it to me. "I've been following her since I heard about the grocery store in Pensacola."

The headline read, **Giant Snake Seen in Produce Section of Supermarket!**

"Florida, Texas, Missouri, Nevada. She sows discord wherever she travels."

There was an understatement. I glanced over at Mr. Davidson and Todd. The manager still crouched on the freezer; the stock boy had sunk down onto a milk crate. They were both stunned stupid.

"I've finally caught up with her. Maggie, if you please, destroy the circle for me."

"What if she runs?" I asked, afraid she would try to possess Todd again.

Eve smiled grimly. "She won't run. Maggie, the circle."

Her voice was still friendly, but firm. I didn't want to find out what would happen if I pissed her off. I slowly rubbed out a section of the salt with my shoe, then jumped back out of the way.

Eve held out her arm, and reluctantly the snake coiled around it. Its green head swiveled around to look at Todd, its black tongue flickering to taste the air.

The pregnant women cocked her head as if listening, then rolled her eyes. "She wants to take care of your rat problem."

"Do you trust her?" I asked.

"Give me that Sudoku book. We won't have to trust her."

I handed her my Sudoku book and a pencil.

"Black ink, please."

"Here you go, ma'am," Mr. Davidson said, pulling a pen out of his front shirt pocket.

She flashed him a dazzling smile and gestured for him to toss the pen. She caught it deftly and began scribbling in one of the puzzles in the back of the book, chanting under her breath in a strange-sounding language.

"Is that Aramaic?" I asked.

"Angelic." She watched the snake slide off of her arm and move slowly towards a large crate of watermelons. Blood sacrifice, rodent problem. Everyone wins.

Arms crossed, Eve watched out the two way mirrors at the sales floor, as shoppers circled up and down the aisles with loaded buggies. It was the circle of life, spiraling through our grocery store.

"Can I get you something to eat or drink?" I asked, not sure of proper deity etiquette. I remembered her purchases last week. "Maybe some apple juice?"

"Ugh," she said, shuddering. "No more apples. What I'm craving right now is a banana milk shake."

Delta: A Story in Verse
by Lily Huang

Preface

Delta: *n*. [1. lit., < Gr. *Delta*, of Sem. orig. as in Heb. *Daleth*. 4th letter of the alphabet, lit. door] 1. the fourth letter of the Greek alphabet (Δ, ∂) 2. something in the shape of a delta (Δ); specif., a deposit of sand and soil, usually triangular, formed at the some of some rivers

The symbol Δ is used in mathematics to symbolize change in a variable (x, y, z).

One should not fail to notice that the letter delta forms an isosceles triangle, with two sides of equal length and two angles of equal degrees. One side (and its corresponding angle) is noticeably different, left out, uninvited.

* * *

Bartered words in the middle of midnight, Conversation #48

      I'm unworthy of your love
God, Eve! How many times do have to go through this? I mean, come on
      No, you come on! Every time we fight, you remind that I was made from you
You're unbelievable
      You're unbelievable. You're a total hypocrite
You're unreasonable
      I'm unreasonable? You believe in God
Not this again
      Oh look at me! I'm Adam and I'm upset! I huff and puff because I'm oh so mad
You're so fucking annoying
      And you just said I was your equal
Isn't that what you wanted to hear
      You're such a liar
Face it, Eve, love is a lie

>   No, love's an emotion
> Emotions lie to be understood
>   You lie to be loved
> You don't get it, do you
>   Yeah, I do. When you named me woman, you wanted me
>   to be below you
> And I was right, you are
>   And you, Adam, you're only human

Complications of equality

   It wasn't always this way. The disputes of love and equality weren't always this aged. It's her fault. Before she was made, there was another. She was the origin of love. I told her she was my equal, but she didn't accept this, and not the way Eve doesn't accept things. Lilith was logical. She made sense. If I ever said the word equal, she'd say, My darling, Adam, you're such a fool. Equality doesn't exist. There is always a less and a more. Two objects, seemingly similar in size and stature, will prove to be either superior or inferior. The moment one shows any sign of defect, the mirage of equality will evaporate like a drop of dew, struggling to drip from a wilting leaf. Choose your role carefully. Would you prefer to be the water, soon to be transformed and forever forgotten, or the leaf, looking at its own mortality in the mirror of the earth? My darling, that's what equality is. Why should we even pretend our love is equal?

   I couldn't argue with her. She was right. We weren't equal. I was hers, and she was free.

   One day, a breeze violently flew her away. God gave her Free Will, and she took it.

   Lilith wasn't even mortal. Even her beauty was complex. She was a mythical creature. I cradled and nurtured her. I tried to capture her, to keep her in my garden, but I am not as strong as she is. I used to believe we were all the same—me, her, Him, His countless minion—each possessing characteristics that the others desired, but life is not so simple now. He gave her the chance and replaced absolute perfection with modified perfection.

* * *

She

Her skin a blanket
Hiding (im)perfections

I can taste the salt of her myth

Her fingers fondle the petals of a lily
Its skin not so soft as hers

I envy that flower
Touching her
Being touched by her

She gave it all her love
And left me
With that blooming bud never browning
To despise
Instead of a kiss

Classifications

Genus & Species: *Lilium lancifolium* (more commonly known as Tiger Lily)

Family: *Liliaceae*

Some common traits:

    Stem over 1 m tall, scabrous, purplish

    Several flowers, nodding, the pedicels pubescent, 6-12 cm long, bracteate

    Perianth parts orange or orange-red, spotted with dark purple

    Some hybrid species known to cause hallucinations if ingested

* * *

Sacrifice

I offered him   my body   that   not enough
my mind   not enough
my God   not enough
He didn't want to own me   not enough
He wanted to be me   enough

But that
I could not offer him

* * *

The Ultimatum, Unanswered

Adam, I said, I have given you everything. I'm finished giving. I'm ready to receive.

He was silent. A tear dwindled near the crevice of his eyes but dared not roll down onto the earth. Gravity lost its strength. He would not bow to me.

* * *

Delta

Rough patch of
Coarse hair
Warmth
Sated
Me

Conversation #75

        Come on, Adam. Be honest. Tell me you still love her
Who
        You know who
Right
        Well do you? Go ahead. Deny it
Do I deny God? Do you think I'm just going deny something because you want me to

> It's not about me. She owns you, Adam, but I guess God
> does too so there's no point

I own myself
> You dream about her

God, you personify cliché
> Clichés exist for a reason

Why are you so jealous? I can't recreate the past, and even if I could, believe me, Eve, if I could rewrite the past, if our love was a story, there wouldn't be a Lilith. I would erase her from the text. No, I would never have even written her down
> But you would do that to avoid pain, to avoid the hurt that
> I feel just so that I would stop fighting with you. You
> don't understand what this feels like

Darling, of course I do. I was jealous once

Back before she left, Lilith planted a garden full of the most perfect flowers. I didn't name them until after she left.
> How can I possibly compete with the ideal memory of a
> wrecked relationship

* * *

The third night alone

I didn't love her too much, nor did I not love her enough. I simply didn't love her at all.

My epiphany arrived too late,
In the wrong packaging,
Without enough postage.

* * *

Classifications

Genus & Species: *Camassia scilloides* (more popularly known as Wild Hyacinth)

Family: *Liliaceae*

Some common traits:

Considerable variation in flower color, from typical pale lilac to pale blue

Bulbs tunicated and leaves basal

Abundant in both hill prairies and railroad prairies

It is interesting that Linneus placed hyacinths in the same family as lilies, as genetically, they are quite different, and they are physically more similar to irises, which belong to the *Iridaceae* family.

* * *

Introductions

I tried to sleep   but the leaves wouldn't keep me warm
                but the leaves were too hot on my skin
                but the leaves still smelled of her
                but the leaves weren't her

Frustrated
I sat up and there was a great burning on my side
Fresh blood moistened the earth
She dipped her white toe in it
Giggled girlishly
And washed my feet with her tears.

But she wasn't Lilith. I cursed God. He waited for me to hollow my thoughts and replied, I call her Woman. You name her Eve.

That day, I met Woman
                    Wife
                  Lover
                  Saint
                  Flawed
And yet, she was still not Lilith

* * *

Desire

I plunged my fingers into the moist ground to extract God's most perfect creation. The green stem nourished a delicately white bud. I had never seen a color so pure. A drop of fresh rain slid along its slender curves, and through that reflective water, I saw every shade of the world.

I rushed the flower to Adam, eager to please him. Surely, if he could not understand my love for opera, or my appreciation of art, perhaps he could find something in this flower.

I thirsted for beauty. I desired more than man. Adam was not enough.

* * *

Crossroad

Why does he reach for the impossible
when his fingers can wrap
around this one moment?

* * *

Classifications

Genus & Species: *Hemerocallis fulva* (more popularly known as the Daylily)

From Greek: *Hemera* = day + *Kallos* = beauty

Family: *Liliaceae*

Some common traits:

Monocotyledons & mostly clump forming

Leaves are strap-shaped, smooth to finely ribbed

> Buds small and round at first, then elongating until its maximum length is reached.
>
> It will then Bloom.

Linneus was incorrect to put these daylilies into the *Liliaceae* family. Modern day DNA analysis has shown that they are more closely related to phormium, putting them in the *Phormiaceae* family and the *Asparagle* order.

* * *

Crossroad (revised)

The past
is a flawless story
                    Distorted

The present
claims her future

But it is a perpetual reminder
of what she has left behind

How could she reach for the impossible
when her fingers can wrap
around this moment?

Content is not synonymous to bliss
And that blissful love
is not offered
Now.

                        * * *

The escape

My flower
slipped
through his fingers
collided
with the sun-cracked earth
to shatter
my love
for him.

In turn,
my feet
automatically
without thought
walked
towards the edge of
his Garden

                        * * *

Power

        God calls me Woman. Adam named me Eve.
          We have been matrimonially united
            Yet she divides the contract of
              our unconditional love
              Sometimes I can try
                to forget that
                  she was
                    first
                     .

                    But
                  I know
              that my love
            can overpower
         this miniscule memory
      that dominates his every thought
   I was made from him and to him I will return.
God calls me Woman. Adam named me Eve. I am powerful.

First step of Knowledge

Accustomed to the gentleness of the soft layer of earth in the garden
My feet burned on blackened asphalt glazed by the brazen sun
I looked down
         suddenly aware of my nakedness
I was not   ashamed
I was   Cold

* * *

Classifications

Genus & Species: *Lilium michiganese* (more popularly called Turk's-cap Lily)

Family: *Liliaceae*

Some common traits:

    Yellow bulbs

    Stem nearly 2 m tall, often shorter, glabrous

    Some or all leaves whorled, lanceolate, roughened along veins and margins

Flowers nodding

If ingested, bodily reactions may occur, such as dizziness, fainting, or hallucination

* * *

Coloration

The whiteness slowly dissolved into technicolored patches.
Her legacy was evolving
                changing
                morphing
                              into something less perfect.

And yet, their flaws made them more beautiful.

I began to obsess over every changing detail. Her flowers were evolving inside my garden just as she was outside the garden. That day, I began to catalogue every lily in the garden, giving everything a distinct and unique name. That day, I fulfilled God's task for me; I became the namer of things.

* * *

Bliss

Dear Adam,

I've missed you.
I think about you.
About us.
Often.
Do you still tend my garden?
How are the flowers I left behind?
Knowledge is bliss.
Come with me.
Come to me.

I love you.
Still.

Lilith

* * *

Myth

How could I respond?

I can still taste
the salt
of
her
kiss

I was wrong

She was not a myth
I can still
feel her skin.

Love is the only myth
I have ever known.

* * *

God, understanding

$\underline{\Delta \text{ Adam}}$ = inevitable knowledge
Δ Eve

* * *

Conversation # 138

Eve, are you still awake
      I'm always awake
What do you think is out there
      Out where
Beyond our garden
      Adam, you used to be satisfied. What's changed

      Adam, please answer me

      Adam, please

* * *

Lilies

Those odious flowers
Offending olfactory nerves
persevering
to remind him of Her

I weed my garden
Thousands of stained lilies
decompose
to appease
my greatest allergy

* * *

Classifications:

Genus & Species: *Lilium superbum* (more popularly known as Superb Lily)

Family: *Liliaceae*

Some common traits:

> White bulbs
>
> Without axillary bulblets
>
> Perianth parts strongly recurved, orange-red or orange, spotted with dark purple
>
> Nectar in stem poisonous, particularly if ingested

* * *

Conversation #435

Do you think the world is any bigger than this
    God, Adam, please stop this! Stop talking this way!
    Please
I was never content, I want you to know, I just learned how to cope
    You're full of shit. You were content with her
That was a different world. A different Eden
    Was it better than this one
Different. Simpler perhaps. We've evolved

>> Why can't I compete with her

You're flawless

>> But I can't satisfy you

She's nothing compared to you. Baby, in a competition for me, you'd win for sure. She can't compete against you

>> Of course she can't. There exists no competition. She's already won

I don't want to talk anymore. I don't even want to know what you're thinking

* * *

Frustration

Under her breath, she whispered, I don't want to know. I could hear her, but I ignored what I was not meant to hear. The intense pain in my side would not go away.

Frustrated,
I climbed the exterior wall
Missing a step
I fell
To bruise
My missing rib.

* * *

The Fall

The day Adam fell
God showed His vengance on us.
He blew away everything.

Our shelter was destroyed
Our sun never rose
Our moon bled maroon
Our food evaporated
Only One tree stood strong

* * *

Classifications

Genus & Species: *Ornithoglaum umbellatum* (more popularly known as Star-of-Bethlehem)

Family: *Liliaceae*

Some common traits:

> Broad green stripe along back side
>
> Rhizomatous plants with a rosette of basal leaves and fewer leaves on the scape
>
> Perianth parts spreading, broadly lanceolate, acute
>
> Used as aphrodisiac in Eastern traditions

* * *

Response to Letter #5, Response #1

Lilith—

Indeed it has been long.
My mind was sickened, but now it is clear. I know what to do.

If I see you again, it would be pleasant.
If it would be pleasant, I would want to prolong the experience.
If I would want to prolong the experience, I would be subjected to love.
If I were subjected to love, I would fall in love with you again.

This scenario, however, is highly improbable.

It would be nearly impossible for me to fall in love with a person in the future, if I were still in love with her in the present. You may interpret this as it suits you best.

Devoted.
Adam

* * *

Self-pity

I used the palm of my foot to crush the flower she left behind
It alone had remained white
The other imitations have changed over the years
I looked down
Its purity was branded by the dirt from my sinned toes

I ran outside
Ingested one   flower
                for every day that
Lilith and I had been separated

A door appeared before me
I opened it
Stepped outside
And realized that I was unclothed

* * *

Crossroad (revised revision)

she stands
        between
lost   losing
the past
is a flawed story
            distorted
the present
can lead to her future   with
                      without Adam
there is a perpetual reminder
of what she has lost   (the emptiness
                   in the garden
                 is) too much
why does she reach for the impossible
when his fingers can wrap
around this one moment
promising her discontent?
(dis)content is not synonymous to bliss and that blissful love is not
offered Now.
her hungry fingers wrap
around that forbidden   fruit
she smiles & takes a big bite

* * *

Crown

The point of intersection between the leaves, flowers, and roots is called the crown. It has been said that if it becomes damaged, part or all of the plant will die. If the lily is ripped from its natural habitat, it will most surely die. The best way to remove it would be to carefully cut it diagonally at a healthy point on the stem.

* * *

Conversation #15033

You awake
      I'm always awake
Did you really miss me while I was gone
      Of course I did
You know, I love you
      Of course you do. I never doubted it.

Death of the Madonna
by Christina McCoy

Nice, France
September 13, 1927

"I can't sell my bed, Mary," Isadora Duncan pleaded.

"I understand," Mary replied, "but it is one of the grandest pieces in the studio. Still quite firm and solid...despite its extensive use. Perhaps that would add to the asking price."

"My children slept here," Isadora said solemnly.

Mary sighed and crossed the bedroom to put her hand on her friend's shoulder.

Isadora leaned her head against Mary's consoling hand.

"Fine, then. Not the bed," Mary said.

"Some things must go, though," Isadora said. She gathered her breath and looked around the room. The ceramics had long since been sold, only a single lamp was left in each room, and all the mirrors and paintings had been taken by the landlord. She'd been allowed into her studio only once she promised she would vacate by the end of the month.

Isadora wandered downstairs into the main hall, flopped onto the last remaining couch, and absently rolled an empty champagne bottle under her bare foot. After a few long moments of thought, she asked, "What about the divans?"

"But where will the guests sit? The chairs are gone."

Isadora's face grew that warm softness, that look she had when she envisioned things others could not yet see. "Yes, but we can take the cushions from the sofas and lay them on the floor. It will be very Greek, very Bohemian. All of Paris will be copying it next year!"

She laughed, and Mary joined in. Their round, wilted faces each mirrored the other's happiness, as once they had when they had both been trim, tight, and pretty.

The aging women's laughter faded as a knock came from the door. The caller opened the door himself, striding in with American purpose and a crisp business suit.

Isadora leaped into the man's arms. "Paris!" she cried, "You've come to rescue us!"

"Mr. Singer," Mary greeted him, "what a grand surprise!"

He pocketed his spectacles and took his old lover by both hands. "Isadora, my dear." He kissed her on both cheeks with his mustachioed lips. "It is good to see you. I thought I'd drop in to see if you have had lunch."

"Oh, please don't speak of lunch," Isadora said, covertly kicking the champagne bottle under the couch.

"Well, I was just about to excuse myself to the hotel for lunch myself," Mary politely fibbed. "So if you would excuse me."

He helped her put on her torn squirrel-fur coat and held the door as she left. As the door slowly shut, Mary could hear Isadora begin her fretful account of the diet Mary had put her on until she was fit to dance again for the public. Mary simply folded her arms against the chill and began her walk to the hotel. She watched the taxis drive past, wished she could hail one. Ah, well. She had walked farther before.

Mary had honestly been surprised to see Mr. Singer, given their last meeting. Isadora had begged her to see him at his chateau to ask his help during her latest bout with financial distress. Mary recalled to him how long he and Isadora had been friends, how greatly she still loved him, how beautiful their child had been.

He told her about Florida, how the great white birds would eat from your hands, how the sunrises sparkled the Atlantic, how the land values went from gold to dust, and how his money was tied into a grand, empty hotel on a beautiful island where the authorities wanted to try him on criminal fraud for his dealings in loans, land, and construction. He said there was nothing he could do. He said that even if he could do something, it would be a waste. Nothing could keep Isadora's wild spending in check. She was on a downward rush no one could halt.

Mary's situation was little better. She had no money for food. Perhaps her waiter would be new and would in his ignorance allow her to charge the meal to her room.

* * *

"But my dear, why did you go away?" Isadora asked Mary.

Her penciled eyebrow rose in reply.

"I should have loved you to hear all things he said. He is a lovely, lovely being, and I love him. I believe he is the only one I really ever loved."

Mary scoffed, nearly spilling her watery afternoon tea. "How can you say that, Isadora?" She shook her head in disapproval, stirring what was left in the sugar bowl into her cup. "Tell me now the absolute truth. Whom above all did you really love the best?"

Isadora thought a moment, "Well, to tell you the real, real truth, Mary, I don't know. I seem to love each of them to the uttermost limits of love, and if Gordon, Paris, Mercedes, and Sergei stood before me, I wouldn't know which one to choose. I loved, and still love them all." Her face took on that distant look of a sibyl. "Perhaps I'm many persons in one. Perhaps many others feel as I do, but won't admit it, even to themselves. And so they go on, fooling themselves all their lives, but I could never fool myself or anyone else for that matter."

"So did you even try to fool Paris out of more of his money?"

"Oh Mary!" Isadora waved the end of her scarf in dismissal.

"You must learn to fool your friends or at least your faux friends out of their money. They won't volunteer to help you any longer. You never think to repay them. You just spend it as fast as you can."

"I did with it just what they expected me to do. What else is money for but spending?"

Mary simply sighed as the maid made her presence known for the afternoon.

Isadora told her of the bottle under the couch that needed attending.

"And besides," Isadora said, "he's promised me a check. He'll bring it tomorrow at four o'clock. And the advance for my cursed book will be here by the end of the week. Once I lose a bit of weight and decide on a dance, Ivan will film it and we'll have money from that too." She exhaled and looked out the window. "There's nothing to worry about at all."

* * *

After Mary had tea, Isadora took her nap so as to be fresh for that evening. Mary lay still in the muted light of the guest room, her stomach twisting in hunger. The waiter at the hotel knew her well enough, so she had spent the afternoon in the park, returning to Isadora's studio after she'd seen that Mr. Singer's car left. Had not her hunger kept her awake, the maid's heavy feet pounded up and down the stairs would have. She could hear the maid occasionally tapping lightly on the master bedroom door, timidly whispering, "*Mademoiselle* Duncan? *Mademoiselle* Duncan?" Then she would run back down the stairs to come back up again moments later.

After the fourth round, Mary peered out at the maid. "*Quel est le problème?*"

"Another young man to see *Mademoiselle* Duncan."

Mary rubbed her eyes and pounded down the stairs. A nervous knock came from the front door. Beyond it stood a handsome young man in what appeared to be a chauffeur's uniform.

"*Bonsoir, Mademoiselle* Duncan," he said uncertainly. "Pardon my attire. I have just come from work. Madame Tetu gave me your address and told me you were interested in buying my car." He pointed to the still-running automobile.

Mary frowned. "I am not *Mademoiselle* Duncan." His face fell. "If you leave your card, I will see she gets it, *Monsieur*..."

"Falchetto, Benoit Falchetto," he said searching his pockets. Producing the card, he handed it to her, tipped his cloth hat, and dashed back to his car.

Watching the car drive away, Mary realized where she had seen the man before.

There'd been an incident at the bistro the other day. Isadora had caught sight of the young man, proclaimed him a Greek god in disguise, and asked the patroness to see that he received her card. Isadora called him "Buggatti," after his car—his disguised chariot, as she insisted. The old woman had smiled knowingly when Isadora explained her interest in his car—Isadora was famously indiscriminate in her choice of lovers—and she assured he would call on her soon. This incident had reminded Mary of the episode with the ship stoker in South America. That had been almost ten years ago, when the world-famous dancer had been young, fit, and nymphal. Mary told her friend any man who coveted a woman not only twice his age but nearly twice his weight was not worth having. She imagined Isadora was still angry, but at least she was behaving herself.

Mary woke Isadora for dinner. It had been some years since Isadora had seen her occasional manager, so this meeting with Georges Hottois and his family was particularly important.

"Up, up, dear," she called, opening the curtains and turning on the lamp. "You must be fresh and beautiful tonight."

Isadora groaned softly, pulling the thin blanket over her head. Mary set out the cosmetics.

"Perhaps if you're looking well, Georges will want to make some performance dates for you."

No response came from the lumps on the bed.

"Isadora," she called, "Bugatti was here while you slept."

She sprung from the bed like a tiger. "I don't believe you, Mary! It's some silly joke. You would have awakened me, you never would have sent him away without telling me."

"Oh, yes I did."

"Well, then, I'll never forgive you. Good heavens, can't you understand how terribly important it is?" Isadora began to pace as Mary calmly laid out the rouge, pancake foundation, eyebrow pencil and eye shadows. "Mary, what have you done? We must find him, the first thing in the morning."

"Isadora," she said, turning to calmly face her friend. "I believe you are losing your mind. What can this chauffeur have to do with you?"

"I tell you he's not a chauffeur, but a messenger of the gods. He's divine."

"That's madness, dear," said Mary. She sat Isadora on a high cushion and began to apply the thick, white foundation with a heavy hand. "You should use your henna shampoo tonight. Your age is showing."

"Ever since I saw him, I see things, Mary. Great visions from the gods…"

"You're not a sibyl," she chided. "You're a dancer, a great dancer and a great artist. You must remember this, or we'll get nowhere tonight."

"Do you remember the birds that were here? The great black ones? And the cats at dinner with Lord Douglas?"

"Not at all, and neither should you."

"I saw three black cats again last night, in the garden this time."

"There are always cats in the garden, Isadora. You feed them, when you can afford some meat." Mary slapped rouge on her cheeks.

"I sense something about the studio…some malevolent influence…a figure in black with those pitiable eyes…"

Mary stiffened. She set her brush aside. "This needs to stop. Nothing is wrong. Tonight you will be beautiful and charming and Georges will ask you to name your price and you'll travel Europe again and you will dance and the world will remember that it loves you."

Isadora took her dear friend by both hands, clenching them. "Please, don't ever leave me alone. I just can't stand it at night alone. You may be sure, Mary, before you've gone ten miles, I shall have walked into the sea, and this time I shall take the precaution to tie an iron around my neck."

The knock at the bedroom door startled her. "*Mademoiselle* Duncan?"

"*Oui, cher?*"

The maid entered, carrying an envelope. "*Madame Desti, vous avez une lettre.*"

Mary opened it, immediately looked to the small slip of paper and then to the letter.

"What does it say?"

Mary smiled. "It's from a dear friend in America. He learned that I was here with you and wishes me to buy you flowers with the monies from this check!"

"Oh, Mary! Surely some kindly god is looking out for us! We'll have money for all the taxis we want and a tomorrow filled with promise!"

* * *

Monsieur Georges Hottois expressed his belated condolences at the untimely death of Isadora's husband while his serving girl refilled his wine glass. "I understand you had some difficulties together, but…"

"*C'est mariage,*" Madame Hottois muttered.

"I am sure you reconciled before now. Has his estate been settled?"

Mary took a deep breath, holding tightly to her spoon.

Isadora's laughter tinkled across the table. "Oh, Georges, always a manager!"

"I always look out for my performers. I want you to wear bedsheets and go barefoot because it is art, not because you must. I learned they have sold all of his poems. It seems he was very popular."

Isadora lifted her champagne flute admiring the golden bubbles. "Sergei was a genius…too large a soul for this world."

"I have not been in the business of poetry. What is the price for that size?"

Georges chuckled to himself.

"Three hundred thousand francs." Mary could not hold back anymore.

Georges raised his bushy eyebrows. "A fair rate for a marriage!"

Isadora stared icily as he laughed. "My marriage was a vulgar gesture and would not have been made any less horrid by divorce. I can't help that their courts decided I was his sole heir. I didn't have anything to do with the proceedings."

"Would all courts be so generous." He lifted his wine glass in a toast.

"I gave it all to his mother and sisters," she said as he drank.

"How kind," replied Madame Hottois.

Mary finished her wine.

"*Maman!*"

Mommy. Isadora gripped her glass. That had been her name, the name her children called her, the boy with golden curls and the girl with her own dark hair and graceful little feet. Patrick, Deirdre… Their tiny hands would hold her so tight while she'd wrap them in her arms so they would feel so loved, so safe. She'd wrapped them in heavy blankets. They would get so cold during car rides.

"*Maman*, my hair!" the little boy shouted excitedly. He ran a chubby hand though his short, blond hair.

"Did *Mademoiselle* Avers cut your hair?" replied Madame Hottois, her voice reaching his same thrilled pitch.

A black woman with round, dark glasses entered behind him.

"*Oui, Madame.*"

"You have made my son handsome, *Mademoiselle* Avers," Madame Hottois said, smiling.

His tiny hands grasped the folds of his mother's dress and he lifted himself onto the tips of his toes as he leaned up to kiss her face. He smiled, and his bubbly baby cheeks swelled like two pink suns setting into the sea. He giggled, and it was music beyond the range of any instrument man could craft. His eyes, two perfect orbs of new sky blue inhabited by darting black birds, set upon Isadora. He was warm and laughing and safe. His eyes were open. Just as she remembered. Just like when she put him in the car with his sister. She had kissed them good-bye through the chilled car window. They drove home for naps. They were tired, said the nanny, the *bonne d'enfants*. They may have been afraid. They had clung to their nanny. Patrick put his arm around his sister, their foreheads pressed together. They fell asleep in the car. The car fell into the river and they went to sleep. Their deaths were beautiful. But they were still dead. The children were dead. Her children were dead and burned to ashes. The girl with the dark hair and light feet and the boy with golden curls were dead.

The fair-haired child asked, "What's the matter with the beautiful lady?"

A cat brushed against her legs.

Isadora fled, her screams distant in her own ears.

* * *

Her toes danced through the dark water. It was cold, just as she had imagined.

"Isadora?"

She had no irons with her, nothing to weigh her down but memory.

"Isadora…"

She could feel herself sinking though her clothes were still dry. She pulled on the long fringes of her scarf, red like heart's blood. Perhaps she could hang herself, like Sergei, or slit her wrists like he had done, and write her last words in her own blood. No, she should go into the sea, into the water, like her children. She'd discover why their faces had been so peaceful.

"Isadora, I'm to take you home."

She continued to watch her toes dip into the cold river.

"Do not flee to the water. God will find you there."

Isadora looked up. The streetlights set a halo about a cloaked figure, her arms reaching out in aid. Darkened by the night, the female form floated silently down the embankment toward her. Two black disks where eyes should be, flashing darkly.

"*Mon ange de la mort!* You are my dark Seraphita come to take me away." She crawled up the muddy shore, grasping wildly at the figure's shadowy skirts.

The figure knelt, stretching thin arms around her. "Poor child," she whispered. "Poor child…"

Isadora could hear the woman's heart slowly beating and feel the warmth of her thin fingers as they swept through her hair. She scrambled free and stumbled back onto the soft, wet earth.

"You're not death! You're…you're the nanny." A sad laugh burst from her slackened mouth. "You're not an angel. *Tu es une négresse!*"

The nanny's expression did not change. "You must go home. Your friend is concerned for you."

"Mary? Why isn't she here then?" she asked despondently. "She's my friend, and she knows me, knows my life. She'll understand why I…"

"She never lost a child," the nanny said coldly. "Her son is a strong young man. How could she understand?"

Running her fingers through the fringe of her scarf, Isadora said, "So you read newspapers?"

"I have never wanted to be ignorant."

"Do you enjoy reading about the tragedy of others? My autobiography is almost finished. You should enjoy that. There's lots of pornography and scandal and the death of chil—" Anger and tears sealed her throat before she could finish.

The nanny stooped down, placing a bony hand on her shoulder.

"You're a vulture, and that's fine," Isadora said after she took a deep breath. "I surrendered to them long ago. I understand your place."

"I do not take pleasure in tragedy," the nanny said as she removed her glasses, "and I am not a vulture."

Isadora had seen these eyes, those pitiful eyes, before. The ominous figure at the foot of her bed...the obscene, bulbous orbs of the dead nanny under the veil...the red, empty gaze from the mirror as she applied her make-up before the cremation...the darting, oily-black birds battering at the window when she was alone...the cat poised in the brush of the garden...

She scuttled back, stopping suddenly when her legs splashed into the cold. Water soaked into her dress, seeping up the cloth, its weight pulling her subtly. "What are you?" she demanded feebly.

Replacing her spectacles, the woman answered simply, "I am *Mademoiselle* Avers, nanny for the Hottois family."

Isadora wrapped her arms around herself, backing slowly into the river. "Then I am mad..."

"If you listen to me, we can help each other."

"Everything is gone. Everyone I love is gone."

"You will kill yourself?"

Isadora smiled distantly. "A thousand times, if I must. It seems no matter how terrible life is I simply won't die."

"If you kill yourself, you will never know God."

"I am a pagan. I don't believe in God."

Avers stood and took Isadora's hands in her own. "I want to tell you of the first woman. I want to tell you of her fear and love of man, the death of her children, her fight with God, and her eternal pain."

Isadora came out of the river, water dripping from her stained robes.

"If I tell you this story, will you dance it?"

She nodded slowly. "I couldn't dance anything else."

* * *

Dawn was coming soon, dimly filling the high arched windows of the studio. The two women sat in the soft light, curled on the floor beneath her eternal blue curtains. Avers let her words marinate in the silence. Isadora folded her hands under her chin like a nun without a rosary.

"Surely someone else should dance this," Isadora said at last. "I am flabby, I am old, and I am certainly not famous enough to attract the number of people who need to see this. I have girls. I'll telegram Irma to pick the best…"

"Girls?" Avers quietly questioned. Isadora paused, puzzled. "Girls cannot tell this story. Girls are children, innocent. They do not know loss or pain. A child cannot dance this."

"Well, not girls, really. Young women…"

"Isadora." Avers ran a skeletal finger along the bones of Isadora's neck. "They would not understand."

Isadora looked away, rubbing the place where the nanny's cold hand had touched. "No, you're right. But no one wants to see."

"They don't. But it's the truth." Avers adjusted her glasses on her sharp nose. "Those who understand will love you and be freed. Those who don't are simply not ready yet."

"They will misunderstand so much. The scandal will destroy me…"

Avers smirked. "Will you care about scandal now? You're Isadora Duncan, barefoot, breast-baring, bastard-baring bolshevik."

Isadora licked her lips and sighed. "No going back."

"Never."

Isadora stood, stepped to the curtain, and stood with her back against them. She unwrapped her long, red scarf from her neck, her shoulders, her arms. She took a deep breath, then flipped her robes inside out. Her naked body was vividly ashen and rounded, emerging like pale sand under a rough wave.

"I've never danced naked," she apologized.

Avers did not move or speak. Her sleek tinted lenses hid her eyes, her mood, her reaction.

Isadora took in her first breath and held it. She became motionless, stoic, One. Fused, there were no desires, no needs. Nothing existed outside. All was complete, unified.

Then the break.

The head and neck snapped into motion. Obscenely aware, she knew part of her was now behind her, a part she loved, a part now separated. Her head and eyes writhed about, seeking him.

The break continued. Shoulders came free. Arms came free. Legs. She pivoted wildly. She stretched and reached behind her.

And he was there. He touched her with his hands. She could feel him still there, but...detached. Her eyes rolled back but she could not see him. She could feel him but could not see him.

She began to pull and he began to pull. They pulled against each other, away from whatever invisible chirurgeon was breaking them. They snapped apart. She fell, tumbled like a child from the arms of its dying mother.

Pain twisted her body and face. Her face contorted as she ran her hands over her new body. It was broken, imperfect. Where they had wrenched themselves apart, she ached. She ached and longed to be one with him again. She wept the first tears. She reached for him again, her arms encircling her invisible partner, seeking his comfort, his love, and wanting to share their loss. She nestled up to him, curling to him.

Her arms and legs burst away from her. He demanded reunification, with a force fast and floundering. She flailed against him, her feet slapping futilely on the ground. The broken pieces would not fit. She cried out. She had no words he could understand.

She leapt free. She fled, dodging unseen plants and waters and animals. Her wild flight slowed. She watched the unnamed beasts, beheld their first ruts and killings and became as they were in their violent purity. She saw the plants' slow rise from the earth, and rose like them for the sun, drinking rain, and dancing with the wind. She saw the first offspring of man, mimics of all his perfection and faults, how they scratched and wept in ignorance. She became as they were, leaping with their joys and comforting them in sorrow.

There was the man again. He recognized her, and she him. She feared him, that first pain he gave her. He spoke words and she could not understand him. She fought again to flee him, and again he caught her, held her down. He whispered to her. Her eyes whipped open with knowledge: It was the name of the One. The joy of knowledge overcame her; she shouted the name to the beasts and plants, wind and waters, and all the children of man.

And the One broke their tongues. And the One spread apart the sea to find her. The One laid her bare for all to see. They saw she was an evil thing and she tried to hide away from their eyes, disgusted by herself.

The servants of the One created an end, and sent this death for her. She bounded out of death's reach, as she had never known birth and could not feel death.

The servants of the One sent death for all she loved. The beasts fell without passing life to another. The plants rotted into the earth. The children of men lay still in the womb and in their beds.

She wailed. She tore her hair. She could not close her eyes to their suffering. Death walked in her footsteps. She cried out again the name of the One, who snatched her up, flying her into the place the One made for itself.

She knelt. She held up her hands. She pleaded for them. She stood in the silence of the One.

Slowly, Isadora's hands touched her eyes. Closing her eyes, she mocked plucking them out like ripe fruit. She held the invisible eyeballs up, offering them. Her mouth warped, her brows knitted. She crushed the rejected offering in her spiteful fingers, impalpable ichors and tears streaming down her arms. Returning them to her fuming face, she stepped away, falling from the stage and back to earth.

Sobbing erupted from Isadora. She crawled to Avers, pressing her forehead against her knees.

"You are a goddess," she said between sobs. She felt reedy fingers sliding through her hair. "You've brought me enlightenment and I can share it with the world. Surely you're Athena or Nyx..."

"I am a woman, just like you, but I have been called those names before," she replied. "I have known what you know now for countless years. You may feel enlightened, but there is no hope. Only the innocent know joy and hope. For us, there is only knowledge." She paused. "I didn't want to tell you when I first saw you. You were too happy. Later, I thought you too lost to despair."

"Nothing can make my pain go away. I'll always mourn my children. But now I understand. It's all clear now. I can focus again." Isadora rushed across the stage, hastily throwing her robes on. "I will dance this for Ivan, he'll film it, and who knows how many will be able to see this? And for all time! Oh, my dear, I will put this to glory!" She fell at Avers feet again, wrapping her arms around her legs like a little child.

* * *

Mary didn't think Isadora noticed that she had not spoken to her, not since she had come down the stairs into the studio that morning and had seen how Isadora had spent the night.

"Now, Mary, if you will only stay by me and see the thing through, just stick with me..."

Mary could hear the dreadful ticking of her friend's mind, like a watch about to break. Isadora had an idea. She didn't dare speak of it fully yet, and it would apparently solve all their problems. Mary began a plan to get them both out of the hairdresser's without tipping.

"We'll go to Russia, get the children from my school, and we'll end in a burst of glory yet. You're grand, Mary. You're just grand."

"*Voilà!*" announced the hairdresser. "*Votre coupe n'est-elle pas belle?*"

"Oh Mary, look at me!" Isadora shook her short, waved bob. "Good enough for an old beau and a young one! See what a little happiness does. Stick on the job, Mary, and we'll ride to glory, I promise you."

They escaped tipping the hairdresser and the taxi driver on their way back to the studio. Mary sat hungry that afternoon, watching Isadora prance around the rooms. Isadora seemed to enjoy passing the time while Mary sat in silence and waited for Paris Singer to arrive at four o'clock with the check he had promised.

Isadora seemed to be nearly bursting with this unspeakable idea, only venting, "Oh Mary, Mary" on occasion. The maid hadn't come, so when the bell was rung, Mary answered.

It was that dark little man with the car. Mary left the door open for him as she turned to don her coat. Isadora swept down the stairs like an angel from heaven, embracing Falchetto in full view of the street.

"Here is your Buggatti," Mary stated flatly as she battled with her coat. Her arm had gone through the tear rather than the sleeve. "I am going to the hotel."

Mary again walked to the hotel, knowing the money she saved on the taxi would be dessert. After assuring the *maître d'hôtel* that she had money, she entered the dining room to find Ivan Nikolenko, the filmmaker. Mary was sure to tell him how pleased Isadora had been with the experimental reel. Isadora was genuinely satisfied and wanted him to film her as he was "an artist." She explained Isadora was "seeing a man about a car" that afternoon, but could join them for dinner that night at the restaurant across from her studio.

Isadora laughingly tore into the dinning room, the *maître d'hôtel* making hot chase behind her. "Mary!" she cried, "I've lost them both, Mary. I've lost Buggatti and I've lost Paris! I always get caught."

Mary excused them, leaving Ivan the bill. Mary held her friend up as they walked back to the studio.

"He says I'm his Madonna and he is my Mercury!"

"Who?"

"Buggatti. He's an aeroplane pilot! He's so daring! We were going to buy an aeroplane and we'd fly together back to America! The three of us!"

"And you lost him?"

"He caught us, Paris. He told me I hadn't changed a bit, but you know I have!"

Mary did not reply.

"So I tried to excuse Buggatti. I said, 'You are coming at nine tonight with the little racing car,' and he took his leave. I told Paris you wanted to buy the car."

"Isadora, why must you bring me into this?"

"He didn't believe me."

"Did he have the check?"

"Well, he said he could only be a moment. His family was going to pick him up in their car. But tomorrow morning he had he would stop by and take me to lunch and give me the check he promised. He just waved good-bye," said Isadora. "I don't believe he will come, or Buggatti either."

* * *

Ivan and Isadora chatted excitedly over their champagne before dinner. Mary stared at the slow-rising bubbles in her full flute. She was tired, having lain awake most of the night worried for her friend. She knew it had been the child, that golden-hair boy, who had sent Isadora flying off into the night.

But Isadora was happy now. She'd agreed to stick to the diet Mary suggested. She had apparently created a dance especially for film, and she was sure it would be a sensation. She would go into glorious history with it. She had champagne, a fellow artist admirer giving her praise, the promise of money tomorrow, and the hope of love tonight.

Yet Mary felt something was wrong. She resolved that after dinner, before they returned to the studio, she would tell Isadora what she had seen last night.

"Will you dance with this scarf? It's so lovely," Ivan said, running the silk between his fingers.

"Isn't it just electric?" Isadora unfurled it for his inspection. "Dear Mary here designed it."

"It's so long!"

"About what, Mary? Twelve feet?"

Mary didn't respond.

"I just love this great yellow bird," Isadora said, smoothing the fabric across most of the table. "And the little flowers. I don't know what the writing is, though. I mean, I know it's Chinese, but...Mary, what does it say?"

Mary gazed at the scarf, its red and yellow swirling patterns reminding her of gore. There'd been a solider in the war hospital where Isadora had volunteered. She remembered his oozing bandages, his eyes peering out like bits of broken glass. How he reminded him of Preston, her son. She'd forget that he was a man now, a grown man, not the babe in arms, not in danger but whole and safe.

He was not in Nice and not a child. What she saw had not been real. Yet there it was, on the shawl. How had she never realized this when she designed it? The huge, bestial bird, the yellow in ichors and red gore stared back at her from the scarf.

Her throat tightened. She shut her eyes, lifted her head up, back straight, knees together, hands on knees. She breathed deeply and whispered, "*A ka dua, Tuf ur biu, Bi aa chefu, Dudu ner af an nuteru... A ka dua...*"

"Mary?" Isadora's brow furrowed in concern. "What's the matter?"

"Is that Chinese?" asked Ivan, still smiling.

"Mary? What's wrong? You're so pale. *Serveur, pourrait vous apporter à la dame de l'eau-de-vie fine?*"

"Is she having a fit?"

"No, this is magick. She uses it when she needs it."

Ivan paused a moment. "Crowley," he surmised.

"You must excuse us. I need to take her home."

"Can I assist you?"

"It's just across the street, but thank you. I'm so sorry. Come by tomorrow, we'll start filming, I promise. Good-bye, I'm so sorry."

After nearly carrying Mary across the street, Isadora managed to seat her on the sofa. She ripped through the kitchen and all her hiding places for brandy. As she crawled out from a cupboard, Mary stood in the doorway.

"I'm sorry, Isadora."

"Sorry? Mary, are you all right? I've never seen a more melancholy face." She hugged her friend tightly.

"I was angry with you for running off last night…"

"Oh, dear, I forgive you."

"Please," Mary begged weakly, "let me finish. I started looking for you, but I was…attacked."

"Attacked! We must go to the police!"

"By a bird…and then a cat… I ran here, to bed. To my room. Isadora, please don't leave me tonight. Don't go with Buggatti."

"Oh, Mary." Isadora laughed. "Didn't I warn you about that cat in the garden yesterday? You told me yourself he's nothing to worry about. Here." Isadora took her friend's hands and walked her into the studio. She turned on the gramophone, and began to dance with those simple leaps and skips that had made her famous. She laughed, "I'm in love again, Mary. This is the happiest day of my life!"

Her movements were magic; Mary could not help but smile.

Two hoots came from a car outside. Isadora dashed out, bouncing merrily into the open back seat Buggatti held for her.

"It's cold. Here, wear my cape," Mary offered.

"I have your beautiful scarf. I don't need anything else!" Isadora gestured at the handsome youth. When he leaned closer, she said in a carrying whisper, "I was visited by a goddess, and her story will save the world."

Buggatti chuckled. "Isn't my Madonna supposed to be visited by the Lord?"

As Isadora adjusted in her seat, Mary whispered to the beaming Buggatti, "I don't believe you realize what a great person you're driving tonight. I beg you to be careful. I'm terribly nervous."

"Madame, when I drive my sweet Madonna," he leaned over the closed door to kiss Isadora's hand, "I drive like Christ."

"We're not going far, dear, just to the Hottois house and back." Isadora smirked dramatically, throwing her scarf over her shoulder for good measure. "Good-bye my friend, I am off to love and glory!"

Buggatti climbed back into the front seat, and Mary turned to watch them leave.

Isadora's scarf fluttered toward the ground, toward the spokes of the wheel. Buggatti started the car.

"Isadora!" Mary cried out. "Your scarf! Pick up your scarf!"

Then the break.

***

Paris knelt at Mary's feet. "They're all gone now," he whispered. "The doors are padlocked. Police sealed the house. No one else should be coming. Please, tell me exactly what happened."

She began again. "Her scarf wrapped around the wheel. It...pulled her out of the car...in the most extraordinary manner...into the street. Buggatti was crying and screaming. He said he'd killed the Madonna. He wouldn't stop saying it, even after I sent him for a knife and scissors...to try to cut her free. I tried not to hurt her. We lifted her into a passing car. They were a sweet couple, but I didn't get their name. I held her poor head...it rolled around so. I tried to get her to breathe... We got her to the hospital. The doctor said she died instantly. Painlessly. No suffering at all."

"Bless him for letting us take her home." He squeezed his lips between his teeth as his tears fell.

Mary gazed at the divan where Isadora had been laid, draped in purple velvet cloth she hadn't yet decided how to use. She was dressed in a scarlet robe and a black cape, shrouded by a fine white veil.

"Bless him," she whispered.

Paris looked away. "You should get some rest. It's three o'clock in the morning."

"She looks like a sleeping child," Mary murmured.

A tap came from the door. Paris wiped his face with his hands. "Damned vultures. Why won't they leave us alone?"

"Answer it," Mary suggested. "Maybe it's a friend."

Paris obliged. He returned with a woman Mary did not recognize. "This is *Mademoiselle* Avers. Isadora was going to see her tonight."

Mary nodded slowly. "The Hottois' nanny..."

"I wanted to see why Isadora did not come to me." The shadowy woman's face softened under her black spectacles. "I can see why now."

"She was getting in the car—"

"I know," the woman interrupted gently. "I didn't come to force you to relive your new grief. If I could, I would like to say some words and then I'll be on my way."

"Certainly," Paris conceded. He sat on the couch next to Mary and took her hand.

"Isadora loved the Greeks. The Greeks once spoke of the Lamia, a woman demon with the body of a snake and wings and feet like a bird. She once had children, and after their death, she could never shut her eyes and thus always could see nothing but their deaths. Zeus, God of gods, blessed her to be able to remove her eyes from their sockets, finding release."

Paris shifted in his seat. Mary remained silent.

"Isadora was a pagan, saying she did not believe in God. There is a difference between having faith in God and believing in him. She did not believe, but trusted. She had no hope, but loved. She had no god, but the One. If one must read from cherished texts when someone dies, then I honor this ritual with some lesser-cited lines."

The woman cleared her throat and began to recite. "'Her house sinks down to death, and her course leads to the shades. All who go to her cannot return and find again the paths of life. Her gates are gates of death, and from the entrance of the house she sets out toward Sheol. None of those who enter there will ever return, and all who possess her will descend to the Pit. One should not sleep in a lonely house, and whoever sleeps in a house alone is seized by Lilith.'"

She placed poppies between Isadora's motionless hands. Mary and Paris lay slumped on the sofa, in as peaceful a sleep as Isadora's seemed to be.

"Isadora, I cannot help what I herald. I had hoped you could dance faster than death. Kiss your children for me."

She closed the door quietly behind her, leaving the three friends together in their sleep. Outside, the slate night sky began to rain.

Screech Owl Serenade
by Lorne Dixon

Verse One

I met her in a song, how all romances start, but the music blaring through those high fidelity bass reflex cones wasn't the honeysuckle sweet hum of Marvin Gaye or the smoky seduction of Sade, it was the sweaty midnight grind of early '80s Prince.

She told me her name was Lilith as she drank pure blue agave tequila straight from the bottle. The rumble of voices thundered through the party, but her words drifted distinctly to my ears. She asked me how she looked and grinned before I could answer. She was reading my thoughts, plucking them out of my telltale eyes.

I checked my pulse, made a joke that might have been clever if she wasn't paying too much attention, and did my best to fill the awkward gaps in our conversation. I asked about her short amber dress and her black pearl jewelry. I complimented her eyes, her hair, her purse, and her posture. I tried not to let my eyes dip down to her curving neck, her breastbone, the perfect cleft of her dark breasts as they pressed out from her décolletage.

The tip of her tongue slid across her top lip and caught an escaped droplet of Casa Noble. Lips still slightly parted, the hint of bright white teeth peeking through, she purred, "You wanna stay here until they dig out the Funkadelic records? Or do you want to remember this night for the rest of your life?"

Verse Two

Indulging, that what she called it, the little dance her fingers did between her legs as I gasped and tried to find my breath. She was unstoppable, a creature of bristling lust that couldn't be depleted of its energy or stamina. She kept her motor running while I sank into the sheets, my pulse bulging in my neck, listening to her purr and whimper, wishing I could keep up. I closed my eyes and strained to hear her body move against the sheets, wet flesh against cotton, every inch of her as delicate as the petals of a tulip. She ran a hand across my chest and it sent out sparks under my skin. I felt myself responding, not eagerly like the first time that night, but grudgingly, like a snake aware of its charmer's mesmerism.

I bit my tongue, gnashed down with my incisors and tried to break her spell. Blood burst between my teeth. Her hand moved down, wrapped around me and I sputtered, sending speckles of blood jetting from my mouth. She licked a smear off my lips with her small, darting tongue. Her saliva tasted like my body. She curled back my bottom lip with a thumb and kissed me deeply, my tongue wrestling with hers, trying to protect my throat from invasion.

She laughed, wiry and bitter, and mounted me.

"This isn't sex," I told her.

She slapped my face hard enough for my eyes to water. Her toes scraped down my legs from thigh to ankle.

She whispered, "You've made love before, but you've just never really been fucked before."

I tried to push her off, but she wrapped her hands around my throat and squeezed. Then she bucked back and I was inside her, I don't know where, damp and tight and hot, but like nothing I'd had before, an untamed place, an organ left out of modern evolution. I could feel her heartbeat from within that chasm, could feel the suction of her blood and the bulge and collapse of her lungs. She rode me hard, back arched, hips grinding, until she began to undulate and shudder.

I felt nothing, not even the hollow-drum numbness of sleeping flesh, or pleasure, or pain. She released my throat and I inhaled sharply.

Afterwards, my body mapped with bruises, scrapes, and bites, I watched her wriggle into her underwear. She didn't glance over at me as she slipped into her dress. She sat on the edge of the bed facing away from me and expertly zipped up. I watched her face in the mirror. She seemed impatient and annoyed.

Before she left, in the moment before the door shut, she finally turned to me. With a quick laugh, the sound of a small animal's death rattle, she saluted me with a single finger. "Bet you'll never forget this."

"Bet not," I mumbled.

Verse Three

I woke with a rockslide in the center of my head. I fought through the migraine's haze enough to hit the alarm's snooze button, collapse back onto my pillow and let myself freefall back into a static-filled sleep.

Fifteen minutes later I repeated myself. Fifteen minutes after *that* I crawled to the kitchen, spilled some of the previous day's coffee into a cup, and sloshed some of it around the microwave.

The microwave's chime reverberated painfully through my pounding head. I tried to tell myself it was the five Herbsaint cocktails I downed at the party but it didn't feel like a hangover. A hangover would have felt positively *friendly* by comparison.

And my side hurt—everything from my left nipple to the peak of my hipbone. I inspected myself in the toaster's chrome body as I waited for a slice of potato bread to pop up. A pink and blue bruise in the shape of a shaky X said hello. If a bruise could sneer, this one would have. *Hey, blood, how's it hangin'?*

Breakfast went down like a handful of miniature bricks and came up as a series of yellow and brown globs. I washed the vomit out of the sink, sat back down at the kitchen table, and waited for my head to clear. Instead, it filled with scenes from previous night. I'd had disappointing sex before and careless, unprotected sex that I'd regretted, but I'd never had *bad* sex. *Bad.* Beyond regret. Beyond Taboo. *Bad.*

And damn it, sitting there in agony, I wanted more.

Verse Four

I fought into a pair of faded black jeans, a ribbed crewneck tee shirt, and my old pair of mid-cut sneakers. I stumbled out into the hall and waited by the elevator for a moment before losing my patience and heading for the stairs. Out of breath and with my bruised side pounding, I stepped out on the third floor and knocked on Lewis's door.

There was an eruption of sound behind the door that could have been mistaken for a china cabinet collapsing. It was Lewis' screaming voice. "I tol' you, I pay rent here an' if I wants to have a party, I'm gonna damn well have a—"

He threw open the door, saw it was me, and dropped the angry black man charade. He snorted out a quick laugh and brought his voice down to his regular church whisper. "Hey man, it's you. Come on in. Neighbors been giving me shit all morning about the noise last night."

Lewis watched me wobble in. "I think they're just jealous they weren't invited... Someone shoot you in the legs? 'Cause you're walking like a crab.'"

Lewis's apartment was one big open loft. I waved to his girl Keo as she sat on the couch and toggled the controls to their game console. I saw her reflection smile in the face of the television set.

"Seriously, you okay?" Lewis asked.

I shook my head. "I'm all banged up. Nothing to ruffle feathers over. I came down here to ask you about Lilith."

"Lilith?"

"Tall black chick." I slid a flat hand a few inches over my head. "She was here at the party. I left with her last night."

Lewis grinned. "She run out on you?"

I nodded.

"You expect her to make toast and coffee?" When he saw I wasn't in the mood for joking his face straightened. "Okay, look, I didn't invite her. I don't really know her. Someone said that she had just moved into the building, but I don't know." He turned and yelled, "Keo. You know the Lilith girl?"

She paused the game and turned. The sight of her petite frame in just a white wifebeater and Lewis's boxers made my wounded body throb, which on most days was a good thing but today just hurt. The brown beauty mark above her right eye gifted her with a dash of innocence, and her devious smile subverted it into something decidedly naughty.

"Lilith?"

"The black chick that was here last night."

"The tall bitch?" Keo winked at me. "The diva that snatched up *playa* here and made a run for the door? She just moved into 8F."

I thanked her, thanked him, refused coffee, and made my way back to the elevator. This time my patience held out.

Verse Five

The hallway on the top floor hadn't been painted in a decade. There were only two rentable apartments, 8B and 8F. The others were too water damaged from the constant leaks that opened in the old tar roof. I ran my hand along the Aubergine wall as I walked, tracing the water stains that reminded me of both spider webs and tie-dyed tee shirts.

I stopped at 8F and took a deep breath. Pain crackled along my abdominal wall until I released the air from my lungs. I steadied myself and knocked. Then I waited, one hand on the door's flat molding, trying to steady my breath.

Down the hall, the door to 8B opened with a click and a squeal. A short, wiry man shuffled out. He clumsily adjusted a pair of correctional lens glasses that magnified his pale blue eyes. "She's not in there."

"Who're you?" I asked, taking a step toward him. White people tended to be more honest when they were a little scared. This one had a little Russian twist to his voice but he was nothing like the loud musclemen that ran the watch shops downtown. He looked weak.

He stepped back, almost retreating into his apartment. Just the iceberg's tip of his head peeked out. "I'm...my name is Alexei. Alexei Andreyev. I'm...I was a friend of Lilith."

"You *were* a friend?" I asked. He didn't answer vocally, but his eyes slid to the floor. "You know where I can find her?"

He slid back out into the hall a little. Since he was shirtless, I could see the massive scar that stretched from his armpit to his waist. "I believe she's walking that dog of hers."

"Dogs aren't allowed in the complex," I stated, though I knew some of the residents kept pets. There hadn't been a superintendent for almost two years, and the owner lived in Florida. "You think she'll be back soon? When did she leave?"

A pale, tiny girl stepped into the hall and curled her arms around his leg. She stared at me with huge green eyes. On her forehead, just above the spot where her eyebrows nearly met, there were two pink birthmarks.

"Please go inside, Zinaida."

Once she slinked back inside, he turned to me, now a little bolder. He started to pull the door closed as he spoke. "She'll come and visit you when she's ready."

He closed the door and locked it several times over.

Verse Six

I considered leaving the building and walking down the avenue to the small park at the end of the strip. It was the most reasonable place to walk a dog in the city. Ultimately, though, my body hurt too badly to walk anywhere. After I left the elevator, I rested in the hall, back against the wall, before finally making it back to my apartment. I collapsed on the couch, thought briefly about getting a glass of water and more aspirin, but then let myself fall asleep.

I woke to the sounds of angry, torch-wielding villagers battering down my front door. It took me a while to get up. My side was now a buzzing hornets' nest of agony. I wobbled to the door, looked through the peephole, and gasped.

Lilith stood outside the door with an extremely tall man. His skin was as dark as black olives but his eyes were even darker, sunken under a massive brow. A single bolt of gray parted his hair. I couldn't help but notice he wore a studded dog collar.

"Open this door. We need to talk," she said.

I unlatched the chain, unlocked the door, and with great effort, opened it. She sauntered in, hands rowing at her sides with each stride. Her companion followed stiffly, staying within a few feet, arms crossed.

"You didn't need to bring a bodyguard," I told her.

He snorted.

Lilith leaned against the back of my couch. She pulled a long, thin cigarette out of her purse and lit it. "Aeshma is not here to protect anyone. That's actually the opposite of his job description."

She was beautiful, even with a face full of arrogance and apathy, as if she now viewed me as no more significant than an easily swatted gnat. I could feel myself becoming aroused just by standing in her presence. I could also feel my side ache horrifically.

"Did Alexei tell you I was looking for you?" I asked.

"Alexei is a worm." She put the cigarette to her lips, a movement so sensual my knees threatened to buckle. She breathed the burning tobacco in slowly, held it, and then exhaled, lips just barely parted as if whistling. "I'm surprised he even groundhogged up out of his hole."

"I wanted to know—" My attention flicked to the tall man she'd called Aeshma, but only for a second. It was impossible to keep my eyes off her for more than that. I somehow conjured up the courage to continue speaking. "Whether last night... I just wanted to know if I would be seeing—"

She shushed me with a finger to her lips.

Aeshma stepped forward and pushed me to the floor with a five-fingered shove. I landed hard, my shoulder blades, elbows, and tailbone clanged against the floorboards like cymbals. An army of newborn pain marched through my flesh, setting fire to clusters of nerve endings like bamboo villages. A sharp, absurd thought flashed through my head, somehow cutting through the intense sunburst of agony: *It wouldn't be so bad if she'd lie down here with me...*

The thought was murdered in mid-synapse firing by Aeshma's foot. He stepped down on my right thigh with an astounding amount of force. I felt a tangle of nerves scream as they were crushed against my femur and felt my leg instantly flush with heat. Continuing to pin me to the floor, he reached down and wrapped his large, flat fingers around my ankle. I realized what he meant to do the moment before he did it. As a small consolation, I did manage to begin my scream before he wrenched my leg straight up, shredding the ligaments attaching my kneecap and dislodging the patella.

People say that once you hit a certain plateau, pain washes away and numbness fills your body as surely as if it were injected with Novocain. Those motherfuckers lie. There's always another depth of pain to descend and I dove deep. I bit down so hard that I chipped teeth. My eyesight blurred and swirled, my stomach heaved, and my temperature soared.

Then he stepped on my left thigh and did it again.

The word helplessness had never meant much to me before but at that moment it might as well have been my name. I passed out but the pain traveled with me into the blackness.

Verse Seven

I wish I could say that the pain had lessened by the time I tumbled back into consciousness but that would be the worst kind of lie, the kind of lie that you tell more to yourself than anyone else. In truth, it hurt worse, a lot worse. The only thing that kept me sane was looking down at my legs bending apart at truly bizarre angles. I thought of the old manhandled rabbit ears antennae on my father's television. I started to laugh. That hurt, too, but it took enough of the edge off that I could drag myself over to the kitchen and prop myself up against the pantry door.

The phone sat on the floor, upside down and shattered, probably only a few inches from my hopes of running in a marathon.

I considered gathering up my strength and making a healthy crawl for the door. But then I merely shifted my weight and the pain flared and I nearly lost consciousness a second time. At the moment, at least, moving was not in the picture. I could scream, of course, yell out at the top of my lungs to my neighbors. But that didn't even seem worth the experiment. People didn't want to get involved—didn't even crack open their doors to look out last month when the dealer from Delancy Street gunned down one of his mules in the stairwell.

I was thirsty.

Maybe some time passed. Maybe I drifted. Hard to tell. The next clear memory I have is my front door opening. My heart started to race as I turned my head slowly, mouth slightly open, and watched Keo sashay in.

She led little Zinaida through the door by her hand and then turned and closed the door behind her.

"*Keo,*" I stammered.

She smiled, came over, and bent down. She was still dressed in the wifebeater and briefs and as she leaned over me I caught a glimpse down her shirt. She glanced down and saw where my eyes were locked. "That's the thing with you men, you know. Could be that your guts are falling outta your belly but a nice pair comes into sight and you still hav'ta look."

I made eye contact with her. "Help me."

"I am helping you," she said and turned to Zinaida.

The little girl held a roll of duct tape in her free hand. She let go of Keo's hand and struggled to pick the end free of the roll. Keo took it from her, dug the end free with a thumbnail, and handed it back. "Now, just like I told you."

Keo stood, moved over to the kitchen table, and dragged it over. Zinaida reached out and scooped my left foot off the floor. I screamed out as she bound me to the leg of the table. She covered my ankle in a thick bracelet of tape and then let it go. My foot was suspended an inch off the floor. Waves of pain hit me in perfect time with each throbbing heartbeat.

"That hurts, right?" Keo asked.

She took the tape from Zinaida and grabbed my right hand. When I went to push her away she plunged the roll of tape down on my fractured knee. I didn't fight her as she bound my hands together. I was too busy sobbing.

"Like a seal's flipper." Zinaida barked, imitating her idea of a seal.

"All you really need," Keo said as her seductive little smile returned, "is a good strong woman in your life."

Zinaida giggled, then pulled up my shirt and put her ear to my stomach. I watched her face blur as my tears distorted my sight. She seemed peaceful, maybe even filled with awe. "I don't hear anything," she said.

Verse Eight

They were gone. The pain stayed behind like an invited guest, brought its luggage and started to unpack a set of muscle cramps into the already crowded space normally reserved for toothaches and migraines. I vomited on myself at some point. I don't remember retching but the evidence was all around me.

Delirium brought guests, too, voices from my past. My mother's shrill voice asking, "*When are you going to go out there and find a nice girl, not these tramps you're always with?*" Leona, the girl I dated for three years in college, not quite the tramp my mother thought she was, but not a nice girl, either, her voice a force of nature, a hurricane: "*What the hell's wrong with you? What are you, afraid of women or something? Maybe you should be afraid...*"

The room was full of women, all asking questions that sounded like judgments, condemnations from my past, reminding me of mistakes I had made, hearts I had broken, girls I had tossed aside. I wanted to scream at them to stop, to shut the hell up, but my throat was too dry and my tongue too lazy.

The bruise on my side must have gotten infected. It began to balloon up and turn an evil midnight purple. I wondered what Lilith had done to me. And still part of me wished she would do more. The voices snickered and mocked.

Verse Nine

Had hours passed or days? My stomach growled and I thought I heard something inside me answer it. My side bulged out like a basketball-sized tumor. Every act of motion, no matter how slight, sent my body into wild spasm of pain. I tried hard not to blink.

The women were no longer just voices. I could see them only as faint outlines and moving shadows, but I could see them nevertheless. They continued to ask their questions and criticize me. Sometimes they would just stare. That was worse. I closed my eyes to block them out but then they would find their way in through dreams and memories.

I wondered why I wasn't already dead. Then wondered if perhaps I already had died and this was my personal hell, filled not with imps and demons but with the woman I'd never bothered to call, the one night stands, the easy barstool pickups, the ones I took advantage of knowing full well they were searching for their daddy's lost love.

I still thought of Lilith, still *wanted* her.

The women laughed at me and wagged their fingers. Their laughter became a roar like saw teeth in lumber. And I wanted to scream but started to laugh, my voice gone. Only a string of croaking sounds escaped from my lips. Tears flowed. I felt madness settle down over my brain like a shower cap.

And the pain somehow just got worse.

Verse Ten

It was night and I was awake and the pain ebbed and flowed like the ocean. My thoughts were a tangle of memories and fantasies. Reality dipped its hard head into the silky folds of dreams and nightmares. The women sang sad songs and my heart broke over and over. I could feel all of their pain join with mine, the angry words that had stung them worse than a slap from an open hand, the agony of doubt and shattered self-esteem, the alcoholic self-derision and bad on-the-mend lapses of judgment.

The room was an ocean of pain and I was sinking.

I felt something move within me and ran my hands over the bulge in my side. I shuddered wildly as I felt something turn just under the tightly stretched skin. The women's singing broke into wild howls and horrible whistles and devilish laughter.

I think my mind finally broke when I felt a tiny hand try to wrap itself around my finger from underneath my own skin. I don't remember but I suspect I joined the women in the next round of song. I think the song was about me and I don't think it was a love song.

Verse Eleven

My world was dark. I heard them enter but didn't bother to open my eyes at first. My entire body had become one raw, throbbing wound. I breathed as shallow as possible to stop my lungs from shrieking, and I concentrated on keeping myself calm. My heartbeat *hurt*.

I felt a small face press against my engorged side and counted backward from twenty to push the new sensations into the rear of my consciousness. Then I heard Keo's voice, gentle and playful, "Do you hear anything now?"

I felt Zinaida's face contort into a gleeful child's grin. It felt as if each eyelash and every flake of skin was tearing into me. "I think so. I think I can hear her."

I opened my eyes and let the light corrode my pupils. How long had it been since I had last seen my apartment? The women came into focus, an army of ghosts standing over me, now silent, watching Keo and Zinaida inspect me.

I felt Lilith come in before I saw her. She wore an auburn, late-nineteenth-century tea gown and a matching cashmere scarf. She looked stunning. If I had been able to speak, I would have told her so.

Aeshma followed her solemnly, arms at his sides, head slightly bowed. In his left hand he held a pair of pruning shears, in his right an eight-inch drop-point blade.

Lilith knelt over me and wiped my face with a silk handkerchief. She cooed as her cold fingers brushed my feverish brow. "Oh, sweet one, you've been through so much, I know, I know. But it's all over real soon now, so just have a little more patience with me."

Her touch sent shivers through me, painful but a different kind of torture, a welcome agony. She leaned down, kissed me lightly on the lips, and then straightened up and motioned for Aeshma to hand her the knife. He placed it gently in her hands and she blew him a kiss. Jealousy raced through me. I wanted him dead.

"After tonight all your debts will be paid. All of these women who haunt you will all forgive you and you'll become a rare male saint among women." She quickly sliced into my skin at the hip and curved the blade, opening a channel up to my nipple. I started to shake violently. She shushed me. "We all make mistakes, honey. I made my first a long, long time ago. I was in love but he rejected me so I fled. Later he had a child, a girl. I left her to be raised by men and treated as little more than a plaything. A toy. She was a goddess but saw herself as a whore. And her children thought the same way. The men as gods, the women as livestock."

She tossed the knife away and reached inside the incision. She smiled as the skin peeled back. Aeshma handed her the shears. She carefully inserted them inside me. I heard the mechanism work and the blades crack through bone. Every nerve cell in my body exploded in a fiery panic.

"But now we both make amends for our mistakes," she said and pulled our daughter out of me. I saw the nib of exposed bone protruding from her tailbone where my rib became her spine. She cried out and the room full of ghostly woman burst into applause. Then one by one they disappeared.

Lilith turned the baby so I could see her. She was a radiant creature with bright blue eyes and coffee skin. And three black birthmarks over her right eye.

"Meet Violet."

"Hi, Violet," Zinaida whispered.

Lilith cradled Violet in her arms and stood up. "Keo will stitch you up and look after you until you recover. I'll take care of Violet until then."

And she left.

Verse Twelve

When Violet graduated high school, she did so as president of her class and prom queen. She had a perfect GPA, perfect SAT scores. Scholarship checks rolled in. I was very proud.

She spent that last summer before college running with a close cabal of friends, the popular kids—a clique of beautiful young woman who excel in academics and athletics. They *all* have birthmarks, but it was always clear that she was their leader.

I can see it in her smile—she'll have one hell of a future.

What Dreams May Go
by Ed Greenwood

The large crate was a surprise.
After it was opened, Bryce had a bigger one.

It had been some years since Bryce Bryce Wildenstone had been truly surprised. He was used to all manner of ideas springing into his head at odd moments. Ideas that were vivid and detailed, like unfamiliar paintings paraded at an auction. Sometimes they were zany, but more often useful.

Wherefore "BB" was now beyond wealthy. Bryce Bryce Wildenstone, rich and successful inventor, fashion designer, and artist. "Restlessly busy," he'd once described his lifestyle; it had been decades since he'd taken a real vacation, because his painting and the fashion shows took him all over the world, and because sitting beside some pool or baking on a beach or parasailing past ancient ruins seemed simply a waste of time.

If he wanted to sit and look at anything, it was the art collection he'd so slowly amassed and hung on wall after wall of his sprawling home—the home that sprawled farther whenever he ran out of wall space and added a new wing. It covered most of a storm-raked ridge in the Poconos now, though he rarely looked out of a window to enjoy any of the views. The ideas were more interesting, more colorful, more…everything.

Still, being surprised was a novelty that BB found himself enjoying. "A *crate*? Well, sign for it, Vandelt. Who's it from, anyway?"

"I'm afraid the courier insists on your signature only. I believe it's from Mister Brandon Corland."

BB blinked. "*Corland?* This isn't some sort of nasty joke, is it? Is the crate ticking, or is something inside growling?"

"No, sir." The butler managed to convey a mild rebuke and complete sympathy for BB's attitude in the same two words. He was already opening the door to usher his master in the direction of the front hall, and BB was striding after him with more urgency than he'd felt in days. More…excitement. A crate from Corland?

It was big, all right. No fewer than four uniformed men from the courier company were standing around it, so it must be heavy, too.

The one with the graying hair and mustache asked BB's name, and when he gave it, held out a clipboard for him to sign, like some of the older art auction houses demanded. No little electronic pads for them.

"Did, ah, Mister Corland tell you anything about this?"

"No, sir. He was very unwell. Died a few hours after we picked it up, I'm told."

"Died? *How?*"

"Sick, sir. What with, I don't know, but he had three doctors looking after him, and they all insisted it was nothing contagious. Signed declarations, too. Otherwise we'd never have agreed to take it, sir."

BB frowned. "But...I don't know that I should accept this. Heirs might come looking for it, if he has any—the usual fuss over a will, you know."

The courier shrugged. "Doubt there are any. We handle all shipping for the law firm that does—did—his stuff, and there's been nothing. So it'll just be the 'anyone out there?' they put in the papers, and then the waiting. No, this monstrosity is yours."

"'Monstrosity'? You've seen it?"

"No, no, sir. I just meant the *crate*."

Which was certainly big and heavy enough to warrant such a description. Reused, of course, as all old, well-built wooden shipping crates tend to be. It was rectangular, taller and wider than a grand old home's front door, towering over the four couriers as they sweated it off their dolly onto his lobby tiles.

Whereupon the head courier came back to BB, holding out a letter. "Almost forgot. This was taped to it, sir. Addressed to you."

Without being asked, Vandelt glided forward, took the envelope, slit it open with a letter knife he produced from somewhere—his sleeve?—extracted a folded piece of paper, unfolded it without looking at it, and proffered it to BB.

Who read the short and cryptic contents, ending as puzzled as ever. There was a salutation and a polite asking after BB's health, followed by: "As for what comes with this: the 'find' of my collecting career. Got for a song, but disappointingly too large for my nest. So enjoy. I can think of no one who deserves this more than you. Cordially, Brandon"

Shakier handwriting than the bold loops BB remembered from atop so many heaps of school tests, a mark or two better than his own efforts—but then, if Corland had been dying...

There was something…"not right" about this. Brandon Corland and BB had hardly exchanged half a dozen polite sentences with each other, ever.

As boys, they'd hated each other's guts, as the saying went. Fierce rivals who'd bloodied each other's noses in fights and striven almost desperately to outdo each other in class and in front of girls.

BB turned the letter over, found nothing on the back, looked at it again, and then shrugged and handed it back to Vandelt. Well, at least it hadn't caught fire, and there was no powder or odd smell…

He shook his head.

After years of sneering at and trying to best each other, he and Corland had turned in different directions in life, and so had fallen out of competition, eventually achieving an uneasy civility. Corland was the increasingly famous painter (whose surrealist daubs BB privately found to be little better than random paint splatters on a canvas; miserly splatters that left a lot of the primer coat exposed, as if Jackson Pollock had been on a tight budget), and Wildenstone the inventor had grown rich and successful enough to buy paintings Corland could not afford the air fare to go and see, let alone bid on.

They both collected art, interested in eras and styles sufficiently different not to ever fight over acquiring a given painting, and so found themselves occasionally at the same opening or fundraiser or art "event," making awkward small talk over glasses of forgettable plonk or worse champagne. Silent at first, then tentatively civil, both finding it hard to let the habit of hatred go, but far beyond times when it seemed to matter. Yet they'd never been *friends*.

So what was going on here?

As the front doors closed behind the couriers, BB found the hall had quietly filled with more than a handful of his household staff.

"Uncrate it here, sir?" Vandelt asked.

"Yes," BB replied, turning away. He didn't want to be anywhere nearby if the unexpected delivery exploded, or splashed paint all over anyone nearby when opened, or was full of dead cats or something. Sometimes having employees to spare was a very handy thing. "I'll be in my study."

Two steps onto its carpet he thought of a new hose-coupling that should be stronger, be cheaper to make, and create a better seal than existing ones.

He was happily humming his way through the drawings the Patent Office deemed necessary when Vandelt appeared at the door. He stood waiting silently to be hailed.

BB got to an easy stopping point and looked up. "Yes?"

"The painting is uncrated, sir, and awaits your inspection."

"Painting? Is it good?"

The butler hesitated. "I cannot say, sir. As you well know, art is very subjective, and I venture to say not all of this work is yet visible."

Not all yet *visible?*

Interest—hell, be honest: curiosity—made him hasten down from the study, eager to see something that could make unflappable old Vandelt hesitate.

The staff were waiting for him when he strode back into the lobby, silently flanking the painting and looking not at it but at him. They wanted to see Bryce Bryce Wildenstone's reaction.

He made himself come to an easy stop, to stand well back from it, studying it. His first thought was that this was Corland's last slap at him from beyond the grave. A taunt, a joke.

Oh, it was a painting, all right. Life-sized, as tall as a door and wider than most. Surrounded by an ornate and heavy gilded Victorian frame, all flourishes and oak-leaves, the largest such frame he'd ever seen. The yellowing nameplate—ivory, of course—read "The Eternal Sisters." Somehow he got the feeling that the frame was newer than the painting itself.

Not that he could see all that much of the painting. At first glance, it looked more like an old paneled wooden wall than a painting—a framed rectangle of varicolored brown mud. At second glance, one could see that its various deep brown mottlings were dirt. The canvas was filthy dirty; it looked like muddy brown grease overlaid with a stuck-on, matted pelt of thick gray dust.

Except for four interruptions that caught the eye—and having caught it, refused to let go.

Staring out of the brown mud, at the right height for eyes to be, if they belonged to standing figures painted life-size, were two pairs of *very* alluring eyes. BB felt himself ensnared, and kept rising eagerness off his face with an effort.

Who were these Sisters, who stared eternally out at the world?

Bryce Bryce Wildenstone ached to find out.

He had the painting moved to the restoring room, set its climate controls *very* carefully—he'd never owned so large a canvas before—and called in his most expensive experts for the cleaning, telling them to take all the time they needed.

Which is when he got his next surprise. A scant few hours later they were knocking on his door to tell him they were finished.

They looked a little…haunted? Sheepish? Only Vandelt dared to loiter within view as he hurried to see why.

BB checked his initial impulse to give his most senior servant the glare that would send him gliding smoothly but hastily away. If the butler didn't see the revealed painting now, so as to spread the word, half the staff would soon come sneaking up to see for themselves—and all of them knew how to deal with the alarms.

With a sigh, Bryce Bryce Wildenstone beckoned to Vandelt to enter the restoring room with him.

It was a measure of his astonishment that the imperturbable butler almost ran right into him from behind, BB stopped so suddenly to stare. Open-mouthed, he knew, but he doubted Vandelt, behind him, was anything less.

"My," he managed to say, long moments later, in what he hoped was a lightly amused drawl, "I knew full well that Corland's capable of *anything*, but I wasn't expecting…pornography."

The huge canvas positively glowed, not a trace of the brown muck left. "Came off easily, sir," the head restorer murmured, as if reading his mind. "In our opinion, someone painted it all over with mud a week or two ago, and then, when it was still wet, put it somewhere very dusty. Like amateur fakers do, trying to make something look old."

"But this *is* old, isn't it?" BB asked, his voice a trifle sharper than he'd meant it to be.

"We're…not certain of anything with this one, sir," the restorer said slowly, "but we believe so. As old as any painting any of us have ever seen."

The palette, with its "still life" brown background cast showcasing an array of rich hues, firmly told any eye "Old Master," but the subject matter looked far more modern in both content and style. The subjects were life-sized, and painted in near-photographic detail. Two impossibly beautiful, mature women—lookalikes; twins, perhaps—with lush bodies and long, long legs.

BB couldn't take his eyes off them.

They were bare but for garments of translucent, flowing light cloth, standing face to face but with their heads turned to stare out at the viewer, cheeks almost touching. They were entwined provocatively around each other like modern-day strippers. BB found himself ensnared by those enigmatic, compelling painted stares. Stares that were full of challenge, lust, and…promise.

Finding his mouth suddenly dry, BB licked his lips and shifted his feet, feeling his body stirring.

Then, with an effort, he abruptly spun away, fighting a sudden and terrifically strong impulse to look back.

Corland hadn't been indulging in the slightest hyperbole. The "find" of a collecting career, indeed.

"Certainly a surprise," he told the restorer calmly, half-turning to address the wall rather than moving to the face the man—and the painting, "but your usual good work. Thanks; Vandelt will pay you. I can't think where to display such a thing. Face to the wall, perhaps?"

Despite those words, Vandelt's eyes betrayed not the slightest surprise at the orders BB gave after the restorers had gone.

BB instructed him to have the Eternal Sisters moved to the upstairs galleries and displayed in pride of place—displacing a Titian—on the wall between the two rooms that dominated the collection.

Even with the display lights off, those painted eyes glowed, the Sisters staring alluringly at anyone entering the galleries.

A powerful, superb painting, to be sure, better by far than anything else he owned. It made the Goya and Chagall sketches look like, well, sketches, and his prized row of Canalettos and Tintorettos and Campis so many tired, dingy old wall adornments. The huge canvas—artist unknown; he'd searched in vain for a signature—seemed somehow *alive*, in a way no painting, not even the Mona Lisa and other masterpieces he'd peered at so longingly in galleries all over the globe, ever had appeared to him before.

After his feet started to fall asleep, BB ordered his favorite chair brought to where he was standing, and a Rémy cognac to arrive there, too.

He sat staring at the painting, sipping cognac that warmed like fire, increasingly certain that the mouths and eyes of the two Sisters had moved, infinitesimally, as if they were focusing not on just anyone standing in front of the painting, but on *him*, their mouths parting in interest as they beheld Bryce Bryce Wildenstone.

After he'd begun his second silken-smooth cognac, BB smiled back.

The ear-splitting crashings of the storm, with lightning striking so close and often that the air tingled and reeked of ozone, roused BB—but it was the insistent ululation of the alarms that jolted him *really* awake.

The flashing red telltale heralded an intrusion in the upstairs galleries. Of course.

He stamped his feet into his shoes and ran, tousled pajamas and all, shrugging on his housecoat as he sprinted down the longest hallway.

Vandelt was waiting for him outside the doors to the galleries, fully dressed and with a gun in his hand, face as expressionless as ever.

"Sir," he murmured in greeting. His voice was as calm as ever, too.

The doors were closed and locked, just as BB had left them when he'd staggered off to bed a few hours ago. Without hesitation he unlocked them and flung them wide. Vandelt flicked on the galleries' lights from the outside switch.

No running masked figures, nothing fallen or out of place—except the windows. Open to the storm, *all* of them, with the heavy blinds billowing and rainwater puddling on the floor.

BB swore with feeling, racing to close them, knowing they had all been closed and latched when he'd left the galleries. And the alarms should have started chirping when the first window was opened, rather than sounding all at once as if windows had been flung open simultaneously....

Vandelt worked one room and he the other, closing and slamming the latch-bars down and sliding the metal dogs into place to keep them there. The carpet was soaked in huge dark patches, the fans in the walls whirring at double speed to soak up the detected moisture.

The last window was closed, bringing abrupt quiet. The lightning storm was fading into the distance, as violent as ever but moving on, and BB devoted himself to having a damned good look around to make sure nothing was missing or damaged.

An intruder—a thief or a vandal—it must have been. Only he, Vandelt, a bonded security firm, and two bank vaults had keys to the galleries.

Vandelt? No...*no.* BB didn't want to think about that, and just couldn't believe it anyway. If Vandelt had wanted to come and peer at the Sisters for himself, he knew how to do so without disturbing anything or setting off any alarm.

The Sisters!

BB rushed over to his latest acquisition and let out a deep sigh of relief. Undamaged, or so it seemed, the canvas right where it should be, unharmed and...

He stopped, frozen in fresh astonishment, standing open-mouthed as a little chill raced around the edges of his utter disbelief.

The two women in the painting had moved.

The Sisters were no longer embracing each other. Now they faced him, shoulder brushing shoulder, leaning forward to stare even more directly at the viewer—at *him*—their hands now off each other and on their own bodices, frozen in the act of wantonly pulling them open as if offering their magnificent breasts to him.

And there were now glints of gold in their wider, hungrier, more flashingly *eager* eyes.

Almost as an afterthought he noticed they were both wearing tiaras. Tiaras whose delicate, upswept silver spires spelled out names. The one on the left, it seemed, was "Lilith," and the one on the right, "Naamah."

BB shook his head in slow, amazed disbelief. Then he bent forward to peer very closely at the paintings.

He was regarding paint that looked as if the brushstrokes that had applied it had always been this way, but he had peered just as closely yesterday—and twice more, in that long, solitary evening of cognac. And he *knew* the photographs he'd taken of the picture after its cleaning would tell a different story.

To say nothing of the step-by-step photographic record the restorers always made. Such things only change by magic in movies and fairy tales.

Bryce Bryce Wildenstone met those painted gazes again—full of warm welcome and warmer promise—shook his head, and forced himself to turn away. Right now, he needed something rather stronger than cognac.

By the end of the day, all of the staff who cared to had trooped up to see the painting. Or so Vandelt had reported, on his way out the door to his sister's.

That bothered BB not a whit. Better they see for themselves rather than spreading wild stories, or waiting until after dark to go creeping around the house to sneak a peek on their own.

Nor had he been idle, either. A quick rummage in the cellars had turned up several old Yale locks from his school days—from lockers and bicycles and such, of the era when you could get only one sort of good lock, and the school sold them and dictated you must use just that one make because there was a master combination for emergencies—and some heavy old chain, too heavy for the bolt cutters, but not for the cutting torches out in the garden repair shed. The window-latches and the decorative door-rings were of "old school" design, he'd noticed, which meant heavy metal construction, forged into loops for just such restraints. BB was going to chain the doors and windows shut at nights.

"Just in case," as they said. And to make it that much more trouble to get into the galleries, if any more vivid dreams of sisters who only had eyes for him awakened him in the dark hours with an urge to just go and sneak a peek of his own. There was something…uncanny, yes, that was the word; eerie, even, about the painting.

He'd have to remember to leave a flashlight or two ready tonight, and find his old gun, too. Vandelt was gone for three nights to his sister's family, and any funny business in the galleries or anywhere else in the house in the wee hours would be his problem alone.

BB oiled and worked the locks repeatedly, to make sure none of them would stick or "go wrong" once it was holding a chain shut. He and Jase Maskell had been reduced to tears once, struggling vainly to open their shared locker. The school janitor—they called them "custodians" these days, after briefly trying on the term "caretaker" —had managed to get the battered, stuck old lock off with bolt cutters and a hacksaw. If anyone did something of the sort to open any of the ways into the galleries, they'd at least leave clear traces behind, and probably give him plenty of time to be awakened by the alarm and come running down.

He trotted up the back stairs towards the galleries, arms loaded with heavy chain. Umm. Something to remember: with no Vandelt to do the watching and listening, he'd have to turn the alarm volume up to max, at his bedside.

Jase Maskell was another watcher and listener. He'd been the one who'd told BB that Corland was ailing, just as he'd told BB down the years about the achievements and calamities of many of their former classmates. Marriages, divorces, remarriages, deaths; Jase kept on top of it all. Some people kept in touch, and some moved on.

The galleries seemed dry and fine, everything in its place and Lilith and Naamah as vivid as ever. At least they hadn't moved again.

BB bade the Sisters a polite goodnight as he backed through the double doors. Locking them, he threaded the last length of chain through their rings, snapped shut the last padlock to firmly fasten those doors together, patted his pocket that held the scrap of paper with all the lock combinations on it until that paper crackled, and headed off in the direction of a good bedside book.

Hadn't Lilith been the name of the storm demon in the old Biblical tales? The seductress, who...er, something or other? He'd have to look her up in the dustier corners of his library. The books he hadn't opened since college.

Though, come to think of it, their stately, leather-bound pages had held tales just as juicy as some of the racier books published these days.

He saw painted hands resting teasingly on painted bodices all the way to his bedroom.

The roll of thunder that awakened him shook the room. He blinked in the blinding flashes of lightning, peering out of habit at the alarm monitor and thankful to see nothing.

Wait. *Nothing*. No green "System Functional" light. No digital clock beside it, either.

Great. Power out, and lightning must have hit the house, somewhere, to fry the backup. Well, there'd be no one firing up the emergency generator except him, with Vandelt sleeping a good three hours away.

At least, BB hoped the old man was asleep. Sometimes he'd wondered if the old butler slept in his suit, stiff and straight, shoes on and all, just waiting to be roused at dawn, like a vampire in reverse; Nosferatu to bed in one direction, exchanging polite nods with an arising butler as they pass each other in a hall.

Lightning stabbed again, close enough that his skin crawled and the darkness around him crackled. Huh. Well, there'd be no getting back to sleep in *this*. He might as well get his shoes and pants back on, scoop up the flashlights, and go on a tour.

A tour that could loop through the kitchens for some ice cream—why let it melt, after all? —and then to the sideboard in the dining room for some more of that cognac. Then he could go up to the galleries and toast Lilith and her sister.

BB was halfway down the main staircase when the night exploded in white lightning, and he suddenly found himself sharing house space with an honest-to-God lightning bolt.

Or *something* that lanced down the stairs blinding-white and snarling, presumably out of the storm.

In its wake, stumbling dazedly against the wall with his housecoat torn away, blinded and with all of his hair standing on end, the stink of scorched wallpaper strong around him, BB heard glass breaking, back on the floor above.

In the galleries, of course.

The lock decided to stick, of course. Or perhaps it was just BB's frenzied, fumbling haste, the paper with the combinations firmly under one foot with one flashlight flaring on the floor beside it, the other trembling in the crook of his shoulder and chin as he turned the dial.

The seventh try got it open. BB clawed the chain through one of the rings with a rattle and let it crash to the floor. Plucking up the paper, he snatched out his keys and got the door open.

The sharp smell of smoke hit him like a wall.

He started cursing even before he had two flashlights trying to pierce the drifting haze. He could hear rain to his right that told him windows were open or shattered, and see gleaming reflections like so many jewels strewn on the floor, that must be fallen glass, but—

Hell and *damn!*

Right in front of him, the great gilded frame hung askew and empty, no canvas within it any longer. The wall behind it was blackened and bubbled down to charred studs and twisted black ribbons that must have been wiring.

He directed the beams of his flashlights to the floor. A few tatters of canvas spilling out of the bottom of the frame, a handful of ashes all around, but nothing that could be salvaged. The two sexy sisters were gone forever.

A storm effing demon indeed! Why—

Something moved in the room where the windows were broken. BB strode towards that half-seen shape, training his flashlights like guns. If someone had—

Jeez. Someone had, all right.

Oh, *God*, someone had.

Facing him with a little smile on her lips, her unbound hair curling and writhing about her shoulders as if with a mind of its own, was Naamah.

Or so her tiara proclaimed. It was undamaged, and so was the rest of her, by what the flashlight showed him, as she glided, barefoot, towards him.

She wore nothing but her smile, that see-through garment of hers now draped over one arm. Her eyes were dark and full of tiny, eager stars.

BB stared at her in wordless astonishment. Then his eyes darted back to the frame and the ruin spilling out of it.

"Huh-how—?" he managed to ask, in the instant before velvet-soft fingers trailed around his ribs from behind, skilled and unhurried, rising to caress his chest before dipping to his shuddering hips...and his belt buckle...

Lilith!

He tried to turn, but by then Naamah had hold of his wrists, her grip astonishingly strong, her mouth warm as it sought his, her breath both sweet and spicy.

She was hungry, but Lilith was hungrier.

Birdsong awakened him, this time. It was bright morning, or so his bleary eyes told him, and Bryce Bryce Wildenstone was sprawled alone on the storm-soaked floor of his easternmost gallery, naked. His shoes, pants, and flashlights were strewn around him, and glass was scattered in profusion on the carpet between him and the now-empty window-frames along the east wall.

Memories came flooding back. Here, on the floor, their caresses, their hot and hungry mouths...

BB rolled over, peering around. He was alone, and just noticing the scratches on his arms and thighs. He could feel them on his back, too.

"Jeez," he muttered, staring at the charred wall where the great painting had been, where its empty frame now sagged. It was the only sign that lightning had done anything in the room. Around the walls, all the other paintings hung in their places, tranquil and unchanged.

Where *was* everybody? Hadn't any of the staff found his room empty and gone looking for him yet?

And found him lying here, like some sort of madman?

Well, they hadn't. He hoped. Or it seemed. And that was *one* good thing...

The birdsong seemed louder than usual, the sunlight different. As if it was full morning. How long had he been sitting here, now?

BB groaned and sat up. He felt tired and empty. He couldn't seem to concentrate, to *think*.

He staggered to his feet, staring dully at all the shards of glass on the floor.

He must...he must...

He must *what?*

Glass. Broken glass. Get it replaced.

Yes. He'd better...he couldn't remember how it had ended, last night.

"God Almighty," he groaned, remembering everything else.

The touch of those fingers, the silken softness of their skin against his, their hot mouths, the tender hunger in their eyes...He groaned again, lust returning, and felt around almost blindly for his pants. Jeez, they'd torn his underwear into a rag.

Lilith and Naamah, who'd said not a word beyond purring murmurs and hissing gasps...their softness, their strength...

He shook his head, wincing. More vivid than any dream, but how soon would it fade?

Bryce Bryce Wildenstone knew one thing. He didn't want to forget any of it.

The firemen met him on the stairs, trudging up grim-faced with a cloth stretcher to find his body. It seemed live wires had burst out of walls all over the house, downstairs, and no one had dared try to get up the lightning-scarred main stair or the spitting-many-sparks back stairs. Until now; the storm had only subsided at dawn, rolling away like a black curtain to reveal the bright morning he'd awakened in.

It would take weeks to rewire his house, the firemen told him, and he'd best move out until the work was done. He nodded agreement while trying to remember where in the cellar the really big box of candles was. And if those coach lanterns flanking the garage doors were really ornamental. No power or not, he wasn't going anywhere.

His work was here, his art, his...obligations. BB wouldn't flee from a little storm damage, damn it.

He remembered little of the days and nights that followed, except for two things.

One was the growing eagerness of twilight and deepening evening, that always ended with him walking through the dark and silent house to the galleries, wearing only his housecoat. The other was what he only dimly realized, through a growing mental haze. New ideas were no longer coming to him. He couldn't think about the ideas he'd already written down, couldn't design anything.

When Jase Maskell finally heard about what the storm had done to BB's house and came by to see how he was, BB discovered he couldn't even concentrate on ideas that were discussed with him.

Listening to Jase read his notes aloud—the jottings he *never* let anyone else see, but now with growing panic had handed to Jase, in hopes that talking them over would bring his brain back—BB couldn't conceive of how he could ever have invented anything.

"They are feeding on my dreams," he mumbled at last, seeing two pairs of hungry and eager eyes full of stars in his mind, Lilith and Naamah smiling at him in the moonlight...

"What's that?" Jase asked, leaning forward over his coffee. "What'd you say?"

"They are feeding on my dreams," Bryce told him, in a horrified whisper. "So I no longer have any." He took a long sip of coffee from his own mug, swallowed, and added slowly, "So my imagination, my creativity, is...shriveling and dying."

His old friend frowned. "That's just what Corland said to me. About two weeks before he killed himself."

BB stared. "Killed himself?"

Jase nodded. "He started taking poison in his coffee. When they did the autopsy, his body was full of it."

Bryce Bryce Wildenstone looked at the mug of coffee in his hand, and slowly, carefully, lowered it to the table.

Then he shrugged, picked it up, and drained it.

Outside, the shadows were getting long. It would be dark soon.

What I Did This Summer
Clara Alvarado-Graham, Age 6
(Mama Elena wrote it down)
by Marcus Ewert

This summer I went to Mount Rushmore with Mama Elena and Mommy Kate. Mount Rushmore is historical and it is a monument. It's all carved up like people's faces. There are four faces on Mount Rushmore, and they are presidents. Not now, but presidents long ago. Mommy Kate said only men used to be presidents. Mama Elena says that's probably changing.

We drove four days to get to Mount Rushmore. We only could stay in campgrounds that allowed kids and dogs. One was called Lake Winnemack, but it didn't have a lake. Another was called Sleepy Pines, and it did have a lake. I got to go water-skiing!

We played Frisbee, too. Mommy Kate says, "Everyone can win," and, "There don't have to be losers." I caught the Frisbee five times! Mommy Kate caught it four times. Gloria caught it three times, and Mama Elena didn't catch it at all. Gloria is our dog. When she jumps high, she stands on two legs in the air, like a person.

When we got to Mount Rushmore, everyone was driving out, very fast. All the cars were honking: BEEP! BEEP BEEEEEP! Some were in accidents. They hit each other's rear ends. There was lots of smoke and one woman was crying.

A man in a Park Ranger uniform came by. It was brown. "Watch out! Watch out!" he yelled at us.

"Watch out for what?" said Mama Elena.

"Watch out for the Mother of Abominations!" he said.

"Who?" said Mommy Kate.

The Park Ranger shouted at Mommy. "Lilith! The Great Whore! She Who Screeches Without Cease in the Wasteland!"

But we kept driving in. Mommy Kate only gets two weeks paid vacation a year. "We're not turning back now," she said, "authority be damned."

"Damned" is cursing.

We drove in as far as we could. Then we parked the car. Then we walked. There was lots of grass. It was sunny and hot. Gloria ran ahead of us, but it was okay, we could still see her. There were no people, but it was loud because of all the woodpeckers. They were eating bugs.

To get to the presidents, we walked two whole miles. Mama Elena said, "You are a good walker, *mijita*."

When we got to the big stone faces, we saw a very huge bird-woman with wings.

She was sitting on Abraham Lincoln, who was a good president. Her big yellow feet held on tight to Mr. Lincoln's nose. Her vagina was showing and she was having babies—lots lots and lots and LOTS of babies. Mostly, they looked like centipedes, but they had people's faces. Some looked happy, and some looked sad.

They climbed all over the presidents.

"Holy shit," said Mommy, which is cursing pretty bad.

Mama Elena said something in Spanish, but she won't tell me what it means, even when I ask her many times.

Gloria didn't curse. She is a dog.

The bird-lady was making even more babies now. Besides the centipedes, there were ones that looked like giraffes plus bats; also, ones that looked like old men in coats; also, ones that looked a little like my old red wagon, once it was rusted with holes, and I wasn't allowed to sit in it.

I asked Mommy Kate in a whisper, "Whose sperm did the bird-lady use?" When I was born, Mama Elena used sperm from Uncle Adelardo, who is gay and lives with Uncle Thùy. That is the recipe for a wanted child.

Even though I whispered, the bird-lady heard me!

She started talking, and the whole valley shook. It wasn't an earthquake, it was just the bird-lady.

"TO MAKE MYSELF GRAVID," she said, "I USE LIES, CLARA ALVARADO-GRAHAM, AND HYPOCRISY, AND THE WORDS AND ACTS OF BIGOTRY!"

Mama Elena said, "'Gravid' means 'pregnant.'"

"Hypocrisy" is when my *abuelo* calls Mommy *una puta*, even though he cheats on my *abuela* and has affairs. "*Puta*" is cursing in Spanish, and is very bad.

"YOU ALREADY KNOW THE MEANING OF THE WORD 'BIGOTRY,' CLARA ALVARADO-GRAHAM!" said the bird-lady.

"Yes," I said, "I do. What's your name?"

"YOU HEARD THE RANGER CALL ME LILITH, AND VARIOUS OF MY TITLES. IN EACH AGE, I ACCRUE NEW NAMES, TRAITS, STORIES—ATTRIBUTIONS AS NUMEROUS AS MY CHILDREN. AND NOW, ONCE MORE I HAVE RETURNED. IN THIS NEW ERA, WHAT WOULD

YOU HAVE ME BE CALLED, CLARA ALVARADO-GRAHAM?"

An "era" means a long time.

I thought about her question for an era. Then I said, "Gloria #2."

Gloria #2 laughed so loud that it hurt our ears. She flapped her wings and it was windy like a hurricane, but we were OK. Gloria #1 started to whine; then she sat down to chew her foot. I told her to stop. It gets sore if she chews it.

After awhile, we said goodbye to Gloria #2. She flew away. Some of her babies flew with her, but most stayed on the presidents.

We drove home and didn't go water-skiing again. Mommy and Mama cried a lot, but when adults cry, it can be ok. Not always is something wrong; sometimes, they just cry.

"You're a very special girl, *mijita*." Mama Elena told me. "Not every little one gets to name a goddess."

We have been home for seven days. I play with Gloria #1 a lot because TV is boring. None of my shows are on anymore. Now it's just Gloria #2 on the news, all the time. She bit the president's head off. A bad president, not a good president. Mama and Mommy cried, though they were also a little bit happy.

Tonight, at dinner, Mommy Kate said, "Now that Gloria #2 is back, everything has changed. Mythology has once again entered History. All bets are off."

"All bets are off" means no one knows what's going to happen, not for 100% sure.

But I do!

In three days, school starts. This year, I'll be in first grade!

So Weeps the Thunderbird
by T. L. Morganfield

Wakinyan the Thunderbird landed in the Kingdom of Heaven's pastel-and-marble city center and shook the rain from his enormous wings. A couple of angels sitting on nearby stools, playing Takhteh Nard, protested him showering them with water, but Wakinyan ignored them, ruffling his golden-brown feathers then smoothing them, making sure he looked proper for his audience with Yahweh. He hopped toward the palace entrance, his talons clicking on the marble surface.

In the hallway he encountered the angel Samael—Yahweh's eldest son—who appraised him with amusement. "Can I help you with something?" Samael asked the giant bird.

The Thunderbird blinked his impatient yellow eyes. "I bring greetings to your father from the Great Spirit. You will show me to him."

Samael narrowed his icy-blue eyes for a moment, then turned and led the way. Wakinyan had met him the summer before, when the Great Spirit invited Yahweh and his young angels to watch the stick-and-ball games on the mighty plains. Samael spent much of the time comparing his wing color with Raven's, absurdly stupid since they both had ill-kept, dingy black feathers that appeared to be crawling with lice. Wakinyan didn't like how Samael smirked at his hopping gait. Not that Wakinyan ever liked anyone; he found it easier to be suspicious rather than happy.

Yahweh sat in the Great Garden with the god Ahura Mazda and more of his sons, regaling them with enthusiastic details of his planned palace expansion. The angels lounged on stone benches or sat on tree branches so their wings didn't drag upon the ground. The second eldest, Michael, sat next to his father on the chaise longue, holding up his enormous emerald wings as if trying to prove his strength. He looked up when Samael and Wakinyan entered the garden, and he nodded to the Thunderbird. They'd spoken briefly at the games, and Wakinyan had yet to find something to dislike about him, though surely given enough time, something would present itself.

Yahweh smiled brightly at Wakinyan, his face slowly shifting through different patterns about every half minute, always human but different in shape, color, and texture. The Great Spirit's did that as well, though at an astounding speed. Such ability was the sign of a powerful god, something Yahweh was well on his way to becoming. Someday he would be beyond description and, like the Great Spirit, spend most of his time in a non-physical form. But for now he favored a strictly human form.

"So good to see you again, Wakinyan."

Wakinyan bowed, twisting his head under so as not to clink his curved beak on the marble.

"I bring greetings from the Great Spirit." He clapped his wings together, and as he stood upright again, he spread them out and they rained white and pink flowers. Samael swatted the pedals with his hands and ruffled his wings, trying to shake them off. A swarm of flowers spun together in front of Yahweh, whispering like wind through tree branches.

Yahweh closed his eyes to listen until the petals fluttered to the ground and turned to pink and white dust. "We're invited to attend the games again," he announced with a smile.

"And what games would those be, Father?" inquired a soft, windy voice.

Wakinyan curved his neck around to see a female angel standing several paces behind him. Like her brothers, she looked typically human, but she seemed unusually curvy under that wisp of a linen dress, and her long, shining-black hair swirled down over her shoulders like cyclones. But her beautiful purple wings—the color of violas in summer—stole Wakinyan's breath. He turned around with a clumsy hop, nearly bowling Samael over with his tail feathers. She smiled as Samael cursed and though she met Wakinyan's hesitant gaze, she didn't say anything.

"The yearly stick-and-ball games over in the Great Spirit's realm," Yahweh answered. "You'll come with us this year, Lilith?"

She stepped up to Wakinyan and asked, "And you will be playing these games?"

"The humans play. We watch," Wakinyan replied. His voice broke on the last word, and just to mortify him further, his eyes bugged in response. He slid his normal scowl back into place and turned away.

"A shame," Lilith murmured. He felt her smile even with his back to her. "What's your name, Thunderbird?"

Wakinyan grunted it under his breath, but allowed himself a quick peek at her again. He then asked Yahweh, "Will you be in attendance?"

"We will."

Wakinyan bowed again and excused himself. He had many invitations to deliver. But as he hopped from the garden, he glanced back to see Lilith watching him, a smile on her sharply curved lips. Samael whispered in her ear and she glared at him while he laughed.

Would he still smirk like that if I plucked him? Wakinyan wondered.

Once he reached the open courtyard where he'd landed, Wakinyan spread his massive wings and took to the skies, cursing under his breath. He hoped Lilith wouldn't come to the games. He suspected that those pesky little fluttering in his chest were the first signs of love, Heaven's most needy, annoying, and unwelcome curse. If the Thunderbird took pride in anything, it was the fact that he loved nothing and no one, and thus far he'd been spared from such stupidity.

But sometimes Heaven had a strange sense of humor.

* * *

Of course Lilith was at the games, and she insisted on sitting next to Wakinyan. As the Great Spirit's messenger, he perched on a thick tree branch behind his master, keeping watch over the small assembly of gods sitting on the platform of clouds, eating pine nuts and ambrosia. Of the dozen or so invitations Wakinyan had delivered, only Yahweh, Indra, Atum, Nox, and Nox's flower-and-leaf-bedecked daughter Gaea were in attendance. Yahweh's angels roosted on the other branches, watching the games. Humans on the field battled with sticks, trying to whack the rubber ball through the goal posts before getting tackled to the ground.

Michael sat on Wakinyan's right side, keeping silent watch over Yahweh. Samael sat three branches below, picking the leaves from his feathers that Lilith kept dropping on him.

And thus far Wakinyan's attempts to ignore her had failed. She wore the most fascinating perfume, lilac or maybe lily—the Thunderbird knew nothing about flowers—and he couldn't help but stare at her when she wasn't looking. She was so small, so delicate, so easily crushed by clumsiness—

"Are you always a bird?" Lilith asked as she reached up to pluck more leaves from the branch above her.

"What?"

She laughed. "Can you take human form? Most gods I know can do that."

"Of course I can." Wakinyan bowed his head then lifted his beak with his wing, pulling his bird head back like a hood to reveal a man underneath. He shrugged off his feathered coat and rested it on the branch above him.

"Ah, and he's handsome too," Lilith said with a smile.

Suddenly feeling hot, Wakinyan looked around for Coyote. Sometimes the trickster turned up the sun, just for mischief.

Lilith threw her leaves on him and laughed. "Have you no idea how to say thank you when a lady compliments you?"

Wakinyan scratched his nape and muttered, "Thank you?"

"You really should be human more often. It suits you."

Personally, he preferred to be a bird, soaring among the clouds, the wind caressing his feathers. If he had to choose only one form for eternity, it would be that. Yet Lilith's words had him momentarily reconsidering.

Michael cleared his throat and glared at Lilith, but she ignored him. She gathered more leaves and handed some to Wakinyan. "Let's see who can get the most on Samael's wings."

So they dropped leaves on the dark angel until even Wakinyan found himself chuckling. When Samael glared up at them, Lilith laughed and clung to Wakinyan's arm. *Perhaps I'll spit on him too,* he thought, but Samael flew off.

"He's such an infant," Lilith said. She smiled innocently when her father looked at her. Wakinyan averted his eyes under the Great Spirit's intense gaze.

"It looks as if it may rain," the Great Spirit said. "Why don't you go sweep away the clouds?"

Wakinyan donned his feathered coat, reforming into the Great Thunderbird. He took to the skies. He'd hoped Lilith might join him, to keep him company, but she remained behind. And when he returned from his duties an hour later, she was gone, and no one knew where she'd gotten off to.

* * *

For the first time in several million years, the Thunderbird considered doing something nice for someone. Ever since the games, he could think of little else besides Lilith's silky purple feathers and soft smile, and he'd hoped for days that the Great Spirit would send him to the Great Garden on some errand, just so he'd have an excuse to see her again. So when the Great Spirit asked him to deliver a thank-you note to Yahweh, Wakinyan decided he should bring Lilith a gift.

He'd had no intension of bringing up the subject to anyone, but in his new insanity he just blurted it out to Raven, Coyote, and Kokopelli during a sweat lodge ceremony. Naturally they were surprised, but they all encouraged him with advice, in hope that maybe now he'd stop being so cranky all the time. Raven told him women favored flowers. Coyote recommended alcohol or maybe peyote, because it "makes it easier to get to the good part." Kokopelli recommended playing some flute for her. "Humans love music and, well, angels are part human."

Undecided, Wakinyan swooped over the plains and forests, thinking and searching. In the southern swamp areas, he saw a magnolia with purple flowers that reminded him of Lilith's wings. *Perfect,* he thought, and ripped it from the ground. He cradled it in his claws as he flew the three-hour journey to the Kingdom of Heaven.

Upon landing, he hid his gift among the marble pillars, then hopped off to deliver his message. Before taking his leave, he asked Yahweh where his daughter was, explaining that he had a message for her as well. Her father hadn't seen her that day. Wakinyan hopped back out to the courtyard and retrieved his magnolia, unexpectedly depressed.

"So you're looking for Lilith?" Samael spoke up behind him. The angel smirked at the gift before turning his icy blue gaze up at Wakinyan.

"Where is she?" the Thunderbird demanded.

Samael walked past, looking slyly over his shoulder at him. "I can take you to see her."

"You *will* take me to her."

As they flew down to earth, Samael told Wakinyan, "She comes down here every day, pining the days away, longing for what she'll never have. You do know she was human once?"

"And how's that any different from you?" Wakinyan snapped.

Samael laughed. "I may have been born of human flesh, but I was never human. Father created her of mud and made her human, for his little play garden."

Yahweh's experimental garden was no secret to anybody. It was his own little microcosm of creation, practice for when he was older and more powerful and would no doubt leave earth to create his own world from scratch. But Wakinyan hadn't known that Lilith had been a part of that. "How did she become an angel, then?"

"She and Adam constantly fought," Samael replied. "She thought him domineering, so Father took pity on her and gave her wings. She flew away from the garden, and she's been our only sister ever since."

They landed in a clearing not far from a small village. Wakinyan set down carefully as not to damage his gift any further than the trip already had. The wind had stripped most of the branches, and only a few of the purple flowers remained.

Turning to Wakinyan, Samael said, "May I give you a word of advice?"

"No," Wakinyan replied.

"Lilith's not interested in you," Samael said, undeterred. "She's only interested in what she can't have, and anyone she thinks might be able to get those things for her."

"I'm perfectly capable of judging people for myself," Wakinyan hissed. *Like you, you jealous buzzard.*

Samael shrugged and set out for the woods, reaching the distant edge in four wing strokes. Wakinyan followed, hopping.

"Lilith!" Samael called as he walked along the tree line. He shouted a few more times before she jumped down out of the canopy, furious.

"Why are you here? You said you didn't want to—" She stopped abruptly when she noticed Wakinyan standing in the clearing, watching her. "What are you doing here?"

Wakinyan held up the Magnolia. "I brought you something."

Lilith stared at it, eyes wide. "It's…a tree."

"It's purple…or at least it used to be. It…uh, reminded me of you, so I thought you'd like it," he finished quickly. He wanted to see that bright smile of hers again, but if anything she looked uncomfortable. He felt as if he'd just fallen prey to one of Coyote's practical jokes.

"Very sweet of him, don't you think, Lil?" Samael said with a smirk. "And what a handsome couple you two make, don't you think?"

"Shut up, Samael. It's a perfectly lovely gift and I like it very much, thank you!" Lilith picked up rocks and started chucking them at him. "Why don't you just flutter on back home and preen your feathers some more, you damn peacock!" Once she ran out of stones, she flapped her wings at him until he finally flew away. She watched him leave, tears clouding her eyes.

"Did you hurt yourself?" Wakinyan asked.

She quickly wiped her eyes. "I'm fine." She smiled at him, and he thought he might melt. "I'm glad you're here. I was just thinking about you, hoping I'd get to see you again. And you brought me this lovely tree—so very thoughtful of you."

Wakinyan beamed. It felt good to be praised for being nice. Perhaps he should do it more often.

"I know just where you can plant it," Lilith said, and she led him into the woods.

They came to a pond shaded by cyprus trees, the banks crowded with reeds and yellow grass. "How about right here?" Lilith pointed to a small clearing near the southern bank where only grass grew. Wakinyan scratched out a hole with his claws and planted the magnolia. He breathed a bit of magic on it, and it immediately took root and the flowers blossomed again. He took off his feathered coat and sat with Lilith it its shade.

"I'm sorry if you didn't like the gift."

"It's lovely," Lilith told him. She wormed her fingers between his and moved closer, blanketing them both with her wings. He felt unbearably hot and nervous about her sudden closeness.

Just then a woman came up to the pond from the trees, carrying an infant in a sling across her chest. She began filling a clay jug with water.

Lilith sighed. "More than anything in this world, I want one of those."

Wakinyan narrowed his eyes at the woman. "A human female?"

"No, you loon. A baby."

"Why would you want one of those things?" He'd heard they cried and made ghastly messes and then cried some more. Certainly no one could truly want something like that.

Lilith shrugged and sighed again. "I suppose you wouldn't understand."

"Because I've never been human?" he asked. She looked horrified, so he promptly said, "Samael told me."

"Of course he would," she muttered.

"It doesn't matter to me," Wakinyan replied, hoping to comfort her.

She smiled at him again, erasing the angry melancholy on her face. "Of course it wouldn't. You're decent and care about other people."

Such words coming from anyone else would have made Wakinyan laugh and caw, but Lilith made him see himself in new, unexpected ways. He sat a little straighter and smiled to himself.

The baby started fussing and the fine hairs on Wakinyan's neck rose. Hopefully the woman would take the noisy thing away soon. "I still don't know why you want such a thing," he admitted to Lilith.

"I had to give up some things to become immortal," Lilith replied. "Things I never thought I'd regret or even miss."

Wakinyan watched the baby for a moment, then looked back at Lilith. She watched it intently, the longing plain on her face. "You can't have any children," he concluded.

She shook her head.

"Why don't you just take one?"

"I don't have the power to turn one immortal. Father would never do it for me. He'd make me give it back," Lilith replied, bitter. She looked at him a moment before sliding that delicious smile onto her face again. "You're quite powerful, yes? You can control the weather with the blink of an eye."

If Wakinyan had been in his Thunderbird form, his feathers would have ruffled with pride. "I don't wish to boast, but I am one of most powerful in my clan."

"Of course you are," Lilith cooed, stroking his bare chest with her fingernails. "You know, if the baby were already immortal when I showed it to Father, he'd have to let me keep it. He can't reverse that, after all. And the one who did such a thing for me, he'd have my heart for all eternity."

"Forever?" he stammered.

She laughed lightly. "Forever," she whispered, and kissed him.

* * *

In the middle of the night, the Thunderbird flew back to the pond and left his feathered coat by the magnolia tree. In human form, he followed the path to the village.

A soldier armed with a spear stood guard near the outskirts, but Wakinyan quickly subdued him with a sleeping spell. He moved to the center of town, throwing dust from his medicine bag on the door of each house.

You shouldn't do this, he thought. *Stealing a human child? If the Great Spirit found out....*

But Lilith wouldn't tell anyone, certainly not if she wanted to keep it. Besides, the child would never know death and disease. There was no nobler gift than eternal life.

Once he cast the last of his sleeping spell on the village, he climbed through windows, looking for a baby. The first three houses proved disappointing, but in the fourth, he found several young children asleep with their parents. The mother cradled an infant in her arms. He carefully unfolded her arms and pulled the child away. He tucked it under his arm and climbed out the window. No one stirred.

He hurried back to the pond and set the baby in the grass. He'd never attempted to turn anyone immortal before, so he took a moment to meditate and pray to Heaven for extra strength. He then breathed upon the infant, filling its lungs with his divine breath.

The child stirred with new life, waving its arms around as it lay half asleep, its fat cheeks puffing as it opened and closed its mouth, searching for something. Now it would be able to breathe in the high altitude of the Yahweh's sky kingdom. Wakinyan set his hands on the infant's bare chest and closed his eyes, summoning all his magic and pouring it into the baby.

An hour later, the child still wasn't immortal and the sleeping spell had nearly worn off. This was much harder than Wakinyan had expected. Already the sun peeked over the mountains, and he had early morning tasks to do back home. The village would awaken soon and discover the child missing, so he sprinkled it with a little more sleep dust and went to fetch his coat from the tree.

He was about to pull up his hood when he noticed the bundle had started rolling down the bank. He lunged after it, unwrapping the swaddling in his panic, but he managed to scoop up the child into his wings before it disappeared among the reeds.

Stupid! he cursed himself. This time he made sure to set the infant away from the pond. He took off his coat again so he'd have hands to rewrap the blankets. Finally he donned his hood and tucked the baby between his claws. He flew up into the early morning sky.

* * *

Lilith waited for Wakinyan at the observation deck farthest from the palace, overlooking the Tigris. "Did you get it?" she demanded when he landed.

Wakinyan set the infant in her hands. "It's not immortal," she noted, a bit irritated.

"I didn't have enough time. I'll come back tonight and finish it."

She nodded and sat on a nearby bench with her new bundle. "What did you get?" she asked, not looking up at him.

"A baby, of course," Wakinyan replied.

Lilith laughed. "Is it a boy or a girl?"

"How should I know?" Adult humans looked different enough for him to distinguish gender, but to him all infants looked androgynous. "Is it important?"

Lilith shrugged. "I hope she's a girl. It's lonely being the only female angel."

Wakinyan wanted to stay longer, to sit with Lilith and maybe hold the baby—he'd grown rather fond of the sleeping child over the last hour—but he couldn't ignore his duties.

"I'll see you again tonight."

She nodded, but her attention was fixed upon on the child. He bade her farewell and headed back home across the ocean.

He'd so hoped she would reward his efforts with another of those wonderful kisses.

* * *

The day dragged endlessly. Wakinyan delivered messages to every city in the southern regions and created rain clouds over all the central plains to feed the thirsty prairies and their hordes of bison. He also had to clear some storm clouds from the north when a whole village prayed for an end to the flooding that had taken the lives of two people. As dark approached, he finally left to meet with Lilith. He hoped his tardiness hadn't upset her.

When he arrived at the isolated deck where they'd met the morning before, he found her waiting for him, her legs dangling over the edge. She was crying.

"Where's the baby?" Wakinyan asked.

Lilith eked out a strangled cry and babbled something incomprehensible. Wakinyan shifted from foot to foot, panic building. "Where is the baby, Lilith?"

"It…Samael…and it died," she managed to hiccup.

Dear Heaven, Samael killed it! he thought. *That was my baby, and that turkey-feathered idiot hurt it!*

Wakinyan's rage built until it erupted into a vengeful screech. He leaped into the air. Lightning shredded the darkness around him. Lilith cried for him to come back, but he ignored her. He would find Samael and kill him.

Wakinyan glided over the city, searching. He spotted Samael sitting in the garden with some of his brothers, laughing and joking. *Bragging about what he did,* Wakinyan concluded. He swooped down, his arched wings whipping up the winds and leaving angry clouds in his wake.

The angels looked up when the Thunderbird's shriek shook the garden walls like thunder. Everyone tried to fly away, including Samael, but Wakinyan scooped him up like an eagle snatching a fish. He thrust back up into the upper atmosphere and pulled into a glide.

"What are you doing?" Samael yelled, trying to wiggle free of Wakinyan's claws. Wakinyan reached down with his beak and snapped Samael's wing at the mid joint. Then he let him go.

Samael screamed as he fell. Wakinyan didn't think the angel had healing powers, but he followed close behind, just in case. Besides, he wanted to see Samael hit the ground.

But the impact wasn't nearly what Wakinyan had hoped. Samael hit a mountain and slid and rolled down the side for a good thousand feet before stopping in a gully. His body was broken and twisted in unnatural shapes, spewing stardust from innumerable wounds. Yet he still lived and even tried to crawl away when Wakinyan pounced on him.

"As resilient as any god, I see," the Thunderbird hissed. "But every divine creature has a weakness, and I will find it." He began plucking Samael's feathers like a raptor tearing apart a rabbit, while Samael screamed for help.

Once Wakinyan stripped one wing to the down, he started on the other, but Lilith's stumbling landing a couple feet away distracted him.

"Let him go!" she screamed. When he returned to his work, she hit him in the side of the head with a rock.

"He killed our baby, Lilith!" he cawed at her.

"Get off him!" She pushed him, and he stepped back, thunder rumbling in the skies behind him. He watched, confused, as Lilith knelt next to Samael and hugged him, saying, "I'm sorry," over and over again.

But Samael shoved her away with surprising strength. "Don't touch me! You told him I killed the brat?"

"I didn't," Lilith insisted.

"You did," Wakinyan said.

"I did not!"

"I never touched the kid," Samael said. He dragged himself to his feet against a boulder. For a long moment he stared at all the feathers lying on the ground. When he looked up, his eyes blazed. "Why don't you tell him who really killed the baby, Lilith?"

"I didn't mean to!" Lilith cried.

Wakinyan hopped backwards, startled. "You didn't...Lilith, tell me you didn't!"

When Lilith refused to answer, Samael said, "It was a lot more work than she'd expected. She got tired of holding the baby all the time, so she set her down on a table. She fell. And because the immortal plain cannot hold up a mortal of any kind, it was a very, very long fall."

Lilith's refusal to look at Wakinyan made Samael's words cut so much deeper. "I risked much to get us that baby—"

"Do you really think you were going to have anything to do with raising that *thing*?" scoffed Samael. "The moment you left last night, she came to me, begging me to help her take care of it. She never mentioned you at all, Thunderbird. It's always been about me, and always will be. I'm that one thing she wants that she'll never have."

He stared contemptuously down at Lilith, still crumpled on the ground where he'd left her. "This fool wanted you, even stole a baby for you, but all this time you'd just hoped to make me jealous. When will you accept that I deserve better than some human's discarded property?"

Samael's cruelty astonished even the hard-hearted Thunderbird. Lilith had betrayed him, but Samael's words recaptured some of his fleeing affections for her. They also reignited his hatred for the black-winged angel.

He fixed his gaze solidly on Samael. Dark clouds formed behind him, roiling and growling. "Lilith, go home," he said softly.

Lilith stared at him, her wet eyes wide and frightened. She stumbled to her feet and backed away. "What are you doing?"

"Destroying evil." When she hesitated, he stepped towards her and snapped at her with his beak. She took to the air but still hovered nearby, struggling against the increasing winds.

"Run, Samael!" she called.

Samael instinctively spread his stripped and broken wings. Pain contorted his face. He turned to flee on foot.

The Thunderbird leaped into the air, wings beating as he gained height. He spread his claws and swooped in. Before he could snatch up his prey, a flash of emerald darted past and scooped the dark angel out from under him. His claws closed around boulders instead, crushing them into gravel.

Wakinyan swiveled his head to see Michael carrying his brother up into the clouds, struggling against the hurricane-force winds. Several other angels followed, guarding the flank. Lilith flew with them, as close to Samael as she dared.

No angel could out-fly a Thunderbird. Wakinyan's wings sent rain flying in sheets as he pounded after them. He knocked the trailing angels aside, sending them spinning wildly off in the wind and closed in on Michael.

Lilith grabbed him by the wing. "Are you crazy?" he shrieked at her.

She wouldn't let go, so he flung her aside, losing a couple feathers to her broken grip. He made sure she righted herself before turning back to Michael and Samael. It seemed to take her a long time.

When he looked back, they were gone.

A distraction, he scolded himself as he searched the skies. A flash of purple drew his gaze downward. He glimpsed Michael's emerald wings just before he and his brother vanished into a cave at the bottom of the mountains. Lilith glided in after them.

When Wakinyan landed at the mouth of cave, the ground shook with the impact. He couldn't see the angels in the darkness beyond, but he could smell Samael's fear and spilled stardust. He couldn't squeeze through the tiny hole. For a moment he considered taking his human form, but he was at his most powerful as the Thunderbird.

"You can't hide from the storm!" he shrieked.

He jumped into the air and flew into the clouds. "Pour your fury on the earth; consume that monster!" he shouted. "Set the land aflame with the wrath of gods and blow them beyond the sky itself!"

The clouds roiled and hissed, disgorging water on the land below. They expanded, spreading from horizon to horizon until the Thunderbird couldn't see an end to the churning darkness. Lightning shredded the skies and scorched the earth wherever it touched. Tidal waves from the sea swelled up and swept over the land, ripping up trees and swamping fields. Within minutes floodwaters gushed into the caves and rolled up the mountains, growing deeper by the second.

Wakinyan watched the cave the whole time, waiting for Michael, Lilith, and Samael to flee, but he never saw them. Even when the water rose above the cave opening, there was no desperate struggle to escape the flood. Part of him hoped to see Lilith break the surface, treading water and calling for help.

Let her drown, you fool, he thought, as the rising waters swallowed the mountains. It was no more than she deserved.

He climbed above the clouds and headed home, his heart filled with the joy and the sorrow and the madness that is revenge.

But when he reached the Great Spirit's realm, he found his own cave flooded, though it was near the top of the tallest mountain in the land. Like the other gods taking refuge from the storm, he ascended above the clouds to the palace of the Great Spirit. He stared at the gods gathered at the palace doors, all arguing heatedly about who would be so foolish as to flood the whole world.

A fool indeed. He lay down on the cloud and wept for what he had lost, and what he had become.

* * *

For all Wakinyan's destructive rage, Samael had survived. Angels didn't need air any more than the gods did. He and Michael and Lilith had remained under the water for days, until their father came looking for them.

Damn those angels! They have no business being so resilient, Wakinyan thought as he stared up at Samael sitting with his brothers on the benches in Great Council Hall, waiting to hear what sentence the Council of Elders would give the Thunderbird for his tantrum. All the feathers on Samael's plucked wing had nearly grown back. He stared back at Wakinyan, his countenance as black as his wings.

Lilith wasn't there, probably fearing questions about the baby and whose idea it was to kidnap it. Of course, in light of Wakinyan's violent attack against Samael and the subsequent flooding that wiped out all but a few dozen humans—and those saved by a couple of diligent gods—the snatching of one mortal child hardly seemed gossip-worthy.

The Council Hall fell silent when the Elders materialized at their cloud benches. The Great Spirit stood to address Wakinyan, who sat on a cloud below.

"The Council has decided on a punishment for your crimes, Thunderbird." He paused for a moment before continuing. "We are relieving you of your duties as my messenger. No longer will the elements obey your beck and call. You shall return to earth and live among men, but never as one of them. And you will leave your feathered coat behind."

"Never fly again?" Wakinyan stammered.

The Great Spirit's ever-changing face looked sad; even Yahweh seemed unsure. The others though—Nox, Atum, Bitol, Huehueteotl, Gao Yao, all of whom had spoken irritably of how much work they had to do now—showed no sympathy as Wakinyan turned over his one true love, shattering his heart anew in ways he'd never even considered.

Coyote escorted Wakinyan back to earth and led him to one of the new human villages along the northwestern coast. "I'm sorry I didn't warn you," he said as they walked through the woods. "Love's a tricky, sneaky game, which is why I play it only for the sex."

Wakinyan grunted. He stopped when they reached the edge of the village. A young woman sat on a mat outside one of the few newly constructed lodges. She smiled at him. He immediately turned around and walked back into the woods.

"Where are you going?" Coyote asked, trotting along at his heels.

"To live by myself."

And so now the once-powerful Thunderbird lived alone. The villagers brought him fish and wove rugs for him to sleep on, perhaps trying to convince him to join them, but he preferred the solitude. He ate only when hunger reminded him to, but he rarely left his house, for the sight of the open blue sky depressed him. But even then, the robins and blackbirds sat on his window and whistled to him, flexing their wings as if to remind him of everything he'd lost because of foolish, self-serving Love. At night he dreamed of the clouds and wind and rain, only to awaken in the morning to remember that they'd never be his companions again. He might have thrown himself into the ocean if he thought it would relieve his pain.

Then in the spring, the Great Spirit came to visit. "You don't look well, my son," he told the once-Thunderbird as they sat in Wakinyan's small, rickety lodge, which smelled of mildewed hides and old fish stew.

Wakinyan shrugged and threw a rock at the crow that landed at his windowsill.

The Great Spirit sighed. "It was a very harsh punishment," he said. "Yahweh and I discussed it privately, and we agreed you should have this." He unfolded a cloak of reddish-brown feathers, much smaller than Wakinyan's old coat. He draped it around Wakinyan's drooping shoulders and gently pulled the beaked hood up over his head.

"It doesn't hold the wondrous magic of your former coat, but I think it will set your heart at ease."

Wakinyan stretched his wings, basking in his beloved form. True, he wasn't the giant, powerful bird he once had been, but that hardly mattered. He would once more feel the wind on his feathers and see the world from above. His heart itself felt as if it might weep with joy. The Great Spirit stroked his head, and Wakinyan stared back at him with his new eagle eyes, bright with gratitude and, yes, Love.

At least he need never doubt the Great Spirit's love for him.

Exiles
by Nancy Schmidt

I heard the man long before I saw him. His footsteps beat heavily through the thicket, a staccato of snapping twigs and dried leaves. Louder came his moaning breath. At first I thought it was an injured coyote pup, but when he drew closer I felt the isolation in the sound. No pup, even one separated from its mother, has the vanity for such loneliness. It was a man, a garden-dweller, one of the sons. By the sound, he darted in panicky circles, losing himself on his own trail.

The movement stopped. I followed the weeping to a mild clearing. He curled in the hollow made by some boulders and an old oak, his knees drawn up against his chest. His hands hid his face, muffling his cries. The wilderness surrounded him awkwardly. Fear shrouded him. He did not fit with chaos and shrank from it. A point fixed in a dynamic space, a point that would fix the space around him, in his own image. Just like his father. My face grew hot.

In him, I saw the forest burning and fish floating on the brown surface of a lake.

His body convulsed as he sobbed. Those sobs would tear apart mountains, spill the blood of the living. A slaughtered landscape lay in the wake of his fear.

He spoke between his moans, a language I vaguely remembered. It was his language, and it surged out of his mouth like a sickness. He gagged on his words.

"...and none to share my pain! Poor wretch...godless... exiled. Woe is my name...cursed Cain...all shame, all despair...this horrid wasteland...."

In his voice, I heard the need, the desperate compulsion to yoke a space around himself, forcing it to conform to the tiny contours of his brain, englobing him in mirrored images. It was a tendency he inherited, a pitiful attempt to reconstruct Eden—his father's little cage-world. He placed himself in the center of (and above) all things.

So, it begins. The servants of order push through the wilderness, invading this wondrous place of exile. I see their walled cities, makeshift Edens, spewed across the land like disease. It begins with that pitiful, huddled figure.

Pain shot through my hands, and I realized I had been clenching my fists so fiercely my nails bit bleeding crescent moons into my palms.

I remembered the day I left the confines of Adam's garden. The sky was full of rain, and the jungle embraced me like a fond parent. Happy reunion!

Then, this sorry creature. It did not surprise me that he could not recognize the Spirit-that-walks-outside in all her variegated splendor. The woman did not either (not initially, not totally). How could I expect anything different from him? But where the woman's fear inspired a respectful awe for the wilderness, Cain's was manifested only as scorn and hate.

It was carved into the creases of his loathsome face.

A spider picked her delicate way up my arm. I softened. *Our gentle night nears the tyranny of day, little sister,* I thought, *and even our shadows will evaporate. Beware the light.* My heart ached as she descended from my hand on an invisible thread. Tiny miracle.

"…Cain! Cain…cursed name…Cursed brother…the soil screams of blood, of murder…."

I could descend into darkness on an invisible thread. I could move deeper into the embracing night. Yes, but it is only time. They will come anyway and sear the night, every corner. And then where would I be? Naked, my eyes filled with sand.

But could I speak that way again, form my tongue around the alienating sounds, words forged like shackles, sentences erected like stone walls? Though I might imprison myself, I said: "Cain."

He jerked his head, wild-eyed, staring at the tangle of boughs and sky.

"O, spirit, have pity…have pity…you promised!" he bawled and pushed himself deeper into the cavity.

I tossed a seedpod at his feet.

He yelped as if it had been a lightning bolt. "Don't hurt me! Don't hurt me! Don't hurt—"

"Cain," I said again as I entered the clearing.

Gasping, he peeked from under the rocky ledge. "Who are you? Did He send you? Are you a demon?"

"I am…of this place," I said, not knowing how else to answer.

"Who are you?" he asked, stretching his neck further from his hiding spot.

He wanted to name me, pin me to a point, make me a stone in his hand. His father had been no different, and he constructed a language that sought to control, a language that assumed the absoluteness of identity.

"I am no one."

"A demon?" he persisted.

Through which set of eyes do you see? The custodian's? The forest-spirit's? His father's? His mother's? Damnable tongue. I forgot how peculiar it is to speak in black and white. How do all the garden-people make their minds color blind?

"No—yes…no." *To your god, your patriarch, and his sons too, I am only a demon. I walked away from his paradise. I knelt by the sea and washed in its waters during my time of seed. The life-color stained its surface. The jealous gods frowned and called it cursed. This color that cannot be caged. Who are they to me? To the dance of light on waters? To your mother? And who am I to eternity? Another vibrant flame.*

"I am Cain, I have protection," he insisted.

"Protection."

He stood. He had scratches on his head as if he had raked the lines there with his own fingernails. "He said, 'Let no man kill Cain,' or else there will be a curse. I'm marked," he said, squaring his chin, straightening his spine.

"No man. Am I man?"

His lip quivered. "Would you kill me?"

I didn't answer. *Would? Yes, and all like you. Will? No. You are only the witless harbinger of a storm far beyond your ken. I hate you for the ashes that rise behind you and conceal the moon. In the dust, I see such things. Someone fingerpaints obscenities in blood and calls it martyrdom. Someone climbs a mountain of bones and calls it triumph. Someone paves the land with tombstones and calls it divine will. Black hearts, sweet amber poison. If killing you could stem the horror, believe that these hands would steal your last breath right now.*

I am already in chains, but you are afraid of me. Cain. In dust, you are only another legend of the hated brother, the brother-killer, the no-brother. Exile. In your language, I am like you—that is, if I let your language stick.

And I know, too, that it will stick. I am a stranger in your world. You are a stranger everywhere.

In that, I could pity him. I could be full of pity.

"You need a place," I said.

He did not say anything for a long time. I thought I had said it wrong. When he did speak, he went back to tears.

"I do," he cried. His knees folded under him, and his body shook. I wondered if he understood the bitter tales posterity would weave of his existence, or was all this only immediate grief? He tucked himself into a ball, finding no comfort in the grasses, the trees, the spiders.

I knelt and drew his hands away from his face. He would not meet my gaze; he kept lowering or closing his eyes.

"Look at me," I commanded softly.

When he did, I saw only his own selfish sadness, nothing beyond this very moment of isolation, Cain's personal isolation. I released him and crossed to the trees, placing my palm on a gently ridged trunk. He was his father. There was no desire for reconciliation with the earth in either one of them.

My own exile had been self-imposed. I escaped the kind of estrangement bred into Cain and the others. After me came the woman. She had it in her to heal, to trade the walls for wilderness. I met her not far from here. She, too, shed many frightened tears, but she wanted to live outside the zoo. Perhaps, if he had not come after her and lured her back into his world, she would be free. She found security—if not solace—in thralldom. I missed her terribly. For a long time, I had hoped she might be released from the fear that made her a slave. Someday.

But Cain... Of him, I had little hope. He brooded in a swamp of shame, a hell in his own image.

One brother's murder was a petty crime in the rage of the encroaching centuries. In a time very close to this one, three thousand will die by their brothers' swords, but those brothers will be justified by a biased history. Time makes heroes of murderers. And villains of outsiders.

"Come with me," I said. Each word felt like a stone in my throat. "There is shelter and food."

He rose, brushing away the tears and snuffling like a force-weaned calf. The shelter had been made for the woman. Though she was drawn to the wilderness, it overwhelmed her. She needed a center, a focused space. So, I made a shelter of palm leaves and fallen branches. It was a loose permanence, and I figured she would not need it after awhile. She spoke a dual language, a hybrid of Adam's and her own words; she no longer knew the difference. He called her Eve, which she despised. We passed hours changing her names, exchanging names: New-Bird-Singing, Leaf-on-the-Wind, Emerald-Fire, Wind-Walker. She never did shake the tendency for designation. Her language slipped easily into Eden-speak; more often than not, she would call me Night-Bird or even his name for me. Alone, she rarely wandered far from the shelter. She wanted me to stay, too.

"We are not trees," I told her. "There is no need to root ourselves to a place."

"We have to be somewhere, so why not stay here?" she insisted. "Or do you know of a better place?"

"Everywhere. Sister-Spirit, why pretend permanence? Homes are just as shadowy as names. Even if we built a house of stone, tomorrow would see only a pile of rocks." I laughed. "Would you be an Eve-pebble in this clearing forever?"

She didn't laugh. Too soon, she left with a man who was better at pretending. Whenever I happened across the place, I'd miss her all over again. I'd rebuild the shelter, in case she wanted to return. I saw some of her in the tentative way Cain held his mouth and in his dark brown hair which glinted shockingly red in certain sunlight. The part of me which loved New-Bird-Song grew tender toward her fugitive child.

"Follow me, Son-of-Morning," I invited, moving into the deeper woods. "You are welcome."

He followed, meekly, more afraid of the shadows than of me. I knew his humility would not last. Soon would begin the excavation of darkness. I gathered food as we went, giving him the chance to catch his breath.

Upon seeing it, Cain moved right into the shelter. He arranged the fronds and wood to his liking, then sat down to the meal I'd collected for him. I watched him eat. His eyes scanned the surroundings. By the calculating look he gave the hardwood trees, I guessed he was already replacing the palm leaves with cut logs.

Food in his belly made him talkative. He held up a berry. "See this? I used to grow an excellent strain of these. Grew almost five rows of it. Olives, too." He nodded toward the dense foliage. "You know, if we burn off that bunch of growth, I'm sure this soil can support some fine plants."

"It already does."

"The seeds will not be difficult to cultivate, not for me. I used to…" He grew sullen, threw the berry instead of eating it. "God does not care much for vegetables. He prefers the blood of animals."

What the spirit would want with material gifts eluded me. I never quite understood the rules, even when Morning-Song tried to explain them. The image of countless carcasses rotting on stone altars for some spoiled child of a deity eclipsed any attempted rationalization. I just listened until he ran out of words.

While he slept, I wandered. I had a destination, but I delayed my progress, lingering at every ridge as if seeing it for the first and last time. I touched each tree with renewed reverence. Each blade of grass, each skittering lizard, each stone stood out with particular clarity, but I was a blur.

The sun had yet to rise as I approached the borderlands and saw the dwindling fires of the camps. The garden-dwellers, in their devotion to order, burned much of the unruly jungle away. Leeched of its fertility, the land of man had become a spreading desert, a growing wound. I moved into the village with the grey morning light.

She was still asleep. Adam was out with the rest of the hunters, pushing into the wilderness like conquerors. She looked worn, liked scarred wood. Even in sleep, her face was strained. I crouched near her and touched her forehead, hoping to erase some of the tension there.

"Wake, now, Tattered-Wings," I whispered.

Her eyelids fluttered open. A mix of fear and delight danced briefly in her eyes, but could not conceal the heavy remorse rooted there. Long ago, those eyes flashed with emerald fire; now, they were like dead moss.

"It's you!" She sat up, glancing about for her husband. "You should not have come. They will hurt you if they find you here."

"*He* already has hurt me, Fading-Fire. He hurts you."

"No, Night-owl, he is good to me, provides me a home, food..." She forced a smile that served only to deepen the sadness of her face.

"And what does he ask in return that has painted so much pain on you?" I asked. Her hair had lost its luster; it hung limply around her thin face.

She wrung her trembling hands together. Her eyes darkened, troubled by storm clouds. "I had a son—sons." She tried to say more, but her voice slipped on the words. Instead, she hid her face in her hands and wept—the same gesture her boy had made when I discovered him. Tears slipped though her fingers.

I touched the wisps of hair at her temple. "You had a son, Cain, who sacrificed his brother to a greedy god."

Startled, she lifted her head abruptly. "You must not—must not use scorn..." She winced as if an invisible hand struck her face. "You must not ever scorn Him!" she hissed. "He'll punish you too."

I made no effort keep the scorn out of my laughter. "You mean Adam-in-the-sky? Oho! Have you fallen so far? Have you forgotten everything?" I stopped laughing. "Are you only, finally, Eve?"

She did not answer. She would not look at me. Then, she said slowly, "Lilith, I do not know how to be brave. I am a mother stripped of her children. I've lost…"

"And, now, I am only Lilith to you," I started, but I let it drop. This was not why I had come. "Urn-of-Sorrows, you have a son. His name is Cain and he is in the wilderness, where you once sought refuge." *And the wilderness withers beneath his feet,* I added silently. What could she do any longer? We were barely the same creature.

"My—my son is alive?" Hope lit her cloudy eyes.

"He is alive. I will look after him as long as he needs it." I took a long breath. "No more grief, heart-friend. You bear too much already."

Someday, I thought fiercely, *someday the she-wolf will awaken inside you. She will be hungry and will devour this woman-puppet you pretend to be.* I said aloud, "May you know flight again, Lonely-Dove, despite your clipped wings." I left her, then.

Cain was awake, busily modifying the shelter, clearing a wider space, already making the earth adapt to him. He never really needed my help. The scenery changes, but the path stays the same. I left him, too, slipping away through the undergrowth.

I wished for ignorance. I wished I could gaze and wander blindly into time like they could. I stood balanced at the moment of this world's decline and tried to see the other side. In the further distance, maybe vines cover the rubble, maybe a sprig of green springs from the blanket of ash.

I could not see so far.

The Girl in the Mirror
by Stephen D. Sullivan

Lady Robyn Fairchild smudged a silk handkerchief across her cheeks, wiping away the tears. She checked her reflection in the mirror. Her face looked flushed, her eyes were slightly red at the corners, and her auburn hair lay flat and lifeless. But no one in the wedding party was likely to notice any of that; they were all focused on far more important things. Robyn fluffed her hair into shape, took a deep breath, and checked again. Hardly any sign of heartache remained. Willing her voice steady, she called, "*Entrez.*"

The door to her tower bedchamber swung open, revealing Drusilla, one of her maids. The girl curtsied. "Begging your pardon, Miss," she began, "dinner is ready, and your father is starting to worry."

"Tell *mi patron* I'll be down momentarily," Robyn replied. She drew her silver-handled brush through her hair, trying not to seem nervous. It would be disastrous if anyone suspected her true plans.

Drusilla curtsied again, said, "Yes, Miss," and exited. The bedchamber door swung shut with a dull thud that echoed through Robyn's chest. She *should* have been ready two bells ago. This dinner was very important to her family, and probably the most important meal of her young life. She needed to play her part to perfection, but could she go through with it?

She gazed at the mirror one more time. Her freshly brushed hair shone like red gold in the late afternoon sunlight. Her white dinner gown, bespeaking her supposed virginity, looked lovely, even radiant. Surely neither her family nor their guests would ever guess the truth. For a moment, it seemed as though a sly smile flashed across the face of Robyn's reflection. A single word, as quiet as a distant breeze, drifted to her ears.

Fly!

Robyn shook her head, rose from her sitting table, and crossed to the tower's western-facing window. Nuvo Castillo, her family's ancestral holdings, lay stretched out before her, green and verdant, full of life, full of everything one could want…except an heir to the Fairchild legacy. In the distance, beyond the family's estate, sunset painted the Azure Sea crimson and sparkling gold. In her mind, Robyn fancied herself flying over those waves, flying far away from her family and this odious obligation.

Taking a final steadying breath, Robyn left her bedchamber and walked down the winding staircase into the castle. As she strode through the twisting corridors that led to the keep's main hall, the sounds of celebration drifted up to meet her: people talking loudly over soft music, people singing out of tune, bursts of raucous laughter, the clatter of dishes and serving platters.

The noise ceased and all eyes turned toward her as Robyn appeared at the top of the ballroom stairs.

"Ah, there she is, now!" boomed her father, Lord Fairchild. "Come down, *filla mia*." His gray-whiskered face broke into a wide grin. Lord Avalard, the man standing next to Lord Fairchild, grinned as well.

Robyn smiled back at her father but turned shyly away from Avalard. Something about the middle-aged lord's smile bothered her. Avalard was tall, broad in the shoulder, well-groomed and well-dressed, with a carefully trimmed beard and shoulder-length dusty hair. Any lady in the land would have considered herself lucky to be his betrothed. But to Robyn he looked like a jailer—the man who held the keys that would lock her away forever.

"By The Eye, she's a pretty little thing, isn't she?" Avalard said loudly; he always spoke too loudly and with a coarseness that belied his fine clothing. "I don't know how I'll manage to wait until the wedding night!"

Robyn flushed as Avalard and his companions laughed. Even her mother and father chuckled. Robyn paused in the middle of the stair, reluctant to continue. Again, the whispered word echoed in her mind:

Fly!

"What are you waiting for, my girl?" Avalard said. "Come down so the other guests can get a better look at you."

Robyn steeled herself and descended to the floor of the banquet hall. Her skin prickled as she went, as though the gaze of the company was ants crawling upon her flesh. There were so many people! Far more than her father could really afford to entertain.

Her parents met her at the foot of the stair and hooked their arms around hers, her mother on the left and her father on the right. Her mother's pale-blue dress glittered silver, like the scales of a netted fish. The thick, golden chains around her father's neck shone red as the last rays of sunset leaked through the hall's high windows. Robyn had never seen her parents looking so pleased. Their pride felt like a dagger in her gut.

Lord Avalard bounded forward jauntily. "H'llo, Robyn," he said. "You look good enough to eat." He took her hand and kissed it. She curtsied, though her knees wobbled as she did so.

Avalard noticed and grinned wolfishly at her. "Don't worry, girl," he whispered. "It'll all be over soon enough. Tomorrow night we'll be honeymooning, and then you'll be setting up house in Castillo Avalard." His eyes gleamed with anticipation.

Robyn's throat had gone dry, but she managed to rasp, "Yes, Milord."

He nodded and said, "Trust me. I know the ways of women. These are going to be the best days of your young life."

Robyn forced herself to smile back at him, though she feared that her best days had just ended.

Somehow, she managed to get through the dinner without passing out, screaming at the top of her lungs, or racing from the hall like a madwoman.

The wedding guests were all unfailingly polite to her, though most of Avalard's friends seemed to possess the same wolfish qualities as the self-made lord. As she danced, Robyn felt that each member of his party was sizing her up, like wolves wondering how a prize lamb might taste.

Most of the courtiers held her at a polite distance during the dances, but Avalard crushed her close. She felt the heat of his body through her bodice and smelled the lusty sweat on his skin. He leered at her, trying to peer down her décolletage.

Robyn turned away from his face, trying not to show her true feelings. For most of the evening, it seemed as though the ball would never end.

When the candles burned low in the chandeliers overhead, Robyn made her excuses and headed upstairs. The castle corridors were dark and seemed strange and foreign to her. How could the arrival of one man—even a powerful lord like Avalard—make her feel so ill-at-ease in her own home?

But, with the wedding imminent, it wouldn't *be* her home much longer. Soon, her home would be Avalard's mountaintop hall.

She'd been there once, visiting, five years ago. At the time, it had seemed like an innocent-enough trip. Now though, Robyn wondered if it had been a sizing-up of her marriage prospects. She shuddered at the thought, and shuddered again at the prospect of living at Castillo Avalard.

Avalard's manse seemed more of a great, stone, hunting lodge than a home. Stuffed trophy heads—boar, bear, stag, delta crocodile, Pelanor lion, iron ox—lined the castle's walls. With so many animals to hunt, it was a wonder the lord of the manor found time for anything else.

Would he make time for *her*? Robyn dearly hoped not. If all went according to plan tonight, he wouldn't have to; he would never see her again.

A man appeared in the darkened corridor in front of Robyn. He stepped from a doorway on the right side of the hallway and grinned: Avalard.

She stopped abruptly, almost running into him. How had he gotten there? How had he found her amid the castle's many corridors? Had he lain in wait along the route to her tower room? Was this some kind of hunter's trick?

Robyn shuddered but managed a polite curtsey. "Lord Avalard," she said. "Are you lost? This is a long way from the banquet hall."

"Just the spot for the feast I'm wanting," he replied, scooping her into his arms. His breath was hot on her face and smelled of sour wine.

"Please, Lord Avalard!" She tried to pull away, but he held her tight.

"C'mon, girl," he said, "call me 'Rolf.' We'll soon be married, after all."

"Soon," she gasped. "But not yet. Not 'til the morrow." Sweat beaded on her skin and trickled down her spine. She tried not to look like a doe trapped in a snare, but Avalard spotted the fear in her eyes.

"Where's the harm?" he said, pressing his face close to hers. "Where's the harm in a little sample before the ceremony?"

He kissed her roughly. His left arm wrapped around her waist, and his right hand groped her left breast. He tasted of sweat and vinegar.

A hundred thoughts flashed through Robyn's mind: images of more tender kisses and a far gentler lover; horrible images of Avalard taking her savagely, right there in the corridor, despite her protests; images of her standing, ashamed, at the altar of the All-Seeing Eye during the wedding ceremony; ever-changing images of her parents, scornful, disapproving, jubilant. Would they be outraged at her violation, or would they think that it merely sealed their compact with the powerful lord?

"My father…!" she gasped, though Avalard tried to smother her words with his coarse lips. "I think I hear my father coming!"

Avalard stopped kissing her, and Robyn struggled free from his grasp. She backed against the wall, cornered, knowing that in her crisp, white dress she could not outrun him.

The wolfish lord wasn't looking at her, though. He was peering down the corridor, back the way she'd come.

Robyn seized her chance. "Can't you hear him?" she asked. "*Mi patron* always checks on me before retiring himself."

Avalard tottered slightly; again, she scented the wine on his breath. "Can't blame him, I suppose," he slurred. "Precious thing like you. Need to make sure you're home safe at night."

"Yes," she said, desperately. "Yes, I need to go. If he were to find us…"

The drunken lord puffed out his chest. "I'm not afraid of him. You're nearly mine, anyway."

"But why risk it? It's only one more day."

He peered at Robyn through the gloomy corridor. She forced a smile, trying to seal her desperate bargain.

"Only one more day, and then it will be sanctioned in the eyes of my parents *and* the church," she pleaded. Her hand strayed meaningfully to the pendant of the All-Seeing Eye hanging at her throat.

Avalard's hand dropped, half-consciously, to the similar church insignia dangling around his own neck. "A day's not that long."

"Not long at all."

He straightened and then sagged once more. "I should be enjoying myself," he said. "This is my last night as a bachelor. Plenty of time to savor you later."

"Yes, plenty of time."

As Avalard leaned back against the wall for support, she hurried away toward the tower stairs.

"I'll taste your sweets on the morrow!" he called after her.

She took the stairs two at a time, not caring that her dress crinkled and bunched up, revealing the smooth flesh of her legs.

Reaching her room atop the tower, she slammed the door and bolted it behind her. Robin stood panting for a moment with her back pressed against the ironbound oak. On the far side of the room, the mirror atop her dressing table shimmered in the light of the chamber's sole lamp. In the glass she saw her own image, framed like a trophy in Avalard's collection.

Something else in the mirror caught her eye, though. She wasn't alone in the reflection; there was someone else with her—a tall, dark woman with pale skin and a crimson dress. The woman was standing beside the tapestry to Robyn's right. A flicker of a smile flashed across the reflection's pale face.

Robyn wheeled and peered into the shadows beside the tapestry. Nothing. She swept her gaze around the rest of the room, but she remained alone. Had she imagined the reflection, or…?

Somehow, the woman seemed familiar, like an acquaintance half-glimpsed out of the corner of her eye, or an old friend met in a dream. Robyn crossed to the mirror, but, as she did, the pale image moved away. The woman had been only shadows, after all. Robyn closed her eyes and let out a long, slow sigh.

The wind danced in through the tower window as Robyn stripped off her ungainly dress. The stiff fabric chafed against her skin and crackled like fire.

Robyn put on a loose-fitting maroon tunic and an old cloak—traveling clothes—and gathered her jewelry from the silver box atop her dressing table. She and Toby would need money if they were to flee Lord Avalard's grasp.

The thought of her handsome young lover brought an involuntary smile to Robyn's lips. For a moment, her arranged marriage with Avalard seemed only a nightmare. Her old clothes felt soft and warm against her skin, like Toby's loving touch.

Fly!

The urgent whisper seemed to come from the mirror right next to her.

"I know," Robyn replied, not daring to look at the glass. "I'm going." She thrust the last of her jewelry into her pockets, and then added her silver brush. She yanked the pendant of the All-Seeing Eye from around her neck and cast it onto her bed. Then she crossed to the door, pressed her ear to it, and listened.

No sound came from without. The story she'd told Avalard about her father checking on her had been just that—a story. Lord Fairchild would be in the hall below, celebrating with all the rest.

Robyn unbolted the door and crept out, keeping to the back hallways and the servants' stairs. Cautiously, she made her way down to the kitchens. The corridors surrounding her seemed colder and darker than ever before. Robyn felt like a stranger in her own home.

To tamp down her fear, she thought about Toby. Images of the first time she'd seen him—delivering bread to the castle—played through her mind. He was tall, strong, and muscular, with a thick tangle of curly black hair atop his head. Making deliveries for the bakery of his father, Toby the Elder, was easy work for the young man, but he enjoyed it. Toby always smiled at the kitchen staff as he unloaded baguettes, sweet rolls, and quick bread. On that particular, wonderful day, he had smiled at Robyn, as well.

She had smiled back. And thus began the most thrilling moments of Robyn's life.

Ironically, because Toby the Elder was the best baker in Nuvo Castillo, he'd been commissioned to bake Robyn's wedding cake.

Robyn felt a twinge of guilt over the cake. What indignities would the old baker suffer when it was discovered that she had run off with his son? It would be bad for him, certainly, but not nearly so bad as the indignities Robyn would suffer at Lord Avalard's hands if she stayed.

A wan, reddish light from the fireplace ovens—still cooking for tomorrow's celebration—filled the kitchen as Robyn entered. The aromas of broiling meat, stews, and savory puddings filled the air. The scents filled Robyn's chest, making it hard to breathe. She hurried across the warm flagstones toward the service door.

Before she reached it, though, Drusilla stepped out of the shadows, blocking her way.

Robyn stopped short. "Dru," she said, "what are you doing here?"

"Begging your pardon, Miss," the girl replied, "but what are *you* doing here?"

"I've an errand to run," Robyn replied, annoyed. "Now, get out of my way."

"An errand?" Drusilla said. "This late? On the night before your wedding? Pardon my saying so, Miss, but you should go back to bed and stay there. You've an important day tomorrow."

More important than you know, Robyn thought. She drew herself up to her full height and glowered at the girl. "Are you my mother now, Drusilla? How dare you tell me what to do?"

Drusilla cowered, but did not step aside. "I only want what's best for you, Miss."

You and everyone else in this old castle, Robyn thought. "Fortunately, *you* do not get to decide," she said. "Now, out of my way!"

The girl didn't budge, so Robyn pushed roughly past. She threw open the kitchen door and surged out into the cool, dark night. A thin fog obscured the furthest corners of the castle's rear courtyard. Mist, hovering just above the dew-sopped grass, crept furtively across the well-manicured lawn.

The service gate in the outer wall would be locked, of course, but there was another way—a disused door, half covered by ivy. Robyn had escaped that way to meet Toby many times before.

She strode purposefully across the courtyard, heading for the hidden exit. As she did, a hulking shape loomed out of the fog.

Robyn stopped, and a chill ran down her spine.

"Father?" she whispered, peering at the figure.

Lord Fairchild nodded and stepped forward. "I have some bad news, Robyn," he said grimly. "Toby, the baker's son, has had an accident. He died this afternoon—run over by a service cart."

All the air rushed out of Robyn's lungs.

"A terrible tragedy," her father continued, seemingly unaware that the castle had begun to fall down around him. "I believe you knew him?"

Robyn barely heard the last words. Her knees buckled. The courtyard spun around her and, with a great, wrenching groan, everything went black.

* * *

Robyn awoke crying, unsure at first of where she was or how she'd gotten there. Gradually, she became aware of soft pillows, warm quilts, a gentle hand running through her hair.

"Toby?" she murmured.

"It's all right now," her mother's quiet voice replied. "Everything's all right."

But everything was *not* all right. Memory of meeting her father in the garden rushed back to Robyn in a flash, and she knew that nothing would ever be right again.

"Is it true?"

"Is what true, dear?" her mother asked kindly.

"Is he...is he really dead?"

Her mother stroked her hair. "There, there, my dear," she whispered. "He was only a servant boy, nobody really important."

Robyn sat up so quickly that her mother jumped back. Robyn glared at her, and Lady Fairchild edged away to the corner of the bed.

"Get out!" Robyn screamed. "Get out!" She seized her silver brush from the bedside table and hurled it.

The brush sailed past Lady Fairchild, barely missing her head. She rose abruptly. "My dear!"

"I'm not your dear!" Robyn shouted. "I'm not anyone's! Get out! Get out of my room!"

Her mother backed toward the door. "Well, if that's the way you feel, we'll talk in the morning. I understand you're excited, but try to get some rest. You have a big day ahead of you tomorrow."

She exited the room, and the key rasped and clicked in the lock. Robyn buried her face in her pillows and cried until the world went away once more.

* * *

Sometime during the night, Robyn became aware of a gentle whispering in the room. At first, she thought that her mother had returned. But the voice was somehow warmer, friendlier, less detached. Robyn couldn't place the tones, but she thought she'd heard the voice before, even though she couldn't make out the words.

"Where are you?" Robyn called. "Who are you?"

"Come to the mirror," the voice replied.

Robin rose from her bed and crossed to the dressing table. She didn't walk, though. Rather she seemed to float, as though wafted across the bedroom on a warm night breeze.

Am I awake, or dreaming? she wondered.

She gazed at her own reflection, wan, tear stained. And behind her, another reflection as well: the pale woman in the crimson dress. The woman was dark, tall, and beautiful. A silver diadem rested on her forehead, and long gray wings sprouted from her back.

Somehow, Robyn didn't feel afraid. "Are you siren mage or demon temptress?" she asked.

"Neither," the woman replied. "I am Lilitu, the Queen of the Night."

"Is it you who've been calling me?"

"No," Lilitu said. "You have called *me*."

Robyn put her hand to her forehead; her skull ached as though it might burst. "I didn't," she said. "I didn't call."

"You call me as you call to yourself. I am the secret that lives inside you. I am a reflection of your desire."

Robyn shook her head. Hot tears dripped from her cheeks and spattered on the dresser. "I don't desire anything," she said. "What I desire is *dead!*"

"No," the woman replied. "Though your lover is dead, your desire lives."

"N-no," Robyn said. "H-he was all I wanted."

"No. He, too, was merely a reflection of your inner self. What you truly desire is freedom."

"I..." Robyn began. Was it true? Had she fallen in love with Toby just to escape her role as a lord's daughter?

"No," she insisted. "I loved him. I *still* love him."

"And always will," Lilitu said. "Take the gift he offered."

Robyn's hand strayed to her belly. Did she feel movement there? Was Toby's gift growing inside her even now?

"That is not *all* he offered," Lilitu said. "He offered freedom. Spread your wings. Fly and be free."

Robyn gazed at the woman in the mirror, at the delicate wings sprouting from her back. "I don't have wings."

"We all have wings. Even if some cannot see them."

"But I'm locked in my room. I can't get out."

"I, too, thought I could not escape," Lilitu replied. "I was shackled by the chains of expectation and love, but I shed them and flew to a new kingdom where I am queen. Here, freedom and love are the only laws."

Robyn reached toward the mirror, as though she might pass through, but her hand found only cold, unyielding glass. "I don't live in your world," she said. "I live in mine."

"Exactly," said the Queen of the Night. "Make it your own and fly free."

* * *

Warm, late-afternoon sunlight streamed through the windows of Castle Fairchild's high tower bedchamber. Robyn's sequined wedding gown sparkled like silvery fish scales as Lady Fairchild, Drusilla, and a maid named Eliza laced Robyn into it.

"It's tight," Robyn protested quietly.

"But very flattering to your figure," her mother countered. "It's important that a girl look good on her wedding day." She led her daughter to the mirror and smiled.

Robyn gazed at her own reflection, hardly recognizing herself. "I can barely breathe. I can barely move."

"You'll get used to it," Drusilla put in.

"Besides," Eliza said, giggling, "you won't be wearing it that long!" Lady Fairchild cuffed the girl on the back of the head. Eliza winced but didn't cry out. "I only meant..." she began.

"We all know what you meant," Lady Fairchild replied coldly. "I won't stand for such vulgarity on my daughter's wedding day. Am I understood?"

Eliza and Drusilla lowered their eyes to the floor, curtsied, and said, "Yes, Ma'am."

Robyn gazed at her own reflection. If there were wings upon her back, she couldn't see them. In the bright afternoon sunlight, no trace of Lilitu remained in the mirror. Robyn's dress crackled stiffly as she ran her hand from her bosom to her belly. Her fingers lingered near her navel, searching for any flutter of movement.

"There now, don't you look beautiful?" Lady Fairchild asked. Without waiting for a reply, she added, "Time to go."

The two servant girls opened the door to the room and Lady Fairchild led her daughter out. Eliza and Drusilla followed after, tending Robyn's train as the four of them wound down the stairs and through the castle to the cliff-side chapel on the far side of the manor.

The day looked like a painting of paradise. Sunlight streamed through clouds overhead, dappling the courtyard in gold. More clouds gathered beneath, filling the green valley below the castle with fine white mist. The courtyard grass shone bright green, and the flowerbeds glistened with all the colors of a rainbow. The air smelled fresh and clean.

Robyn marched across the court quickly. Before her rose the chapel of the All-Seeing Eye—marble steps, gleaming white walls, towering columns, ornate doors, and wide windows, all topped by a graceful dome. The golden scrollwork decorating the church gleamed like fire in the sunlight. The chapel was the most ornate and beautiful part of Castle Fairchild, but Robyn barely saw it.

Her dress rustled like dry leaves as she walked up the steps. Her father, adorned with gold and sparkling jewels, met her at the top of the stair. He linked his right arm through the crook in her left elbow.

"Almost there," he whispered. "I'm very proud of you."

Robyn cast one last, longing glance at the cloud-swept valley behind her, and then both of them stepped inside.

Guests filled the chapel nearly to overflowing. Dignitaries from fifty leagues around, resplendent in their wedding finery, turned and gazed at Robyn as she entered the hall. A white carpet led from the entryway, past the polished oak pews, to the golden altar of the All-Seeing Eye on the far side of the nave. The chamber's wide, tall windows cast a grid of slanting shadows across the carpeting.

Lord Fairchild led his daughter down the aisle. The sunlight coursing through the windows felt warm on Robyn's skin, though the shadows felt cold, like iron bars—the bars of her wedded prison.

As Robyn reached the chancel, the white-clad bishop standing before the altar smiled warmly at her. Lord Avalard, waiting beside the bishop, turned and grinned as well. His smile was far more predatory. Soon, Avalard would have what he wanted.

Robyn took her place on his left, though she did not take the lord's hand. Her father stepped back three paces, beaming. Lord Avalard seized Robyn's fingers and held them tight.

"We are gathered here today, in the sight of the All-Seeing Eye, to join this man and woman in holy wedlock," the bishop began. "Who gives this woman to be joined to this man?"

Before Lord Fairchild could answer, a sudden gust of wind caught one of the chapel windows and thrust it open. From outside, Robyn heard a single word whispered on the breeze:

Fly!

With a cry of joy on her lips, Robyn pulled herself from Lord Avalard's grasp. She sprinted to the window and threw herself out. Her dress rustled like the wings of an eagle as her white-garbed body soared over the castle parapet, and she vanished into the mist below.

* * *

Drusilla ran from the high tower screaming, her face pale and her eyes wild.

Lord Fairchild met her on the stairway and seized the girl by her shoulders. "What is it?" he bellowed. "Is the tower ablaze? Are we invaded?"

Deep lines of worry creased his face—a face that seemed to have aged a decade since his daughter's sudden disappearance a year previous. All of Nuvo Castillo had searched for months, but no trace of Robyn Fairchild's body had ever been found.

"I've seen her!" Drusilla screamed. "I've seen her!"

"Who?"

"The mistress!"

For a moment, hope suffused Lord Fairchild's aged face. "My daughter?" he gasped. "My daughter is alive?"

"N-not alive," Drusilla replied. "In the mirror. Mistress Robyn is in the mirror!"

"Make sense, girl!"

"I swear! She's in the mirror!"

Lord Fairchild let go of the maid and dashed up the stairs, his heart pounding. He threw open the door, nearly tripping over the mop Drusilla had abandoned at the threshold. His gray eyes took in the entire bedchamber.

There was no one there. The room looked exactly as it had on the day Robyn disappeared.

Something caught his eye, though, a movement in the large looking glass atop the dressing table. What had the foolish girl said about the mirror?

Lord Fairchild crossed to the dresser and his mouth dropped open. In the mirror, he saw Robyn standing next to his reflection. In her arms, she held a babe with curly black hair, swaddled in a blanket of blue and silver. Behind Robyn stood a company of girls, hundreds strong, with a tall, pale woman at their head. All of the women smiled at him.

Anger and confusion filled the lord's belly. How had so many people entered the chamber without him seeing? He whipped around, but, to his astonishment, found no one behind him. The room remained empty.

Musical laughter filled the bedchamber; the sound seemed to emanate from the mirror.

The blood drained from Lord Fairchild's face. He seized Drusilla's mop from the floor and, hefting it like a lance, thrust it into the glass.

The mirror shattered into a thousand pieces. As the last of the shards tinkled to the floor, a single word drifted through the open window to Lord Fairchild's ears.

Free!

Lord Fairchild shook his head and muttered, "Witchcraft."

He left the tower and locked the door behind him, never to return.

When Hell Comes Calling
by Jackie Kessler

She'd been in the tree for hours, sitting in the low-hanging bough and staring beyond the silver gate, when the Man finally found her.

"Eve! There you are!" The Man's voice held both pleasure and contempt—he was happy to have found her, it would seem, but annoyed at her choice of location. Probably because he couldn't climb for shit. "Come down!"

She ignored him. She refused to answer to that name. It wasn't the Man's to give her. He could name all the animals and the birds and the stars and the plants to his heart's delight. But no one could name her. It was *her* name, after all. Hers. When she was ready, she'd decide on her own name. Something that spoke to her. Something powerful.

"Eve! Come down, I say!"

Make me, you self-centered ass. But she dared not speak that aloud, so she said nothing.

"Eeeeeeeve!" Whining, now.

She sighed. If she pretended not to hear him, he'd keep yammering at her until he finally asked God to bring her down from the tree. He'd done it before. Gooseflesh dotted her bare arms as she remembered. Last time, she had hidden herself in a cave at the far end of the Garden. When the Man missed her, God had sent a bear into the cave to frighten her out of it. And into the Man's waiting arms.

So the Man had told her later, after he'd fucked her. He'd laughed as he explained, as if the whole thing were incredibly amusing.

Ha fucking ha. Sometimes, when she closed her eyes, she still smelled the bear's rank breath, felt the beast's claws raking her thigh.

She rubbed her arms, tried to work away the chill. It was a conspiracy. When the Man complained, God answered. When she complained, she got silence. God was probably a Man, too. God and the Man, in their own Man's club. If God were a Woman, She would answer. Or at least She would have things make sense.

Swallowing the lump in her throat, she thought that maybe what the Man always said was true, and God loved him best.

Or maybe the Man was full of shit. It didn't matter. If he complained, God would answer. That was the way of things.

Better to not have him complain.

Stretching, she looked down at him. His earth-colored skin gleamed in the morning sun, slick with either sweat or water. Knowing him—and after all this time, she knew him far too well—it was sweat. He did so love to run and jump and play, rolling on the ground with the dogs, staring wistfully at the sheep.

When she finally acknowledged him, he grinned at her, his teeth bright against his dark lips. "Come, Eve."

Eve. Stupid, ridiculous name. "What do you want?"

"You."

Frowning, she slowly climbed down, feeling his heated gaze on her long limbs. She didn't mind sex, but it always stopped just as it was getting good. He'd grind on top of her, pushing himself into her as far as he could, and a few thrusts later he'd grunt and shudder. Sometimes, he'd rub against her *just so*, and for a delicious moment she'd feel herself catching fire from that touch. But then he'd shift, and the feeling would ebb, and then he would grunt and shudder and the whole thing would be done, and she'd lie next to him, feeling strangely cheated.

Being the Woman sucked.

As soon as her feet hit the ground, the Man grabbed her and groped her, his hands clumsy and his kisses sloppy. He had his way with her, and she bore it, and when he was done he rolled off of her and let out a contented sigh. She lay in the grass, staring at the clouds above. So many clouds, free to drift wherever they chose, even beyond the silver gates.

Before she could stop herself, she asked, "Do you ever wonder?"

The Man snorted, already half-asleep. "Huh?"

"Do you ever wonder?"

"Wonder what?"

"What's beyond the gates?"

After a pause, he rolled over to face her. She wouldn't look at him, but she felt his gaze roaming her face, considering. Finally he said, "Why would I do that?"

"Aren't you curious?"

"God gives us food. God gives us drink. He gave us animals for companionship. He gave you to me for sex. Why would I think on anything else?"

Her voice low, she said, "So you never wonder what else there is? Even after all this time?"

"Why would I need anything else?"

Why indeed? The Man had everything he wanted.

And her? What did she have, other than a steady ache in her chest and rage bubbling in her belly? No, quash it, kill it, before he decides to complain. "You're right," she said. "There's nothing else." The lie came easily, and it felt right on her tongue.

"Of course I'm right," he said, laughing. "You're silly, Eve."

She flicked him a hard smile, then gave him her back as she rolled away from him and pretended to sleep. Only after he left her did she allow herself to cry.

* * *

When she saw Him beyond the gates, she thought she was dreaming; how else could she explain this tall Man with black hair and white skin and startlingly green eyes? He was standing just beyond her reach, His chiseled profile stark against the backdrop of night. She felt strength emanating from Him, warming her like the sun, and she intuitively understood that He was obscenely powerful—far more so than the Man.

Her heart beat faster, and her breasts tingled, and she felt something in her belly that she didn't know was anticipation because she'd never experienced it before.

She must have made a sound, because He turned to regard her. His eyes were kind, and sad, and hinted of flame. "Hello, First Woman."

Such a soft, melodious voice—so very different from that of the Man's. She stammered a hello. When He said nothing more, she said, "You're like me. You're outside the gates, and You're like me." Faster, now: "There are others like us! And You're outside!"

He smiled. There was nothing mocking in it, but neither was there true mirth. A sad smile. "I am not like you, First Woman, although you are correct when you say there are others like you, outside of the Garden."

She clutched the silver bars of the gate. "Please, I don't understand. If You're not like me, what are You?"

"I am called many things. Most recently, as those things go, I am called King."

"King?"

Now humor touched His smile. "You need not address Me as such. You are not answerable to Me."

"I don't understand…"

"Of course you don't." The...not-Man...sighed, shook His head. "You're His first, you know. First Man, first Woman. First Animals, first Plants. And because He likes to keep things, you are kept."

Her stomach clenched painfully, and she whispered, "Kept?"

"Here, in this menagerie." He nodded at the silver bars of the gates. "Safe in the Garden. Safe from time. And outside, beyond the Garden, time moves forward. The world moves on."

"Time." She grasped at the concept. "The way the sun comes and goes, you mean?"

"Indeed." He stared at her with those bright green eyes, and she felt herself sinking into His gaze. "In the Garden, you do not grow old. In the Garden, you do not get with child. In the Garden, you are perfectly preserved for all time."

Here, with the Man, forever. The thought made her want to scream. "Outside of the gates, there are others like me?"

"Oh yes."

"Not just ones like the Man? Ones like me, too?"

"Men and women alike," He said. "Entire nations of people, who live and procreate and die." Something in His eyes gleamed as He spoke, hinted of bitterness and rage and, oddly, joy. "They love and they hurt, they wound and they bleed. They build and they destroy. And so it goes."

"Let me out," she whispered, squeezing the bars of her prison. "Please. Let me out."

The hard look in His eyes softened. "Why do you want to subject yourself to the evils of the world? Here you are safe."

"Here I am trapped." Her next words spewed from her mouth like venom, and as she spoke she gave birth to the fury hidden so long inside of her. "Here I am forced to subject myself to the whims of an arrogant, selfish Man who isn't capable of dreaming of greater things, who can't see beyond the gates or think beyond his belly or his cock. Here I am doomed to be his receptacle and nothing more. There—" She motioned to the world beyond the gates. "—I would be free to be whatever I wished."

"The world is not as welcoming as you make it sound."

"Let me take my chance!" She fell to her knees, bowed her head until her forehead touched the ground. "Please, oh King, I beg You. Please set me free."

"Raise your head, First Woman. I am not your king. You should not bow before Me."

"I'll serve You," she insisted, keeping her head down. "I'll do whatever You wish. Please, *please*, release me from the Garden."

He laughed softly. "Despite My reputation, I do not barter for souls. The evil find their way to Me, all in their time."

"Then I'll be evil, whatever that means. I'll do whatever You want, if You would just free me."

"Look at Me."

Keeping her body down, subservient, she managed to raise her head to look at Him.

He stared deeply into her eyes. "You would serve, and yet you would call yourself free?"

She nodded vigorously, said, "I would happily serve anyone, anything, that let me escape from here. It would be my greatest pleasure to do the basest task, if it were beyond these gates. Please, I beg You, please free me."

They looked at each other, the First Woman and the King of Evil, and she was certain He would help her.

"I should not have shared the knowledge of the world with you," He said at last. "Ignorance is bliss."

"Knowledge is sweeter than bliss," she said. "I'd rather know with certainty that there's more to life than the Garden. Please release me."

"I cannot, First Woman. There is only one who can set you free."

Her voice breaking, she asked, "Who?"

"When the time comes, you will understand. And then you will do what you must."

And He smiled, and He reached out to touch her forehead—

—and she woke up, tears streaking down her face. The Man's arm was wrapped possessively over her, his dirty hand cupping one of her breasts; one of his legs draped over her hip. Sick of the feel of him, she snarled, elbowed him off her body. He muttered and rolled over, blades of grass clinging to his back.

She rose and walked to the edge of the Garden, grasped the silver bars of the gates.

A menagerie, He had said. Kept.

Fuck that.

"I'm getting out of here," she whispered. "Do You hear me, God? I'm not a pet. I belong in the world."

Nothing answered her but the sound of her own heartbeat, thumping wildly in her chest. Maybe that was all the answer she ever really needed.

She closed her eyes and saw His face: white and chiseled and strange, with eyes like green fire and hair black as the night.

"I'll find You and call You King," she swore. "Somehow, I'll find You."

* * *

His hands were rough on her body, and she slapped him away. "I told you," she said, "I'm not in the mood." *The pet doesn't feel like performing.*

"Mood?" The Man let out a laugh, then groped her again. "I don't care about mood. Come on, let's have sex."

"No." Once again, she pushed his hands away, being none too kind with her nails in the process. Served him right if she cut him; the prick had pinched her nipples. She kept staring beyond the gates, looking for a Not-Man with green eyes, or maybe something else—a hint, a clue, a sign that told her how to escape.

The Man whined, "What do you mean, no?"

"No," she said. "Noooo. Nuh-ohhh. No."

"Eve…"

"That's not my name." She glared at him over her shoulder. "You can't name me."

"But I already have," he said plainly. "You're Eve. I'm Adam."

"You're stupid. And I'm not having sex with you. Go get a sheep and leave me alone."

"But I want sex."

"And I want to get out of the Garden," she said. "Looks like neither of us is getting what we want."

He stomped his foot. "You can't say no! God made you for me to have sex! I want sex, now!"

"Stick it up your ass," she suggested, still peering beyond their slice of Paradise.

"It won't reach."

"Take a lesson from the dog and lick your balls. Or use your own hand. Just leave me alone."

He grabbed her shoulder and spun her around, then pinned her against the bars of the gate. "You're mine to have sex with," he said, still angry, but already his eyes were glazing with a look she knew all too well. "I want sex now. You'll do as I say."

She spat in his face.

His eyes wide, he touched the runner of spittle staining his cheek. Then he growled, the sound low and deep in his throat. He backhanded her, hard. Her head rocked back and hit the gate, and stars burst behind her eyes.

"I'll tell Him!" the Man snarled. "I promise you, I'll tell God everything." He grabbed her chin and forced her to face him. "He'll punish you. God loves me best. He'll punish you if you don't do what I say. He made you for me. And I'm sure," he added thoughtfully, "He could make me another one, if you're broken."

Like that, understanding came.

"So give me sex," the Man said, his hands squeezing her shoulders. "Now."

It wasn't just about being kept. It was being kept subservient. Kept in her place. Here in the fucking Garden, where time stood still and she had all she needed to eat and drink and survive. Survive, but not truly live.

There are others like you, He had said, *outside of the Garden.*

And she finally knew how to get past the gates.

The Man thrust his shaft against her belly. "Sex," he demanded again. "Now!"

A smile curved her lips, and she reached down and grabbed his erection. She paused long enough for him to grin and relax just a touch—just enough to stop crushing her shoulders. And then, still smiling sweetly, she kneed him in the balls.

He squealed—and oh, how the sound shot through her as if he'd accidentally stroked her *just so*—and he released her to clutch himself. She shoved his chest with all of her strength. Off balance, he toppled to the ground.

"Sex," she hissed. "Now."

And she climbed on top of him and forced his hands away from his sack, and she rubbed herself over his softening cock.

"No," he cried, "this isn't sex! I won't lie beneath you!"

"No?" She grinned, delighted in repeating his asinine question: "What do you mean, no?"

"You're supposed to be in the bottom position. I'm the superior one."

She burst out laughing.

"Eve," he whined, "what's wrong with you?"

"Nothing. For the first time, nothing." She rocked over him. "I won't lie beneath you, *Adam*," she said, turning his name into a sound of pure derision. "If I'm not on top, we're not having sex. And if you ever try to force me again, I'll bite off your cock when you sleep."

"You're mad," he said. "I'm the Man. I'm supposed to be on top. God said so."

She leaned down until her breasts pressed against his chest and her mouth was a breath's length above his ear. "So go complain to God. Or get yourself another Eve. I'm done with being your fuck toy."

She pushed herself off of him and stood tall. The First Man squirmed in the dirt, as low as the dust he'd been made from. "You're broken," he said. "God will make me a new Woman, one who does what I tell her to. One who comes when called."

"Enjoy your new bitch," she said, and upon those final words, she walked away from him.

* * *

"First Woman."

She turned away from the bars of the gate and saw Him—no, not Him exactly, but close. This not-Man was tall, and white—and even His hair was white as the stars in the nighttime sky, white as many of the flowers in the Garden. Massive bird's wings spread behind Him, and His eyes burned with green fury. He stood—no, floated just above the ground—right there in the Garden. Anger rippled off him like rain beading off of skin.

In His hand He held something long and silver, and it looked very, very sharp. Staring at it, and at Him, made her knees weak and her stomach hurt and suddenly she wanted to vomit.

Her first thought was to run, shrieking in terror.

Her second was to throw herself to the mossy ground and beg; for what, she didn't know, but that didn't matter.

Her third was that He was a pale imitation of the King of Evil, who had needed no wings and no sharp thing in His hand to convey His power. And that thought gave her comfort and strength.

And that, frankly, made her feel horny. She smiled at the not-Man and said hello.

"You have broken the covenant."

His voice rolled like thunder, and as much as she wanted to be afraid, she refused herself the luxury. Her chin high, she repeated, "Covenant?"

"To be the Man's companion in all things."

The words were like a punch in her belly. "I never agreed to that."

"You did. When you first drew breath, you did. God told you your role, and you accepted."

"I don't remember."

"Of course you don't." He sneered down at her, His cold face twisted with such haughtiness and self-importance that He made the Man seem selfless. "You cannot possibly remember the Voice of the Almighty. You were not created for such things."

She wanted to ask Him what His purpose was, with His bird's wings and clean feet that didn't touch the earth, but instead she said, "How can I be held responsible for something I don't remember?"

"It is the way of things."

"It's a stupid way."

He narrowed His eyes. "Do you remember declaring yourself to the Man the first time you rutted like animals in the Garden?"

"I never…"

"'You're mine,'" He said, His voice mimicking the Man's panting declaration from that night so very long ago. And then her own voice followed, equally breathless, drunk from the first sips of life: "'I'm yours.'" Pausing, perhaps to let the words sink in, He watched her as if He thought she would try to flee. "You agreed."

Yes, she had. Bowing her head, she said, "I didn't know any better."

"That doesn't matter."

"That's unfair."

"You are not allowed to judge what is and is not fair."

She ignored the tears stinging her eyes, and met His furious gaze. She crossed her arms over her breasts and tapped her foot on the dirt that He refused to touch. "I say it's unfair! And it's unfair to keep me here, trapped, used by the Man!"

"You agreed to be his."

"He needs a new toy." She motioned to herself. "This one is broken."

"Broken toys get thrown away. You prefer to be discarded and left to rot?"

"I prefer to live on my own terms, not on his. And not on God's, if all He means is to keep me here, locked away from others like me."

"Blasphemy."

"Even so." She took a deep breath and said, "I want to leave the Garden and taste the world."

The not-Man's eyes flashed. "You think you're used poorly here. If you leave, you'd wander a land you don't know, filled with humans who'd use you and destroy you, and wouldn't mourn you when you died. For what purpose would you leave the safety of the Garden?"

"Freedom."

A smile worked its way across His face, and it was filled with hateful things. "Freedom," He said, mocking her. "And what will you do with your freedom, First Woman, when you are hungry and you don't have any food to eat, or any money to pay for food? What will you do when you're cold, and your nakedness won't do anything but show your vulnerability? What will you do in the world?"

What indeed?

But the answer was as clear as the God-kissed skies. Thinking of her place with the Man, she said, "I'll have sex."

The not-Man threw back His head and laughed.

"Sex will keep me warm," she said over the sounds of His laughter. "And through sex I'll get food when I am hungry, and this thing called money. The Man has taught me that sex makes me strong, for he was reduced to begging for it. Sex will lead me through the world."

"Sex will make you a whore," He said, His laughter dying, "until you are fat with child. And then what will you do when you're burdened with a baby?"

"Take all my babies and drown them," she hissed, "a hundred babies and throw them into the water!" She slammed her fist against the bars and screamed her frustration and resentment to the skies above. "You chain me with safety, you chain me with babies! Fuck your chains, not-Man! I'll not be trapped here a moment longer! Give me my freedom!"

No longer a request, or a wish, or even a want. A demand.

And because even His kind were made to bow before the humans—no matter how much that chafed, and how much He despised it, if He were to ever admit such a human thing as feelings—He replied, "Then go, little whore. Work your way through the world. And when your breasts sag and your back aches and your looks have left you, however long it takes—a day, a month, a year, a lifetime—there will come a moment when you understand just what it is that you are doing now." He stared at her, hard, His eyes burning hot. "By God, you are a fool."

Maybe so. But if she was a fool, she was a happy fool.

And, finally, free.

* * *

As these things go, it didn't take long—especially after the timelessness in the Garden.

It came to pass as He had said: her looks had left her, and disease had marked her, and her body was old and spent. She hadn't fucked anyone for weeks. She hadn't eaten in days.

Even so, she smiled as she lay dying in her pauper's bed.

The King of Evil approached her as He had that fateful night, and once again she didn't know if He were a dream. "First Woman," He said.

"You," she whispered. "My King."

His smile was soft, and warm, and lovely. "You do not serve Me."

"I would. Gladly. You gave me freedom."

"No, First Woman. I merely gave you knowledge. You freed yourself."

"Because of You. Thank You."

He arched a dark brow. "You've lived a short life as a whore, barely making enough to survive this long. And for this, you thank Me?"

"You opened the world to me."

"Was this worth sacrificing your safety behind the gates?"

Her smile stretched. The Man was probably still ensconced there, with his latest Eve, woefully ignorant. The thought made her chuff out a crone's laugh. "Worth that, and more."

"Worth dying for?"

"Yes. Again and again, yes."

"First Woman," the King said, "instead of dying now, would you serve Me? Would you use your sex as your strength and swear yourself to Hell?"

She looked into His green eyes, saw worlds swimming there. "Would I be trapped?"

"Yes. Your freedom would forever be tied to the land Below. But you would be one of thousands of demons who exist to seduce evil men and send their souls to Hell."

"You wish the company of evil men?"

He let out a surprised laugh. "If you agree to serve, one day you would learn the role of Hell, and of Good and Evil."

She felt her body slowly shutting down. A gray haze covered her eyes, and she could not take in enough air. Blind, her voice a bare whisper, she said, "I will serve, with all of my heart."

"And so."

As her breath left her, she felt His kiss on her brow.

* * *

He holds her hand and helps her to her feet. Her form shifts, ripples like water, and she laughs in delight.

"You will be a fine succubus," He says, and He smiles. "But you need a name."

She thinks of words that feel seductive, at combinations of sounds that hint at something powerful. And finally, her lips curve into a wicked smile.

"I am Lilith."

When the Wind Blows
by Eirene Donohue

My mother died before I was born. Eight and a half months pregnant, she was driving to the store to fetch some food before the storm set in. But the storm was early. The twister came hard and fast, ravaging a path across the fields, scooping up the wood-paneled station wagon and tossing it into the air where it was caught by the branches of an old oak. The only tree on that entire five-mile stretch of road. When the wreckage was removed, there was hardly a scratch on the tree, just some broken glass sprinkled among its roots. A hidden threat sifting in the dirt, just waiting to cut the skin of the innocent traveler who might someday seek solace beneath its leafy shade.

She was brain dead by the time they finally got her to the hospital. They kept her on life support long enough to deliver me by C-section. It was a miracle, the doctors said. I was a little underweight, but besides that I was perfectly healthy. Ten fingers, ten toes. No sign of the trauma that had birthed me. Those bruises would take years to reach the surface of my skin.

My father named me Mallory, which had been my mother's maiden name. People tell me that it is a beautiful name, but I looked it up in a baby name book when I was ten and I know that it means unlucky. I tell people this when they hear the story of my birth and they tell me how lucky I am to be alive.

As soon as they released me from the hospital, my father packed me into his truck and drove east, leaving the flat open plains and my mother's freshly buried body behind. We shifted from state to state for the next thirteen years, just the two of us. He worked at whatever job would have him, in whatever town he could find some kind, old woman to watch me while he was gone. We never stayed for more than a year in one place. One day he would be staring out onto the horizon, and his eyes would squint with fear and a hint of recognition, and by sunrise the car would be packed and we would be on the move again. We lived like fugitives on the run, not realizing that we had already been caught. From plains to mountains, from deserts to the sea. There is no escaping the wind.

* * *

"I like it here," I say to my father as we unpack the last of our boxes inside the small stone cottage. It is old and musty, cluttered with mismatched furniture and rusty gardening tools, but the ceilings are high and crosscut with thick wooden beams. The front window is large and south facing, thick streams of sunlight illuminating the swirls of dust that seem to kick up from every surface. "It feels like it's out of a fairy tale or something, like there should be a witch living here, or maybe a princess in hiding."

He looks over at me and smiles, but my father's smiles are more like an involuntary reflex than a display of emotion. Like blinking. Words might invite conversation, and my father has a talent for silence.

The cottage is on the edge of a rundown estate on the southeast coast of Massachusetts. Two weeks ago we were living in Maine, my father working for some fishermen on the docks. He had picked up a weekend job varnishing the yacht of a lawyer on vacation with his family. At the end of the weekend, the lawyer offered him a job as a caretaker on an estate that he managed. There was some sort of ongoing family dispute over the property, and no one had lived there for years. He needed someone to look after the grounds and maintain a presence on the property. Local teenagers had taken to breaking into the main house and holding parties. There wasn't much of a salary, but the rent on the cottage was free and the work was solitary. There was still a month left of school, but that had never stopped us before. By the end of the week we were gone again.

* * *

The guidance counselor looks down at my file and then back up at me with a nervous smile. "Well," he says, taking off his glasses and setting them down on the desk. "You certainly have moved around a lot."

I nod and give him a tight smile. He looks almost exactly the same as the guidance counselor at my last school, even down to his tie. Brown, striped through with flaky gold thread.

"It says here that you are living on the Primrose estate, but your last name is Borasco. Is your mother a Primrose?" he asks. I can tell by the way he lifts his chin that he is hoping the answer is yes. He is hoping there is some reason for him like me more than he does. If I am a Primrose he will give me a tour of the school himself, otherwise it will be some hall monitor with body odor and veiny hands.

"My father is the new caretaker. We don't live in the main house." I don't mention anything about my mother. If I tell him she is dead, it will fill him with pity, and then he might take a "special interest" in me and tell me that he is here for me if I ever need anyone to talk to.

"Well then," he says, picking up his glasses again and glancing at my file. "All this movement doesn't seem to have affected your academic studies. From the looks of it, you should have no problem getting up to speed with your peers here. If anything, you are probably a bit farther along than most of them." He gives me a searching, sympathetic stare. "Twelve schools in nine years. That must be hard on you."

He waits for me to respond, to seek his counsel, but I don't need guidance from anyone. A tight smile and a nod is all he will get.

* * *

After dinner I close myself into my bedroom and check the barometer I keep by the window. The pressure has been dropping steadily all day, and the air is wet and thick with heat. The storm is almost here.

Drops of sweat furrow and pool on the backs of my thighs. The humidity creeps through every surface, a wet residue trailing its tongue across my skin. I wait patiently and listen to the soft slapping sound of cards being laid out evenly across the dinner table. One more game of solitaire and my father will be ready for bed.

Tap, tap. He squares up the cards against the table before sliding them back into their case. *Screech.* His chair scrapes against the stone-tiled floor as he stands. Every night it is the same, no matter how many houses we have lived in. He pours himself a glass of water from the sink and sets the glass down on the counter, where tomorrow I will find it, wash it, and return it to the cupboard. *Swoosh.* The curtains slide closed. *Thwack.* The deadbolt is turned.

His footsteps pause outside of my door as he debates whether or not I am still awake. If he thinks I am awake, he will say a soft goodnight. Otherwise he will continue silently to his room. I am always awake.

When I hear the hum of his fan, I know that it is safe. He is done for the night, and I am gone.

I slip silently out the window and set off through the woods behind the house. The solstice is a week away, and there is still enough light to see the thick white clouds rising up against the moon, fat with rain and anger.

The wind is kicking, and the air tastes metallic. I make it to the clearing in ten minutes. I found this place the day after we moved here. While my father cleared brush and weeds from our front lawn, I had wandered the surrounding woods and stumbled upon an open field, hemmed in by tall pines, a twisted weeping willow soaring and isolated in its center.

The first droplets of rain hit just as I take my place about ten yards from where the willow branches skirt the ground. I pull a large metal cross out of my back pocket and hang it from my neck. The sky lights up, white with heat. I throw my head back and stretch my arms open in invitation.

I live for these storms, for the wind and the rain, for the electric current pulsing through the atmosphere. The rain soaks into me until my clothes hang wet and heavy from my skin. Then the numbness melts away. I feel my pulse beating steadily through my veins.

Hoooo hooooo! The screeching hoot of an owl cries out from the woods, and I spin towards it, my hands wiping the streams of water from my eyes.

And there she is, at the edge of the pines. Her long, red hair, an angry serpent writhing against the wind. White nightgown clinging to her bony frame. Staring back at me as if *I* am the apparition. That is all I see in the split second before the night goes black again. By the time lightning strikes twice she is gone.

* * *

A set of abandoned train tracks runs along the outskirts of the estate. I follow them until they reach the edge of the pond. There is a rusted out No Swimming sign posted on a tree. The shoreline is a tangle of marsh grass and muddy debris—crumpled packs of cigarettes, empty bottles, and candy bar wrappings. Out on the water, three white swans float in circles around each other. They look bored and malicious, as if they have seen it all. But this is a pond, not a river, and there is nowhere else for them to go.

I leave the tracks and follow a small dirt path that leads along the water. I'm still watching the swans and don't notice the group of kids sitting on a couple of fallen logs until it's too late to avoid them. I stop in my tracks, and all four of them look up at the same time. I recognize them from school. The girl is Ava Sanders. Her father is the one who hired my dad. I remember watching her on the docks in Maine and being fascinated by the way she seemed to glow, a blonde halo shimmering around her. Even here beneath the trees she somehow manages to catch the sunlight in her hair.

The boy sitting next to her stands up and pulls a pack of Marlboro Reds from his back pocket. Adam Farris. He sits in the back row of every class but at the center table in the cafeteria.

"You got a light?" he asks, squinting his dark eyes at me in question. I nod and pull a pack of matches from my jean cutoffs. He puts two in his mouth and lights both of them with the same match. He pulls one from his lips and hands it to me without even asking if I smoke, which I don't. Only I do. Now I do.

He looks at the other two boys and jerks his head to the side, motioning them to make room for me on the makeshift bench. He sits opposite from me, and Ava immediately lays a possessive hand on his thigh.

"You're the new girl," he says. "The one living on the Primrose estate." I nod.

"Your dad is the new caretaker, right?" says Ava with what I imagine she thinks is a warm smile. She throws a little extra heat into her lips. "He's really nice, your dad. I met him in Maine when he was scrubbing down our boat."

"Yeah, that's right," I reply. "I think he cleaned out your shitters too." Her smile disappears into cold shock. "I remember him saying that you guys had the cleanest shitters he'd ever seen."

The boys laugh, and Ava recoils in anger, but she is too cool to show it. She just smiles again and cocks her head slightly to the side.

"I'm glad he thought so. I'll make sure to pass the compliment along to my father."

"So have you been inside the big house yet?" Adam asks, changing the subject. "Is it all haunted like everyone says it is?"

"I didn't know it was supposed to be haunted," I reply.

"Oh yeah," says Ava. "It's like, totally haunted. Two girls died in there. One was a really long time ago, and then another one died about fourteen years ago, and no one has lived there since."

"How did they die?" I ask.

Ava leans in and replies in a whisper, "They were murdered."

"By who?"

Ava looks over her shoulder across the pond. "Goddess Lilly killed them."

Now everyone looks across the pond, leaving me to ask the question they are all obviously waiting for me to ask.

"Who is Goddess Lilly?"

"She lives in that little cottage over there," says the boy next to me. "She only comes out at night, and even then usually only if it's raining."

"She's crazy," chimes in Ava. "My dad says before the second girl died she used to walk up and down Brick Street all day dragging a suitcase behind her because she wanted to be ready for when the aliens came to get her."

"When I was little," adds Adam, "my mother used to tell me that if I was bad Goddess Lilly would come and take me away when I was sleeping."

"So did mine."

"Mine too."

Goddess Lilly doesn't sound like the only twisted woman in this town. "Did she really kill them?" I ask.

"They could never prove it," says Ava. "She was a maid on the Primrose estate way, *way* back in the day. She tried to kidnap the daughter or something like that. They caught her with the girl at the train station in Boston. She said that she was just taking her for a day trip and that the mother had given them permission, but the mother denied it. A week later the girl collapsed in her bedroom with fever and was dead by the next morning. The mother went crazy and had to be institutionalized. She was convinced that Goddess Lilly had cursed her child."

"And what about the other girl? What did Lilly have to do with that?"

"Same age girl, same mysterious circumstances. Totally healthy kid comes down with a fever and is dead the next day. The mother swore that a week before the girl died, she had caught Lilly looking in through one of the windows at night. But there was no proof, so the police couldn't do anything. She just lives there in her cottage now like a witch, all crazy and evil." Ava shivers as if cold. One of the boys picks up a rock and skips it across the surface of the pond.

I don't tell them that I have seen her. I don't tell them about the storm and the owl and the way she had looked at me as if she knew me. Maybe she is a night demon. Maybe she does eat little children. But there was something familiar about her. Maybe she does know me.

* * *

My father comes home on Friday afternoon with a paycheck and an invitation. It's hot pink with purple glitter hearts and stars.

Wet n'Wild! Summer starts now! Be hot and stay cool! Ava is having a pool party, and for some reason she has invited me.

"Mr. Sanders asked me to give this to you," he says, wiping the stray glitter off the kitchen table.

"Do I have to go?"

"Only if you want to."

"And if I don't?"

He just shrugs and continues to wipe the table with his fingers, even though it is clean.

"You're not going to make me go so I can get in good with the boss's daughter?"

He sighs and looks up at me, defeated though he never even started the fight. "I'm not going to tell you what to do, Mallory. You do what you want to do."

He always says things like this. *You do what you do. It's your life. It doesn't matter what I think.* Most kids my age would kill for this lack of restriction, but it doesn't feel like freedom to me. If I fall, it is because I was the one who jumped. If I get lost, it is because I am the one who ran the wrong way. He will not hold me back. He will not hold me at all.

* * *

Ava lives in a big boxy house across the pond from the estate. Her backyard slopes down to the water's edge, where two kayaks and a canoe are tethered to a large wooden post. The pool is directly adjacent to the back of the house, surrounded by a large stone patio. Above the garage, overlooking the pool, is a deck that leads into a small, open, studio apartment. This where Ava lives—during the summer at least. When it gets too cold, she moves back into her bedroom in the main house. I learn all this from a girl with French braids and blue sparkle fingernails. She relays this to me in a hushed whisper over the potato chip and onion dip platter.

"Her parents are so cool," she says, nodding her head toward where the father stands manning the grill, and the mother lounges beside him sipping chardonnay out of a giant wine glass. "They let her get her ears double-pierced when she was ten."

I spend most of the party in the shallow end of the pool. Most of the kids are curious but friendly. I recognize them from school but haven't spoken with most of them. I know that they are wondering why I am here, but there is no animosity. If Ava has invited me, then I must belong here. I must belong with them.

Ava, strangely enough, since this is her party, rarely interacts with the other guests. She holds court over by the hot tub with Adam by her side. She sits on the edge with her feet dangling into the steaming water. Every once in a while she goes over to the trampoline and bounces for a few minutes. She bounces perfectly.

When it starts to get dark around nine, people start leaving. I slide my cutoffs over my damp suit and grab my bag.

"Were you just going to leave without saying goodbye?"

I spin around, and Adam is standing there holding my towel in his hand.

"Yes," I reply. I reach out to grab my towel, but he doesn't release his grip.

"C'mon. We're just getting started." He pulls me over to where the few remaining kids are seated around the fire pit. Ava has started a game of truth or dare. She does not acknowledge me when I join the circle.

Dare. One of the boys leaps from the balcony into the pool. *Truth.* Blue sparkle nail polish admits that she watched a porn movie once, but it was by accident and like, totally gross. *Truth.* Ava stole a hundred-dollar pair of earrings from a jewelry store when her mother told her they were too expensive for a fourteen-year-old. She wears them every day, and her mother has never noticed.

My turn. *Dare.* Everyone turns to Ava and waits for her pronouncement. She smiles with anticipation, and I can tell that she has planned this whole game just for this moment.

"I dare you to knock on Goddess Lilly's door."

Blue Sparkle gasps beside me, but I'm not shocked at all.

"That's it? Just knock?" I clarify.

"Just knock."

"Fine." I get up and start down towards the water. "Is it all right if I take the canoe?" Lilly's cabin is directly across the pond. Walking through the streets would take too long. It's agreed that Ava and Adam will come with me to witness.

On the ride over, no one talks. There is only the soft rhythmic slapping of the paddles against the surface of the water. Halfway across the pond, the wind begins to quicken. Looking up, I can see clouds rolling in across the moon.

Adam pulls the canoe up onto the embankment and offers me his arm when I climb out. My feet sink into the mud, and I nearly loose my balance, but Adam sets me steadily onto the shore. Ava does not bother to dirty her feet. She climbs onto his back and lets him carry her to dry land. The reeds give way to grass, and then Lilly's cottage lies before us, dark and quiet.

The garden is thick and overgrown, a tangled bramble of white roses and poppies. Off to the side of the yard, there is a rusted miniature windmill creaking slowly with the breeze. There is no movement from within the house, but I can feel its silent menace beating through me like a pulse.

Ava nods her head towards the back door. "Go on then," she whispers. Her eyes dilate with fear and anticipation. "We'll stay here and watch."

I move steadily up the path. My stomach is tight and twisted, but not with fear. This place feels somehow familiar. That smell of roses mixed with summer heat, aggressively sweet and cloying. I know that smell. It smells like my mother. This thought pops into my head, and it makes no sense, but I know that it is true. This is exactly how she smelled.

I make it to the door and look back once at where Adam and Ava are hiding at the edge of the yard, crouched low behind a leafy bush. Raising my arm, I swing my knuckles hard towards the door, but before they can make contact, the door swings open and I fall forward into the empty space, the momentum of my arm pulling me over the threshold.

Behind me I hear Ava scream, and then two sets of quick feet scrambling through the reeds towards the pond. Still on my knees, I can hear the splash of oars against the water as they race away without even an attempt to wait for me to catch up. Save yourself. Of course.

I pull myself up by the doorframe. Inside the house it is dark, darker than it is outside, where at least there is a moon to cast shadows. Here there is no depth of vision, only a deep and grasping blackness.

From the back corner of the entranceway a figure begins to emerge, pale white fabric picking up the light from moon, as it moves closer to the open door.

I should run. I should turn and run and not stop until I am home and the door is dead-bolted behind me. My left foot makes it as far as the back step, but there is something stronger than fear rooting me to the spot. I want to see her again.

She stops about a foot away from me and looks me over with confusion. She is older than I thought she was, in her seventies. Her red hair makes her look younger, but up close she is frail and worn. Her pale skin is wrinkled and smooth at the same time, like a blank piece of paper that has been crumpled up and then rubbed flat again. Her black eyes are deep set and framed by thick brows and lashes. She was beautiful once.

She leans in until her face is just next to my cheek and she inhales deeply. Leaning back again with her eyes closed, she releases the breath in a slow hiss. Opening her eyes, she stares at me with a look of sadness and resignation. She reaches her hand out and cups my cheek in her palm. Her voice comes out in a whisper.

"Sweet child, how many times must I kill you before you let me rest in peace?"

And that is when I run.

* * *

The next night after dinner Adam shows up on my doorstep and asks me to go for a walk. I shout to my father that I will be back later and close the door behind me without waiting for a response. There is never a response.

I lead him into the woods towards the willow tree. He says nothing about what happened last night. He doesn't apologize for abandoning me, and he doesn't ask me what happened. He keeps rambling on about the weather, about how strange it is and how unusual it is to have so many storms this time of year. He talks about the heat as if it is an intruder trespassing on his soil. He doesn't seem to understand that it is summer time. By definition the temperature must rise. The heat belongs here more than he does.

I part the branches of the willow, and we settle ourselves amongst the roots, leaning back against the trunk. It is cool here in the shade.

"I can't believe I've never found this place before," he says, looking up at the thick canopy of leaves and branches that form this hidden cavern. "What a great hiding spot."

"Have you got something to hide?" I ask. He glances over at his knapsack.

"Maybe." He unzips the bag and pulls out a small bottle of gin. He takes a sip and shivers involuntarily. Then he hands the bottle over to me. I take two long gulps and set the bottle on the ground. He is very impressed. He would be.

"Wow, you sure know how to drink."

"Yes, my father is very proud," I reply.

He takes another sip, this time no shiver. "You never talk about your mother."

Here it comes.

"What happened to her?"

"She's dead," I reply, reaching for the bottle. I can see the sympathy forming on his lips, that random apology people give when they find out someone is dead, as if they had something to do with the death. But I'm the only one with blood on my hands, and I don't want his condolences. "I killed her."

His face moves from sympathy to confusion. "I don't get it."

"She was pregnant, and she had cravings. Apparently I had quite an appetite for sardines and strawberry ice cream. So she went out to the store in the middle of a storm. She crashed into a tree and died. They cut me out of her while she was on life support."

I take two more swigs from the bottle, but it brings no relief. I am looking for oblivion, but instead all I get is heat, the gin seemingly skipping my blood stream and seeping automatically up through my skin in little beads of clear sweat. I wipe my face against my sleeve.

Adam mistakenly takes the sweat for tears. He lays his arm across my shoulder. "It's okay," he says softly. "It wasn't your fault."

I have to cover my face with my hands to hide my smile. "It wasn't your fault," he repeats as he strokes my back. I am laughing so hard that my body begins to shudder, which he thinks are sobs. This poor boy. Does he really think that's all it takes? If only it was that simple. I compose myself and pat him on the knee. "Thanks, I really needed to hear that."

He leans back against the tree and looks up. "That's a crazy story. I mean, do you have any idea how lucky you are just to be alive?"

No, Adam, I say to myself as I lean back against the tree and close my eyes. I have no idea.

* * *

Adam and I start meeting up at the willow tree a few times a week. He tells me that I am not like other girls, which is what all boys say when they are hoping that you will do things that other girls won't do. So I do. I always do.

I like it best when he is flat on his back with his eyes closed and his arms tossed wide to the side. I could do anything and he would not be able to stop me. I run my fingers over his pale hairless chest, tracing the outlines of his ribs. I could kill him if I wanted to. I could drive a knife between his bones into his heart, and as the blood and life drained slowly through my fingers I could look him in the eye and ask him to tell me again how it wasn't my fault.

Afterwards he is always quick to leave. He pulls his clothes on and brushes the twigs and dirt from his hair. He has to be home in time for Ava's phone call. She's gone to her beach house on the Vineyard for a few weeks, but she calls him every night before bed. Leaning in to give me a kiss, he always says thank you. I always say you're welcome.

Sometimes he walks me home, but usually I stay behind. I lie beneath the tree as the night comes creeping. I wait for the wind, and when it comes it carries the smell of roses and the low hooting cry of the owl.

She is near. She is waiting.

* * *

I wait for an hour, but Adam never comes. Lilly does.

"No show tonight?" she asks as she steps through the willow curtain. I rise slowly to my feet and brush the dirt from my hands.

"Sorry to disappoint you."

She is dressed in her white nightgown and barefoot as usual. She walks by me and goes to stand by the trunk of the willow, laying both of her hands on the bark. She presses her cheek against it and releases a sigh and a slow smile.

"I remember the first time I found this place." She looks over her shoulder at me. "I was your age, or around it. I used to come here to hide."

There is a foreign edge to her voice, though I cannot place the accent. The vowels are slightly drawn out and there is a low hiss that slips out behind her words.

"What were you hiding from?" I ask.

She turns around and leans her back into the tree. "From life," she replies. "But life can find you anywhere, even here." She smiles. "And so can death." She takes a few steps towards me. "But I don't need to tell you that, do I?"

"What do you mean?"

She laughs. "I can smell death on you, child." She leans in and sniffs. "It's like perfume, only sweeter." She takes another step closer. "You look like her, you know."

"Like who?" For a moment I wonder if it is possible that she had known my mother.

"Like the girl I killed."

"Girl?" I reply. "I thought there were two of them."

"So far," she says.

I can't control the goose bumps that rise up on my skin. "Are you afraid of me?" she asks.

"I'm not afraid to die."

"That's not what I asked." That low hiss creeps between her syllables.

"Did you kill those girls?"

"It's my fault they are dead."

"That's not what I asked."

She chuckles softly and steps back. "Of course I killed them."

"I don't believe you."

She looks at me with darkness in her eyes. "You are not the one who must believe it for it to be true." She walks back towards me until her face is inches from mine. "You think you are so high, so strong. Lying here with that boy every night as if you were the first person to ever use your body in such a way. You think you are untouchable; I can see it in your eyes. Well, I was untouchable, too, once."

She grabs both of my wrists in her hands and shakes me. "You don't believe me? Who asked you? I killed those girls. I killed them because I loved them and we all kill the things we love. If you loved yourself even a little you would be dead already!"

She moves her hands to my shoulders, her bony hands surprisingly strong, digging into my flesh. Her eyes are black and snapping with anger. "Not afraid to die? You stupid, ungrateful girl! How dare you step in front of me, looking like her and tell me that you are not afraid to die! You dance for the thunder and lightning like a demon seeker, but there is no life to steal from your veins!"

She pushes me to the ground and turns back to the tree. "Go home," she says breathlessly. "You're not the person I thought you were. You're not her."

I scramble to my feet and move quickly away from her. By the time I step outside of the willow she is on her knees, her body shaking in silent pain.

* * *

Adam meets me at the end of the driveway. There is a storm rising and he doesn't want to get caught in it. He leads me towards the main house where a basement window has been pried open. He slides in first and then reaches his arms up to catch me. Without a word he leads me up three flights of stairs, then down a dark hallway.

The house seems bigger than it looks from the outside. Echoes skip away, and we are gone by the time they return. Rooms open onto each other endlessly, empty and neglected. Wallpaper falls in cascades from moldy walls. Remnants of past intruders lie scattered throughout the house. Crumpled beer cans and empty wine bottle candelabras. Dirty blankets and an old issue of *Playboy*. It's all very romantic.

We come to a small room at the western edge of the house. It looks as if it had once been a nursery. There is a faded mural painted along one wall, of a castle set amidst the sweeping sand dunes of a desert, camels caravanning across the landscape. In the highest tower, the silhouette of a woman can be seen in the window. An owl is perched on the turret. A pair of lions stands guard on either side of the castle gate.

"This is so cool," I whisper as I trace my finger across the paint. Adam tugs at my hand and leads me towards the French doors that open onto a small terrace.

"Check this out," he says. Outside the sun has set, and the sky burns out in a rash of bright orange. From this high up, we can see over the trees all the way to the ocean, the whitewash of the surf, flashing like sparks every time a wave breaks. A wall of clouds moving in from the north tumble over one another. It won't be long before the rain comes.

"It's beautiful," I whisper. He wraps his arms around my waist and pulls me back inside.

"You're beautiful," he replies, and then he leans in to kiss me.

It's too much. The sunset, the haunted mansion, the candles he has lit around the room somehow when I wasn't looking. I don't like to be shown the things I can't have. I only like to have the things I don't want.

I push him away. "More beautiful than Ava?" I ask. She comes home tomorrow. This will all be over soon enough.

"Why do you have to do that?" he asks, his face darkening.
"Do what?"
"Ruin everything."
"It's what I do best," I reply.

He sighs and pushes his hands deep into his pockets. He flips his head to get his hair out of his eyes, even though he is not looking at me.

"What do you want from me?" he asks.

I shake my head. He doesn't get it. "Nothing," I reply honestly. "There is nothing I want that you could ever possibly give me." He looks hurt by this statement. "But I can give you what you want," I continue, pulling my shirt over my head and dropping it on the floor. "And that's enough for me."

It's enough for him too. He walks over and runs his finger across my collarbone. I turn my back to him and he begins to kiss my shoulders. On the wall in front of me, there is a giant floor-to-ceiling mirror. The frame is intricately carved, twisted vines and serpents tangled together. It seems like a strange piece of furnishing for a child's room. It looks old and expensive. I'm surprised no one has stolen it.

The candles flicker and send soft shadows licking across my skin. Adam kisses my neck and reaches his hands around to cup my breasts. I reach behind me and unhook my bra, then pull my arms free of the straps. I watch myself in the mirror as his hands roam over my body. My reflection shows no response. This is who you are. Untouchable. There is nothing here for anyone to touch.

"Mallory."

The voice is low and rises from the darkness of the doorway. Adam jumps back, but I remain where I stand. I cross my arms over my chest and watch in the mirror as my father's figure is illuminated. Adam curses and apologizes in the same breath. He grabs his bag and runs past my father, the echo of his footsteps on the stairs ringing out its hollow goodbye. And this time it is definitely goodbye.

My father turns his head as I pull my top back on. "You shouldn't be up here," he says finally. "You could have burned this place down. It's my job to keep this place safe."

"This place?" I reply. "It's your job to keep this place safe?"

"Yes."

"That's all? You find me in here half naked with a boy you've never met, and that's all you have to say?"

He sighs and finally looks me in the eye. "What do you want me to say?"

"Say anything! Say you're angry! Say that you're disappointed in me; say that I'm nothing but a dirty whore and that no daughter of yours is going to disrespect herself like that."

He just shakes his head. I know exactly what he is about to say. "I'm not going to tell you what to do. It's your life."

The rage rushes up like vomit from my guts and explodes in a scream. I grab a wine bottle from the ground and throw it at the mirror. I watch our reflections shatter as broken glass cascades to the floor.

"*Stop saying that!*"

I clench my fists at my sides and walk towards him. There is a look of shock on his face. "It's not my life. It never has been." A wave of pain rises up from my spine as my confession tears itself free and escapes through my lips. "I took it from her and you've never forgiven me for it."

"What are you talking about?"

"For killing my mother."

Now he looks genuinely confused. "You didn't kill her."

"She had cravings, that's what you said, she went to the store because she had cravings for ice cream and sardines. It was my fault she was out driving. It was my fault..." My voice trails off, and suddenly I feel much younger than my fourteen years.

His entire body sags and deflates, then a deep breath refills him as he rubs his hands over his face. "You didn't kill her. No one killed her. She left me. She left us."

Now I'm the one who is confused. "I don't understand. The storm. The car accident."

"That part is true. She was going to the store and got caught up in the wind. The doctors delivered you while she was in a coma." He takes another deep breath. "Only she didn't die. When she came to, she told me we were through. She said I was too controlling, that this was her second chance at life, and that there was no way she was going to waste it living beneath a man who smothered her and told her what to do all the time. There was no changing her mind. As soon as she was healthy she up and left."

"And what about me?"

"She took you with her. I don't know where. Three years later she showed up on my doorstep. I think she'd been through some rough patches. She said she couldn't take care of you anymore. She said that the storms wouldn't stop chasing her and that it wasn't safe for you anymore. That was the last I ever saw her. I haven't heard from her since."

"Why didn't you tell me?" *All this time,* I think. *All this time.*

"I thought I was protecting you," he says with apology in his eyes. "I didn't want you thinking that you were the reason she left.

I thought it would be easier if you just thought she was dead, but if I'd known that you blamed yourself..." His voice catches. "I'm so sorry."

I look at him now as if seeing him for the first time, this stranger I have known my entire life. The regret weeping from his eyes, a lifetime spent holding me at arm's length so that he wouldn't push me away. There should be anger here. Recriminations and hatred and fingers pointed in blame. But I have lived with those emotions for long enough already.

I stand in front of him and reach my arm out, pressing my palm into his chest. He takes one hand and lays it over mine. He reaches his other hand out and lays it on my head, thumb stroking my forehead as if in absolution. It is not his fault.

"It's not your fault," I whisper. Sometimes it is that simple.

* * *

I wait for him to go to bed before I slip out the window. I don't want to worry him, but there is something I need to do. The rain is falling in sheets, and the clouds have blacked out the moon, but I make my way quickly through the woods. The storm has risen. I know where to find her.

As the thunder begins to rumble, I pick up my pace. The wind pulls at me, and the mud sucks at my bare feet, but I don't slow down. I push my legs harder until my lungs heave and my muscles burn. I need to see her, I need to tell her that she was wrong. I am not untouchable. There is love here. There is love inside me. There is no death on me.

I reach the willow and force myself through the curtain of thrashing branches. The wind howls through the canopy, a screeching whistle that tears at the ears.

"Lilly!" I scream. Her back is to me, her hands against the trunk, head hanging between her shoulders. "Lilly!"

I run to her and spin her around. "She's alive! You were wrong, she's alive. I didn't kill her."

Her hair is tangled in a wet heap around her face. Her nightgown is soaked completely through. She shouldn't be out here. She looks confused, her eyes glassy and swollen.

"You can't be alive," she says. "I killed you."

I shake my head, "No, no, my mother. My mother is alive."

She reaches out and runs a finger down my cheek. "That's impossible. I am your mother." She smiles at me. "They're trying to take you away from me, but I won't let them, not again. Tomorrow we will take the train to Boston. As quick as the wind, we will be gone before they know it."

The realization of what she has told me hits, and I wrap my arms around her tiny frame. I don't know if it is the truth or delusion speaking. Either way, she is too fragile to be out in this storm.

"C'mon Lilly, I'll take you home." She follows after me for a few steps. A loud thunderclap snaps her head back, and suddenly her eyes are clear.

"You're not her!" she cries. "What have you done with her? She's sick, she needs me!"

She pulls herself out of my grip and races back to the tree. She beats her fists against the trunk. "Where is she? Where is she?"

Her voice is raw, her shouts barely audible above the wind. I stand behind her and wait for the fight to subside. She sinks to her knees in quiet sobs.

"Where is she?" she whispers over and over.

"It's time to go," I say and reach for her.

As my hand touches her skin there is a loud crackle in the sky. Both of us look up in time to be blinded by the white flash of lighting streaking towards us. I see the flames erupt from the top of the tree at the same moment the heat surges through my body. I am lifted through the air, caught by the wind. Behind the smoke of the tree I smell a hint of burnt roses. Electricity pulses through me, and in that last moment before everything goes black, all I can think is that they were right. All of them were right. How lucky I am to be alive.

Mother of Vampires
by Jennifer Greylyn

"But it's just not sexy!" wailed Lionel in protest.

She sighed to herself at her prospective editor's intransigence. Vampire fiction was hot these days. Bookstore shelves were stocked with countless stories of vampires in the modern world, in alternate realities, in a post-apocalyptic hell, even in space. If all of those variations could succeed, why not hers?

It had started off so promisingly. Within a week of submitting her manuscript, she had received a call from Ishtar House (a good omen, she had thought, as she had worked well with a goddess by that name in the past) from an editor who called himself Lionel Something-or-Other, wanting to set up a meeting. She didn't pay much attention to his last name, but she liked his first. She had always been fond of lions.

They agreed to meet at a coffee shop near the publishing house. It wasn't the whole-hearted official response she'd been hoping for, but, as Lionel had said, almost apologetically, "It's less formal, you understand." Which she did. It meant they wanted her to know they were under no obligation to proceed any further. "But I'm quite looking forward to meeting you, Ms. Adams," he added, his voice gaining strength with his anticipation. "Your work is very…compelling."

That last word was spoken rather breathlessly, and she smiled to hear it. She'd exerted just a little of her will to make sure her book got a favourable response. Not so much that anyone who read it loved it mindlessly. She had never been interested in thoughtless worship. She just wanted to make sure what she'd written was given a fair chance. She had a way with words. It was part of her heritage. She couldn't imagine writing would be any different.

She began to have her doubts, though, when Lionel walked into the coffee shop. She knew it was him because he was the only customer in a business suit, oxblood-leather briefcase clutched protectively under his arm. He looked very little like the regal creature that was his namesake, being rather lank and scrawny, with receding grey-blond hair. But she didn't let this put her off. She was used to men disappointing her.

"Ms. Adams?" he asked when he saw her looking at him from the corner table. There was a nervous quaver in his voice that hadn't been there on the phone. She smiled at him. The rest of him trembled then. Her smile deepened as she inhaled his desire. Unprepossessing he might appear, but she thought she could work with him.

"I prefer to use my ex-husband's name as little as possible," she told him as he sat down, almost missing the chair because he was unable to take his eyes off her. He managed to find it but dropped his briefcase. "Please, call me Lilith."

His balding head shot up as he was reaching for the briefcase. "Er…that's your real name? I mean—"

She cut off his stammered explanation with a throaty chuckle. She'd had many names over the years, some of her choosing, some not. She considered this one very apt for the series she was contemplating. It didn't bother her if Lionel thought she was crazy. Unlike last century, they wouldn't try to lock her up, or burn her for heresy as they might have done several centuries before that.

"It's the name I want you to call me."

Putting just a little of her will into her voice had him nodding eagerly. "Of course, of course."

His submission was very sweet, but she resolved not to let it go too far. She wanted the world to know the truth about her, and it wouldn't do to seduce her editor to accomplish that. It would only confirm all the old lies.

The server, a slim young man with the coffee shop's logo emblazoned on his apron, appeared to take their orders. He was open in his appreciation of her, smiling so charmingly that she had to smile back. It was just her everyday smile, but their drinks arrived in record time, barely giving Lionel a chance to lay out his papers on the circular silver table.

She suspected all that fuss was for nothing, but she was willing to allow him the comfort of a routine that appeared to steady him. She even went so far as not to interrupt him, letting the effect of her will wane. Still, she was surprised when Lionel seized his cup almost urgently before their server could set it down and took a long swig of the black coffee, although she would have bet he normally added loads of cream and sugar. He winced as if he burned his mouth, but his expression was firmer. It seemed, in some distant corner of his brain, he might have sensed how she'd influenced his thoughts and knew the stimulant would help to clear them. She sipped thoughtfully at her green tea and wondered if she'd misjudged him. A lion would recognize a greater predator.

"So…er…Lilith," he said, trying and failing to meet her gaze, a sign of his good sense. "Tell me about your story."

He knew all about it already. She saw her manuscript in one of his carefully arranged piles. But, thinking he wanted to put her at ease, she was happy enough to discuss it. She explained how her heroine, Lilith, was born of the desert, child of wind and fire, and how she was spurned by her first love, a cruel man, because she could not conceive. Leaving him, she wandered the world in despair until the wind brought her news that he had taken another wife and had children by her. She could have borne that, albeit painfully, if the wind had not also told her that he was spreading false stories about her, saying that she was willful and defiant and responsible for every ill. Filled with righteous anger, she called on fire, also her kin, and prepared to burn the liar out of his garden home. But, by the time she found him again, he had angered someone much more powerful than she and had been cast out anyway. His kind were spreading all over the earth. Seeing them, his sons and daughters, she decided on a different revenge. She would make them her children instead.

"And this is where Lilith—that is, your *heroine*—turns them into vampires?" asked Lionel, somewhat awkwardly.

It amused her to wonder who he thought she thought she was. The reincarnation of the original Lilith? A medium channelling her spirit? She doubted he would believe the truth.

"Yes," she confirmed, relishing that long-ago triumph—that moment when Adam's wrath turned to impotent fury, when he realized he could do nothing to stop her save tell more lies. "The first generation of vampires."

"And she does this by—" Lionel shuffled some papers, coming up with a list of handwritten notes. "—breathing on them when they're children?"

He sounded so incredulous that she felt she had to say more. "Infants, actually. It works better the younger they are."

"By breathing on them," he repeated.

She tried to be patient. Men could be so exasperating. "That's right. It can be done to anyone of any age, but children adapt more easily."

"But-but…*breathing*? It's so ordinary." He shook his head in disbelief, and she fought not to grind her teeth or snap at him. What she was telling him wasn't so hard to understand. Wasn't he listening to her?

"No, it isn't 'ordinary.' It's a special kind of breath: the breath of fire. You don't think she'd want to go around turning everyone into vampires, do you?"

And that was when he said it. Wailed it, really. "But it's just not sexy!"

Sighing to herself, she arched her brow at him. "And you think blood-sucking is?"

He shifted uncomfortably in his seat. "Well, no, but it's…er…an intimate act." A flush crept into his wan cheeks. "Between adults." He pinched the bridge of his nose as if to keep the blush it from spreading up to his forehead. "And it's what our readers expect!" The last was said with a great burst of effort that reddened his whole face and caused him to sag back against his chair.

She sat back much more slowly, frowning slightly. In principle, she could not disagree with him. Drinking blood was something almost all the vampire fiction she knew of had in common. The movies, too, and even the plays that had come before movies were invented. She'd have liked to blame it on Bram Stoker, but he only popularized the idea. It was that damnable Lord Byron who'd first introduced it to the English-speaking world in a poem. Not even a very good poem. It'd made her laugh at the time, thinking any of her children could be so crude. But then the idea spread, and it seemed to be everywhere, and she wondered if some of her children weren't actively promoting it. She discovered a few of them at it—one of them, for instance, was behind that dreadful *Nosferatu*—and admired their initiative and thought that the myth-induced fear provided a bit of protection in a time when some humans still believed in vampires. Now that almost no one did—not in real vampires, anyway—she just found the idea tiresome and decided to set the record straight. It didn't hurt that she could refute the lies her spiteful ex-husband had spread about her at the same time.

Shaping her face into an expression of innocent bemusement, she leaned across the table, elbowing some of Lionel's precious papers out of the way so he could get a good look at her. "Surely your readers are sophisticated enough to appreciate something different, something subtle." She wasn't certain of that, actually, but she believed in flattering the male ego.

As she hoped, Lionel puffed out his chest and assumed a more supercilious air. "Of course, but—" Then he looked her in the eyes again and flinched. Truly, there was a little of the lion in him. He knew to be scared of her.

She liked the taste of his fear, a cool tingling on her tongue, but she needed him calm. She could enthrall him, but she would rather persuade him. Straightening up and adopting a demure tone, she ventured, "Of course you would know best, Lionel, but I hoped you'd be open to something new."

She sighed aloud, letting him hear her disappointment. He leaned forward, moving to take her hand. She allowed it because it made him think he was comforting her. "My company is open to new ideas, Lilith," he assured her, almost urbanely, but then he ruined it. "It's just…turning someone into a vampire by *breathing*? It sounds about as sexy as CPR."

He snickered at his own poor joke, and she withdrew her hand, giving him a cold look that wasn't feigned. "I can see you are sadly lacking in knowledge of vampire lore. There are many potential ways to become a vampire." She didn't add that they were all untrue. That wouldn't help make her point.

"Vampire lore?" he asked, baffled. He tried to recapture her hand, but she kept it out of his reach. He colored again when he almost knocked over what was left of his coffee.

"Vampires exist in almost every culture around the world," she informed him, quite sincerely. "I'll just stick to the East European variety, which are probably most familiar. Take Romanian lore. It says that someone can become a vampire by being born with an unusual physical trait like a caul or extra hair. Or if their mother, when pregnant with them, sees a black cat. Or if she doesn't eat salt. Or if her child is born out of wedlock."

"Give me strength," muttered Lionel, almost inaudibly, raking impatient fingers through his thinning hair. She could see why he had such a sparse mane.

But she had the ears of a cat (not literally anymore; they were too noticeable, so she gave them up along with her wings) and she heard what he did not mean for her to hear. A wicked smile crossed her face.

"Careful, Lionel. In Bulgaria, talking to yourself is a sign you're doomed to become a vampire."

He darted her a reproachful look and began to gather up his papers. "I think we're done here, Ms. Adams. As compelling as I found your book, on further reflection, I don't believe it's right for us at this time…"

She stopped listening to his words after that. He was rejecting her. *Him*! Daring to reject *her*! An ancient anger stirred inside her, vast and smouldering. She closed her eyes to make sure he didn't see them flicker with flame.

This wasn't right. She knew readers would love her book if only they had a chance to read it. She could not disappoint them.

She opened her eyes and fixed them on Lionel just as he was putting the last of the papers back in his briefcase and getting up from the table. She intended him to see the fire in them now. He did, blinked and looked again, unable to believe it. Then he went as pale as snow and tried to turn away, but she caught him and he melted under her gaze.

In a whisper steely with her will, she instructed him, "You will tell your company that you must publish my book and every other one I care to write. You will tell them my ideas are innovative, especially the way humans are turned by the fiery breath of a vampire. You will not rest until my book is on the shelves. Now sit down."

Lionel sat, slack with oblivion as her instructions burned into his brain. When she was finished, she closed her eyes and let the fire sink back into the depths of her being.   A delighted smile swept over Lionel's sweat-sheened face. As he gushed about what a success he was sure her book would be—just the first of many, he hoped—their server returned to ask if they wanted anything else. She had to hold up her hand to make Lionel stop talking.

"No, we're fine," she told the young man. Her mood must have shown on her face, because he lost his charming smile and hastily withdrew. It was too bad he believed that twinge of dissatisfaction was directed at him. She meant something else entirely.

She'd wanted to sell her story without exerting her power, and she wasn't pleased that she'd had to resort to it. But as she inhaled the sweetness of Lionel's newfound enthusiasm, she couldn't stay sorry for long. She already had an idea for her next book. It would be about how her children learned to feed on human emotion, which was so much cleverer than draining veins.

Propping her elbow on the table and dropping her chin into her hand, she gestured with the other for Lionel to resume his spate of praise, and then basked in it, feeling the beginning of a happy glow.

Motherhood, in any form, was never easy. In the end, any effort was worthwhile. More than worthwhile—it would be forgotten, once she saw her child.

In hardcover. In the front window of every bookstore.

The Right Thing
by Hannah Goodman

I sit on the edge of the tub with the window open and watch the pink line on the stick get thicker and darker. Suddenly, I notice the wind and turn my head to feel it. I put the stick down on the counter and close my eyes for a second. When I open them, I see brilliant sunlight reflect off the blue sky. The leaves on the trees shimmer and sway in a slow dance. My belly feels warm and my breasts tingle. I feel the warm ball, the warm tornado of life in my belly, and as the breeze lifts my hair from my forehead and shoulders I feel that She will be born and nothing, no one, will stop it.

When I tell my parents later that evening, I do it properly, just as a good girl like me would. I sit them down on our plush, cushy beige couch in the family room. The soft light from the Victorian lamps casts a comforting glow around the room. Dad puts his feet up on the oversized ottoman. I walk across the burber carpet, as soft and cushy as the couch. In the kitchen, I fill the kettle with water for Mom and go to the pantry to retrieve an apple-cranberry tea bag.

"Can I help?" Mom calls.

"No," I call back, making sure my tone is light.

"To what do we owe this doting?" My father asks. "Is there some very good news you wish to share with us?"

I pour water into the coffee maker for him and try to swallow the tears that spring up suddenly. He thinks I am going to tell him I got the letter from Brown.

I did. A packet. It's still sitting unopened in the bathroom, near the window.

I blink the tears away, rub my eyes and swipe at my nose before walking back out into the family room. "Just another minute, okay?" I flash a smile and read their faces. Normal. Tired, but normal.

I go back into the kitchen and fix Mom's tea, no sugar or sweetener, and Dad's coffee, cream only.

Moments later they are holding their mugs and sitting straight up on the couch, waiting.

I open my mouth, which tastes like dry crackers, like saltines without the salt or the yummy yeast taste. I press a mental pause button on the moment. The last moment they will be proud of me, the last moment I will be their perfect daughter. The last moment they would look at me and think *Brown University, Doctor, change the world, make the universe better.*

Mom's hair is tousled, the fluff replaced with frizz. She has a hair and nail appointment tomorrow, every other Wednesday. I picture Stella scrubbing Mom's hair in the sink, asking in her loud voice, "How's Saint Lilith?"

But I can't imagine how Mom will respond. The few imperfect moments of my life have always been kept between us, and never have I done anything as imperfect as this. Knowing Mom, she just won't go tomorrow. That just makes me feel guiltier.

Mom's feet are bare, the toenails decorated with chipped pink polish. She's wearing her after-work attire, a brown, crushed velvet sweat suit, making her look years younger than fifty-six. My father is still in his shirt and khakis, but his shoes are off, and he rolls his ankles, which make popping noises. My parents' eyes are red and puffy. The day seems to wear out their eyes the most.

I want to savor this last moment of normalcy at the end of a work/school day. My belly feels cold and empty now, yet I can feel my heart, swollen, like it is too big for my chest. The beats pound my chest.

I scan their faces, wonder if maybe I should ask Dad how his presentation went today. See if Mom's showing was successful. That would be a normal way to start a big talk with them. Then I realize I've never had a big talk with them.

My heart hurts, burns. I pictured it in my chest, bright red, violent blood red. Beating and pulsing. So I stop thinking and just open my mouth.

"I'm pregnant."

Then I wait to see. Mom freezes, her mouth in an O shape. Then she leaps up and her hand flies over her mouth. She is right next to a tall lamp, and her glossy red nails glimmer in the soft light. I worry she will fall into the lamp.

Dad crosses one leg over the other, cracks his ankles again, turns his head to the side and curses, "Goddamnit." Then he stands up and runs a hand over his hair, which doesn't ruffle or move.

I stand with my arms loose, dangling by my side. I'm cold and hot at the same time.

Silence follows.

During the silence, they reposition themselves back to the couch. Perched upright at the edge. Waiting.

When I do speak again, all I say is, "I have to tell Adam." Which is not what I want to say. I want to say, *I am having this baby. I'm keeping it.* But it's like I am two people—the me that they're staring at would never say that to them, but the me inside, with the swollen heart, would.

I stand alone, my whole body pulsing and warm now.

"Lilith," My mother says each syllable drawn out. "You know, you don't have to tell him." She looks at my father, who nods and sighs.

"We can help you take care of this." She clasps her hands onto her lap and leans forward, like I'm years younger than my seventeen years.

"Adam doesn't even have to know, honey." My father puts his hand out as if he is going to rub my arm.

The shock of what they are saying, what they are really saying underneath the words, punches me right in the chest. I take a step back, and I do something I can't remember ever doing. I go to my room and slam the door.

And they do something they've never done before; they don't come to check on me, even when I know my sobs are loud enough to echo through the house.

* * *

I call Adam at midnight.

He answers immediately. "Did you do it?"

"Yes." My voice is hoarse from crying but I feel calm.

"Oh, shit. You've been crying–"

"I'm pregnant."

I hear a muffle like he's covering the phone. I swallow the lump in my throat and wait, pulling at a loose thread on my bedspread.

"Sorry— Shit! Okay, okay. We can take care of this, right? I mean no one has to know, right?"

Just like my parents. The tears fall again silently, and I hang up the phone.

He doesn't call back.

* * *

I hear other lockers creaking open and slamming shut, I smell eggs and toast floating up from the cafeteria, and I know other kids are weaving in and out of classrooms. I know the rhythm of the school morning, the early morning before the buses arrive, dumping the rest of the population, the unfortunate ones who aren't old enough to drive, or the even more unfortunate ones who don't have enough money to have their own cars. It's a comfortable rhythm that floats around me like the music I play when I study; it's background noise, a comforting buzz of sound. I hate silence. I love this part of the day when the background noise is bright and cheerful.

Cece, Mimi, and I stand in front of my locker discussing abortions.

"When Jewish girls get knocked up–nice Jewish girls, that is–they get abortions, Lil. That's what they do when they get themselves in trouble. They have it taken care of. They don't actually have the baby; they don't give it up for adoption like maybe a nice Catholic girl would do. They don't discuss it or any other options other than get rid of it."

I slam my locker shut. "Doesn't the Bible, the Torah, say anything about this?"

"This has nothing to do with our religion, Lil. It's our culture. The whole education-slash-success thing." She sighs. Mimi's father is a Jewish Studies professor at a nearby university. Dinner conversation at her house usually involves a debate. Like, is being Jewish a race, a religion, or both? Another favorite is why, throughout history, are Jews hated? So I know her mini lecture is not in the spirit of trying to advise me, but to give information. I take a deep breath and make myself listen to the rest.

"Your parents have a plan for you. You are going to Brown in the fall and then off to med school. You'll wait until your residency is over, marry a nice Jewish boy, preferably a doctor or lawyer, preferably Adam." She ticks each item off on her fingers. "Come on, you know the drill."

I think of the unopened large envelop from Brown tucked away in my desk drawer. I shift my backpack from one shoulder to the other, reminding myself that this is Mimi's way of being here for me right now. But it's hard to ignore the lump forming in my throat. I feel Cece eyeing me. She's an emotional barometer. If your breath changes she notices.

Like right now.

Cece glares at Mimi. "Can you save your abortion lecture for later?"

Mimi shakes her head. "Okay, I'm not saying I think you should do it…"

I nod my head, but it's apparent by the way Cece holds her hand to cut Mimi off that I am not doing a good job of hiding my feelings. "Enough, Mimi."

The Right Thing

"I'm just saying, I kind of understand why your Mom and Dad want—"

Mimi stops herself before Cece lunges at her. She frowns and grabs one of my hands. "I am sorry, Lil. If there's anything…"

The lump in my throat is about to explode. I shake my head.

* * *

At the end of the day, Cece and I walk slowly, elbows and shoulders bumping. We alternate between looking ahead and sideways at each other. I look down at our feet, in perfect synchronicity. Her navy-blue Crocs to my brown ones. God, does she make me feel safe.

"It's kind of ironic, you know," I say softly, looking up at the bright hallway stretched out in front of us, kids darting out of classrooms, arms loaded with books.

She glances at me, brushes the curly hair out of her eyes. "That the valedictorian is pregnant?"

"Yeah. My whole life has been about doing the right thing, the good thing, the proper thing, and now here I am faced with a decision to make, and the right thing is to kill my baby."

We stop at my locker. I feel her staring at me as I work the combination. She holds the door open as I put my calculus book away and pull out a stack of notebooks.

"I don't know what to say."

"Tell me I should do what I want, not what good Jewish girls should do." I bend down and put the notebooks carefully into my open backpack. Finals start tomorrow, and since I have a perfect GPA, I'm exempt from them all. So I am emptying out my locker today.

"But Lil, aren't you pro choice?"

I'm glad she can't see me when she says this. I put my hand on my belly, as if her words could hurt Her. I gather myself before I stand up.

I close the locker and we are eye to eye now, just inches apart. I can smell her lavender perfume. "Let's say I am. Pro-choice means just that—pro *choice,* as in, this is *my decision*. Not my parents. Not Adam's."

She turns so her back is against the row of lockers, her head is bent down.

But I step even closer now. "You want me to do it too, don't you? It's too embarrassing to say your best friend has a baby, right?"

She looks up, her pupils large. "Lil, come on," she says in a whisper. "That's not fair. I just…I just think that you…you need to really think this through. Abortion is an option, you know."

"Not an option for me, Cece. I want this baby."

"You may want this baby, Lil, and you may hate me for saying this, but nobody else wants you to have that baby."

"Including you?" I can barely get out the words.

Her whole face changes. It's like the screen just went black and white on a TV. All the color gone. I can't tell what she is thinking now.

"I don't know, Lil."

"Including you." It's not a question.

"Okay. I mean, I just think you might, well, ruin your life." She glances away, smoothes her ponytail. "And Adam's."

There's another moment of silence. I exhale slowly, envision myself pushing my chair back from my desk and saying, *This is the best I can do.* That's what I do when I've worked on a paper for so long my eyes ache and my fingertips burn. Sometimes I can work and work and still not get where I think I need to be, where I should be. Sometimes I've run out of time and it just has to be enough, so I push back the chair, turn the computer off and go to bed.

Cece has seen me do that throughout high school, nights where we've worked or studied together. She's watched me let go of trying, cross my fingers, and say a quick prayer to G-d. *Please let this be enough.* She knows my secret desperate moments, when I feel like all the hours and days of working on something has made me dumber instead of smarter, and I'm certain this is the time I will see a red F on a paper or exam.

But standing there now, I don't say any quick prayer to G-d in my head, and I don't worry if what I have said to her is enough for her. It's enough for me and my baby.

When I drop her off at home, she holds the door handle a beat and says, "Lil, I know you've made up your mind. But remember, this isn't just about you."

That's where she is the most wrong. Because of course it's about me. But I don't say anything. I just nod and watch her leave.

* * *

"I'm keeping her."

The bed is only a few feet from the bathroom; the door is wide open.

"Honey, I can't hear you."

Good. I can try to breathe this time when I speak.

The faucet stops running. I sit on the edge of my mother's bed, waiting. I picture her drying her hands quickly and pausing by the mirror to fluff her hair. She's always fluffing her hair—wavy chestnut hair that she doesn't have to color like most of my friends' mothers do.

She pops her head out of her bathroom, her hair perfectly fluffed. "What did you say, sweetie?"

I can't look at her. I can't stand up.

I can't breathe.

"I'm keeping her," I whisper into my hand, which cups my chin. My elbow digs deep into my knee.

Silence. I hear the rustle of her movement, her billowy, lacey nightgown swishing. I move my hand from my chin to my knee.

"Honey, speak up. I can't hear you."

Now my right knee bobs up and down and makes my entire body bounce on the edge of her bed.

"I'm keeping the baby." I say it in my normal voice, but it sounds like an echo coming from somewhere far away. I seem to be able to breathe easily, steadily now.

She makes a noise, an aggravated, disgusted noise. Like when she is on the phone and I ask her if I can borrow a shirt or the car. A noise that says you're annoying me, you're in my way. Scram.

"We've discussed this, Lilith." She says my full name, reserved only for when she is pissed off.

"No, you and Dad discussed it."

My voice is steady and calm and even. I look right into her eyes, which are narrowed, beady. It always seems odd to me when she does that. Blue is such a gentle color. You wouldn't think those gentle-colored eyes could get so small and mean. They don't seem capable of that until she is angry. She doesn't let anger seep into any other part of her body. The rest of her looks relaxed and soft, leaning against the doorframe of her bathroom, her posture tall but comfortable. The bathroom light casts a soft glow through her nightgown, which is a painful, angelic white.

"It's my body, Mom," I tell her as I stop my shaking knee with my hand. I force myself to continue to look at her. I want her to see me as an equal, a woman, with the same parts as her—life-carrying, life-giving parts.

But my mother's eyes shove at me, like they want to push me out of my woman's body.

I don't want her to look at me any more.

I don't want to be me in my body any more.

I feel my breath whoosh out of me as her eyes shove, shove, *shove* at me and suddenly I fall, I fall out of my body and I float away, up and away. I hover somewhere above it, looking down at a seventeen-year-old girl, with straight brown hair, athletic, firm body, clear skin.

That's me? I seem so young, so untouched, so perfect.

But I'm not.

I watch from above as my mom clutches her own body, wrapping her golden-tan, firm arms around her golden-tan, firm tummy. Her mouth is moving but I don't make out the words.

My mother. She grew me in her body. She carried me, nursed me, held me.

I fall back into my body. Inside it I feel clunky, thick.

"…you have your entire future, your entire life depending on this decision. Lilith, don't be stupid, don't be impulsive."

"There's nothing impulsive about having a baby. An abortion is impulsive, Mom."

"Blowing away your future, Lilith, is impulsive. You see that, don't you?"

She always says *you see that, don't you?* To me, to Dad, to her clients.

"Don't do this to yourself. If you go through with this, you will be making a huge mistake."

"No, not a mistake. This is a *gift*." My voice is strong, stronger than my heart, my brain.

"No, don't kid yourself, Lilith. This was nothing but an *accident*. A gift is something thought out, something intentionally given. Don't kid yourself. This is nothing but an accident." She corrects me like I spelled something wrong.

Fury erupts from my belly and shoots up my body like fire. "How can you call a baby an accident? My baby! Your grandchild!" I wring my hands together.

She's in front of me now, glaring down, brown arms folded, white nightgown billowing.

"Now listen to me, young lady. I will not be a grandmother. There will be no grandchild, not now, not for a long, long time." She points a finger at me, the nail red and shiny. Her brown and white and red overwhelm me.

I can feel the tears start. I try to swallow them but instead make a whimpering noise. Nothing can stop the sobs.

Mom lets the sound fill the room, and then she lays a cool smooth hand on the top of my head, the side of my wet cheek. She tilts my chin up and her expression is soft, cotton-like. It's amazing how she can go from monster to angel so quickly.

"Honey, listen to me. It was a mistake, a mistake that can be easily fixed."

I close my eyes and let her hold my chin a bit longer.

We are silent.

In the silence I feel a stirring in my belly. I picture the inside of my body; I see Her growing. The stirring inside becomes a tornado, a whirling ball of energy that lifts me up, lifts my hand up.

"No," I say as I smack her hand off my chin.

Her eyes widen, and her mouth forms a circle of surprise.

I leap up and shake a nail-bitten finger right under her nose.

"You can't tell me what to do. You can't make me kill her!"

My mother takes a step back.

"What are you going to do, Mom? What are you and Dad and Adam going to do?" She puts her hand over her mouth and shakes her head. Her nightgown is flat against her body. She looks smaller, skinnier, weaker to me. Her brown skin looks like an overdone pancake, and her red nails are like shiny plastic.

"Are you going to force me? Tie me up? Drag me screaming and yelling to the abortion clinic? Or will you just kick me out? How will that look, Mom? How will it look to your friends, the gossips at Temple, your colleagues, when you send me away or kick me out?"

Now *she* won't look at *me*.

* * *

"Lil?"

The room is dark. I can't see Adam, but I know the hand brushing my cheek—large, warm, gentle. I know his aftershave. Spicy. Musky.

"I just wanted to see if you were okay."

My eyes adjust. Adam's glasses gleam in the moonlight that streams though my bedroom window. It must be late. How did he get in?

"I called your parents, told them I had to come over."

Even when Adam feels desperate, he is responsible.

"I was such a shit." He strokes my cheek. I can feel my heart and the tiny tornado in my belly. "Listen, I know what we should do."

My heart stops and the tornado spins away.

He sits down on the bed and strokes my hair. "I want you to have our baby."

"What?"

"Yeah. I'm scared, and I was freaked when you told me, but I get it Lil, I get it."

I try to sit up, but my body is heavy and achy. I let myself melt into Adam's hands, which are roaming all over me now.

He bends down and kisses my flat belly. "I watched this show, on TLC–" His voice catches. "After you hung up on me, I was all freaked out and I turned on the TV and man, there it was."

"The Baby Story?"

"A Baby Story, Lil. Like a friggin' sign from G-d or something."

I can see his smile clearly through the dark. I want to kiss him. I had to watch that show for my child development class—a class I wound up in by accident. I couldn't get Sociology, which is the class where they have an abortion debate. My heart and belly hum. I grab his face and kiss him all over.

"This is going to be hard, Lil."

I am kissing and nodding. "I know, I know." My voice soothes.

"You'll have to take time off school to go somewhere and have the baby, but then we'll find the perfect family for it. I Googled adoption agencies–"

I stop kissing. I stop breathing.

He cups my face in his hands. His brown eyes are satiny in the moonlight. "And you know what? I don't care what my parents say, or your parents. For the first time, they are wrong. It's wrong to kill this baby–"

I push his hands off my face. "It's wrong to give up this baby, too!"

He sighs and stands up. "Look, your parents think I am in here setting up a time to take you to the abortion." He puts his hand up. "But I'm not."

I cross my arms and look up at him. "But you still want me to get rid of her."

He looks confused, sad, like a puppy that's been tricked. "I thought no abortion meant–"

"Adam, I want this baby. She is mine." I jump out of bed and swipe at my flying hair. "I am going to raise her."

The silence that falls is so loud, like a judge's gravel.

Now he's a puppy that's been kicked. "How?" he whispers, tears darting from the corners of his eyes.

I want to reach for his hand but I don't. I just clasp mine together. "You mean how are *we* going to do this."

His eyes drop to my belly. He grabs my hands and then together with his, he puts all the hands on my belly.

"We made a mistake," he whispers, still looking at my belly.

"It's too late to be a mistake, Adam."

He begins to cry. He drops to his knees and puts his head to my belly. The tornado stirs. I know he can feel it.

"It's warm," he murmurs. "The baby is there. She's tiny."

I resist soothing Adam with my fingers in his hair. I don't want to soothe him. Instead I say, "You said 'she.'"

"I did." He straightens up and wipes his eyes. "I did."

He sighs, pushes his glasses up on to his forehead, and rises to his feet. Rubs his cheeks, mouth, and eyes. The sigh continues to flow through his body. I sit back on the bed and curl my knees up to my chin and lean against the headboard, watching him. The small dark mole on his forearm, the trace of a vein on his neck pulsing, the honey color of his skin. I know his body as well as my own. This realization makes this baby even more important—I will know all of her, and yet she will be completely new. Her skin, her moles, her veins, will not be mine or Adam's but her own.

I am aware of my heart beating again, and I grip the sheets with both hands and lean forward, my knee pushes into Adam's thigh. "I want to keep this baby. I *need* to. I *have* to." I twist the sheets. "It's primal. I can't put words to it." The sheets feel wet in my hands. I twist again. "I don't know... I don't know... It's like I am being born or maybe being reborn...."

Adam's mouth hangs open—soft, pillowy. Vulnerable. His eyes shoot back and forth, searching my face like a map, trying to find the right destination, trying to find where he wants to be or maybe where he is.

He touches my knee with his fingertips. "But this baby isn't you."

"She is growing in me. She's part of me right now." I slow my breath down, feel my chest rise and fall and the beats of my heart slow down. "She's part of both of us."

He takes my hand, and his eyes relax, the pupils stop shifting. He is thinking, deciding.

"And when she comes out, the moment she comes out, I am reborn, Adam, and so are you. We are no longer the people we've always been. We're parents. We're more than just who we are now."

He doesn't have to speak. I see his answer on his face. So I sit back and look out the window next to my bed. The stars are dots of brilliance, the moon a yellow slice, and the sky a sheet of velvet. Calm, reliable. Stars, the moon, the midnight sky, every night reliable, no matter what.

He brushes his lips across my forehead.

I listen to the click of the door after he shuts it.

Confirmation
by Tracy Woelfel

Red-gold sunset light streamed sideways through the broad windows of the airport terminal, lending nostalgic warmth to the advertisements for hotels and car rentals. At the security gate, those who were just beginning their travels stood in queue while weary but satisfied travelers emerged from the cordoned hallway. The arrivals scattered as they reached the lobby, some into joyful reunions, some glancing up at the signs for baggage claim and parking.

A bank of screens listed arrivals and departures in ever-shifting order. People paused to glance for familiar numbers. Among them stood a man who looked to be in his late thirties, but for the threads of grey dulling his dark hair and the exhaustion deepening the lines of his face. He reached into the pocket of his crumpled suit for a pack of cigarettes. His hand stilled, as if he'd suddenly remembered there was no smoking in airports. He sighed and ran his hand through hair that was in dire need of a trim.

She moved to his side, standing companionably close but looking at the screens. "Jude," she said softly.

"Thecla."

The exchange of names served as sufficient greeting. Too much conversation might draw attention. The contrast between them was notable enough. His suit was rumpled, but it was at least a suit. She wore faded jeans with a denim jacket faded nearly white. She looked her age—middling twenties—and her smooth chestnut hair had been disciplined into a short, neat braid.

"Is he in yet?" she asked, not looking at Jude.

"On the ground." He cast a look toward the arrival gate.

They drifted closer to the clumps of people who searched for familiar faces among the latest surge of deplaning travelers.

"Where's Peter? Shouldn't he meet the new kid?"

"He's not feeling well today." Jude said. He caught her sharp look and hastily added, "We're behind in the count. S3's flagship had trouble and they're being towed to dock. We're just lucky we still have contact with them and S2. We'll do what we can to catch up."

"Hell of a day to call in sick."

Jude shrugged, but his phone rang before he could comment. He flipped it open and grunted something noncommittal. He waited a moment for the call transfer to come through, then demanded, "Where are you?"

"Um...I'm here. I don't see anyone."

Tecla heard the response in stereo—coming softly from Jude's phone, and from a new arrival, a kid with dusty blond hair and a cell phone clamped to one ear. He looked like a student returning to college, complete with backpack and duffle bag. In addition to looking much too young, he also looked lost and—judging from the way he was openly searching the crowd—completely clueless.

"Walk to the nearest Arrival/Departure screens," Jude instructed.

Now the kid's searching look had an air of purpose to it. He spotted the board Thecla and Jude had been watching and walked past them to the listed screen. And there his intent ended, replaced by the default confused search. Jude and Thecla exchanged a wry glance. The kid was about as subtle as an announcement over the PA system.

Jude lowered the phone and turned to Thecla. "I'll get the car. We'd better get him out of here before he holds up a sign."

With a sigh, Thecla walked over to the kid and extended her hand. She received a blank stare until Jude instructed the kid to be polite and shake her hand already. He did as he was told, then shut his phone—which emitted the steady hum of a dial tone—and tucked it into his pocket.

"How was your flight?" Not that she cared, but that's what people said in airports.

"Fine," he said. "I'm a little hungry, though. Is there any place to eat around here?"

"Probably, but we're running behind." A grim smile thinned her lips. "And trust me, you don't want to eat on your first night out."

* * *

Thecla slid into the passenger seat of Jude's car and kicked aside a crumpled fast-food bag to make room for her feet. She twisted around to regard the rookie. "How much do you know about the Bible? Enough to pick out an alias?"

At least the kid knew better than to reply to a rhetorical question. It wasn't until the parking fee had been paid that he answered the real question. "I'll try Matthew."

"Okay, Matthew." With effort, Thecla kept her tone coolly professional. "Forget everything that happened before you got off that plane. You have no name from before, no family from before, no friends, no hometown. You are here because you have no ties to be severed. You're going to see and do horrible things, and it will all be for the good of others. Tell me what you know about S1."

He looked a little overwhelmed by the brief lecture, but his answer came quickly enough: "They hunt demons."

"*We* hunt *Lilim*," Thecla corrected. She gestured for him to continue. He didn't.

Jude glanced at him through the rearview mirror. "How did you come to be in S1? Everyone has a story they're dying to tell when they start. Might as well get yours out of the way."

Matthew shrugged. "A hooker tried to hijack my car, and two S1 agents dragged her back out. When she started growing wings, I jumped in to help them. We wound up talking afterwards. I joined S1."

Jude and Thecla exchanged a quick, speaking glance. No one spoke lightly about their first incident so soon after it, except for those unbalanced few S1 accidentally recruited every now and then.

"How long ago?" Thecla asked.

Matthew bowed his head in embarrassment. "Almost a year. I didn't... I had to think about it, midway through the training."

Thecla couldn't decide whether that was good news or bad. She shrugged, flipped open her phone, and dialed the same number Matthew had dialed in the airport.

"Where's our first?"

She listened attentively and snapped the phone shut. "Confirmed at Johnson Medical Center. Room 325 West. S2 will be waiting."

Jude nodded and pulled onto the highway. "We'll see if they can line up another one after this. We'll call at location."

She gave him a sharp look. "What's the count?"

"Thirty-seven."

Thecla slumped back in the seat. "So you were understating when you said we were behind. What's wrong with the East? They're better than that."

Jude just shrugged and shook his head.

"What's the count?" asked Matthew. "I mean, besides being thirty-seven. What I mean is—"

"We get it," Thecla broke in. "A hundred Lilim a day, starting at sunset in the holy city."

"Usually S3 has a good start on it before sunset here," Jude said. All three of them glanced out the windows at the brilliant last traces of sunset. "And Europe's S1 usually does pretty well."

"What's S3?"

"S1 you know—patrolling and purging. S2 is eyes and informers. They find Lilim for us. Sometimes they will contact us in an emergency. Sometimes, like today, we contact them if we're desperate for the count. S3 isn't something you hear about during training. They connect us all, in addition to doing their own hunting. They're at sea, deep undercover. Merchant ships, navy, coast guard, even pleasure cruises. They usually pull in half the count with their fishing, you should pardon the expression."

Matthew blinked in silent amazement. "Is there anything else I don't know?" he asked as Jude pulled up in front of the hospital.

Thecla's smile held no amusement whatsoever. "Looks like we're about to find out."

* * *

To Matthew's surprise, Jude made no move to leave the car. Instead, he tapped out a cigarette and pulled a lighter from his pocket.

"Don't smoke in the car," Thecla reminded absently as she unbuckled herself. "Come on, Matthew."

She moved fast. Matthew had to hurry to keep stride. Just before they passed through the automatic sliding door, he glanced back. Jude was leaning against the car, holding the cigarette idly. There wasn't time to see if he was actually using it or just letting it burn.

"Everyone has a story," Thecla said. "Jude's story is that his child died at three days old."

Matthew didn't know what to say to this, so he didn't try. Thecla wouldn't have heard him, anyway, since she was back on the phone, telling someone that they were on location.

Thecla walked through the hospital as if she owned it. She led him through mostly-empty halls and up a back stairwell. They emerged from the stairwell into a quiet institutional hallway. Clean, seamless white tile floor gleamed underfoot. She paused, tipped her chin toward a direction sign.

"Jude still can't bring himself to get revenge on her level."

Matthew glanced at the sign. *Maternity*. So that's why Jude was sitting this one out.

Understanding swiftly gave way to horror. What sort of creature had been born? He shuddered as Thecla knocked on the door to room 325, looking calm and professional.

The door opened, and a short, mousy woman in a doctor's coat admitted them to the small recovery room. The new mother slept peacefully in the railing-bound hospital bed, an IV dripping steadily into her arm as small machines hummed. Beside the bed stood a tiny crib in which slept a swaddled child. The only other furniture in the room was a chair that rocked gently. Obviously the S2 doctor had been sitting there, watching the baby as she waited. She closed the door behind them now.

"Both are sedated. The mother is tainted. The infant…" The doctor trailed off and shook her head. Thecla nodded, obviously understanding.

The only thing that was immediately apparent to Matthew was that the baby had beautiful black and curly hair. It looked like a perfectly healthy, normal baby to him.

Thecla reached into the crib and gently turned the infant. She pulled back the blanket to show two extra folds of skin growing from the infant's back.

Matthew recoiled, startled by the deformity.

"If the birth has dark hair and wings, the mother is unclean," Thecla recited. "This child is one of the Lilim."

She turned the infant on its back once more, then carefully pinched its tiny nose and held its mouth shut. Aside from one sleepy, sedated twitch, the baby gave no struggle.

Thecla straightened and leveled a grim look at Matthew. "If you're going to be sick, get it out of the way now. We have a long night before us."

Matthew shook his head dazedly, still staring at the baby as he tried to reconcile his ideas of slaying demons with suffocating newborn infants. "I'm fine."

Thecla responded with an unconvinced snort and turned to the doctor. "It's done. What of the mother?"

"Tainted, as I said. She has already had an emergency operation and will have no further children. It remains to be seen if she will be a target for you one day."

Thecla studied the sleeping woman, her face thoughtful. For a moment, Matthew could almost hear the words "thirty-nine" and "pre-emptive strike." She shook her head slowly, then strode to the door.

Matthew fought down a wave of nausea and followed. He'd heard that dealing with demons had risks beyond the danger to life and limb. Already, he was starting to understand what that meant.

* * *

The sky was dark when Thecla and Matthew returned to the car. She was already flipping open the phone and dialing as she buckled in.

"Confirmed down," she told S3. "What's the count?"

"Forty two."

"Looking better then. Where's our next?"

"2230 Sylvan Boulevard. Unconfirmed."

Thecla lifted the phone away and scowled at it, then clapped it back to her ear. "S2 waiting?"

"S2 waiting."

She nodded to Jude, trying not to notice that his face was as ashen as the kid's had been upstairs. He crushed a cigarette beneath his foot and dropped into the driver's seat. Several miles down the road, she broke the silence. "The best they can manage is an unconfirmed. You're taking the kid in on this one."

"But if it hasn't been confirmed..." Matthew protested weakly.

Jude glanced back at him through the mirror. "On-site decisions are tough, yeah, but fortunately they're not common. Tomorrow you'll ride with Peter, so you can meet the whole S1 presence here and get a feel for normal days."

"If Peter is feeling well tomorrow," Thecla reminded. "And if Matthew makes it through tonight."

"Did I do something wrong?" Matthew asked tentatively.

Thecla didn't answer, instead staring out the window at passing streets and lights.

* * * *

Sylvan Boulevard was in the "better part of town," but Jude found it claustrophobic. Houses were grand, divided only by narrow spaces made narrower still by grand old trees emerging from the strip between the sidewalks and road. The branches interlaced over the road itself, blocking view of the sky and holding the light of the few streetlamps underneath. What grass survived was neatly manicured, but the strip was barely wide enough for two people to stand side by side. Two lines of parallel-parked cars reduced the road to one lane and promised vengeance of a judicial nature should the slightest scratch appear on these expensive models.

Jude pulled into an open spot at 2230, between two cars with bumpers that cost more than his entire car had been worth new.

The kid was looking around, his expression puzzled. Obviously this wasn't the sort of place he expected to find demons.

"I'll watch the door," Thecla volunteered, adding to the reasons for her staying with the car. Jude headed for the door, motioning for Matthew to follow.

"Did I do something wrong back there?" Matthew asked quietly as they waited for someone to answer their knock.

"Thecla? No, she just hates the unconfirmed ones." Jude took out another cigarette, considered it for a moment, then stuck it back into his pocket unlit. "Don't let her get to you. She's one of the most dedicated S1's you'll ever meet, but she's only out for Lilim. Not knowing is just a waste of her time."

"What's her story?"

"You'd have to ask her. Or Peter. I transferred in a couple years back."

The door opened. The man who answered had gone grey artistically—just around the temples—and the dark suit he wore was a few rungs up the fashion ladder from Jude's. The man waved them in and closed the door.

"Suspected Lilim?" Jude prompted.

The S2 butler tipped his head towards the staircase. "Three weeks ago the teenaged daughter's personality changed. She went from a model student to promiscuous delinquent."

Matthew's jaw dropped. "That sounded like teenage hormones, not demonic possession."

Jude quelled him with a sharp glance. "Are we talking about your observations of this girl, or something a little more personal?" he asked bluntly.

The butler shifted uncomfortably. "She...offered. I turned her down, of course."

With a sigh, Jude looked up the stairs. "About three weeks ago, did she receive or purchase a mirror? Secondhand or antique, perhaps?"

"I have not been able to find one."

"Oh, Sam!" The singsong call drifted down the upstairs hall. "Get the car ready so we can go!"

"I am still working, as you know," the butler called back.

A girl dressed in club attire started down the stairs. Her top was a sequined dragonfly laced over her chest, accompanied by a short black skirt and knee-high boots. Between the bangles and body glitter, she sparkled.

Her eyes skimmed over Jude and settled on Matthew. "Oh, we have guests!"

"Keep her here," Jude told Matthew in a low voice. He looked to the butler. "Sam, I hate to be rude, but could you show me to a washroom?"

As they passed her on the stairs, Jude made brief eye contact, broken as she looked down at Matthew and grinned.

The butler showed Jude not to the requested bathroom, but to the girl's bedroom. The cluttered confusion testified to the abrupt shift in its occupant's tastes. The unmade bed had both a pastel comforter and scattered flashy clothes. A bookshelf held textbooks, trinkets, stuffed animals, and a row of voodoo dolls studded with pins. On the walls, framed photographs showed family, friends, pets, and a shy, well-dressed girl who never seemed to be looking at the camera.

Jude started rifling through the drawers in search of anything that might indicate this was something other than a teenage phase. No diaries, no dark poetry. There was a hand mirror on the vanity and a full-length mirror on the door to her personal bathroom, but neither looked ominous.

"I wish we had a week more to watch her," Sam muttered.

Jude looked up. "Some days I agree with Thecla about the unconfirmed."

Sam gave a nod and started on the closet. Jude's phone rang. He hit the mute button quickly, not wanting to alert the girl to the search, then almost dropped it when he recognized the number. "Peter, is everything all right?"

"Peter is here," responded a distinctly female voice—a voice that was smooth, calm, and entirely unmistakable. "And everything is as it should be."

She began to hum a lullaby.

The last his son had ever heard.

For a moment Jude stood frozen by memory and grief. Then he dropped the hand mirror and bolted from the room. Sam said...something; Jude wasn't paying attention. He thundered down the stairs, drawing alarmed looks from Matthew and the girl who was draped over him. He seized Matthew's arm and dragged him away as the girl protested.

*　*　*

Thecla flipped her phone open and checked the time again. She knew better than to call Jude to ask how it was going, but she was tempted. Better to stay in the car than be forced to decide whether she was looking at a human or a Lili. Sometimes the line was uncomfortably narrow, and if S2 couldn't figure it out, who could?

She shoved the phone into her pocket, only to pull out a pocketknife from another and begin the fidgeting process as before.

Before she could flick it open, Jude bolted from the house. He nearly fell over the hood in passing, and all but threw himself into the car.

"Lili or human?" she demanded as Jude roughly jockeyed the car out of parallel parking, not waiting for Matthew to shut the door, much less buckle in. He ignored her and peeled into the street.

Worried now, Thecla demanded, "Jude, did you kill a human?"

"Peter," Jude stated, as if the name was sufficient answer. He whipped the car around a corner, tires squealing. Thecla cast a sideways glare at him. This was not professional, no matter what had happened to Peter.

"It's already too late," she pointed out. "If you don't slow down, someone else could die."

He merely scowled and accelerated. Thecla gave up and braced herself for the ride ahead. To his credit, Matthew didn't ask a bunch of questions. Maybe there was some hope for the kid, after all.

* * *

They pulled into a neighborhood of modest older houses with long-established, overgrown landscaping.

Thecla frowned. Peter didn't own or rent a house. Why would he be here, especially when he was supposed to be home sick?

Before she could raise either point, Jude pulled sharply into a driveway and slammed the car into park. Then he was gone, leaving the headlights on and the motor running. Thecla cursed under her breath as she followed.

Jude burst through the front door and down the entry hall, moving like a man who knew the house well. The family pictures lining the hall were obscured by cracked glass. The television and several pictures in the living room were also shattered, but Thecla would see no further damage. A woman lay on the couch, apparently oblivious to the shattered glass around her. Jude went to her immediately, checking her breathing and pulse. Only then did Thecla notice the prescription bottle on the end table, along with a half-empty glass of water.

There was no sign of Peter. Thecla returned to the hall as Matthew cautiously entered, his face tight with dread. She jerked her head, indicating that he should follow her up the stairs.

She paused at the door of a bathroom, staring in disbelief as her suspicions jelled into certainty. There was no mirror, not even here.

A faint sound drew her attention down the hall, to the one room with the door left open. Thecla crept closer. Although the room was in shambles, it had unmistakably been a nursery. Peter sat on the floor, leaning against one wall. His eyes were open and sightless. How he had died was not immediately apparent, but his phone was on the floor beyond his fingertips.

And standing next to the window was a woman, tall and curvy, with black ringlets of hair dangling to her waist. Her wings were even darker than her hair.

"Lilith," Thecla murmured, her voice barely a whisper.

The winged woman turned at her name. Her eyes passed over Thecla and Matthew and settled on something beyond. She smiled.

"He has your eyes, Jude," the mother of Lilim observed.

Jude sagged against the door frame. "But how? You have no power over him. I took the precautions…"

Lilith's smile turned mocking as she lifted a small bronze medallion. "You don't even remember their names, do you? The three I bargained with for my life and freedom." She tossed the ward aside. "They didn't stop me then, and you cannot stop me now, any more than your comrade-in-arms could."

Thecla turned away from the anguish on Jude's face. It was easier to face Lilith.

"Let my son go," Jude begged.

"Oh, I plan to."

Something in her tone made Thecla's flesh crawl. With narrowed eyes, she watched Lilith walk to Jude and place the baby in his arms.

"I have not harmed him," the demon said, her voice as soothing as a lullaby. "He will live, and thrive, and his daughters will be blessed with beautiful dark curls."

She turned to Thecla, and her smile curved into the shape of pure evil. Then she was gone. A small, dark owl winged out of the broken window and out into the night.

"Thank god," Jude murmured over and over as hugged the sleeping infant.

Thecla laid a hand on his shoulder. "Give me the child, Jude."

Realization hit him then. For a moment he stood very still, then he twisted sharply away from her. "He's my son!"

"He *was* your son," she snapped back. "Now he's unclean at best."

"Unconfirmed!"

"Lilith herself told us." Thecla caught Matthew's eye and glanced into the hall. The kid was sheet white, but he understood her signal and moved out of view of the doorway. When he got out his cell phone, Thecla stepped into the room.

As she'd expected, Jude pulled a handgun from the back of his belt. Thecla narrowed her eyes at gun and wielder. "What's your plan, Jude? Are you going to kill me? You'll have to shoot Matthew, too. And if you do, S3 will send a new S1 unit here. If you run, S2 will find you. No matter what, the child will die."

The handgun was trembling badly. Jude attempted to readjust his grip without releasing his son. Thecla took another step forward.

* * *

Matthew was wrapping up his panicked call to the S3 number when he heard the gunshot. He spun back toward the nursery, fully expecting Jude to emerge and shoot him as well. But after a few terror-frozen moments, Thecla emerged, holding the still-sleeping infant.

"There are very few guarantees in S1," she said quietly, "but understand this: None of us will see old age, and none of us will ever raise a child."

She shifted her hands. In a few failed breaths, the child would never wake. When it was finished, she set the babe next to his sleep-medicated mother. The poor woman was going to awaken to a nightmare.

Matthew swallowed hard. "Jude?"

"Pretty sure he's gone. Go look, if you think you can handle it."

* * *

The kid thought he could. Thecla went outside. She leaned against the porch railing and stared at the dark sky. Less than a minute passed before Matthew stumbled out and vomited into the bushes.

She resumed her study of the sky and waited for him to finish. It didn't take him as long as some. He was trembling when he stood, but he looked as if he was holding together.

"The first time I saw Lilith, I was pregnant. She tore the baby out of me and tainted it. I survived, the baby didn't. The attack left me sterile, which, all things considered, is a twisted sort of blessing. That's my story."

She let that sink in as she pulled out her phone to report. "Jude and Peter are dead. We encountered Lilith, and we got an unnoted male carrier." She gave them the details and the address. "Unless there's an emergency, we're done for the night."

Thecla glanced at Matthew, expecting to see relief. But the kid shook his head and held up Jude's keys. Thecla noted his grim set to his baby-face jaw and the look in his eyes, and approved both. She turned back to the phone.

"What's the count?"

A Day at the Fair
By Clint Collins

Two pairs of feminine eyes scanned the crowd, all but hidden by hooded windbreakers and the Lilith Fair hats purchased at a Village booth.

"Do you think she will come?"

"Names have power," said the other. "These events bear her name. And some of the Daughters have reported sightings."

Her companion nodded. Indeed, there had been reliable reports the goddess had been seen swaying with the crowd at past Lilith Fairs. She certainly wasn't easy to miss, not with that long cape of auburn hair.

"This could be the last Fair," she continued, watching with disinterest as the Dixie Chicks launched into "I Can Love You Better" on the main stage. "And we know this is the last show on the tour. This may be our best chance for a long time."

The two angels exchanged a glance of mutual, deadly intent. In their backpacks each carried a knife with a wavy, serpentine blade, a shape recalling the trickster of Eden. Getting the weapons through security inspections at the gate had been easy, as Eve had made the knives invisible to the eyes of men.

As the Indigo Girls and Sheryl Crow came and went to thunderous applause, the two angels moved among the crowds in Edmonton's Commonwealth Stadium. Despite the chilly, lingering rain on this last day of August, the crowds were sizable. Lilith could be anywhere, anyone.

They decided to do another pass through the Lilith Village, a cluster of booths and stands offering everything from handmade jewelry to artist CDs to tee shirts. They stopped to watch a woman arrange boxes of blueberries on tables protected from the rain by a wide green canvas awning. The tee shirt stretched tautly over her ample bosom read "Goddess Orchards."

"I don't recall seeing her here before," said one of the assassins, shrugging off her backpack.

"No, someone else was here earlier. She's new."

They edged in for a closer look. As if obliging them, the woman stepped out from behind her table. Long auburn hair fell like autumn sunlight to ankles sporting owl tattoos.

The angel known as Arkalia pushed back her hood. "The goddess of storms cannot prevent rain on her namesake festival? How ironic."

Lilith's silver eyes met angelic blue. "Even the Daughters of Eve should know what every garden needs from time to time." She cocked her head slightly. "And speaking of Eve, when will my old friend abandon this senseless pursuit?"

The angel shook her head. "Some transgressions are not easily forgiven, Lilith."

With a slight wave of her hand, the goddess quelled a breeze threatening to scatter the brochures on her table. "Eve still claims I urged the Serpent to deceive her?" She let loose with a lusty laugh. "I was banished to the desert long before then. When she was talking to snakes, I was consorting with demons in their caves. I recommend it." Her smile turned sly. "Still virgins, girls?"

The angels frowned and pressed unkissed lips tightly together.

The goddess's smile faded, and her impressive bosom rose and fell with a heavy sigh. "Look, I know Adam, and I'm sure he blamed that silly bitch for the Fall. Eve had to pass the blame along to someone, am I right?"

The angels shifted uneasily as some concertgoers splashed up to the booth and rushed away with colorful cartons of various organically grown berries. Sarah MacLachlan was to be onstage at ten, only a few minutes away.

Lilith tossed the angels a couple of strawberries. "These are really good this year."

Arkalia batted hers away into the mud, but the other angel, Serenissima, stained her lips crimson with a single bite before catching a glare of disapproval and dropping the bleeding fruit.

"But the very best from my orchard are these." She extended a gleaming, red-skinned apple.

The angels stepped back. Certain curses still lingered, and apples and snakes were to be avoided.

Lilith took a crunching bite. She chewed as she regarded the rain glistening on the angels' hats and windbreakers. "You two wearing Lilith gear? Now *that's* irony."

Arkalia responded with a snarl and a drawn blade. Lilith merely motioned toward the crowd. "The Lilim—remember them?—are out there dispensing some very expensive free love." She touched the owl pendant at her throat. In response, several women among the throngs pushed away from the men in their grasp and turned silver eyes toward the angelic assassins.

"Better be on your way, girls. They remember the days in Mesopotamia, when you came down in flocks to attack my temples. But we are simple folk now. We keep a low profile and tend to our own paradise. I advise you to do the same."

The angels looked nervously around. With hurried, sidelong glances they made their way to the nearest exit and out of the Fair.

Taking another bite of the apple, Lilith turned toward the main stage. The music began, and the goddess smiled in recognition. All of the succubi knew all the words to this one. "Possession" was every demon's favorite song.

Man-Underground
by Kate Riedel

The night wind kept me awake, but if I didn't sleep, neither did I dream.

At dawn I put on my boots, rolled up my sleeping bag, strapped it and my toolbox onto my bike, slung on my backpack, and wheeled the bike onto the footpath. I knew where there were a couple of benches that got the sun this time of morning.

One of them was already occupied.

I didn't need both.

I propped my bike against the unoccupied bench, unslung my pack and dropped to the seat, stretched my legs out in front and my arms along the back, tilted back my head and closed my eyes.

"You look as if you've had a tough ride."

I opened my eyes. The woman on the other bench wore a yellow sweater that set off dark hair, swept back and pinned up. Dark green slacks. She looked forty, maybe. Or maybe not.

She expected an answer.

"Tough night," I said. "Got kicked out of my room."

Now why did I tell her that? Next thing I'd be whining for spare change.

"At least you have transportation," she said, indicating the bike. "And a trade?" she added, noting the toolbox. "What kind of work do you do?"

"Handyman. Repairs. Gardening, if you can supply the tools. Carpentry. Basic plumbing and wiring, good enough to pass inspection."

She pulled a little notebook and a pen out of her bag, and began to write. "You do garden work?" She tore the sheet out of her notebook and handed it to me.

Her physical age might have been hard to pin down, but those eyes were old. So had my mother's been.

"I've just moved in at this address," she went on. "I need a nice garden and patio put in, in time for…an event. I have all the tools you'll need. There's a room over the garage. Do you know where this address is?"

I looked at the paper. "I should. I grew up a couple of streets over. So what do you pay?" If she thought I was going to do it for nooky….

She named an amount that was neither nooky nor peanuts. "Are you interested?"

"Maybe. There's a couple other things I might have going for me." There weren't.

"Think about it."

"Paid in cash?" I asked.

"Cash," she said, turning to go.

"Wait," I said. "Any kids?"

She turned and looked at me. Those eyes might have spied on Adam and Eve.

"No. No kids."

"Good. I hate kids."

"I know," she said. "So do I."

* * *

Our old house had been re-sided, a garage attached, and a second story built over all. There was a solid-looking tricycle on the front porch, and a kiddy-car, and one of those heavy molded-plastic wagons filled with smiley-face balls and hockey sticks and so forth. Far cry from the balloon-tire bike and beat-up tin wagon Jimmy and I'd had. What Mom made after Dad died hadn't stretched to new toys.

A woman was watching me from the house across the street, and I remembered I was no longer Mrs. Daugherty's nice, hard-working boy, ready to shovel walks and clean gutters and rake lawns to help Mom stretch the grocery money. I was a Suspicious Character.

I rode on. As I turned the corner I nearly ran into a kid, about ten years old, on his skateboard. "Ya fuckin' asshole!" he yelled after me.

"Stay on the sidewalk and watch your mouth, you little shit," I yelled back.

The address she'd given me was the kind of house you'd expect to find in a working class neighborhood, solid brick bungalow, not tarted up like my mother's was now. She was waiting outside.

She led me through a narrow gate that connected house and garage, into the long back yard, isolated by the garage on one side, and by a fence of weathered planks that was well over regulation height on the other two. I could just see, over the back, the tops of walls that were probably commercial buildings backed onto an alley. Weeds choked every inch of the place. She opened a door in the side of the garage and turned on the lights. There was no car, just a collection of garden tools.

"Are these suitable?" she asked.

"Just fine," I said.

She indicated a flight of stairs, not much more than a ladder with an open trap door at the top, and I climbed through into a loft with a window at either end, bed, table and chair, space heater, and a walled-off corner with toilet, wash basin and shower.

"It's fine," I said, leaving my pack and coming back down.

She handed me some bills. "An advance," she said, and turned to go.

"Just a minute, Ms...."

"Ardat," she said.

"All right, Ms. Ardat. Don't you want to know my name?"

"If you want," she said with a shrug.

"Denis Daugherty," I said. I felt as if I was throwing down a challenge, but I wasn't sure what the challenge was.

* * *

Next morning I began battling garlic mustard, nightshade, henbane, and man-underground, as the older folks call the white-flowered perennial morning glory that strangles every other plant it touches; all the rank-smelling weeds that are the hardest to get out and keep out. But there had once been roses—I could see yellow-green leaves struggling through thorns.

And there was a nice little apple tree. I whacked my way through to unwind the nightshade strangling it. The nightshade left a foul smell on my hands.

The tree had grown out of another, broken off some years ago. Pale dead-man's fingers grew from the old tree's roots; the fungus would darken to black stubs later in the summer.

An apple tree...roses...

"You're up early," she said behind me.

She wore yellow slacks today, and a leaf-green top.

"I like to earn my keep, Ms. Ardat," I said. "Do you want the apple tree and the roses left?"

"Of course," she said. "They remind me of old times."

Lots of yards have apple trees and roses.

I felt someone behind me, elbow-height. "I thought you said you didn't have kids," I said. Or started to say, for when I looked, there was no one there.

I thought she smiled, but I couldn't be sure.

"Remember, I have a deadline," she said.

But before I could ask when, she walked away.

I worked until the sun hit the top of the sky, then I went for lunch. I avoided the old greasy spoons I remembered from when I was a kid and chose a new, anonymous fast-food franchise.

I'd finished and was stacking the containers to dump in the trash when a hand dropped on my shoulder.

"Denis Daugherty, by God!"

The older man plopped himself and his cup of coffee down at my table. "Denis! Haven't seen you since...since..."

I didn't say anything.

"You remember me. Dave? Dave Johnson. I used to go out with your mother. How ya doin'? How's your mom?"

"Dead," I said.

I crumpled the food containers so I wouldn't crumple his face, and dropped them in the trash as I walked out.

The ground I'd cleared that morning was a yellowish mess of cut and broken stalks. Already, in just a few hours, the man-underground was putting up new tendrils. Again I felt someone standing behind me. Again, there was no one there.

I began to rake up the trash. The tines of the rake caught on small objects, like tiny bones. Not bones—bleached-out bits of plastic. Toy soldiers, the kind you could buy by the bag-full. Jimmy had had some—I never found out where he'd got them. This soldier knelt with his gun braced against his dirt-crusted shoulder. I dropped it into my pocket and picked up another, and another. The lost patrol.

I went back to weeding.

"Leave that—it will have big white trumpet flowers."

"It's jimson weed, Ms. Ardat."

"It's datura." She walked away. I shrugged and left it.

That evening, feeling through my pockets for change for supper, I found the toy soldiers and set them up on the windowsill. There were half a dozen, most missing heads or limbs—probably not enough plastic for the molds. A lot of Jimmy's had been incomplete. Probably some other kid had sorted the incomplete ones out of his bag and given them to Jimmy.

For supper I bought some stuff at a deli and ate in a nearby park, as far away as possible from a bunch of kids practicing stunts on their skateboards, including the little creep I'd nearly run down the day before.

He recognized me, too.

"Hey, Mister," he yelled, "where's that pile of shit you call a bike?"

I stood and started to walk away; it was getting dark anyway.

"Hey, shithead!" he called. "I'm talkin' to ya!"

"Better run home, sonny, before the boogey man gets you," I said. "Isn't that your mamma calling?"

Unfortunately, it was, and it was the same woman who'd been watching me from across the street.

I dreamed that night, not the usual dream, but about something heavy and soft, moaning...

It wasn't a dream.

As I came awake it found the open window. I stumbled over to look out. An owl, silhouetted against the full moon, flapped its wings and circled out of sight.

It had knocked over the toy soldiers. I set them up again.

Next morning I tackled the far end of the yard. I found old patio stones here and there and pried them up and set them aside, in case Ms. Ardat wanted to use them in the new patio. The man-underground grew more thickly toward the center of the old patio, and when I cleared it away I found a base and column, white marble, as if for a fancy birdbath. Digging around the base I found a toy car, one of the good kind, made of heavy, still brightly painted metal, with wheels on solid axles that turned freely once the dirt had been knocked out....

Jimmy, where did you get that?
Oh...found it.
Where?
Oh...around.
Look, Jimbo. Isn't that the car Andrew said he'd lost?
Maybe.
And that was just after you'd been playing with him.
No answer.
Stealing's wrong, Jimbo.
I didn't steal it. I...I accidentally put it in my pocket.
We're going to give it back to Andrew, right now.
Do I have to?
Yes. And you be darn careful you don't have that kind of accident again.

So Jimmy had given it back, and Andrew seemed to accept the explanation. After I'd got paid for mowing Mrs. Kapinski's lawn I took Jimmy down to the local Woolworth's. Mom was short of grocery money that week, but I could afford a ball, one of those red on one side and blue on the other with a white stripe around the middle. He bounced it all the way down the sidewalk, chased it when it rolled out into the street. I finally took a shortcut down an alley just to keep the damn kid from getting run over…

Again, I turned. I was sure someone was watching me.
I shrugged and set to cutting thistles.
Once I caught myself turning to ask Jimmy if he wanted to help by hauling the weeds in his old wagon to the growing pile. I felt like a fool. But of course, that was it; that was why it felt as if there should be someone there. I'd almost always had Jimmy along when I did this kind of work. I could almost see him running that toy car over the bumps and ruts of the turned soil.

Ms. Ardat turned up for inspection after lunch. She wore a yellow sundress printed with green leaves.

"I'll have the patio blocks delivered tomorrow," she said.

"I'll need to dig these out before the blocks go in," I said. "Otherwise, end of summer you'll be right back where you started."

"Don't bother," she said.

* * *

Next morning I went after the rest of the thistles. When I reached the fence I found a gate, with some boards nailed across it. There was an iron bolt in decorative cast-iron fittings, and the joints of the hinges were also cast iron.

I stepped back for a better look and nearly tripped.

Under more thistles I found a low dome of white marble, like the end of a large egg sticking out of the ground. This had to be the missing bowl of the birdbath. I found a trowel and shoved the blade under the edge of the bowl.

"Hullo? Anyone home?"

I rose and looked toward the front gate.

"Got a load of patio blocks for you," the man at the front gate said. "Where d'ya want 'em?"

I walked over and looked at what was in the truck in the driveway.

"Need it at the back," I said.

"Good lord," he said, "I'm not gonna haul this stuff across that." He waved a hand at the stubble and rough ground.

"Me neither," I said. "Tell you what: there's a gate at the back. If you can drive around there, maybe we can get it open."

It took a hammer to get the bolt back. I heard the truck pull up outside as I was oiling the hinges. The driver pulled and I pushed, and finally the gate swung open enough so he could back the truck right up to the opening.

I signed the receipt and looked over the copy, trying to decipher Ms. Ardat's first name on the delivery instructions. I gave up, shoved it in my pocket, and stepped out into the alley to push the gate closed.

The oil had finally sunk into the hinges; the gate slammed shut. I looked at the outside of the gate and went cold...

Jimmy, you're gonna lose that thing before you even get it home.

Jimmy was in the alley, bouncing his ball off the fence, trying to catch it on the ricochet. Finally he tossed it so high it went right over a fence—a fence with a big, solid, wooden gate with huge wrought-iron hinges, like someone's idea of a door for a dungeon in a castle. Right in the middle of the gate, at the top, was a round grill, also wrought iron, sort of like a hot air grate, only fancier, just too high for me to see through. I pulled at the gate—it wasn't as if we'd broken a window or anything. But it was locked.

Lift me up, Den. Maybe I can see it.

So I lifted Jimmy up until his face was level with the grill.

A lady has it. She wants me to come in and get it.

Well, if she says it's all right.

I heard a bolt go back on the other side of the gate, and it opened just a crack.

Wait. You're not going in alone.

The lady said just me! She said she has a present for me.

No! You don't take presents from strangers.

But Jimmy ducked past me, or tried to. I grabbed him by his belt and pulled him back and kicked the gate shut.

But it was a lady!

Look, Jimbo, tomorrow I'll figure out what house that yard belongs to and knock on the door and ask the lady to give me your ball.

She won't give it to you.

She'll give it to me. Come on, we'll be late for supper, and Mom will worry...

Now I stood looking at wrought iron hinges—big, like hinges for a castle dungeon—and a fancy round wrought-iron grill, boarded over inside.

I went back through the gate and gave a really hard push on the handle of the trowel I'd wedged under the edge of the upside-down marble bowl. It flipped over to reveal its stained inside.

Nothing underneath but dank earth, tunnels of roots and beetles, and a circular imprint left by the rim of the bowl.

I sat back on my heels, breathing in short gasps. What had I been expecting, anyway?

I rolled the bowl over to the garage, propped it against the wall, and went back to digging. If she wanted the blocks in tomorrow, I'd have to get out as many of the roots as possible today. Even the smallest bit would send up shoots and start the whole thing over again. Of course I'd never get the main root of the man-underground, that could be six feet under, but if the shoots were kept pulled, finally it would starve.

I felt something that wasn't a root, and, curious, knelt to brush away the loose dirt.

This was what I had expected to find under the marble basin…

"I told you not to dig!" Ms. Ardat said over me.

"And now I know why," I said, on my feet. "You didn't want me to find—"

"That?" she finished for me, smiling.

"Yes, that!" I turned to point.

It wasn't a dead child. It was just a doll, one of those molded, soft plastic dolls of the cheapest kind, nylon hair worn to frizzy stubs, painted eyes blank with dirt.

"I don't think I need your services any more," Ms. Ardat said. "Here's the rest of your pay. Please go now."

"Delighted." I shoved the money into my pocket and walked away, up to the room above the garage, washed, and packed my backpack.

As I wheeled my bike from the garage, something touched my arm.

I dropped my bike and whirled around. Too late again.

But something bumped against my boot.

* * *

I counted my money. There was enough. I got on my bike and rode slowly down the nearby business street until I found a strip mall that had what I wanted.

* * *

We have nothing to talk about," Leah said when she opened the door and saw me standing there. "Go to the Sally Ann. Go to hell, for all I care."

"I just need a favor." I held up the flyers I'd had made at the copy shop, and the cell phone. "I had to give a billing address for the cell phone. I just want to use your address until I get one of my own. That's all."

She narrowed her eyes, looked me over, then said, "Whatever your other faults, you were never a liar. But one condition."

"What's that?"

"You tell me what this is all about. Because you never ask for favors, either."

My turn to think a minute.

"All right," I said.

I followed her up the stairs to her apartment.

"Okay," she said, sitting at the table. "Tell me about it."

So I told her about meeting Ms. Ardat, straight through to when Ms. Ardat had fired me. I didn't tell her about whoever was playing the vanishing act.

"So?" she said.

"So what?"

"I said, you had to tell me all."

All. I took a deep breath. "You know my mother killed herself."

She leaned forward. "The reason you never had to lie was because you never talked. Why did she do it?"

"Because of my little brother."

"You never told me you had a little brother, either."

"There were already too many people who knew."

She waited.

"Dad died early," I said. "Stroke. Mom couldn't afford a babysitter while she worked. I wasn't quite old enough to hold down a regular job, but I could do odd jobs around the neighborhood, and I could look after Jimmy while I was doing them. I'd rather have been out bumming around with the other guys, talking about cars and girls, but we needed the money."

"So what about Jimmy?"

"He disappeared."

"Ran away? Kidnapped? Killed?"

"As far as anyone could tell, he got out of bed during the night, got dressed, and left the house. They never found him."

"But that wasn't your fault."

"The day before, I'd bought him a toy. A rubber ball."

I didn't tell her why. That was between Jimmy and me, and it was going to the grave with me. But I told her the rest.

"I got a look through the gate as I grabbed Jimmy. There was a garden, with an apple tree, and a fancy birdbath, and patterned walks of some kind of stone—marble, maybe—and roses, and all kinds of other flowers, like something out of the Arabian Nights."

"There's something else you never told me—that you'd read the Arabian Nights."

"I didn't. Our fourth-grade teacher read us stories. Anyway, this Arabian Nights garden even had a princess, a beautiful woman who just stood there, tossing Jimmy's ball up and catching it. She was dressed in yellow and green…"

"So did you tell the police about this?"

"Of course I did. They didn't believe me. I guess everyone thought I'd gone a little nuts what with Jimmy missing and my mother in a bad state."

"Surely they checked it out."

"Of course they did. No one lived there. The garden was just an old overgrown lawn with an apple tree."

"You were sure it was the right place?"

"I couldn't forget a gate like that. That, and the apple tree. A young tree, but growing out of an old stump. And this."

I pulled it out and handed it to her, the thing that had bumped against my boot.

Leah looked at the weather-pitted rubber ball that still retained traces of its red, white, and blue paint, but she didn't touch it.

"You keep saying Ms. Ardat. Doesn't she have a first name?"

"I guess so, if you can make it out. I can't." I dug out the receipt for the patio blocks.

She looked at it carefully, then shook her head. "Denis," she said, "you can stay here tonight, if you want."

"No," I said. "Thank you."

I wanted to. But when you're scared is not the time to go soft.

"Call me," she said.

* * *

I slept, dreams and all, in a park. I got my first call the next day.

"Denis Daugherty? Is that really you?"

So there were still some of the old folks left in the neighborhood, besides Dave Johnson. "Mrs. Kapinski," I said.

She wanted me to dig up her garden for spring planting. She offered me her garden tools for any jobs I might get in the neighborhood, as if I would be doing her a favor by using them.

She let the new people in the neighborhood know I was okay. I had another job before the day was over.

Every day I rode my bike through that alley behind Ms. Ardat's and looked through a knothole I'd found. She had a younger man now, who worked shirtless, whose muscles gleamed with sweat. I judged, from the way he smirked, that he wasn't getting paid in cash. But I knew there was still a deadline.

It began to look more and more as I remembered, as the roses leafed out and the sod went down. But I knew that the rank weeds lay below, waiting to reclaim their space.

In a couple of weeks I had enough cash tucked away to pay for a room at a cheap motel.

I called Leah.

"The invitation still stands," she said.

"Thanks, but no."

The next evening, someone was in the alley before me. He had his back to me, his eye to the knothole, but I recognized his skateboard.

"What are you doing here, you fucking pervert?" he said.

"I could ask the same of you," I said.

He smirked, rather like Ms. Ardat's new gardener. "Boy, the jugs on that piece of pussy—major megafuckable. Wanna look?"

"Do you talk to your mother like that?"

He jumped on his skateboard and pushed off.

I slept badly that night, but that was nothing new. There was a lot of wind, enough to shake the wooden frame of the motel unit, or maybe it was just the usual dreams.

Just my luck, Dave Johnson was at the donut shop where I went for breakfast. I headed for a table at the other side of the shop, and then, even though I knew he hadn't seen me, I changed my mind and went to his table instead. It might have been because a bunch of noisy, whiny brats had taken the table where I'd planned to sit.

"Look," I said, "I'm sorry about the other day."

"Forget it, kid. I honestly didn't know about your mother. I'm sorry. She was a good woman."

"Forget it," I said.

"Hear you're back in the old neighborhood."

"Doing okay."

"Look, I hear all you got for transportation is a bike. I got this pickup truck I ain't using—" He broke off when he saw the look on my face and added, "You could kind of, you know, rent to own…"

"I'll think about it," I said.

That evening, the patio blocks were laid out in the fancy pattern I remembered, with the marble basin on its pedestal in the center and bright-colored bedding plants around it. It was just like I remembered it from the first time. Just like the Arabian Nights. Except…

Something leaning against the garage cast a long shadow in the lowering sun.

They didn't have skateboards in the Arabian Nights.

"Son of a bitch," I said aloud, and since that didn't seem sufficient, I said it again.

* * *

Back at the motel room I put a week's rent for the room into an envelope and the rest of my cash into another envelope, for Leah.

I placed the envelope with the rent in plain sight on the dresser. I put Jimmy's ball in my jacket pocket.

I arrived at Leah's at dusk. I didn't ring the bell, just left the envelope in her mailbox and walked away from the lights in her apartment.

Only when I had reached Ms. Ardat's did it occur to me that, since I had no idea what was going to happen, a weapon might be useful. The garage wasn't locked, and I knew my way around inside well enough to lay my hands on the shovel, even in the dark.

At first I thought it was my own footsteps, then I realized the sound came from the room above. Some kind of movement. A whimper. Pain or lust? The young man taking his payment? Was the skateboard a false alarm? Had I come too early for the deadline?

I heard a noise and flattened myself in the shadows next to the door.

Ms. Ardat stepped inside. She paused; she'd noticed the open door. But then she walked over to the stairs and climbed them, and slid back a bolt on the trap door.

The upstairs room had been locked. From the outside.

She raised the trap door and stepped through.

I slid empty-handed out the door, and around the corner of the garage. I could smell the jimson weed, just as I could feel that I wasn't alone out here in the dark.

I heard steps across the garage floor. Giggling.

Ms. Ardat stepped out of the door. The kid was with her, the brat with the skateboard. He was the one who was giggling. They were both stark naked. He had an erection. But whatever she wanted I had a feeling it wasn't sex.

She led him across to the patio. She made him kneel beside the birdbath, with his head over it, as if she were going to wash his hair. The kid was passive, except for the occasional giggle.

The moon glinted on the blade of the knife she unwrapped from a white linen napkin.

I never found out whether I would have gone to the brat's rescue, or remained frozen in the shadows, watching his blood drain into the basin, because Ms. Ardat looked straight at me and said, "Come out, Denis Daugherty."

So I stepped out, and whatever else was there stepped out behind me. I didn't try to get a look at it. I didn't have to.

"You gave me your name. Voluntarily. Although I already knew it. We are much alike, Denis Daugherty, you and I."

"How are we alike? Because we both hate kids?"

"Because we're both proud."

The brat giggled again.

"Me? Proud? Scraping by with the help of an ex-girlfriend and a little old lady?"

"Why did you never tell your ex-girlfriend, while she was your girlfriend, about your mother and little brother?"

"Because there were already too many people who knew," I said, as I had said to Leah.

"Oh, yes," she said, stroking the brat's hair. "Shame is the reverse of pride, anger is the solder between them. But you made yourself accept help from them both. Why?"

"The same reason I came to work for you. I knew you. I needed to know how."

"I think you needed more. As did I. I don't often..." she hesitated, smiled, "...come back for seconds." She held out the knife to me. "Here, you do it. An eye for an eye, a child for a child."

I felt the presence behind me stir.

"Will you let Jimmy die?"

"You're the one who wouldn't let him die. But if you kill this one, Jimmy will die, too."

I knew she lied.

"It isn't as if this is a particularly loveable child," she went on.

"Hell, *I'm* not particularly loveable. But his mother shouldn't die of grief."

"Over one child?" she asked.

"That's all it took for my mother," I said.

"One child!" she repeated. "And the neighbors came to mourn with her, and yet she could not continue to live. I lost hundreds, and no one mourned with me. And yet I still live."

"Hundreds?" I said weakly. I had to keep her talking.

"There were giants in the earth in those days," she said, her voice sharp with scorn.

"And why did no one mourn with you?"

The kid giggled again. It was starting to get irritating.

"Because like you, I'm proud. Didn't God make me from the same earth as my husband? But my children were all destroyed—all! Because I refused anything less than equality with him. And no one wept with me. So now they weep because of me."

Her hair had loosened in the storm of her words, a dark wind, locks writhing like live things, like wings.

"Why did you drug him then? Why not let him scream?"

She laughed. "They're my…performance pieces. Each one the same, each different. I get plenty of screaming oh, say, in Darfur."

"Supposing," I said. "Just suppose you had your own child."

"What? Are you offering to sire one for me? I have produced the children of men." She grinned. For the first time I noticed her teeth. "They're delicious."

Behind me, I could feel movement, like someone shuddering. She touched the brat's throat with the tip of her knife. He giggled.

My cell phone rang.

I could have giggled myself. "Excuse me," I said, as calmly as I could, and reached into my jacket pocket, trying to act as if it were the most natural thing in the world to answer a cell phone while a naked woman was about to slit some damn kid's throat.

When the phone came out, the old rubber ball came with it, hitting the ground and rolling away.

She slashed my arm before I could push the talk button. I dropped the phone and grabbed my arm. Blood ran between my fingers. She picked up the phone and threw it over the fence. I heard it clatter on the pavement of the alley. It continued to ring.

The brat was restless now. The drug was wearing off.

The phone continued to ring. I tried to move, but whether from the loss of blood, or because there had been something on the blade of the knife, everything had gone into slow motion.

Out in the alley, the phone rang. And rang. And rang…

From behind me, a rubber ball lofted into the air and over the fence.

The phone stopped ringing.

She put the knife to the brat's throat.

At first I thought it was the brat I heard, but he was giggling again. The screams came from behind me, the screams I had been hearing in my nightmares for years, the screams I always heard every time I relaxed even a little, because then I'd start imagining how Jimmy might have died, and how he must have screamed before he died.

She threw the knife. The screams went silent.

The presence behind me was gone.

The brat was whimpering now.

The sound of a car in the alley, the glow of headlights, silence as the car stopped. Car door opening. Moving beam of a flashlight.

"Here's the phone," a voice said.

Ms. Ardat began to grow. Not physically, not in body, but in presence, like a black whirlwind hovering over the brat and me, a roaring and a darkness that rose and increased…

…and suddenly shrank to a bird that flapped away.

"Look at that friggin' big owl," I heard someone say as the flashlight beam pointed into the sky. "You think that's what she heard?"

I managed to push back the bolt and yell for someone to open the gate.

* * *

So what happened?

The ball tossed over the fence had hit the talk button, and Leah had heard the scream, and guessed where I was, and that I was in trouble. She called the police.

The neighbors hadn't heard any screams.

Why? Go figure. Maybe the same reason Jimmy's aim had got so good.

The crushed leaves of the jimson weed had been enough to induce the state the brat was in. His mother told the police about me, the Suspicious Character, and when they found Jimmy's bones under the patio blocks, I was the first suspect.

Then the police uncovered more bones, children's bones, that went back far before I could ever have put them there. Back to before the neighborhood was there. Bones furrowed with tooth marks.

After all the excavating was over, the backyard was an expanse of dirt and rubble. Only the apple tree, now setting on fruit, rose above it. But jimson weed seed can last for years in the ground, and I know they didn't reach the main root of the man-underground.

The police never found Ms. Ardat. How do you capture the night wind?

Leah thought the name on the receipt had to be Lilith. She had looked up Ardat, on her computer at work.

Maybe Leah was right. I don't know. I'd always thought Lilith was about sex, you know?

Oh sure, she was sexy. I'd felt it. My replacement sure felt it. Not to mention the brat. But. It's hard to explain. Which came first, the chicken or the egg? Which is more important, intercourse or issue?

We were much alike.

The brat and I did not become best buddies.

Leah and I didn't get back together. She figured, I guess, that if this experience didn't turn me into father material, nothing would.

Dave Johnson told me he was fed up with retirement, and seeing as I'd already built up the clientele, how about he'd contribute the transportation and we'd go into partnership. It's worked so far.

So I guess maybe that's a happy ending. After all, I don't dream about Jimmy screaming any more.

I do dream sometimes about Ms. Ardat's children.

The dead ones.

Not the ones the police found.

Her children.

Reconciliation
by Lynn Hawker

The young man moaned and arched his back. A soft cry escaped as he reached his climax. He reached his arms out but clasped only emptiness. He turned over, tangling the sheets around him.

She stood by the window, her full red lips curving with a slight smile. Her long red hair swirled around her face and shoulders as she turned to look at the bed where the young man was beginning to awaken. He couldn't see her; they never could.

He groaned, and his breath caught in a sob. He sat on the edge of the bed, holding his head in his hands. Soon he put on his robe and slippers and padded out the door, down the long hallway and through an arch into the sanctuary where he knelt on the cold stone floor and prayed for the rest of the night.

She stood in the room, the smile fading to a look of unutterable sadness—then she dissolved into the moonlight. An owl flew into the night, hooting softly.

* * *

She leaned against the crib in the pink and white nursery. The night light shone on a small sleeping figure. Gently she picked up the tiny child and kissed her. As she kissed the infant, its breath stopped. Tears ran down her face as she placed the dead baby back in the crib.

They used to know words that would fend her off, amulets that would keep the newborns safe. All that had been forgotten. Only the curse remained.

* * *

The fat businessman thrashed in his sheets. His nightly glass of Scotch stood on the bedside table. His wife, long absent from the bedroom, slept down the hall. He grunted and panted in the throes of his passion.

The flame-haired figure leaned over the bed. She smiled, watching. In his dream she was short, slight, and blonde. Finally the release came and he woke up. "What a dream," he muttered.

His gaze turned wistfully to the bedroom door. *Well, I suppose it's good to know I can still get it on.*
He sighed, turned over, and went to sleep.
A soft hoot, a flapping of wings, and the night was still.

* * *

As the first light of dawn appeared in the sky, a small owl squeezed through a broken window in a deserted warehouse. It landed on a floor white with droppings and littered with mouse and rat bones. The owl shook itself, and suddenly a tall woman stood in its place, pale and shivering slightly. She went to the stairway and descended two flights. There, in a sheltered space no bigger than a closet, was a sleeping bag. She lay down, pulled it up to her chin, and drifted into sleep.

* * *

There is a moment between day and evening, and again between night and morning, when the world stands still. Those who know of it can meet Outside—a place beyond now-and-then, a place not subject to Time. In that space someone came to her in the tiny room in the deserted warehouse—a woman, dark of hair and dusky of skin. She squatted beside the sleeping bag and waited with immortal patience until Lilith awoke.

"Eve!" Lilith sat up abruptly and pushed her back against the wall. She pulled the sleeping bag around her. "What are you doing here?"

Eve looked around. "I might ask the same."

"I always was a creature of the waste places. Once it was the desert, now this. What do you want?"

"Only to talk to you."

"Why? It's been centuries."

"The sun is setting now. Meet me tomorrow at sunrise, Outside. Promise?"

"We have nothing to say to each other."

"I thought so too, once. Promise."

Silence.

"*Promise.*"

"All right," Lilith said grudgingly. She didn't trust Eve, but it seemed prudent to find out what she was up to.

Time shifted back into place, and Eve was gone. Lilith frowned and shrugged. A moment later, an owl flew into the gathering night.

* * *

They sat together Outside in that moment between darkness and dawn, Lilith with her ghost-pale skin and Eve, dusky and dark.

Lilith spoke first. "Why come to me, when you could be in heaven with *Him*, singing the glories of the Unnamable." She smiled slightly as she said that, remembering that moment at the beginning of time when she had spoken the Unnamable Name.

"It's the apple," Eve said, and sighed.

"What?"

"They're still talking about the apple. Not all the time, of course, and not to my face, but they've never forgotten it. Even with the sacrifice and the atonement of my great-however-many-great-grandson, it's still about the apple, and how it's all my fault."

"I see," murmured Lilith.

"Some of them watch what's going on down here. They see the wars, the killing, the hatred. And they blame it all on me and the apple." Tears were rolling down her cheeks now. "They're all my children, the sons and daughters of the earth. And they fight and kill, just like the first two. My heart breaks with it."

Lilith sat in silence.

"I thought you'd understand," said Eve in a small voice.

"I do." Lilith sent her a sidelong glance. "You know what they blame me for. Their lustful dreams. I am the lamia and the succubus; I seek out men and cause them to sin. I am the demon who draws men to their destruction." She laughed bitterly. "I create nothing. I only shape what I find in the depths. Some of them enjoy it."

This time, they both sat in silence.

"How is Adam?" Lilith asked.

"He stays in the Presence and sings praise eternally."

"And you?"

"I grieve for the earth, for the water and air, and most of all, for my daughters."

Lilith watched Eve closely. "Do you know there are some women—few, very few—who call themselves Daughters of Lilith?"

Eve nodded, eyes downcast. "It's the apple again."

"Yes, I guess in a way it is."

"I must leave," Eve said. "No one in Heaven notices me much, but I doubt this is allowed."

"But you'll do it again. If I agree to meet you, you'll come again."

Eve met her eyes. "Yes."

* * *

"You know, I never saw Adam again after I flew away."

A long silence followed. Finally Lilith asked, "Did you think I had?"

"He said you came back and visited him in his dreams."

"After I spoke the Name, I grew wings and flew to Lucifer and Samael and the others. Fallen angels go downhill over the centuries, but let me tell you, in those days Lucifer was glorious. Would I leave an angel, even a fallen one, for a man made out of clay? And a stubborn one, at that?"

Eve's lips curved in a small, wry smile. "I should have known Adam wasn't being quite honest. He never was good at taking responsibility."

Her eyes grew distant, thoughtful. "I imagine Lucifer was glorious. The serpent was the most beautiful creature I'd seen, shimmering and sinuous, with such a thrilling voice…"

"Did you know about the naming of the animals?"

Eve shook her head.

"I tried to tell Adam they already had names, that they knew their names and all we had to do was sit with them very quietly and each creature would let us know its name. We argued about that, he said, 'No, I get to name them,' and went around saying, 'That's a tiger, that's an elephant, that's an aardvark,' and on and on."

"That explains something," said Eve. "I asked him once if I could name a couple of the animals. He said, 'Don't *you* start!' and stamped off."

Eve regarded Lilith for a long moment. "You and I should have talked eons ago."

"We couldn't. We never trusted each other enough. Then, when you went to Heaven, I thought you were caught up in singing the praises of Him, and that was that."

"I was, at first. But it does get tiring. I thought I could get to know Mary, but she's sad and crying all the time. It isn't as if she's the only one to lose a son. They'll be reunited eventually—she's gradually moving up the line, you know, but it takes forever. Partly because she's a woman, no matter how sinless, but mostly it's just Heavenly politics."

As if in response, dark clouds began to form in the skies Outside.

"I'd better get back," Eve murmured. "I didn't think He noticed I'd gone. What if He has? What if He's heard?"

Lilith patted her hand. "Don't worry. After all these centuries, why would He start listening now?"

* * *

The meetings continued, and two women, once ancient enemies, listened to each other. And listening is always where it begins.

* * *

"I have to ask about the babies," Eve said tentatively. "Why do you kill them? If there is hate in you, I don't see it."

"You know the stories. I'm said to be the mother of demons."

"Yes…"

"Well, it's true. As I said, the fallen angels were glorious and I'm not bad myself, but every birth was a demon. And newborn demons fly away—or crawl or slither away." She shuddered, remembering. "That's why I finally left Lucifer. The more demons, the happier he was, but I couldn't stand it. I just want to hold a baby, to feel the softness and innocence. I don't *do* anything to them. I just touch them and they stop breathing. They call it crib death now," she said, swiping the back of her hand across a tear-stained cheek. "People used to have charms and amulets to protect children. The old prayers are forgotten, but if the parents just ask for protection, from Him or from Mary—or anything of Spirit, for that matter—then I can't get close."

"I'm sorry," Eve whispered. "I didn't know."

She put her arm around Lilith. Her dusky cheek rested against Lilith's pale face, and their tears mingled into a single, shared sorrow.

* * *

"Could you just look at the babies and not touch them, not kiss them?"

Lilith's smile was sad, but filled with wonderment. "You, who have lost millions of children, can think of my pain?"

"I care for you."

It struck her, suddenly, that no one had ever said that before. Millions of men had lusted for her, but no one, not even Lucifer, had ever said that he cared.

* * *

A small white owl fluttered to the windowsill, and then a tall woman with red hair stood by the window. She looked around the room, with its pale blue blankets and crib canopy. A small mobile was attached to the crib railing, little wooden angels that moved gently.

Was that protection?

She moved toward the child and felt…nothing. The angels meant nothing but decoration to this family. No prayers, no petitions, nothing holy protected the infant.

She reached out, her hands almost touching the tiny boy. Her whole body yearned for the feel of a child in her arms. Sobbing, she turned and stumbled toward the window. An owl flew erratically across the night sky.

* * *

"What is it like to be the object of desire, of lust?" Eve questioned.

"You should know that well enough."

"Not as you do. I was created for Adam. I was a part of him. You were always yourself." Her eyes grew wistful, and she repeated, "You were always yourself. I wonder what that is like."

* * *

Two women, one dark and one light, stood in the young priest's room. The dreams came to him and he cried out with lust.

"So that's what it's like," Eve whispered, trembling.

They watched unseen as he went to his desk and began to write frantically. His breathing gradually quieted, but he wrote on through the night, fashioning a sermon. By the time the housekeeper brought his morning coffee, he was quite cheerful.

* * *

The women came next to the bedroom of the fat businessman. They watched as his breathing became rapid, heavy. He woke and sat up abruptly. He shook his head, muttering. Again he looked wistfully at the bedroom door, and after a few minutes he went down the hall to his wife's room. There was some quiet conversation. He did not return.

"He knew the dream spoke of his own desires," Lilith whispered. "It was not me. It is never me."

"I understand," Eve answered. "And his wife?"

"Perhaps this will heal the emptiness in her and help her move into her own life. Perhaps some pains can be healed only when they are shared."

Something dawned in Eve's dark eyes. "Perhaps that is so."

* * *

That Sunday the priest spoke for over an hour on the curse of Eve. He quoted St. Paul's warnings about the weakness of women and the sins of the flesh. After the sermon, he stood by the door of the church and watched as most of the parishioners hurried by him with only a perfunctory nod. Only his mother, always his greatest supporter, stopped. Her lips were set in a firm line and there was no warmth in her eyes.

"Eloquent as always, but considering the current condition of the world, the church, and humanity, I consider such a sermon to be a waste of your time and talents. It was positively medieval, and more than a little insulting."

He recoiled in astonishment. "Mother, you know I was not speaking of you."

She met his eyes with a stern, direct gaze. "You were speaking of me, and your grandmother, your aunts, your sister, your nieces. We are all women, and every one of us is tired of hearing about that wretched apple." She brushed past him and strode away, not looking back.

His housekeeper tramped out of the church without saying a word. Judging from the grim set of her face, there would be no hot dinner tonight.

Eve and Lilith stood together beyond the churchyard, watching, smiles on their unseen faces.

* * *

The small, dark woman, mother of millions, carefully bent over the sleeping infant. She slowly handed the baby to her companion, keeping one hand on Lilith's shoulder, another on the baby. Lilith bent her head and gently kissed the small face. The infant stirred, stretched, and settled into sleep again, breathing evenly.

The women stood with their arms around each other, both faces wet with tears.

* * *

In the place Outside of Time they sat, watching the dark clouds scuttle across the sky.

"It will take years," said Eve. "Centuries, perhaps."

"Yes, but we have begun," answered Lilith.

The dark clouds surrounded them, but as they looked up they could see brightness beyond.

Nocturne
by Lester Smith

Amazing, nothing less, at this gray age,
Across the dusty distance of such years,
To waken from a dream in youthful tears
For an old love, "the one who got away,"
While she who sleeps beside me holds me here,
In comfort of the history we share.

Sleep deeply, Eve. I'll marvel while I may—
In grip of earnest passion I had feared
Forgotten—and imagine, if I dare,
That somewhere Lilith also lies awake.

About the Authors

Robin Bridges, who thought she had seen everything working nights at a grocery store, now works nights as a nurse and sees even weirder things. She lives on the Mississippi Gulf Coast with her husband, two kids, and two English Mastiffs named Grendel and Monster.

Clint Collins lives and writes in northern Virginia. He was previously published in *Under The Fang*, an anthology of vampire tales.

Elaine Cunningham is a *New York Times* best-selling author who has published over twenty fantasy books and nearly three dozen short stories. *Shadows in the Starlight*, the second book in her urban fantasy series Changeling Detective (Tor), appeared on the *Kirkus Review* list of Top Ten SciFi Books of 2006. This anthology is her first time on the editorial side of the desk.

Eirene Donohue was born and raised in Rhode Island. A class of 2000 graduate of Brown University, she has spent the past eight years traveling, teaching, and learning. She is currently at work on her first novel.

Lorne Dixon lives and writes somewhere off an exit of Route 78 in residential New Jersey. He grew up on a diet of yellow-spined paperbacks, black-and-white monster movies, and the thunder lizard backbeat of rock 'n' roll.

Marcus Ewert is a Capricorn who lives in an honest-to-god turret. His first children's book, *10,000 Dresses*, is coming out in 2008. He also created the fantastical animated series *Piki & Poko*, currently playing on MTV's LOGO channel.

Ed Greenwood is a librarian, avid reader, and a writer. He created The Forgotten Realms® fantasy world and has written over a hundred and fifty game adventures, sourcebooks, and novels, including the bestselling Spellfire and the Elminster series, and (with Elaine Cunningham) *The City of Splendors: A Waterdeep Novel*. He keeps busy writing fantasy novels for Wizards of the Coast (Forgotten Realms® books), Tor Books (the Band of Four saga and his current Niflheim series), Solaris (his Falconfar stories), and for fun, lots of short stories for anthologies like this one.

Hannah Goodman, M.Ed, is the author of five books, the first of which, *My Sister's Wedding*, won the first-place award for The Writer's Digest International Self-Publishing Contest, 2004, YA division. The second, *My Summer Vacation*, won an IPPY in 2007. Visit her website for more information: www.hannahrgoodman.com.

Lara Gose lives with her husband, Ed Gentry, and two cats in the Midwest, where she works full-time as a university administrator and part-time as a freelance editor. Unclaimed hours left in the day are given over to writing, reading, knitting, or cooking.

Jennifer Greylyn has been writing almost as long as she's been reading—that is, most of her life—but it's only recently that family and friends have convinced her she should share her stories. (She hopes this will stop them nagging, but she doubts it.) In another life and under another name, she works as a university lecturer and publishes nonfiction in the fields of medieval and early modern history. She lives in Canada.

Lynn Hawker has worked as a newspaper reporter, a psychotherapist, and as clinical manager of the counseling department at a women's domestic violence shelter. She is co-author of *End the Pain: Solutions for Stopping Domestic Violence*. An avid reader of fantasy and science fiction, she has had two stories published in *Triangulation*, an anthology by Parsec, the Pittsburgh area science-fiction group. She first wrote about Lilith fifty years ago for her senior tutorial at Chatham University.

Lily Hoang is the author of *Parabola* (Chiasmus Press, 2007, winner of the Chiasmus Press First Book Contest) and *Changing* (Fairy Tale Review Press, forthcoming late 2008). Her writing has recently appeared in *Black Warrior Review*, *Quarter After Eight*, and *Fairy Tale Review*. She teaches writing and Women's Studies in Indiana.

Jackie Kessler is the author of the Hell on Earth series, in which Lilith (or Lillith) plays an important role (loosely defined as pulling out all stops in trying to destroy the heroine, the former demon Jezebel). Jackie lives in Upstate New York with her Loving Husband, her Precious Little Tax Deductions, and two geriatric cats, one of whom is senile and caterwauls at three in the morning, every morning, until Jackie picks her up and cuddles with her (so it's little wonder that Jackie is grumpy and is all too happy to write about demons). For excerpts of Jackie's books, and for more information about Jackie than you probably want, visit her website: www.jackiekessler.com.

Twenty years ago, **J. Robert King** earned a degree in Theology and the Humanities. He didn't go into the ministry, so his Theology degree hasn't had much use, and acquaintances often question his Humanity. *Lilith Unbound* has finally allowed Rob to use his degree—for all of six thousand words. Rob has written a few million other words, including the *Mad Merlin* trilogy and the recently-released Sherlockian hardcover: *The Shadow of Reichenbach Falls*.

Since the time she was born in Hollywood, in the late 1970's, **Christina McCoy**'s life has become only more eccentric and intriguing. She currently resides in southwest Florida and has conceded that she will never experience seasons. Her occupations include teaching high-school students how to pass state exams, co-owning Mad Scotsman Games, and being entertained endlessly by her husband. Christina has a BA in English Literature with a background in Mass Communications. Her interests include high fantasy, low humor, and too many role-playing games. "Death of the Madonna" is much in debt to Peter Kurth and his marvelous book, *Isadora: A Sensational Life*, and is dedicated to Irene, the greatest martyr she knows, and Najila, her dancing grandmother who taught her of their divine ancestor: Miss Duncan.

Jonathan Moeller lives somewhere in the trackless wastes of Minnesota. He wrote the novel *Demonsouled* from Gale/Five Star, and occasionally writes short fiction, most recently in *Sword & Sorceress 22*. For obvious reasons, all the mirrors in his apartment are covered.

T. L. Morganfield lives in Colorado with her husband and two children. She attended Clarion West in 2002, and her short fiction has appeared in *Dragons, Knights & Angels*, *Dark Recesses*, *Atomjack*, and *Paradox*. Her website can be found at www.tlmorganfield.com.

Mike Resnick is the all-time leading award-winner, living or dead, for short science fiction (according to *Locus*). He has won five Hugos, a Nebula, and other major awards in the USA, France, Spain, Japan, Croatia, and Poland. He is the author of 53 novels, 12 collections, almost 200 stories, and two screenplays, and he has edited 46 anthologies. He is currently the executive editor of *Jim Baen's Universe,* and recently served a stint as science-fiction editor for BenBella Books. His work has been translated into 22 languages. In his spare time, he sleeps.

Kate Riedel was born and raised in Minnesota but is now a card-carrying Canadian and lives in Etobicoke, Ontario, Canada. Her most recent publications are in the anthologies *Tesseracts 11* from Edge Press and *New Writings in the Fantastic* from Pendragon Press, and stories in *On Spec* and *Realms of Fantasy*.

Marsheila (Marcy) Rockwell is a Rhysling-nominated poet who lives in the desert in the shadow of a sacred mountain. She is also a Seabee wife, the mother of two precocious sons, the curator of a sizable collection of Wonder Woman/Wonder Girl statues, and the author of *Legacy of Wolves* (Wizards of the Coast, 2007). You can find out more here: biodegradable.blogspot.com.

Lawrence Schimel is a full-time author and anthologist who's published over 80 books, including *Fairy Tales for Writers*, *Vampire Stories from the American South*, *Two Boys in Love*, and *Little Pirate Goes to School*. He's won a Lambda Literary Award and the Rhysling Award for poetry, and his children's books have been chosen for the White Ravens by the International Youth Library in Munich and for IBBY's Outstanding Books for Young People With Disabilities 2007. His writings have been translated into 22 languages, including Basque, Esperanto, and Icelandic. He lives in Madrid, Spain, with his husband, Ismael Attrache.

Nancy Schmidt's M.A. in literature and fiction has set her on an itinerant career path of freelance everything. Her publications include several speculative-fiction pieces that explore manifestations of the Goddess, particularly the insubordinate ones. She is currently working on a novel that brings the ten Mahavidyas, wisdom goddesses from India, into modern-day Vancouver.

Nisi Shawl's story "Cruel Sistah" was included in *The Year's Best Fantasy & Horror #19*. Her work has also appeared in *So Long Been Dreaming: Postcolonial Science Fiction and Fantasy* and both *Dark Matter* anthologies. With Cynthia Ward she co-authored *Writing the Other: Bridging Cultural Differences for Successful Fiction* (Aqueduct Press). Nisi's 2008 story collection *Filter House* (Aqueduct Press) received a starred review in *Publishers Weekly,* and Ursula K. Le Guin calls it "superbly written." A board member for the Clarion West Writers Workshop, one of the Carl Brandon Society's founders, and a guest speaker at Stanford University and Smith College, Nisi likes to relax by pretending she lives in other people's houses.

By day, **Lester Smith** is a writer and technologist for the Sebranek Group, an educational design house that creates textbooks for the Houghton Mifflin Company. In that capacity, he has written poetry chapters for children from third grade through high school. By night, Les fights crime as president of the Wisconsin Fellowship of Poets, as a founding member of the Alliterates, and as a member of the One Campaign and Amnesty International. You can learn more about him at www.LesterSmith.com.

Stephen D. Sullivan is the award-winning author of over 30 books. He is married and has two children, a son and a daughter. He has never locked either of his children in a tower—though, since they have become teenagers, he has been tempted to do so more than once. Steve and his non-captive family live in haunted Wisconsin. He dedicates this story to Joss Whedon and Ang Lee, for reasons that seem obvious to the author. More information about Steve and his work can be found at www.stephendsullivan.com.

Tracy Woelfel is a lifelong Alaskan and graduate of Montana State University. If asked, she will attribute her storytelling to research and her family's tendency to provide events that are worth retelling.

About Popcorn Press

Popcorn Press is a micropublishing house based in southern Wisconsin, devoted to publishing fiction and poetry that is both genuine and unique. We are a coalition of professional writers who know from experience how books normally get to market. Many deserving texts aren't published simply because they don't fit a current trend. Our aim is to get such texts before an audience in ebook and paperback format. If we can match a good book to the right reader, then our efforts have been worthwhile.

Visit us on the Web at www.PopcornPress.com.

Made in the USA
Charleston, SC
09 January 2014